redemption

A Story of Grace

a novel by

Renee Propes

The Kimmer Group

The Kimmer Group
Publisher's Note: This is a work of fiction. Names, characters, places, and incidents are a product of the author's imagination. Locales and public names are sometimes used for atmospheric purposes. Any resemblance to actual people, living or dead, or to businesses, companies, events, institutions, or locales is completely coincidental.

Cover and Design-Aaniyah.Ahmed

Redemption: A Story of Grace Renee Propes. -- 1st ed.
ISBN 978-1-7348219-6-3 PB
       978-1-7348219-7-0 HB

Library of Congress Control Number: TXU002315579

Dedicated to the memory of my mother,
Lois Cape Ladd,
who encouraged my love for the written word. She
graced this world with a saintly presence, exquisite beauty, and
an unassuming elegance.

May 4, 2022

A field of ten champion Thoroughbreds, nine colts and one filly, each worthy of the opportunity to compete, slowly galloped around the track.

Shivering, a tall, dark-haired Italian man buttoned the top of his Giorgio Armani jacket. He watched the sunlight peek through gray clouds as the heavy fog dissipated. A residue of dampness from the previous day's rain and the brisk eastern winds created a chill in the air as the horses continued their pre-race workouts. The humidity also enhanced the sweet fragrance of the rich Kentucky soil.

He watched each horse's movement around the track through binoculars. Beside him, a shorter, older man of similar heritage clung to a cup of hot coffee as if the twelve-ounce cup of steaming liquid could warm his chilled body.

To a casual onlooker, the men could've been a father and son, two friends, or just two interested bookmakers attempting to set the betting odds for the following day's race.

The tall man lowered the binoculars, "You know, that little filly doesn't look like a champion Thoroughbred in my opinion."

"True. She's small, but she's got a presence. Just look at her—she prances around that track like she's royalty." The older man rubbed the altered lanyard hanging from his neck. "According to our friend, she has the heart and speed of a winner."

The tall man chuckled, glancing once more at the track. "He may be right, but I'm betting the house she loses on Saturday," he said as if he already knew the outcome of the race. Then, he placed the binoculars back inside the case and continued, "We better get going. We have a lot to do."

"True. We've got a long twenty-four hours ahead of us. Besides, I'm chilled to the bone."

"I can tell. You've hugged that cup since we came out here. Are you ready to go inside?"

"Lead the way," the older man said, draining the last of his coffee. "I'm right behind you."

Chapter One

March 2021

Teddy Williams arrived at the bank at precisely eight-thirty. He'd hoped to meet with the bank manager early to get to Andrew Byrd's law office by nine o'clock. Glancing around the parking lot, Teddy remembered once again that today would have been Andrew's son and his best friend, Drew Byrd's, birthday. Reaching over the console to the passenger's seat, he grabbed the envelope, which contained a blank check and a statement of interest he owed for the farm's state-of-the-art remodel.

Teddy raked his fingers through his blond hair as he entered the front of the bank. As usual, his windswept hair suggested he drove a convertible. He did not.

Manager Don Johnson, a wiry little guy with a slick round head and watchful eyes, walked through the lobby. His dark glasses perched on his nose, Don was reading a document he held in one hand while balancing a coffee cup in the other. Johnson walked past Teddy and into his office without looking up from the paper.

Teddy flashed a boyish grin as he approached the receptionist's desk. "Hi, Pam. I'm here to see Don. Does he have a few minutes?"

Pam slipped the nail file under a stack of papers, turned toward Johnson's office, and called, "Don, do you have a few minutes to speak with Mr. Williams?"

He looked up and a smile formed on his face. "Of course."

Johnson hurried from his office to the receptionist area. "Hi, Teddy. What brings you in this early?"

Teddy looked around the lobby area. "Do you mind if we talk in your office?"

"Sure. Come in." Johnson gestured for Teddy to enter first. "You want a cup of coffee?"

"No thanks."

They walked into the office, and Johnson shut the door behind him.

Sinking into the leather chair in front of Johnson's desk, Teddy explained that he was there to pay the quarterly interest payment on the loan he'd taken out to finance the racehorse business he'd started for Katie and Sammy.

Once Teddy handed over the check, Johnson relaxed a little. "How are Mr. and Mrs. Byrd? Are you still checking on them from time to time?"

"Funny, you should ask. I'm on my way over to his office for a quick visit this morning. Today would have been Drew's forty-third birthday. His birthday is always a tough day for his parents."

"I can imagine. You know, Drew and I were rather good friends. I think of him often. But I still can't understand his disappearance."

He pulled open the bottom drawer of his desk and pulled out an old newspaper. "I've still got a copy of the local newspaper article." He held it up and read over his glasses.

"Local police have no clues about Mr. Drew Byrd's mysterious disappearance. Mr. Byrd was married to his high school sweetheart, the former Colleen Brock. They have three children and reside in the town's historic district. At the time of his disappearance, he was a partner in his father's law firm."

Johnson folded the paper neatly and dropped it back into the desk drawer. Then, shaking his head, he said, "His lifestyle certainly didn't fit the profile of a man who would disappear and fall off the grid. But, evidently, that's what happened."

Teddy gazed out the window. "I know. It's a mystery. I wonder if Drew's even alive. After all these years… you'd think someone would have heard something, wouldn't you?"

Johnson nodded. "Not even his wife has heard from him since the day he vanished."

The two men were silent for several moments.

Johnson spoke first. "So, you're going over to Mr. Byrd's office when you leave here?"

"Yeah, that's my plan." Teddy glanced back at Johnson. "I try to stop by Andrew's office at least once a week to check on him."

The banker took off his glasses and reached for the handkerchief in his coat pocket. As he carefully polished the lenses, he said, "I must say, Teddy, you're a bigger man than me."

"How do you mean?"

"If someone had plotted with my wife against me, I'm not sure I would take on the burden of comforting the guy's parents. Don't get me wrong; I liked Drew. But he took the cowardly exit."

Teddy did not respond. There was no need, really. It was his first marriage, but it seemed like eons ago.

Johnson placed his glasses back on his face. "What would you do if Drew suddenly resurfaced?"

Another quiet moment passed.

Teddy stood, extended his hand, and said, "Thanks, man. I appreciate your seeing me on such short notice."

Johnson gave Teddy a measured look, then shook his hand. "Sure. Anytime."

As he reached the door, Teddy turned back and said, "Andrew was my dad's best friend. I'm just trying to do the right thing by him. This situation hasn't been easy for anyone involved."

"I understand, my friend. I'm sure it's been difficult."

"But to answer your question," Teddy paused, looking at the floor. "I'm not sure how I'd react if Drew suddenly returned. All I can say is, we'd certainly have a lot to discuss."

Chapter Two

Andrew looked up from his desk and motioned for Teddy to come into the office as he wiped his nose with his monogrammed handkerchief. His white hair emphasized his ruddy complexion, causing it to appear redder than normal. Then, pointing to a chair across from his desk, he asked, "What are you doing out this early on a Monday morning?"

"I thought I'd come by for a short visit before you got busy."

"Glad you did! I have someone coming in at ten o'clock this morning, so we have a few minutes." Andrew gestured again to the chair. "What's on your mind?"

"When I woke up this morning, I remembered it was Drew's birthday, and I thought I'd stop by on my way to the office."

"I appreciate it, son. Daisy was in tears during breakfast this morning. We still can't get our heads wrapped around his disappearance."

Teddy looked over at the older gentleman and realized he'd be pushing seventy-five years old by now. The same age as his dad.

The weight of that tragic day wore heavily on them both. "I'm sure not knowing what happened to Drew is troubling," he said. "Believe me, Andrew, there's not a day goes by that I don't think about that weekend."

Andrew got up from his desk and walked over to the window to peek through the blinds. "I've been meaning to call you. I ran into Tommy Parker last week at the barber shop. Someone has been vandalizing his farm."

Teddy sat up in his chair, "Does he have any idea who is responsible?"

Andrew shook his head. "It started as a small thing. One morning, Parker found red spray paint on a section of the fencing around the property. A month later, there was severe damage to the same area. It looked like someone had plowed through the fence with a four-wheeler or tractor. There were wood splinters everywhere. Two weeks ago, he discovered a large red circle painted on the roof of his barn. Then last week, while driving around the property looking for a lost calf, there was an acre of pine trees cut. You know he sells wood from his farm as pulpwood."

"Thanks for letting me know. I'll be on the lookout."

Andrew looked over his glasses as he sipped from his coffee cup.

"Thank you for making your visit a priority this morning." Andrew walked around his desk and sat in the chair next to Teddy. "And for understanding how difficult Drew's birthday is for Daisy and me." He reached over and patted Teddy's arm. Fresh tears filled his eyes. "I'm so grateful that you and Drew were such good friends; otherwise, I'm not sure we would've made it through this nightmare." Andrew's lips quivered as he said, "I don't know about you, but I have to believe my son is still alive, and if he is, I intend to find him."

Chapter Three

When he left Andrew's office, Teddy went straight to work, but he couldn't get Andrew and Daisy off his mind. The conversation with Johnson and his visit with Andrew had left him in a dreadful mood.

He had several appointments with families of children who were waiting for operations. As a pediatric surgeon, he scheduled the surgery appointments in the morning and worked the wellness checkups during the afternoon.

After speaking to his staff, Teddy went into his office and closed the door. He stared at the wooded area behind his office.

If only I'd stayed in Abington that weekend, maybe I could have prevented the hostage situation, which ultimately cost the life of Uncle Freddy, Nancy Leigh, and her boyfriend.

Finally, he glanced at the first couple of messages and made notes about the physicians that required a return call. Then he checked the children's charts they would be discussing.

The next message was from Colleen Byrd. Rebecca woke with a fever and complained of a sore throat. He'd been treating Rebecca since opening his practice, and her mother wasn't one to overreact. So Teddy placed Colleen's message on top.

As he got to the end of the messages, there was one from Frank Nordstrom. His voice was strong and upbeat as he left a number and the nature of his call. Teddy scribbled his number on the pad and wrote real estate beside Frank's name.

Later in the afternoon, when Teddy turned onto the road to their farm, he came upon the long white fence covering the outside parameters of the property. From a distance, he saw Sammy and Katie walking a horse around the large riding ring.

Teddy was in his study making calls when he heard Katie's footsteps on the back porch. He looked at the time—she must be done for the day. The interest payment he'd made to the bank had nagged at him like an annoying splinter. He put the phone down and considered speaking with her about their finances.

The backdoor slammed when she came into the house. He caught a glimpse of her long auburn hair as she rushed through the kitchen and ran upstairs. Then the water bolted through the pipes when she turned on the shower. Teddy stretched his arms over his head, looked down at his list of messages, and made the next call.

Teddy waited until they were finished with dinner and enjoying a glass of wine on the back porch to ask his wife about the horse they were training.

He watched Katie's body language as he slowly opened the bottle of wine.

She was quiet. But that was okay, too. With Katie, sometimes her silence was a sign she was working through her thoughts and emotions.

But he couldn't be sure.

He handed her a glass of wine and then settled himself in the chair opposite her. "Cheers!"

"Cheers."

They sat in silence for a few moments and enjoyed the cool evening air.

"On the way home this afternoon," Teddy said. "I saw you and Sammy training a horse. What are his chances to race in the equestrian event in June?"

Katie scrunched her nose. "I don't think he'll be ready by then, but hopefully by the September event."

Teddy stood up and walked over and leaned against the post as he looked out over the pasture. "Do we have any horses ready to race in June?"

Katie shook her head as she sat up straight in her chair. "No, I'm afraid not, Teddy. Only one horse we currently own comes from a championship bloodline."

"I was hoping out of those horses we bought back in the fall, more than one of them would show promise as a winner." Teddy turned around to face his wife, "I tied up a good bit of capital in that purchase."

"I know you did, sweetheart. It just takes time to find the right horse."

Teddy turned back around and looked across the pasture. He didn't understand this horse racing business. Unfortunately, he had no previous experience to draw from, and he had trusted his wife and her uncle's instincts. They shared a love for animals, and both were skilled at training horses.

Since they had married, Teddy and Katie had remodeled the farmhouse she'd inherited after her grandmother passed away. When they finished the remodeling project, he took out a bank loan to purchase the five horses the previous fall and make some upgrades to the farm.

The horses were all sold to them as potential winners. The most impressive of the five had suffered a torn ligament in his leg shortly after they bought him.

Katie and Sammy wanted to use the farm to train horses to race. One night, seeing the excitement in his wife's eyes as she and Sammy discussed their plans for the property, he offered to finance the renovations needed to bring the farm up to current racing standards.

When it was all said and done, the price tag for the farm's upgrades was more than the renovations for the one-hundred-year-old farmhouse.

Teddy was clearly out of his league.

Although he didn't regret the investment, Teddy was concerned their horses were taking too long to train, and the expenses were mounting. He wasn't used to being indebted to a bank.

"I don't know, Katie, this business is pricey. I thought one horse would be ready to race by June, and the others would all be ready by the September race. Did I misunderstand you?"

She shrugged. "It just takes time, Teddy. Be patient."

He looked sternly into his glass of wine and said, "Patience. Okay. Well, this morning, I paid the quarterly interest payment to the bank for the loan to finance this little business of yours. So, I suggest you get with Sammy tomorrow and figure out how you're going to make this business profitable."

Katie froze. What did he just say? Her fingers tightened on her wine glass. Her narrowed eyes and flaring nostrils signaled an impending explosion. Instead, she set her glass on the side table and jumped up from the rocker. By the time Teddy had formed a more rational response, she was off the porch, striding toward the stable.

Teddy knew he had spoken too sharply to her, but she needed to understand that horse training was no longer a leisurely hobby as it had been while her grandparents were alive.

Things had changed.

The dynamics of the farm had changed when they completed the modifications. With the purchase of more horses, they now needed a return on the investment.

He stayed on the porch until just before dark and waited for Katie to return to the house. As he scrolled his phone, he remembered what she had said about having only one horse with a championship bloodline.

Why had she recommended buying those horses if they weren't championship caliber?

Finally, he saw her and Sammy walking up the trail from the stables, his limp slightly more pronounced. His sandy blond hair, heavily streaked with gray, stuck out from beneath his ball cap. Sammy waved as he climbed the steps to his garage apartment, and Katie walked onto the back porch.

"Listen, Katie, I'm sorry. I was a little short with you earlier."

Katie turned and looked at him with her piercing green eyes. Hurt and anger flickered across her face. "You think?" She said as she walked into the house and slammed the screened door.

Teddy released a deep breath and drained the last of his wine. He knew there would be no point trying to explain his frustration now. He'd already screwed up, and she would never listen to his reasoning tonight.

As he leaned back in his chair, he decided he would take a few days and go down to Savannah to clear out the offices of his deceased Uncle Frederick's law firm. He had been delaying the trip for several months. There were no surgeries scheduled for the next four days, and he could quickly reschedule any of the wellness checkups over the next couple of weeks. He hated to leave while she was mad at him, but he really needed to attend to this business.

The following day when Teddy came downstairs, Katie, Mattie Grace, and Sammy were already in the kitchen eating breakfast. Katie gave him an icy stare and stabbed a bite of French toast with her fork. Teddy looked over at Sammy, who shrugged and stirred his coffee.

Mattie Grace was the only one of the three who displayed any semblance of normal conversation throughout the meal. When she saw his suitcase next to the stairwell, she asked, "Daddy, are you going on a vacation?"

"No, princess. I need to make a quick trip to Savannah to take care of some business that I've been putting off."

Mattie Grace clasped her hands in a pleading pose she must have picked up from a Disney princess character. "Oh, Daddy, I want to go with you. Please, can I go?"

She even looked like a princess with that long auburn hair and the long flowing nightgown. "Not this time, sweetie. I promise you I'll be home for Friday's pizza night." He gave her a playful wink. "You know I can't miss my little girl's birthday!"

Mattie Grace ran into his arms and said, "Daddy, please don't go. I'll miss you so much."

Teddy looked over his daughter's head. "Do you hear that, Katie? Mattie Grace will miss me."

Katie rolled her eyes as she began to load the dishes into the dishwasher, but as she turned away, he thought he saw a glimpse of a smile.

Chapter Four

S tate Road 16 going toward Savannah scrolled before him as his eyes stayed on the white Honda Civic that he'd trailed since leaving the outskirts of Macon. Teddy replayed the previous night's conversation with Katie. "How had they gotten to this place? And where did this go so wrong?"

He'd only wanted to make her childhood dream become a reality. Still, somewhere along the way, he had taken on the role of the CEO, which meant he was subconsciously treating his wife as an employee.

Spotting a restaurant up ahead, he changed lanes to exit the interstate.

Still stirring his coffee, Teddy walked outside and stood next to his car for a few minutes to enjoy the warmth from the morning sun. A few spaces over, a couple stood next to their vehicle, talking in a quiet tone. The man held the woman's hands close to his chest, and every so often he would lift her hands to his lips.

That could be he and Katie when they first married. He missed those days.

Teddy shook it off and allowed his mind to return to the present.

He had to get a handle on the situation. Katie was a smart woman. He had to make her see that the racing business did not differ from any other business she provided services to when she worked in public accounting.

If, and if was a big word! If they won the Derby one year, their winnings could be huge. Then he could pay off the debt to the bank.

But all the horses they currently owned would be too old to compete in the next Derby.

What was more important, a healthy balance sheet or a healthy marriage?

Katie had been wrong to freeze him out, but he'd been wrong, too. He should have never spoken to her in that tone of voice. Why had he let the interest payment upset him? He knew there were payments involved when he took out the loan. He should have waited a couple of days before bringing it up.

Now, he could never take those words back—never get that evening back.

He glanced once more at the young couple, who continued to gaze into each other's eyes.

Of course, he wanted Katie to be happy. He also wanted the business to be successful. Was it too much to ask for both?

Teddy unlocked the car and placed his coffee in the cupholder. As he merged back onto the interstate, he decided to contact a realtor and discuss listing his uncle's office building while in Savannah. He'd meant to list the property for several months, but he had been so busy he'd put it off. Selling the property now would eliminate some of the financial pressure.

When his uncle and aunt moved to Savannah fifty years earlier, he'd rented a two-room office suite until he could save up enough money to make a down payment on a house in the downtown area. Once he made the modifications to bring the house up to code, he settled in and stayed. He'd never even moved his desk from where it was placed by the furniture delivery team.

Teddy reasoned that since the law office's location was in the landmark district of Forsyth Park, he should get an updated property appraisal. The most recent assessment was done in 2015, the year after his uncle and aunt had died. He'd kept the law office as a rental, and it had been worth keeping as long as the young attorney was renting it. Now that he had moved out, it just seemed like the perfect time to sell.

On the way back from dinner that evening, Teddy called home. Katie answered on the third ring, but her voice was heavy. She was already in bed and had fallen asleep while watching television. They didn't talk long. Teddy promised he'd call her earlier the following night.

The next morning, while cleaning out his uncle's filing cabinet, he received a call from a man who had shown interest in purchasing his dad's real estate company several years earlier.

"Mr. Williams, this is Frank Nordstrom. I've spoken with Frederick Simpson on numerous occasions regarding your father's real estate business. I was wondering if you would have time to sit down with me for a few moments this afternoon?"

Teddy remembered the message from Mr. Nordstrom still lying on his desk at home. He'd meant to return the call earlier, but he kept putting it off. "Yes, sir. I can meet you this afternoon."

At precisely three o'clock, a black Mercedes pulled in front of the law office. A professional-looking gentleman with straight black hair peppered with gray removed a briefcase from the sedan's backseat and walked toward the front door. He wore a navy blazer, white button-down shirt, and gray dress slacks.

Tall. Above-average build. Fair complexion. Nothing that stood out or attracted attention.

There was something in the way he carried himself though, a confidence in his gait, which reminded Teddy of his father.

Nordstrom smiled as he looked around the business district and moved toward the walkway.

The bell above the door jingled, signaling he had arrived. Teddy went into the reception area where the visitor stood. "Good afternoon," he said, extending his hand.

After the introductions, Frank added, "My condolences on your loss. I had the privilege of meeting both your father and your uncle several years ago."

"Thank you, Frank. As you can imagine, it was tough losing them both in the same year."

After his uncle passed, he immediately found a guy fresh out of law school who needed a place to work. He'd been renting this office to the young man for the past six years. But the freshly minted lawyer secured a job with a big New York law firm, and he left at the end of December. It was time to put the place on the market.

"I've been watching for you to come down. You haven't been back to Savannah in a while."

"It's been a while."

"Your uncle was an interesting man," Nordstrom said. "I thoroughly enjoyed talking to him. In fact, I sat in this office one afternoon for over two hours listening to his stories about Savannah. He could really spin a story."

"That's for sure." Teddy smiled, savoring the memory. He and his siblings were often spellbound as Uncle Frederick spun a ghost story certain to keep them jumping at noises all night. "My uncle mentioned that you'd contacted him after my dad's stroke and again in November before his death."

"That's right. I've wanted to purchase your family's business since before your father got sick." Nordstrom was a licensed realtor, he explained, and was looking for an established business in the Abington area. He admitted the growth in that area of the state was skyrocketing. He'd driven through Abington several times, but he fell in love with the area one autumn day when he flew over the city in a helicopter looking for large tracts of land.

"The town surrounded by the lake and sitting at the foothills of the Blue Ridge Mountains, oh well—I'd like to move there permanently."

"Well, I appreciate your interest, but Mom is now helping me run the business." Teddy said, motioning to a seat on the sofa, and explaining he'd been showing her the ropes while establishing his pediatric practice. His mom had a degree in interior design, but unfortunately, when she married and started having children, she never pursued her dream.

Once Teddy's dad became incapacitated, she spent her days by his side until his death. Now that she had all this time on her hands, learning the real estate business helped to fill those lonely days.

Nordstrom said, "Your mother's name is Claire, right?"

"That's right."

"Does she have her license?"

"No, but she plans to take the test next month. I'm showing her the administrative part of the business now. I'm afraid she'd be disappointed if she thought I was trying to sell the business out from under her."

As soon as the words came out of his mouth, he thought of Katie.

Teddy was relieved Nordstrom understood his dilemma. Frank suggested asking his mom to meet with them at the office in Abington. Frank explained that he would welcome her involvement if they could reach an understanding, either as a consultant or an associate if she was interested in selling properties. Or maybe she would consider an administrative position. He thought this could be a good deal for all of them.

Teddy felt relaxed with Frank and remembered his uncle's remark about his being a 'man's man, and comfortable in his skin.' Teddy offered Frank a cup of coffee. Then they moved into the break room while Teddy brewed a fresh pot.

"I must admit, Frank," Teddy said as he measured the coffee into the filtered basket, "I would like nothing more than to sell the business. Real estate was my dad's profession, and he had planned to groom my younger brother, Bobby, to take over at some point. Unfortunately, when Bobby and our sister were killed in a car accident, Dad hoped I'd take over for him," Teddy paused, "but it just wasn't right for me."

"Excuse me, Teddy. Did you say you own a pediatrics practice in Abington?"

"That's right. I realize this must sound absurd. A medical doctor running a real estate office." Teddy laughed. "Actually, it was a bone of contention between my dad and me for many years."

"How about your mom?"

"Mom just wants me to be happy. She knows I've dreamt of practicing medicine since I was a young boy following my grandfather around town." Teddy smiled at the memory. "My grandfather would let me carry his black bag for him." Teddy reached for two mugs and said, "I don't know what made me tell you that story."

"I have that effect on folks. People I barely even know will share their most private secrets with me." Frank grinned and pointed to his head. "It must be the gray streaks in my hair."

Teddy chuckled. He liked Frank. Somehow, Teddy knew they could be great friends. Frank was wise and thoughtful and showed no signs of arrogance. He appeared to be aboveboard.

While Teddy and Frank finished their coffee, they decided to meet in Abington. Teddy warned Frank that he might be unable to convince his mother to sell the business. However, he would be remiss if he didn't arrange a meeting for them to discuss the details.

Two hours later, when Frank left the office, Teddy had a good feeling about the upcoming meeting. He was hopeful his mother would keep an open mind.

Teddy went back to work cleaning out the filing cabinet. When he finished, the streetlights were on. He reached for the phone and dialed Katie. Mattie Grace answered the phone and spent fifteen minutes telling him about her day at school and describing the cupcakes she wanted for her birthday party.

"Can I speak to Mommy, please?"

Katie picked up the phone. She seemed distracted. Teddy asked about her day, but Katie just yawned and said she needed to get Mattie

Grace ready for bed. He asked her to kiss Mattie Grace goodnight. Then they hung up.

Teddy rocked back in his chair. His wife and his mother were both strong women. He needed to talk his mom into selling the business to Frank, and he'd like to get out of the doghouse with Katie. Somehow, he needed to restore their relationship to where it was before they went into the racing business.

He could think of no reason why the racehorse business shouldn't work. They were both mature adults.

But first, *he* had to change the way he was looking at this investment.

Chapter Five

On Friday morning, Teddy met with the realtor and handed over a key to his uncle's law office. He was encouraged that the realtor thought the property would sell quickly.

Frank Nordstrom had given him an unofficial review of the property the previous afternoon. The commercial realtor's appraisal came within ten thousand dollars of Frank's assessment. Teddy felt the price he was asking was in line with other properties listed on the historic site.

When the meeting ended, it was already ten o'clock. Finally, Teddy was ready to get on the road and head home. As he backed out of the parking lot, he remembered his conversation with Frank. He was careful to point out any problems that could arise with a building of a certain age. It happened all the time.

Frank seemed to have an innate ability to read people's emotions, and he seemed to care as much about the purchaser's interest as he did with the sellers. On the surface, Frank was a good, solid man.

As Teddy reached the interstate, he thought about how perfect Frank would be for his mother. But, unfortunately, she'd never known a partnership like she would have with someone like Frank.

Mattie Grace had spoken to him on the phone both nights and reminded him of his promise to be home in time to celebrate her birthday. Sammy usually joined them for pizza night, too. It was a casual meal, marking the end of another week. When the weather allowed, the adults sat in the rocking chairs—often in front of the rock fireplace, they'd added to the back porch—and watched Mattie Grace chase lightning bugs.

As Teddy reached the city of Atlanta, the bumper-to-bumper traffic slowed to a snail's pace. He crept along for over forty-five minutes until he reached exit 249D, the North Avenue location of one of Atlanta's oldest iconic drive-in restaurants. He called Katie's cellphone to let her know he was running behind schedule because of the traffic.

He left a message.

An hour later, she still hadn't returned his call.

Now that she wasn't answering his call and hadn't called him back, he realized that perhaps two and a half days wasn't enough time for Katie to get over being mad at him.

Guess I'm still in the doghouse, but what can I do about it?

Well, he knew when he married her that she was a feisty girl, and they'd just have to work through it.

He looked over the horizon and saw that traffic was moving steadily up ahead. If he could get around the stalled traffic jam, he could make it home with plenty of time to spare.

Chapter Six

B randon Stone stood in line at the gate, waiting for the
security guard to open the heavy steel gated door to the
grounds of the federal penitentiary. One thing he'd learned
about the employees at the prison: no one ever got in a hurry. They
had a shift to work—an eight-hour shift, and for that period, they
could not leave the premises without special permission from the
Warden.

The Warden didn't permit special favors—for anyone.

A heavyset guard, possibly in his late sixties, got out of his car and
started across the parking lot. He seemed obsessed with the toothpick
he moved around in his mouth. Finally, he looked toward the gate and
raised his finger to Stone, but he didn't move any faster.

It really didn't matter, though. Stone wasn't in a hurry to get inside
the prison. The ten o'clock meeting with Fitz Ramona and his uncle,
Nic Suarez, was not something he was looking forward to—he'd
rather be anywhere else in the universe.

Finally, the security guard unlocked the gate, and held the door for
Stone to walk through.

"Thank you, sir," Stone said as he walked past the armed guard.

He reached inside the guardhouse and grabbed his clipboard.
"Name?"

"Stone. Brandon Stone. Counsel for Fitz Ramona and Nic Suarez."

The guard motioned toward the door to the prison. "Go on in.
They'll finish the security check at the first door just past the
entrance."

Stone walked through the prison door. Nervous sweat drenched his freshly laundered shirt. Immediately, the smell of greasy food hit him like a ton of bricks. It reminded him of being a young boy at camp again. He'd never been able to eat those powdered eggs and half-cooked sausage patties. The smell was the same. He swallowed hard, trying to keep from gagging.

At the next security check, a skinny little fellow with a gold-capped tooth greeted him. The guard checked Stone's credentials and puffed on a cigarette held between his teeth. As he busily completed the paperwork attached to the clipboard, gray ashes drifted over the desk like snowflakes.

Stone glanced at the guy's yellow-stained fingers with disgust. All he had to do was get these two yahoos off. He just had to prove *beyond a reasonable doubt* that the rogue Special Agent Bill Bowen had acted alone concerning both the kidnapping and human trafficking charges and that he was not a member of the cartel. It sounded simple enough, and if he weren't working for the cartel, he might even enjoy defending this case. But the Suarez Cartel, well… that was a different story. If he failed, he could die, or someone close to him could get hurt. On the other hand, if he succeeded, he could find himself under their thumb forever. Those guys weren't known for letting you go if they found you useful. Stone looked up, and the cigarette was still in the guard's mouth. The guard smiled, his gold tooth shining in the overhead light. "You're good to go," he said with a chuckle. "Enjoy your visit."

A natural comedian, that guy—the highlight of his day was telling the visitors to enjoy their visit. The man probably didn't even understand the irony of his statement. It didn't matter. Stone was inside now, and hopefully, within an hour, he'd be walking out the door. He walked to the visitors' area and signed in. In a few brief minutes, they called his name from an electronic device and directed him to room 8A. He'd been there six times previously, and somehow he'd always met with his clients in the same room.

What were the chances?

When he became a defense attorney, he understood that many of the people he would represent would be guilty. That was what made the legal system work. He did his best job, and that kept the prosecution honest. They couldn't just railroad an innocent man; they had to play by the rules and bring their A-game. Real evidence. I's dotted. T's crossed.

Afterward, win or lose, they'd all—defense team and prosecutors alike—go out for drinks. Because they weren't really on opposing sides. They were cogs in the same machine, each doing their part to make sure justice was served.

At least, that was the way it was supposed to work.

But this case was different. He couldn't afford to lose, but he wasn't sure he could win without compromising his ethics. He'd often heard the thing a defense attorney feared the most was an innocent man. It had sounded true at the time, but now he knew it was wrong. These guys were anything but innocent, and Stone was terrified out of his mind. He'd heard stories about the cartel. They didn't take failure lightly, and when they decided to dispose of someone, they did so swiftly.

Stone could not fail.

He straightened his shoulders and walked into room 8A, where Fitz Ramona sat in a chair with chains attached to his ankles. The handcuffs were still in place. Something Stone and the Warden had agreed to the first time he visited the prison.

Stone greeted Fitz, sat down at the table, and removed a vanilla file from his briefcase. It took him less than thirty minutes to hammer out the information he needed from Fitz. He just hoped Fitz was telling the truth—or at least some semblance of the truth.

But these guys wouldn't recognize the truth if it hit them in the face. Maybe he just needed to settle for a facsimile of truth that couldn't be refuted.

As a courtesy, when the meeting was over, and because Stone liked Fitz, he stood and thanked him for his time.

In a few minutes, they escorted Nic into the room. Again, his ankles were shackled, and his hands secured in cuffs. Nic was a polite enough guy when he wanted to be, and Stone could almost like him, but he always seemed to do or say something that unnerved him.

No Mr. Nice Guy today, though. Nic started making threats the moment the door closed behind the guard. "You better damn well get us out of here, Stone. I don't do well inside the pen."

"I'm working on it. Let's get busy going through these questions."

Stone began by asking Nic about Special Agent Bill Bowen.

"You know he wasn't one of us, man. Bowen was a moron! That's the reason he got killed. The FBI didn't even want him."

"That's fine, but I have to prove it, Nic. That's what the court system requires of me as your defense attorney. I have to prove beyond a reasonable doubt that Special Agent Bowen was not working on behalf of the Suarez Cartel."

Nic's eyes narrowed. "Listen, Dude. You can hire someone to testify in court for the right amount of money. Credible people—that will say whatever you tell them to say."

Stone asked a few more questions and then took a moment to review his notes, ensuring he'd left nothing unanswered.

"Did you hear me? You can hire someone…."

Sweat broke out on Stone's forehead. "I could get disbarred for that kind of unethical conduct."

Nic jumped up and kicked the chair backward. It banged against the cinderblock wall like a gunshot. Nic glanced toward the door. Then he towered over Stone and whispered, "Would you rather be disbarred or dead?"

The door opened, and the guard looked first at Stone, then at the chair lying twisted on the floor.

Stone nodded. "Everything's fine here." He was surprised to find his voice was steady.

The guard, looking grateful for the evasion, remained just inside the opened door.

"We're done here," Stone said. "I've got everything I need." He stood and stuffed the papers into his briefcase. Then he paused and looked Nic squarely in the eyes. "Nic, I believe I can win this case without it."

He licked his lips, trying not to think about what the cartel would do if he failed to deliver.

Nic's eyes were cold and flat, his voice barely audible. "You'd better!"

Chapter Seven

April 2021

The morning passed too slowly as Katie counted the hours until Teddy got home. She'd decided earlier they'd finish up around noon because she needed to go to the market, clean up the house, and decorate for Mattie Grace's party. Looking at her watch, she said to Sammy, "I've got a ton of things to do before Mattie Grace and Teddy get home. Let's walk the horses around the track once more and call it a day."

Sammy's distracted smile told her he was lost in his own thoughts. She'd learned to watch his facial expressions when she spoke to him for clues to his mood.

After a moment, Sammy said, "Can you believe we got a real racetrack on these thirty acres?"

"I know, right?" Katie said. "And not just any track. A track with the same level and distance as the one at Churchill Downs."

Looking out over the property, a sadness swept over Katie. The conversation with her grandparents about their will still brought tears to her eyes, even after all these years. She'd known immediately that she wanted to convert the property into a horse farm—a real racehorse farm. She had more than enough room to raise fifteen racehorses and keep a decent number of riding horses, too.

Sammy interrupted her reflection. "Have you heard from Teddy this morning? Is he on his way back?"

She scrunched her nose. "Not yet. I know it's only been two days, but I'm ready for him to get home. I've missed him."

"Me, too." Sammy looked toward the barn. "Remember that night we told him about our dream for the farm?"

Katie nodded and smiled. It was thoughtful of Sammy to try to distract her from the fact that her husband hadn't called.

Sammy went on. "Me and you were talking so loud—Teddy covered his ears with his hands."

"I remember." Katie recalled the conversation around the dinner table as Sammy explained his plan to divide the property between three separate fields: a twenty-acre field for summer, a twenty-acre field for spring and winter. They would build a racetrack on the final thirty acres. It was a well-devised plan. She'd been impressed with it, and apparently, so had Teddy.

"When Teddy told us he'd finance the farm," Sammy said, "that's the night he became my brother. Until then, nobody but you had believed in me since... since the accident."

It had happened before Katie was born when Sammy was only fifteen. He'd been begging his parents to let him drive the tractor. When Sammy finally got the chance, somehow, when he turned the tractor at the end of the row, he'd miscalculated the distance to the nearby ditch. The tractor flipped, and it had partially trapped him underneath. They'd air-flighted him to a hospital in Atlanta that specialized in brain injuries, and it had been touch and go for a week or so. Physically, he'd recovered quickly, except for a stiff leg, but his mental struggles had affected his speech and self-confidence.

She marveled at how far Sammy's conversational skills had advanced since Teddy had been in their lives. Before Teddy, she and Sammy would work in the stables all afternoon with no measurable exchange.

Teddy's influence had improved Sammy's life—all of their lives.

Katie rubbed her uncle's arm, her throat suddenly tight with gratitude for her husband's loving, accepting nature. His condescending remark about the ranch was out of character. Now she wished she'd explored his reasons with him, instead of shutting him out. She'd just been so hurt and angry, she knew if she'd tried to talk to him then, she'd say things she'd regret.

"Teddy Williams is a good man, Katie," Sammy stated as if there were multiple meanings to the remark.

"I know he is." Katie beamed. Teddy had never once resented her assuming responsibility for her Uncle Sammy's wellbeing, which allowed him to continue to live in the apartment above the garage behind the *big house*—a term coined by Mattie Grace during the renovation.

Because Nana and Papa had protected Sammy after the accident, it had stifled his social and cognitive development. He could live alone, but he had little understanding of money and budgets. Katie paid the few monthly bills he incurred and invested his money. He'd learned to operate the microwave and coffeemaker, but he still hadn't mastered cooking a simple meal. However, he had an innate ability to communicate with horses.

As they returned the horses to the barn, Katie was grateful her grandparents had left the house and twenty-five acres of property to her. Even so, they couldn't have done it without Sammy's twenty acres and the thirty extra acres they'd bought from her uncles, Stephen and Roger.

Or, of course, without Teddy.

Closing the door of the barn, Sammy looked around and said, "Looks pretty good, huh, Katie? Now we've just got to figure out a way to make this thing work, so you and Teddy can get back to being a happy couple."

****

Katie stepped back and spread her arms, admiring the shiny foilstreamers and brightly colored My Little Pony balloons that transformed her kitchen into a wonderland. She and Sammy had spent the afternoon decorating the room for Mattie Grace's birthday celebration. A few packages strategically placed at the end of the table completed the tableau. The glitter-infused ribbons shimmered in the light.

Mattie Grace was going to love it.

Sammy finished attaching the last balloon and gave her a crooked grin. "Looks good, Katie girl."

She nodded, then glanced at her watch. "I'd better get showered and changed before Colleen drops Mattie Grace off. They'll be leaving for Angie's soccer game in about thirty minutes." She paused, "Thanks for your help."

He waved a dismissive hand. "Happy to. You still mad at Teddy?"

"I'm not sure yet. I guess we'll see when he gets home."

He met her gaze with troubled eyes, and she realized how much her argument with Teddy had bothered him.

"Oh, Sammy..." She laid a hand on his forearm. "Couples get angry sometimes. It doesn't mean they don't love each other. Now, let's go get ready for the party."

Katie was coming down the steps from their bedroom when she heard Teddy's car coming up the driveway. Her heart skipped a beat, and she smiled in spite of herself. That charming, infuriating man— after seven years of marriage, he could still make her stomach flutter.

She watched from the window as he got out of the car and walked toward the back porch. Then she moved to the sink and pretended to be washing the few utensils that lay on the counter. Would he put his arms around her waist and kiss her neck as he always did? She hadn't heard from him all day. Maybe Sammy was right, and her anger had created a rift in her marriage.

When she felt her husband's arms encircle her waist, the knot in her stomach unclenched.

"You still mad at me?" Teddy asked, his breath warm against her ear. "You haven't answered my calls today."

"Calls?" Katie reached for her phone in her pocket. It wasn't there. "Oh, my gosh! I must have left my phone in the car when I brought in the groceries."

"Oh, okay." He sounded relieved.

Katie turned around to face him, "Yes. I'm still mad." She was careful to add a little sass to her tone for emphasis. "But it'll just have to wait until after the birthday party."

"I look forward to it," Teddy said. The warmth in his tone sent a tingle through her. As he turned to walk away, he looked over his shoulder and winked.

Suppressing a smile, Katie wagged her finger at him. "Don't think you're getting off easy, Mister!"

He chuckled.

Then, walking toward the refrigerator, he asked, "What's on the birthday menu?"

"Mattie Grace wants cheese pizza, fried pickles, and Cheetos. She also asked for miniature cupcakes with chocolate frosting and colorful sprinkles instead of a traditional birthday cake."

They laughed at the absurdity of the menu. But Mattie Grace was their only child, which afforded her the luxury of anything she wanted to eat on her birthday.

"Ooh," Teddy said, "looks like someone made a charcuterie board. Is that for me?"

Katie smiled. She'd hoped they'd have a chance for some adult time after Mattie Grace went to sleep. With a flirtatious toss of her head, she batted her eyelashes at her husband and cooed, "Maaaaybe,"

After supper, they sat in the big black rockers on the front porch of their farmhouse while Mattie Grace played on the top step with her wooden horses, a birthday gift from Sammy. She looked every bit the part of an equestrienne with her new camel-colored riding pants and tiny western mountain boots, both gifts from her grandmother, Claire.

Katie watched their daughter with growing pride. Mattie Grace was tall for her six years of age, and her vocabulary was more advanced than children two years older. Katie and Teddy had included her in all aspects of their lives, and she was mature for her age. Katie nudged Teddy and nodded toward the side of the house.

Just as they had arranged, Sammy rounded the corner leading a Shetland pony. When Mattie Grace saw the big pink bow tied around the pony's head, she squealed, "SAMMY!"

She turned to her parents. "Is that for me?!" At their nods, she screamed with delight. Teddy reached down and took her hand, and the three of them left the porch to meet the new pony.

The horse was a beautiful animal, smoky-black hair with a white blaze running from his forehead to his nose. Sammy had chosen and trained the even-tempered animal for this special little girl in his life. Katie knew Mattie Grace was the closest thing to a daughter Sammy would ever know.

Teddy lifted his daughter onto the small saddle, and Sammy instructed her on the proper way to sit on the horse. Then he carefully took the rope and led them for a few feet. Unaccustomed to having a rider on his back, the pony bucked a little. Katie held her breath, poised to intervene if necessary, but Sammy gently murmured a few words that immediately calmed the animal.

Mattie Grace seemed unruffled by the pony's behavior. Her little hands continued to stroke his neck.

Katie stepped back to allow the men time with Mattie Grace, both clearly excited with the thrill of her first pony ride.

Teddy grinned. "Sammy, look how well Mattie Grace sits that pony. She's a natural."

"She got that posture from her grandmother."

"It must be genetic," Katie said. She moseyed back to her seat on the porch and enjoyed a sip of tea as she finished her chocolate cupcake.

While Mattie Grace was getting to know her pony, Sammy glanced at Teddy and said, "Hey, did you ever have a pony as a kid?"

"No. I grew up a city boy."

That was a good answer. Teddy was indeed a city boy, but he'd adapted so quickly to farm life. Watching Teddy give his full attention to their daughter, Katie smiled. He never looked away from the little girl, and his arms wrapped around her small body, even as he told Sammy about his parents' idea of farm life, which involved an annual trip to a pumpkin patch each fall. A few weeks before Halloween, Teddy explained they would drive out to the country to get a pumpkin to carve into a jack-o'-lantern. Katie laughed as Teddy told Sammy the closest he came to a pony was the hayride led by two horses.

Sammy gave Teddy a sly grin. "You know, Teddy, Katie's always wanted a Thoroughbred racehorse. And her birthday's coming up soon."

Katie turned her head away before Teddy could see her face. There was no way they could afford the kind of horse she'd always dreamed of, especially considering Teddy's comments about making the business profitable.

No, her dream horse would have to stay just that—a dream.

****

Teddy forced a laugh. "Yeah, well. I want a beach house, but you don't see me running off in search of one, do you?"

Part of the research he'd done in Savannah involved a little digging on the costs of a Thoroughbred racehorse. He'd learned it could cost up to one million dollars. As much as he'd like to, he'd need to sell the other horses before he could sink that kind of money into a horse for his wife's birthday.

Grinning, Sammy glanced at Katie. "I'm just the messenger. Katie's been talking about getting a racehorse ever since you agreed to get Mattie Grace a pony for her birthday."

"That wasn't the same." Mattie Grace's gift had pretty much fallen into their lap. "You said it yourself; we just lucked up. The pony's temperament was perfect for Mattie Grace."

Sammy shrugged. "I'm just trying to help you out here. But—if you want to get out of the doghouse, you best start looking for a racehorse to run in the Derby next year."

Shaking his head, Teddy spat on the ground. "And that's the only card to get out of jail?"

Sammy shrugged. "Pretty much."

Katie was watching Mattie Grace trot from one end of the house to another, grinning so wide it looked like her head might split when a light flashed from the woods at the side of the yard. At first, Katie ignored it. There were no houses nearby, and the woods were clearly marked *No Trespassing*. Her eyes must be tricking her. A few moments later, though, the light reappeared.

"Teddy," she called, "do you see that light over in the woods?"

No answer. His intense expression told her he was completely focused on Mattie Grace's safety. When he got like that, nothing else existed. He probably hadn't even heard her.

When the child grew tired, Sammy returned the pony to the stable. Mattie Grace and her father returned to the porch.

"Daddy, do you think Domino is a good name?"

Teddy glanced at Katie and grinned. "Yes, Mattie Grace, I think Domino is an excellent name."

Katie rolled her eyes at her husband and mouthed, "You're such a pushover."

Beaming at her father's approval, Mattie Grace turned to Katie and asked for another cupcake. Katie hesitated. Sure, it was a special occasion, but an extra cupcake might be enough to send her daughter bouncing off the walls. Funny, the experts claimed there was no evidence that sugar made kids hyper. In Katie's opinion, the only people who thought that were people who didn't have children.

Mattie Grace put on her pleading face. "Mommy, pleeeease?"

"Tell you what," Teddy said. "Why don't we each have another treat? To celebrate the addition of Domino into the family."

Katie suppressed a flash of annoyance. He wouldn't be the one staying up with Mattie Grace if she was too wired up to sleep. But, hey, there would only ever be one, sixth birthday. No harm in living a little, right?

When Teddy returned from the kitchen, he winked at Katie as he handed her a cupcake. Then he knelt beside their daughter and placed one into her tiny hand.

Mattie Grace grinned and dove into the cupcake face first. Katie shook her head, laughing. Their daughter looked just like her, with her long auburn curls and bright green eyes, but she had her father's playful spirit—one of the many things Katie loved about them both.

As Teddy bit into his cupcake, he lifted his head and looked toward the woods, a thoughtful expression on his face.

"What is it, Teddy?" Katie followed his gaze toward the woods, where another flash was fading.

He walked to the end of the porch and stared intently toward the trees. "Did you see that light, Katie?"

"Yes, I mentioned it to you earlier when Mattie Grace was on the pony."

Mattie Grace looked up, her face smeared with chocolate frosting. "Domino, my pony's name is Domino!"

Teddy chuckled at her rebuke. As he walked back to his seat, Katie watched the last of the light recede.

"That is weird," Teddy said. "It could be an image from the sun. Anyway, the light has moved on."

****

The man in the woods watched the young family as the father boosted the child onto the pony. Through his binoculars, the little girl's smile looked radiant. The father's jawline had the faintest trace of stubble. Apparently, with the tension of the previous few days gone, the woman looked relaxed. The watcher wondered what had happened to have alleviated her temper.

He had developed a pattern of sitting on a tree stump where the front yard was visible through the foliage. The family spent most warm evenings on the porch following their evening meal. Tonight, however, they appeared to be enjoying a celebration.

He wondered how long they'd been married. Not too long, he imagined, by the way the woman gazed at her husband. Even from afar, it was obvious she adored him.

Once the woman looked his way, as if she sensed his presence, her face became stern. He realized she wasn't the kind of woman you would want to cross.

The man went inside and came back with three cupcakes. As he bit into one, he stopped and stared into the woods. The watcher shivered. They were looking right at him. But that was impossible. He…

Oh, crap.

He stared down at his binoculars. The sun had shifted, and the angle of the light hitting the lens of his binoculars created a glistening reflection.

Quickly, he jerked the binoculars away from his face, slapped the caps over the lenses, and moved deeper into the woods.

Chapter Eight

S aturday afternoon, when Teddy finished his rounds and walked through the hospital portico, he stopped and looked up at the sky. It was a brilliant blue, almost a cobalt color overhead, fading as it edged toward the horizon. As the warm Georgia sun shone on his face, he decided to grill dinner for the family. He'd stop by the market on the way home and pick up four steaks. Nice, thick ones, with plenty of marble.

An hour later, driving up the blacktop driveway to the farm, he thought of the crooked, graveled trail he'd traveled the day he met Katie for the first time. The remodel, which had started two years after Teddy and Katie married, totally changed the house's exterior facade. It transformed the two-story farmhouse into a modern-day home with an additional wing that included a master suite, an office for Teddy, and a sunroom.

The contractor suggested increasing the back porch size to fit the house's length, beginning with French doors opening from the sunroom to the long-extended porch, and that suggestion alone had been worth the investment. The enlarged structure with its white-sided exterior, black shutters, and soft black architectural roof stood positioned to oversee the large farm surrounded by white fencing. Moreover, it made for a picturesque setting worthy of gracing the cover of any prominent southern magazine.

Besides the rock fireplace on the back porch, Katie designed a fireplace to fit the corner of their master suite.

At first, Teddy brushed her off, but, while they were still in the planning stages, a storm swept through from Canada one snowy night and knocked out the power and the heat. They'd stayed up past midnight, huddling in front of the fireplace in the kitchen. They considered sleeping in the recliner and on the sofa, but both were so uncomfortable, they had second thoughts. Teddy had a surgery scheduled the following morning, and he was afraid he'd pull a muscle in his back if he slept in the chair.

As they shivered in bed that night, Mattie Grace lying between them to keep her warm, he decided a fireplace in the bedroom would be a practical addition.

Teddy parked his vehicle in the detached garage and removed the bag of groceries from the trunk. As he walked toward the backdoor, he spotted Sammy slowly strolling up from the stable.

"Hey, man. When you get cleaned up, come on up to the house. I'm going to fire up the grill in about an hour, and you can keep me company while I cook the steaks."

Sammy rubbed his hands together. A grin spread across his face as he went up the stairs, taking the steps two at a time.

Teddy went inside and laid the steaks out on a wooden board on the granite island. He seasoned the steaks with garlic salt, Worcestershire sauce, and freshly ground pepper and prepared the potatoes for baking.

Katie came into the kitchen, she looked over his shoulder and rested her chin on his back. "You're cooking dinner tonight, I see."

"Yeah. It's going to be an epic meal. There's nothing too good for *my* family." Teddy turned and kissed her cheek.

While Katie went over to the refrigerator and gathered ingredients for a salad, Teddy sliced the mushrooms and chopped some onion to sauté.

He needed the black iron skillet to sauté the mushrooms, the one Katie's grandmother always used for cooking cornbread. Teddy looked on the middle shelf of the island and glanced over at the stove.

"It's on the bottom shelf."

After Katie finished the salad, she suggested they eat on the back porch.

"Sounds good," Teddy agreed.

She grabbed the blue and white checkered tablecloth and napkins from the drawer and went out to set the table. Then she came back in and poured herself a glass of chardonnay and pulled up a stool next to the island. "Teddy, what do you want to drink while you're grilling those steaks? Can I get you a water or a glass of tea?"

Carrying a platter loaded with tongs, paper towels, and other items needed for grilling, Teddy walked toward the back door and said, "A water would be great. Would you bring Sammy one, too? I see he's already showered and on his way over."

Seeing the joy on Sammy's face as he walked toward the porch, Teddy suddenly realized the ranch was much more than a place to live for Sammy. It was a form of therapy. The consistency of living on the farm and training the horses since his parents' death had made an enormous difference in his development. Maybe, just maybe, that was enough to make the endeavor worthwhile, even if it wasn't profitable.

Everything in life shouldn't be about profits.

After dinner, they lingered at the table, watching Mattie Grace play with her plastic horses. During a lull in the conversation, Katie said, "I'm thinking about investing in a horse to race in The Kentucky Derby."

Teddy glanced over at Sammy and raised his eyebrows.

It was a great idea. He'd been having the same thought.

"I've done my homework, Teddy," Katie said, with a sassy tilt to her chin, "If that's what you're thinking."

"Well, I'm glad to hear you're looking around for a good deal on a horse."

"I'm not just looking for a good deal. I've found the horse I'm interested in buying. Talking Jack is a two-year-old Thoroughbred, and he's one of the fastest horses in Kentucky. A former Belmont winner sired him."

Trying to suppress a smile, Teddy wiped his mouth with his napkin.

Sammy cleared his throat and said, "Teddy, she's looked into it—and if everything she's saying is true, I may invest, too."

Teddy shot Sammy a questioning look. Sammy had contributed his share of the land to this endeavor. Still, he had never shown an interest in investing in anything before. "Okay, fine. I see what you guys are doing here. You're going to railroad me into this little purchase of yours."

"There's nothing little about this purchase, Teddy," Katie said.

"Well, just so you both know, I met with the accountant about filing our taxes for last year, and we're operating in the red. Fortunately, we set up an LLC for the farm, which should help us some. We should be able to carry some of the losses forward to another tax year. But if you want to invest in a champion racehorse, we'll need to sell the horses we purchased last year."

Katie glanced at Sammy and then at Teddy. "Excuse me, Teddy. What did you say?"

"I said if you want to invest in a champion racehorse ..."

"No. No, before that, it sounded like you said you'd set up an LLC."

"Yes. That's correct. That's exactly what I said. You know the drill, Katie. People set up a corporation to protect themselves."

She finished her iced tea in silence. Red splotches appeared on her neck. She turned to Teddy and asked coolly, "Why would you even think about establishing an LLC without our input?"

Sammy drained the last of his tea and took his plate into the kitchen.

Teddy and Katie sat in uncomfortable silence as Sammy came back to the porch and kissed Mattie Grace goodnight before heading to his apartment.

Then Katie reached for her plate and stalked away from the table. When she turned around at the door, the vein on her forehead bulged. She pointed to Sammy's retreating back, and said, "Sammy and I own this property, Teddy! You can't keep making decisions without consulting with us."

Chapter Nine

The next morning, Teddy awakened early. After so many years of waking at the same time, his body naturally sprang to full consciousness at 5:30 a.m. each day. On Sundays, however, he would slip out of bed and let Katie sleep late. Today, he tiptoed downstairs and made coffee and then walked down to the mailbox. By the time Katie and Mattie Grace woke up, he had already read the morning paper.

Katie's silence during breakfast told him she was still upset. Fortunately, Mattie Grace's chatter filled the void, and Teddy was glad she didn't seem to notice the tension between himself and her mother. Katie picked at her food for a bit, then pushed her plate away and said, "I'm going up to take a shower." When she came back downstairs, she had on her riding clothes.

"Are you going riding this morning?" Teddy asked. As soon as he said it, he wanted to slap his own forehead. What a stupid question.

"Yeah, I'll be down at the stables."

While Teddy finished cleaning up the kitchen, he thought about Katie's position. It was true that, although he'd used his own money left to him by his Uncle Frederick and Aunt Mary to renovate the house, Katie was technically correct when she pointed out that the property belonged to her and Sammy.

When he'd decided to update the farm for raising racehorses, he knew it would cost a fair bit of capital. His only intention was to make his wife happy. Now, it seemed that ever since he agreed to finance the renovation, he and Katie had done nothing but fight about the farm.

Looking around the kitchen, Teddy remembered the old Formica table where he sat the first time he visited the farm. It was the day he met Tom and Nora Hawkins and their granddaughter, Katie. Although the kitchen now included all the fancy appliances of the twenty-first century, it pleased him that the renovation did not destroy the kitchen's character.

As soon as Katie inherited the property, he knew this would be their forever home. The reason he'd poured a bit of himself into the remodel of the old house, trying to preserve as much of the history of the century-old structure as possible while installing many modern-day conveniences, so they both would be proud to call it their home.

Their home.

All right, maybe he should have consulted Katie about creating the LLC. But that was sound business sense. It had never occurred to him that she would disagree.

Her words from the night before still echoed in his mind. *Sammy and I own this property.* It stung that, after all the time and money he'd spent on this place, *their* place, she'd been so quick to cut him out of it.

Teddy stood at the kitchen window looking out over the pasture where the horses grazed in the morning sun. The freshly painted fencing accentuated the horses' gleaming coats and graceful beauty, and the morning dew glistened on the carpet of thick green grass. The sky was a blue so rich and deep it looked like you could drink it. It was a spectacular setting, and he wished he knew an artist who could paint it.

It was at this same window that he'd learned to appreciate the solitude of farm life. Standing in that comfortable but antiquated kitchen, he'd noticed the graceful movements of the horses grazing in the schooling ring for the first time.

He touched the glass of the window and closed his eyes. He could almost smell the fried chicken Katie's grandmother had cooked for lunch that day. A small plate of the leftover chicken pieces had sat on the stove next to a bowl of freshly sliced lemons. The smells permeated the room. How he'd wanted a piece of that chicken. The brown crunchy drumstick had seemed to call his name.

There had been a pleasant breeze flowing through the open window as he sat at the Formica table with Katie and Mr. and Mrs. Hawkins, sipping iced tea as they crept around the subject of selling their farm.

No wonder he remembered every detail of the meeting. It was the day he fell in love with Katie. It wasn't just her beauty that caught his attention; there was an underlying toughness that one could easily miss. She'd described how her grandparent's lives had revolved around the farm they inherited from her great-grandparents. As Katie refilled his glass of sweet nectar, her tone held a measure of grit beneath the sweetness of her voice that reminded him of his grandmother Simpson.

Teddy laughed and opened his eyes. If Katie had it her way, that magnificent white fence would have remained an ugly brown. The upkeep for the house trim and white fencing required a maintenance contract for fresh paint every three years. A price Teddy was more than willing to pay.

Teddy shook his head and looked at the floor. One of the many things he'd learned about real estate was the importance of curb appeal. The external renovations completely changed the façade of the farm. Now, the view coming up the driveway was nothing short of spectacular.

But all the improvements he'd made to the farm couldn't erase the fact that he'd formed a corporation for their business without consulting his wife. As a licensed CPA, Katie might not know much about real estate, but she knew far more about establishing a corporation and interpreting tax laws than Teddy would ever know.

No wonder she was livid!

He thought of an idea as he poured the last of the coffee into his mug. Then he grabbed his phone and called his mother.

"Mom, can Mattie Grace spend the day with you? We've got a few things we need to handle today."

Half an hour later, while Mattie Grace set up her plastic horses in her grandmother's family room, Teddy pulled his mother aside in the kitchen and asked, "Mom, did you ever feel that Dad made decisions without consulting with you?"

His mom laughed. "Did I ever! Almost every decision made around here, your father made without my consent."

"Seriously?"

"Yes. If the refrigerator tore up, guess what? He'd buy one and have it delivered... usually without even telling me when it would arrive. Same for a new washing machine or dryer. He just felt it was his job to make those decisions."

"Did..." Teddy hesitated, choosing his words. "Did that make you mad?"

She laughed. "Madder than a wet hen in a spin dryer. But I realized I could either stay mad at Theo or just accept the way he was. So, I chose the latter."

Teddy frowned and leaned against the counter.

I've become my father.

He kissed his mother and thanked her for watching Mattie Grace, but as he pulled out of the driveway, his thoughts lingered on their conversation. Katie, of course, was from a different era than his mom. Women were more independent now, and Katie seemed more independent than most. His wife wasn't likely to be as patient as his mother had been with his dad, but even if she were, he didn't want to make her feel shoved aside, like his mother had.

Teddy stopped by the market and picked up some chicken salad and a fresh loaf of sourdough bread, along with a container of cheese straws and lemon squares. He picked out a nice bottle of chilled rose wine and headed back down to the farm.

When he'd set the groceries on the counter, he rummaged through the large closet in the old mudroom used for storage space. Finally, he found the picnic basket on the bottom shelf. Not too dusty. Not even a cobweb. Perfect. He wiped it down with a damp cloth. Then he filled it with the wine and food he'd bought. When he finished packing their lunch, he rushed upstairs and slipped on an old pair of jeans and work boots.

He loaded the picnic basket onto the Gator and drove down to the stables, where he found Katie grooming a brown mare just inside the opening of the door. Teddy stopped the Gator twenty feet from the barn door and just sat and appreciated the competence with which she brushed the animal. The circular movement of her hand as she removed the dirt and dead hair, was graceful and unhurried. She was in a zone, her happy place, and he didn't want to disturb her rhythm.

Katie looked up at the sound of the Gator in the drive. As Teddy climbed out, her gaze flicked to the tattered picnic basket in his hand. A brief smile flitted across her lips.

That was a good sign.

"Hey pretty lady, how about a picnic? It's such a beautiful day. I thought we'd eat down here at the stables if you like." Teddy grimaced as a pungent odor filled his nostrils. He sniffed at the air and looked around for the offending manure pile. Not exactly the most appetizing fragrance, but Katie didn't seem to notice. He gestured to an open expanse of grass a sufficient distance from the barn.

"Teddy, honey, have you forgotten that we have a six-year-old daughter at the house?"

"No, we don't," Teddy said playfully.

Her eyebrows arched. "Where is Mattie Grace?"

He walked toward her and sat the picnic basket on the bench. He pulled her close and said, "Relax, sweetheart. She's spending the day with Mom."

Katie's face softened. She fluttered her green eyes. "You're a bad boy, Teddy Williams."

"I know." He winked. "I just thought we needed some time together. I know you have a good reason to be angry with me, but I'd like for us to get back to where we were last weekend."

"Is that an apology?"

Teddy nodded. "It hurts me to see you upset. Besides, I just wanted you all to myself for a few hours."

Katie slipped her hand around the back of his neck and gently pulled his head down for a kiss, and then drew away, smiling. "Let's saddle up a couple of horses and ride down to the creek. There's a flat spot by the creek bed, and it'll be a perfect place to enjoy our picnic."

He gave the horse a sidelong glance. "You know I don't ride. My only interest in horses is this business of yours."

Katie's smile faded. Her shoulders slumped.

Damn. Trying to regain the mood, Teddy laid a hand on her arm and conceded. "Okay, but only if you find me the slowest horse in the stable."

Eyes shining, Katie clapped her hands and gave a happy little leap. Teddy had seen the same reaction from Mattie Grace thousands of times, but he'd rarely seen Katie express such delight. After a week of her continuous anger, her excitement was a far greater reaction than he'd expected.

It was even worth a trail ride.

Teddy helped saddle Brie, the brown mare Katie had just finished grooming. Then she brought out Hershey, a dark bay gelding. She smiled as she handed Teddy the saddle.

He wrinkled his nose. "What's that awful smell?"

Katie giggled. "Are you kidding?" She leaned close to the horse's neck and took a deep breath. "Horses smell amazing."

"That's one word for it."

After showing him how to climb onto the horse safely, Katie took the picnic basket, balanced it on the saddle, and they headed out of the stable.

Immediately, the clip-clop of the horses' hooves on the blacktop drive became a fascinating, almost hypnotic sound. It immediately calmed Teddy's nerves. When they reached the end of the pavement and moved onto the dirt, his horse strolled along in a trot as he followed Katie's lead. Then, without warning, the jarring unbalanced trot became the smooth, slow lope, but something changed in Teddy when their speed increased to a canter.

As he relaxed in the saddle, he forgot all inhibitions about the horseback ride. His body released the weight of the burdens he'd carried around since the tragic weekend when his first wife shot herself and his best friend disappeared. Sitting high on the back of the massive animal, he felt in tune with the nature surrounding him. While pressing the horse's body with his legs, he felt every fiber of the horse as they moved as one with a graceful rhythm.

Katie glanced back at him and grinned.

Teddy had to admit it felt like a power trip—an experience unlike anything he'd ever known. He suddenly understood his wife's love for horses.

He followed her down a hill to a grassy area near the creek. As soon as he saw the flat area, he instinctively knew it was the place Katie had described. When they dismounted and ground-tied the animals, Katie spread out the checkered tablecloth under the giant oak tree. Then she knelt down and unpacked the picnic basket while Teddy uncorked the wine.

The sunshine was warm. Katie looked up at the sky. "This is perfect weather. Thank you for putting this meal together. You know how much I love a good picnic." Teddy and Katie enjoyed their lunch while the horses meandered and grazed around them.

When they finished their meal, Katie sat with her back to a tree and while she finished her wine, Teddy stretched his legs and rested his head on her lap. The soothing sound of the water rushing down the creek bed lulled him to a state of relaxation.

"You know, Katie, I could never understand the reason you love horses so much, but after that ride, I finally get it. It's a powerful feeling when you mount a thousand-pound animal. I could feel Hershey's muscles bunch and release. As his hooves hit the ground, there was a hypnotic rhythmic motion of the animal's head. It was exhilarating."

"I told you it would be fun."

"He's a beautiful animal," Teddy said.

"Yes, he is. Hershey's sweet-spirited too."

Teddy watched her face as he listened to the passion in her voice.

Katie ran her fingers through Teddy's hair and said, "I knew he'd be gentle with you once he sensed your anxiety."

"Maybe you wouldn't mind if I go riding with you more often."

She kissed two of her fingers and pressed them on his lips. "That's like music to my ears."

When they got back to the stable, Teddy hesitated before going inside, mainly because he was fearful the hay would upset his allergies. The clean, sweet scent of new wood shavings crunched underfoot. Teddy strolled from stall to stall, looking at the different horses while Katie finished her chores. There were three blocks of fresh hay in each stall, and when he went into an empty one, he recognized the smell of the fresh alfalfa. He reached over to the blocks and picked up a piece of straw, and placed it in his mouth. Remembering the offensive odor from earlier, it surprised him he hardly even noticed the manure smell anymore.

At the end of the stable, Teddy saw a beautiful black colt. Looking into his big black eyes, something stirred in him. The horse made a soft sound, and it was like he had whispered his name.

Teddy reached up and stroked his muzzle. To his surprise, the horse nudged him and rested his head on Teddy's shoulder. Even as a novice horseman, Teddy knew he and the horse had communicated. He wasn't sure of the meaning, but it felt good. It was an intimate act that Teddy would never have thought could exist between a human and a horse. But there was no denying it: the horse's head was on his shoulder.

"Katie!" he called softly, so as not to startle the horse.

"Yeah. What is it?"

"What's this horses' name?"

Katie's eyes danced as she approached the end of the stable. "So, you found Mr. Zee. Isn't he beautiful?"

"Yes, he is. What's that marking on his forehead?"

Katie stroked the white marking between Mr. Zee's eyes. There was a tenderness to her touch, and the horse responded with a nudge of his head on her face.

"It's a star," Katie said. "No two markings are the same. It's like no two people have the same fingerprint. Each marking you see on a horse is unique to the individual animal. If that makes sense?"

"Yes, of course. Why don't you name him Star?"

Katie grinned. Then she explained his official race name was Kentucky Star because of the prominent white star on his forehead, but they called him Mr. Zee. Zeke was the name of the trainer who had brought him to the farm.

"Zeke never named the horse, but he always said watching the horse run was like watching butter melt."

Teddy chuckled. "Maybe he was going to name him butter or some derivative of butter."

"Could be. We started referring to him as Mr. Zeke's horse because we expected him to come back and get him." She patted his back. "Then one day Mattie Grace was down here, and she misunderstood Sammy. She called him Mr. Zee, and we've called him Mr. Zee ever since."

Teddy loved the story about how he got his name. As he continued to rub the horse, he asked why they kept Mr. Zee at this end of the stable.

She motioned to the section of the barn where they kept the racehorses. "We keep the ones in training over there. But Mr. Zee hasn't raced in a while. He hurt his leg one day when Zeke was riding him on the uneven gravel drive and injured a tendon in his lower right leg." The colt needed rest and rehabilitation, she explained. But when he worked out, he still gave it a hundred percent. Of course, it was ingrained in him. His sire, one of the country's top Thoroughbred stallions was a former Kentucky Derby competitor. Even now, after his injuries were healing, it was like he was pushing to become a champion.

Teddy moved around to the side and continued to stroke him. "In your opinion, do you think Mr. Zee can recover enough to be competitive?"

"Maybe. With the right amount of attention. Sammy spends so much time with the horses you bought last year that he doesn't have the extra time to devote to Mr. Zee."

Teddy ran his hand down Mr. Zee's legs. They seemed strong and sturdy. It sounded like he just needed some extra love and attention to get him back to the place he was before his injuries.

Maybe he and Mattie Grace could take on the colt as a project and nurse him back to total health. It suddenly occurred to him that an investment in a champion racehorse was better than the five less proven horses he'd purchased the previous year. "I've just made an administrative decision."

Katie frowned. "You have…" Then she seemed to register his teasing tone and laughed. "What's that?"

"We're going to sell those five horses we bought last year, and then I'm going to match yours and Sammy's investment in that racehorse you've been looking to buy."

Chapter Ten

A ndrew frowned. Daisy had lost interest in her orchids. At one time, she had over thirty orchids in various colors, placed randomly throughout their sunroom—and even more sitting on tabletops, bookshelves, and sideboards in other rooms. It was like a tropical oasis of beauty. In some cultures, orchids were thought to bring warmth and happiness to a home. Daisy's babies, as Andrew affectionately referred to them, were a source of pride and pleasure for her... until Drew disappeared. As he looked around the sunroom, Andrew counted four orchids. He stopped to check the soil of the pretty lavender plant—he shook his head... dry as a bone.

He went to the kitchen and dispensed several ice cubes into a small bowl, which he divided among the four plants in the sunroom. It was the third time he'd watered the plants in the last month.

Daisy yelled from upstairs, "What are you doing, Andrew?"

"I'm about to read the paper. Why do you ask?"

The house was silent.

Andrew looked at the folded newspaper and considered how their lives had changed since their son had disappeared. Drew's cheerful personality lit up any room he entered, and when he stopped by to check on the "old folks," as he would affectionately refer to them, it was like he brought the sunshine indoors, along with a lot of noise.

He was their life. The most important person in their life, for sure.

A few minutes later, Daisy stuck her head around the door frame as she cleaned her bright blue glasses with a tissue. As usual, her silver hair was pulled back in a large hair clasp, and the fuchsia-colored lipstick had been recently applied. "I thought you were about to make lunch?"

"That's a thought." He glanced at the folded newspaper and settled back into his chair. "But there's not much in the fridge. Do you want to run over to the sandwich shop for a quick bite?"

Thirty minutes later, Andrew placed their order, grabbed their drinks, and found his way to the table where Daisy sat. She scrolled through her phone, looking at family pictures.

Again.

He set her iced tea on the table in front of her. When she looked up, there were tears in her eyes.

This wasn't good.

The server arrived at their table with a tray. "Here's a turkey club...."

Andrew pointed to Daisy. "... And I got the Reuben."

"Do you need a refill on those drinks?"

"No. Thank you. We're fine."

Andrew cut his sandwich and glanced at Daisy. "We need to get that declaration notice filed so Colleen can find closure and heal." He took a big bite of his sandwich and wiped his mouth with his napkin.

Daisy bit into her sandwich and chewed slowly. She took a sip of her tea. "So you've said. But how about me, Andrew? How am I supposed to find closure and heal? I'm his mother!"

Andrew reached for her hand. "This may not be much consolation to you, but you've still got me to help you through it. Colleen has three children depending on her, and she deserves all the help we can give her." He smiled to remove the sting from his words. "Colleen told me just last week that she thought she was ready to move forward."

Daisy's spine straightened. Her mouth opened as if to protest, but before she could speak, Andrew patted her hand and said, "She loves Drew, honey, but she's a smart gal. She knows if he were alive, he would already have found a way home."

Daisy slumped in her seat. "He... could be..." She closed her eyes as if she could conjure another explanation. Then she choked out, "I know."

Well, that was progress.

They'd been down this road several times in the past few months. But until now, the conversation would end with Daisy fleeing the room in tears. Of course, she was in tears now, but at least she seemed ready to face the truth.

Chapter Eleven

On a Wednesday afternoon in mid-April, Teddy met with Frank Nordstrom at the real estate office. As promised, Claire agreed to meet with Frank to hear his proposal.

He had prepared PowerPoint illustrations with charts and graphs as he explained his five-year plan for the business. Frank gently described a position for Claire in the role of administrator. If she agreed to his proposal, she'd supervise the staff and manage the office, allowing him the freedom to build the business. He went on to explain, when time allowed, she was welcome to list properties in the area.

Claire looked up and stopped picking at her freshly manicured nails. Suddenly, her demeanor changed when Frank mentioned his plan to develop a high-end condominium complex adjacent to the downtown area. When he asked if she knew of an interior decorator/designer he could hire for a full-time position, his mom sat straight and tilted her head. Her apparent interest in the project encouraged Teddy.

He watched as Frank led up to the proposal. He had thoroughly explained his vision for the business. When he presented a contract to purchase the real estate company, his mom took a few moments to review it.

Claire's dark brown eyes darted from Teddy to Frank and back again. "You aren't serious, are you? This contract includes the property along with the business."

Frank's eyebrows lifted, and after another moment's hesitation, he said, "Yes, Claire, that's correct." He looked at Teddy for confirmation and continued, "My discussions with Theo and Frederick included the property."

She locked eyes with Teddy. "I can't believe you and Theo would think you could sell the property without my permission. It's part of my parents' estate, and I'm disappointed you'd try to sell it without my consent." By the time she'd finished talking, her voice had lost its edge, and her eyes sparkled with sweetness.

****

The confidence Frank had displayed when he came into the meeting turned to disappointment as his mom finished explaining her reason for holding onto the property.

Finally, his mom smiled sweetly. "Frank, this property is valuable, and I plan to pass it down to my grandchildren."

Teddy suppressed a smile as he realized Frank had just fallen under the spell of his mother's southern charm.

When the meeting wrapped up, his mom looked at her phone and said, "Well, it's almost five-thirty. Frank, why don't you join us tonight for dinner at Scott's?"

Frank glanced over at Teddy. His face puckered with confusion.

Teddy shrugged and smiled, "If you can join us, I'll call my wife, Katie, and ask her to come, too."

His mom said, "You can ride with me, Frank." Then she looked at Teddy and said, "Why don't you pick up Katie and meet us at the restaurant in about an hour? Frank and I will go over and have a drink while we wait for you."

Frank removed his car keys from his pocket and said, "I'll drive, Claire. If you'll point the way."

Later, when Teddy and Katie walked into the restaurant lounge, they saw his mom and Frank sitting at a small table. His mom laughed at something Frank said. They seemed oblivious to anyone else in the room.

After the maître d' directed them to their table, the four of them enjoyed fresh bread with silky blueberry butter while Frank shared his interests outside the real estate profession. The others peppered him with questions. Katie then asked if he had any family members living in Georgia.

"No, I don't. I have a sister and brother-in-law who live on Nantucket and one brother up in Kentucky who owns a Thoroughbred horse farm. He mainly breeds his world-class mares to top-notch stallions."

"Are you serious, Frank?" Katie asked. "Your brother breeds for a living?"

"Yes. That's right. Philip owns a 950-acre, full-service Thoroughbred breeding facility complete with 13 barns and over 200 stalls. It's an impressive operation–they're currently training my horse for competition."

"Do you mind me asking the name of the farm?"

"Of course not," Frank said. "It's Nordstrom Farms."

Katie placed her hand on Teddy's arm and said, "You're not going to believe this, Teddy."

"Is that the farm where you found your horse?"

Katie smiled.

As the server delivered their meal, they discussed the horse racing business, and Katie explained to Frank that the horse she wanted to buy was sired by a former Belmont Winner.

"You must be talking about Talking Jack."

"Yes," Katie said. "I understand that's his barn name."

"He's an impressive animal."

Frank told them about the horse's famous bloodline and confirmed he had been at the race the day Talking Jack's sire, Jumping Jack

Flash, won the Belmont. He suggested they take a weekend and go up to the farm and spend some time with the animal before making a final decision.

He also gave them the name of a B&B outside of Lexington, within a few miles of the farm.

While they finished their coffee, the conversation turned away from horses and back to the real estate deal.

"Claire," Frank said. He had to be sure she hadn't forgotten about his offer. There had been nothing in her body language that showed him she was definitive in her answer. "Have you given my offer any more thought? I know you said earlier that you weren't interested in selling, but you didn't seem sure. Would it make a difference if I increased my offer twenty grand over the earlier price?"

His mom placed her napkin next to her plate. Then, she patted his hand. "I admit, your offer for the business is reasonable, but I'll never sell that property. Besides, with my background and interest in properties, I have as good a chance as anyone else running our family business. You know, Teddy's still involved with the operation of the business."

Teddy shot Katie a sideways glance as Frank placed his other hand on top of his mom's and said, "Well, I appreciate your honesty. Keep in mind, if you ever decide to sell, my offer remains." He smiled as though his disappointment had vanished.

Chapter Twelve

May 2021

When they pulled off the main highway onto the secondary road, Katie knew they were about to embark onto hallowed ground. It felt like something big was just around the bend.

She looked to the left side of the road as they waited to turn into the long blacktop drive. A rock archway extended from one side of the wide entranceway to the other. Nordstrom Farm was prominently displayed in black at the top of the archway.

Katie touched Teddy's arm, "Sammy, Mattie Grace, y'all pay attention. It isn't every day we get to visit a Thoroughbred breeding farm."

As they continued down the blacktop drive, the beautiful plush grass, which spanned as far as the eyes could see, was an Easter Egg green. Trees of every conceivable type dotted the grounds. Red maple, tulip poplars, and Kentucky coffee trees provided shade, prevented erosion, and regulated temperature extremes. Off to the drive's right, in the far distance, were thick patches of the native eastern white pines. Of course, Kentucky's native Virginia, yellow, and patch pines were also abundantly visible along the route.

Katie pressed her nose to the car window. "This is an impressive operation,"

She'd used her cell phone to do some research while Teddy drove and Mattie Grace entertained Sammy with her crayons and coloring book.

Katie had learned that Frank's family bred, raised, trained, and prepared Thoroughbred horses for championship competition. As impressive and exciting as the horses and stables were, it was the far end of the property that visitors were prone to ask about throughout the tour. Specifically, the equine cemetery where several Kentucky Derby winners and one Triple Crown winner were laid to rest.

The Nordstrom Farm was initially one of the big four Thoroughbred race farms in the United States.

Over the years, a security check station was installed one-eighth of a mile from the road, equipped with satellite cameras that picked up motion for up to five miles around the perimeter of the farm. Only those who had been pre-vetted could enter the facility.

Katie's pulse quickened as they passed the Hall of Fame/Welcome Center with life-like statues of each champion produced by the Nordstrom family throughout their one hundred-and-twenty-eight-year history. Nordstrom Farms was an extraordinary equine facility. The white stables with the green trim were separated by a cobblestone drive and divided by sex and purpose—one for colts, another for broodmares, along with a separate breeding barn just a stone's throw away from the foaling barn. She wondered which was which and where Talking Jack would be.

As Teddy crept up the drive, Katie drank in everything, filing away ideas for their own enterprise. Each building on the farm was uniform. She'd read that of the hundred thousand visitors to the farm each year, more than half commented on the aesthetic birds-eye view as they flew in from neighboring states and from all over the continental United States and beyond.

What would it be like to create a dynasty like this?

She forced herself to wait for Teddy to park. Then, with Mattie Grace at her heels, she hurried to explore the barns where the horses lived. Each stall door displayed one or more metal plates, each engraved with a horse's name that had lived in that specific stall. Several doors bore as many as six names of Thoroughbred horses, and the mere number of horses bred and raised by the Nordstrom's family facility overwhelmed Katie. She touched the inscription on the metal plates and tried to comprehend how each champion had influenced the history of horse racing.

She was captivated by the cleanliness of the facility. The Nordstrom's had a reputation for maintaining strict regulations to reduce infectious diseases from the animals. Katie overheard one of the maintenance crew say they hosed out the cemented barn flooring twice each day and cleaned it with a specially formulated cleaner. Then, after the large industrial blowers dried the concrete, they sprinkled each stall with fresh hay.

Katie stopped in mid-stride and drew in a deep breath. God, she loved that smell. She glanced over at Teddy. Even he didn't seem to be bothered by it.

Teddy placed Mattie Grace on the top plank of the wooden fence and held her by the waist. Katie and Sammy stood next to them. Together, the family watched several Thoroughbred horses train in the nearby arena at Nordstrom Farm in Lexington, Kentucky.

Teddy glanced toward Katie. Her fingers clinched over the top rail of the white wooden fence, and her eyes danced with excitement. Her childhood dream of training a colt to race in the Kentucky Derby was about to become a reality. Teddy smiled at his wife's non-stop chatter as she watched Talking Jack work out. He could tell she favored the tall, two-year-old colt, at least sixteen hands, maybe more, with large black eyes, a shiny chestnut color coat, and a white snip between his nostrils. The only other white marking on his body was a half pastern on each of his four legs. Otherwise, he was solid chestnut.

A few short months earlier, Teddy hadn't even known what a hand was. Now the language of horse breeders was starting to come naturally to him.

Maybe Katie would make a horseman out of him after all.

The horse finally ambled over to the fence near where Katie stood. She gently placed her hand under his mouth. Teddy watched Katie melt at the feel of his silky mane. He had only seen that facial expression one other time, and that was the first time Katie had held Mattie Grace in her arms.

After a few moments of talking to the animal, Katie noticed Mattie Grace's filthy hands clinging to the white fence. She nudged Teddy. "We're going to the restroom so Mattie Grace can wash up. That chocolate bar Sammy bought for her from the concession machine melted onto her hands."

When they were out of earshot, Teddy turned to Sammy. "Well? What do you think about Talking Jack?"

"He's a beauty," Sammy said. "That's for sure."

He could tell Sammy wasn't completely sold on the large horse. Teddy moved closer to Sammy to determine which horse he was watching.

"I need your help here, Sammy," Teddy said. "This is a big investment. I'm wary of making an investment of this size without one hundred percent assurance this horse will compete well."

Sammy scanned the horses in the pasture. "Let's look around a little more before we decide."

On the way back from the restroom, while Mattie Grace intentionally ambled along, she spotted a pretty, young filly on the other side of the fence, heading her way. Mattie Grace eased closer and waited. When the filly finally reached her, she stopped in front of the child and arched her neck over the rail for a caress. Mattie Grace was entranced. She'd never seen such a gorgeous horse, not even her birthday present came close.

When they returned to the arena, Mattie Grace grabbed Sammy's hand. "Come over here, Uncle Sammy. I want to show you something."

When they got to the fence at the adjacent paddock, Mattie Grace looked up at Sammy and beamed. She pointed to the filly standing near the tree. "Isn't that the most beautiful horse you've ever seen?"

"That silver horse over there?" Sammy pointed. "Mattie Grace, that animal is a little on the small size to race in the Derby. She couldn't be much more than 15 hands. 15.2 at the most."

She looked up at her uncle with tears in her eyes. How could he not see how beautiful the horse was? A little horse could be fast, too.

****

He looked down at her trembling chin. After a moment, he turned to the trainer. "Could we climb over to get a closer look?" It took Sammy a moment to get his stiff leg over the fence, then he reached for Mattie Grace's hand and helped her over, too. They watched for a few moments as the filly pranced around the pasture. It seemed the animal was performing for their enjoyment. The longer they stayed inside the fence, Sammy observed a natural intelligence in the animal. The filly suddenly stopped prancing and looked at Sammy with those large, intelligent eyes. Finally, Sammy lifted Mattie Grace onto the horse's back but held onto her in case the horse became startled and decided to buck.

The filly didn't flinch.

He lifted his niece from the animal's back and pointed to a nearby bench. "You sit there, Mattie Grace, while I check this little lady out."

He walked around the horse, one hand trailing over her hindquarters as he passed behind her, checking the conformation. Strong, straight legs. Deep heart girth for vital oxygen exchange. Topline shorter than underline, indicating a strong back.

Well-balanced. Evenly muscled. Beautiful.

He pulled back her upper lip and checked her mouth and gums. Healthy and well cared for.

The more he looked, the more he liked what he saw.

As Sammy and the trainer talked about the filly, a large stallion wandered toward them. The presence of the stallion would be another test.

The trainer motioned to the stable boy to bring the stallion closer. He smiled at Sammy as he removed the toothpick from his mouth. "Watch this."

Although there was fencing separating the two animals, the stallion walked right up to the fence. The little filly's ears went back and she kicked at him. The stallion stretched himself until his head was as close to the filly as he could get it. As the stallion moved closer, the filly raised her neck and moved closer to her side of the fence.

"She's got spunk," Sammy said. It surprised him because she was so gentle with Mattie Grace.

He pointed toward the track on the other side of the arena and asked if this was the same horse they'd seen working out an hour earlier.

"Yep. She's the one... don't know if you spent much time watching her train, but when this little filly trains, she never gives less than a hundred percent."

"And yet," Sammy said, "she doesn't seem too tired right now."

He gestured for the filly to move toward him. "Come on, girl. Come to Sammy."

The animal followed his simple command.

When a shiny black horse walked down the blacktop drive led by a stable boy, the filly reacted the same way as she did toward the previous stallion.

Gently, Sammy placed his hands on both sides of her muzzle and looked into her big eyes. The horse moved her head toward him.

"What does this pretty little thing eat?"

"Same as every other horse on this farm; oats and good quality hay. Of course, while they train, they also get the necessary supplements recommended by the veterinarian on staff."

"So, you have your own veterinarian on staff?"

The trainer nodded as he rubbed the horse's back. He explained that every horse was tested weekly for foreign substances, and the testing was performed daily for the two weeks leading up to a big race.

"Sounds like a lot of testing to me," Sammy said.

"Yeah, well, I'm sure it does. But we must be certain, going into a big race, that all traces of drugs used to fight inflammation caused by exertion—have cleared the body. Otherwise, we could get scratched from the race... and, if for any reason they detect an illegal trace of betamethasone in a post-race test, the winner could lose its standing. It's a chance we're not willing to take because it would smear the name of our facility. We have a reputation to uphold."

Sammy turned and nodded toward Mattie Grace. She came over and reached up to stroke the horse.

"This here's Mattie Grace," Sammy said.

The trainer reached inside his pocket, removed a piece of peppermint, and placed it in Mattie Grace's outstretched hand. Surprisingly, the filly dropped her head and rubbed the child's face before taking the candy.

Sammy nodded. Then he winked at the trainer.

"Mattie Grace, I think you've found us a racehorse."

Chapter Thirteen

Teddy looked around the farm for Sammy and Mattie Grace and saw them petting a silver-colored horse in a separate arena. He reached for Katie's hand and made their way over to where the horse was grazing.

"Look what Mattie Grace found over here," Sammy said. "Isn't she a beauty?"

The four of them stood watching the silver horse while Sammy explained the intelligence he had observed.

When Teddy asked about the cost of the animal, Katie gave him a stern look. The trainer told him three-hundred-thousand dollars and excused himself to check on the stables.

Teddy realized there was no way they could afford both the horse Katie wanted and this unexpected find Sammy felt could be a contender in the Derby.

He ran a hand over the filly's neck and said, "What do you think, Sammy?"

Sammy continued to inspect the animal. "Well, this filly has the four most important qualities we've been looking for."

"What four qualities?" Teddy asked. "And remember, I'm a layman."

"Soundness, appetite, constitution, and desire. A Thoroughbred horse usually has all four."

"So, what do you think about this little filly?"

"Honestly, Teddy," Sammy said. "I think she's a contender. We need a horse that won't run from a fight. I don't think this one will back down."

"What do you mean?"

Stroking the little horse's withers, Sammy explained that it wasn't just about the speed or the strength of her legs, the length of her stride, the level of intelligence, or her gut instincts. It was a matter of the heart.

"When racing Thoroughbreds, the winning horse is all about heart. Nothing else."

Mattie Grace tugged on Teddy's sleeve. "Daddy, this is the one. I know it is!"

"Well..." Teddy smiled down at his daughter. "Maybe we should ask a few more questions. After all, this is your mother's investment."

While Teddy questioned Sammy about the animal, Katie watched the beautiful chestnut-colored horse in the other field. And, although Sammy and Katie had the rare gift of looking a horse in its eyes to see the genius in them, Katie was hesitating, wary of getting too close to the silver horse. She feared Sammy had already detected the animal's brilliance.

Teddy frequently glanced at his wife, who kept looking over her shoulder at the larger horse in the next arena.

Each time Katie looked toward the filly, Teddy averted his gaze.

She wanted the big horse. Regardless of the cost, she wanted what she wanted and would not settle for anything less.

Teddy struggled with the possibility of spending one million dollars for the big, gorgeous colt. Even with Sammy's part of the investment, Teddy's household would be responsible for three-quarters of a million dollars. Three hundred thousand for the silver filly was much more palatable.

He was impressed with how well Sammy explained his thoughts about the horse. Teddy grinned as he shook his head. "Sammy, I didn't know you knew so much about Thoroughbred racehorses?"

Sammy chuckled as he reached down and picked up a piece of hay and placed it between his teeth. After a moment, he removed it and said, "There are some talented horses that are unsound, and that's why they never reach their potential." He turned back to the trainer. "Has this little filly ever had any soundness problem?"

"No, sir. She's never had so much as a limp. She's as sound as they come." The trainer turned to Teddy, "Soundness issues can be anything from bad feet to ankles, soft bones, and weak joints. A racehorse has got to have good conformation—or at least conformation that is manageable. Also, the horse must be able to manage itself through the training."

Sammy picked up an apple from the barrel, broke it in half, and fed it to the horse.

The trainer went on. "Another important thing is a racehorse must eat a well-balanced diet to maintain their ideal weight. Without a good appetite, a horse can't build the muscle mass necessary to fulfill their athletic ability."

After a few moments, Katie slowly walked over to the silver horse and started checking out her hindquarters. "A racehorse must also have a strong constitution," Katie said.

"That's true," the trainer said. "It's important for a racehorse to have both a mental and physical constitution. The magnificent horses of the world do not worry."

Teddy looked over at Sammy. "What does he mean by worry?" Teddy asked. "It's a horse!"

"They don't walk their stalls," Sammy said. "They don't weave or crib. They come home, they eat, rest, and train. They're like us, Teddy. They're straightforward animals, and these are the mental traits of a good constitution in a horse."

The trainer added, "There are a few physical traits one must have to compete for The Triple Crown. A strong heart, a big pair of lungs, and sound limbs. A sound body goes right along with a sound mind. I'm not sure I should be telling you this, but Mr. Nordstrom and a few of his buddies think this little filly has what it takes to win The Triple Crown."

Teddy went over and stood next to Katie. "What do you think, sweetheart?"

"Well, she must have the desire to win," Katie said. "It's difficult to persuade a thousand-pound animal to run to its maximum potential with a 115-pound man on its back when they don't want to do it."

They discussed the silver horse for over an hour. Katie and Sammy were conflicted. Katie wanted the chestnut colt, and Sammy thought the silver filly would be the most competitive. Teddy just wanted to get the most horse for his money.

Finally, Teddy walked off from the others and went inside the nearby stable to spend a few minutes alone. He spotted the horse's owner entering the opposite end and walked over to ask about his silver filly.

The owner smiled.

"That's a fine animal," the owner said, "but unfortunately, I've got to sell her."

Teddy picked up a piece of straw from the ground and placed it in his mouth. Silence, he'd learned, was a great psychological tool. People tended to be uncomfortable with it—and tried to fill the empty spaces.

Sure enough, the owner said, "I'm going through a divorce, and my wife no longer wants the animal." He removed a handkerchief from his jacket pocket and wiped his nose. "The missus, she's the one that loved horses. Not me. It's been a lucrative business these last few years, but I'd just as soon sell the filly and put the money into a real estate investment."

They talked for a few moments about several other horses in the nearby stalls. Teddy explained he was looking for a horse to race. It was a toss-up between the silver filly and the chestnut colt.

The owner talked about the previous races the filly had won and was optimistic about the future.

"Our trainer is convinced the horse could win the derby, or at least finish in the top three. But the missus isn't willing to put in the time to find out. She's done with the racing business. Besides, she's moving to France at the end of the month."

Teddy took mental notes of everything the owner told him, and then he explained he hadn't yet decided which one to purchase.

That is—until the last comment the owner said before walking off.

"Well, she may be small, but if you want to win the Triple Crown, I've been told by several people up here that this horse has the heart and the stamina to get it done."

Teddy sat on the bench outside the stall. He stretched his legs and placed his arms behind his head. Katie had been upset with him for so long that he hated not to give her the horse she wanted.

It was a big step.

And a hefty price tag for their first Thoroughbred purchase. Of course, there was Mr. Zee, but neither Sammy nor Katie seemed interested in training him for the race.

He kept thinking about the owner's remark, noting the conviction in the guy's voice. Teddy released a deep breath and stood. For better or worse, he had decided.

He left the stable and found his family at the track. He told them about his discussion with the filly's owner, but he quickly added that he was open to debate.

"It's our first big-ticket purchase," he said, "so I suggest we offer three hundred thousand dollars for the silver horse." Mattie Grace squealed with excitement, but Teddy looked from Sammy to Katie, waiting for a bomb to drop.

Katie tore her gaze away from the chestnut colt and looked from Sammy's earnest face to Mattie Grace's shining eyes. Slowly, she said, "If you guys feel that the silver horse is the best purchase, then so be it."

Teddy smiled, surprised she'd given in so easily. Then she turned away, but not before he saw the glint of tears in her eyes.

Teddy waited for an objection from Sammy.

When no one else spoke, Teddy wrapped his arms around Katie and whispered in her ear.

"Seriously?" she said. "You're going to buy the silver horse for my birthday present?"

Teddy nodded, hoping the financial windfall would make up for the loss of the colt.

Katie looked at Sammy, a question in her eyes.

He shrugged. "This is your deal."

Mattie Grace said, "Daddy, let's vote on it. We can be a democracy."

Teddy smiled. "Mattie Grace, I think the word you're searching for is democratic."

"Democratic." Mattie Grace frowned, trying out the word. "Yeah. Okay."

"That's a good point," Teddy said. "Let's form a circle, and Mattie Grace can count the votes."

They formed a small circle and agreed to raise one finger to represent their vote. Then Mattie Grace made them close their eyes before they voted.

Teddy opened one eye and quickly closed it. It was tempting, but he resisted the urge to peek and see how Katie voted. At the last minute, he surprised himself by voting for the chestnut horse.

When she counted the votes out loud, three favored the silver horse, and one did not.

Mattie Grace pulled at Katie's hand and whispered, "Daddy voted for your horse."

Katie smiled as she cut her eyes over at Teddy. He gave her a casual shrug and looked away, glad that his gesture had pleased her.

Katie turned to Sammy. "Are you sure about this?"

Sammy shrugged. "Racing in the Derby is your dream, not mine— but if you're going to race at this level, you've got to trust people. It's not every day a horse comes along equipped to win The Triple Crown."

She took one last, regretful—look at the chestnut colt and said, "That's true. We'd better take advantage of this opportunity."

Chapter Fourteen

Mattie Grace ran over to Teddy and wrapped her arms around his legs. "Daddy, are we really taking her home?"

Katie smiled. The joy on her little girl's face was almost enough to make up for the loss of Talking Jack.

Teddy picked up Mattie Grace and said, "Looks like the silver circle has spoken."

"Katie, girl..." Sammy smiled. "It looks like you've just got yourself a birthday present."

Teddy put Mattie Grace back down and added, "Katie, are you sure?"

She placed her hand on her husband's face. "It's not what I wanted, but I see how much our little girl wants this horse."

Teddy kissed her nose.

His genuine concern took the edge off her disappointment, but losing the chestnut colt still hurt her heart. She'd fallen in love with him the moment he'd nuzzled her hand. But sometimes you had to give up what you wanted for the people you loved. "Besides, everyone else thinks she'll win The Triple Crown." She laid her hand on his chest. "I love how you try to make us all happy. You're a good man."

Mattie Grace was dancing around. "I love that name! Silver Circle is a perfect name for our horse."

Katie laughed at her daughter's antics. Silver Circle. It really was the perfect name for the little filly.

And the perfect name for a Triple Crown winner.

The decision, met with a majority vote—was final.

****

It was time to meet with Frank's brother. Together, they walked to the main house, an eighteenth-century variegated orange-reddish and brown brick mansion with cream-colored wooden accents. Four cream-colored columns balanced each side of the magnificent porch and provided stunning access to the regal entranceway, which included doubled beveled glass doors encased in wood.

The left wing on the bottom floor of the three-level structure served as Philip Nordstrom's presidential office suite.

He met them at the door of the suite, a hand outstretched, a broad smile on his face. He had Frank's square jaw and broad shoulders, but the creases around his mouth and eyes spoke of long hours working in the sun. "Welcome to the great state of Kentucky! Come right in here and have a seat. Frank's told me all about you guys."

Teddy introduced himself, then Sammy. He told a little about his uncle-in-law's history with horse training.

Then he introduced Katie and said, "My wife's childhood dream is to race a horse in the Kentucky Derby."

Philip chuckled. "Well, Mr. Williams, that's all well and good, but I want to meet the little princess standing behind you."

Everyone turned to Mattie Grace. She stepped forward primly and said, "My name is Mattie Grace Williams. I'm six years old, and I have my own pony. His name is Domino."

Philip was a large man, and his laugh was robust and bellowing. "Little Princess, you and I are going to become good friends. I can feel it in my bones."

He led them to a mahogany-paneled meeting room. The brick on the fireplace mirrored that of the house's exterior, and a marble hearth stood flush with the floor, convenient to pulling over a side chair to enjoy a good book or a cup of cocoa.

Two caramel-colored leather sofas faced each other in front of the massive fireplace. Philip offered them a seat on the couches. Teddy sat on one sofa with Katie, and Sammy sat opposite them, while Philip sat in one of the armed chairs that faced the ends of the couches. Although it was mid-May, the air was still brisk, so the warmth from the fire felt good. While the adults settled in for their conversation, Mattie Grace stood in front of the fire to warm herself.

Philip said, "Please tell me about your tour of the farm. We exceeded your expectations, I hope?"

Teddy immediately liked Philip. There was something about his easy-going spirit that made one feel comfortable. But comfortable or not, they needed to remember this was a business deal. Teddy shifted in his seat and said, "Mattie Grace has found us a little filly to race in the Derby. I've talked to the owner already, and he said to let you know when we decide."

Philip got up from his chair and dragged it over to the fireplace. "So, you've picked out a horse. Can you tell me a little bit about her, Princess?"

"Yes, sir. She's a silver horse, and bigger than Domino. She sure is pretty."

He pulled out his pipe and filled the bowl with tobacco. "Well, then. Have you talked it over with your mama?"

"Yes, sir. We voted, and it was three to one for the silver horse."

"But you came here today to look at a different horse, isn't that correct?"

Mattie Grace looked at Katie, her smile fading.

Katie smiled and said, "Mr. Nordstrom, we took a vote."

"I understand."

"Honestly," she went on, "buying this horse might be a good idea, since the price is right and it's our first official racehorse."

Philip dragged his chair back over to face the sofas. "I spoke with Talking Jack's owner a few days ago, and he thinks that 'big ole' colt could take the Derby."

"Thank you, Philip," Teddy said. "I'm just not sure the three of us are financially prepared to buy that horse. We found out a few moments ago that they're asking over a million dollars."

"I understand what you mean, it's a lot of money to spend on something that has no guarantees. The little filly is a good choice."

Chapter Fifteen

Claire's assistant buzzed her office. "Ms. Williams, a Mr. Nordstrom is holding on line three."

Claire looked up from the real estate comps she was working on. Frank Nordstrom? What could he possibly want now that she'd turned down his offer? "What did he say, Sally?"

Sally hesitated and said, "He just asked to speak with Claire Williams. Should I put him through?"

Claire tapped her fingernails on the desk. She didn't really want to explain again why she wouldn't sell her business. On the other hand, what would it hurt to hear what the man had to say? "Yes, put him through. Thank you, Sally."

She reached for a mirror from the bottom drawer, then laid in on the desk, laughing at herself. It was a phone call, not a video chat. She put a smile on her face and picked up the phone. "Claire Williams."

"Well, hello, Claire. This is Frank Nordstrom. Do you have time for lunch? I have something I need to discuss with you."

His rich baritone voice sent an unexpected thrill through her. She quickly tamped it down. "I appreciate your call, Frank, but I'm not interested in selling."

"Of course, Claire. I'm on to another project. If you remember, when I met with you and Teddy, I mentioned a condominium development adjacent to Abington Square, downtown. Well, I've just learned the seller wants to meet with me on Friday to sign the contract."

"That's wonderful news. Congratulations!"

"Yes, I know. But I'd like to talk to you about hiring a designer. I already have drawings for the property, and Since you served on the Beautification Committee for the downtown area, I thought you might give me some input for the brochures."

Claire couldn't hide the excitement in her voice. "I'd love to have lunch with you and discuss the brochures. Where should we meet?"

"I'll drop by your office around twelve-thirty, and maybe we can go over to Scott's."

"I'll be ready at twelve-thirty. If you pull around to the back of the building, I'll be watching for you."

Claire hung up the phone and leaned back in her chair. It had been almost two weeks since they met to review his proposal to purchase their business.

She opened the compact on her desk and looked at herself. Well, she could use a few more highlights in her hair, but otherwise, she looked okay for a woman of her age.

Why was she having these thoughts?

She and Theo had made a good life together, although their conversations mainly revolved around their three children. Theo ran his business, and she ran the household. Perhaps not the best of situations, but it had worked for them.

However, when Bobby and Beth died in the car accident on that dreadful afternoon, Theo became more distant and withdrawn, and regardless of what she did, she couldn't penetrate that wall he'd erected around himself.

That is... until that weekend before his second heart attack and stroke. On Saturday morning, Theo had left home sullen and distant and returned home later in the afternoon—a changed man. He'd experienced a complete personality change. The next day, a beautiful Sunday afternoon in autumn, with the crisp air and crystal blue skies, while watching the Atlanta Falcons football game, Claire experienced one final blissful afternoon with the sweet and kind man with whom she'd fallen in love.

When Sally walked into her office, Claire quickly snapped the mirror closed and shoved it into the desk drawer.

Sally pursed her mouth in a self-satisfied smirk. "Well, Mr. Nordstrom doesn't seem to give up too easily, does he?"

Claire tried to suppress a smile. "He needs my advice about a brochure for a condominium complex he has plans to build. The closing for the property is on Friday, and he wanted to ask me a few questions, that's all."

"Oh, yeah. That sounds legitimate. He's a successful developer in the Savannah area. Sounds to me like he needed a good excuse to see you again."

"Let's not make this into something more than it really is." Claire waved away the thought, ignoring the warmth that crept across her cheeks.

****

Risking the midday rush, Teddy strolled into Scott's, his taste buds set for a big, juicy gourmet steak burger. Many young professionals from businesses around town frequented Scott's at lunch.

As he headed to the lounge, Teddy saw his mother and Frank sitting at an intimate table in one of the three alcoves. The only items remaining on their table were the two half-filled glasses and the opened wine bottle. His mother leaned forward, hanging onto Frank's every word.

As he walked toward them, Frank raised a hand and waved him over to the table. His mom's eyes danced with joy, as they always did when Teddy was around.

Frank stood as Teddy approached. "Hello, young man! Please, come and join us." He motioned for Teddy to have a seat. "It's good to see you, Teddy. We're just finishing up a discussion about The Abington Square Condominiums."

Reluctantly, Teddy took a seat. "I don't want to interrupt your luncheon, but I couldn't pass by without speaking. Mainly, I wanted to thank you for introducing us to your brother."

Frank grinned. "It was my pleasure. Phil told me you found a horse for Katie. He was quite taken with her and your little girl."

"Yeah." Teddy glanced at his mother. "Like most southern women, they can be quite charming."

"Yes, like your mother." Frank winked at her and then nodded at Teddy. "I trust your wife is happy with your purchase?"

Teddy grimaced. "I'm not sure happy is the correct word in this situation."

"What do you mean?"

"Well, it's not the horse Katie wanted, but she does think it might compete in the Derby."

Frank paused. Then he wiped his mouth with his napkin before saying, "Teddy, you're new to this business, but I want you to know that when the first Saturday in May rolls around, I'll put my money on your horse. Many people will bet on Talking Jack, and he'll be the main attraction leading up to race day."

"Well, I admit, he's a beautiful animal."

Frank placed his napkin on his lap and said, "I agree. There's no denying that big boy has the look of a winner, but as you well know, looks aren't everything." He looked around the restaurant and lowered his voice. "By the way, my brother agrees, if trained correctly, Katie's little filly could be the winner and may possibly go on to win the Preakness and the Belmont."

Teddy raised his eyebrows. "I hope you're right about that."

His mom excused herself to the ladies' room. Frank and Teddy stood as she walked away.

When they settled back into their chairs, Frank said, "Tell you what...I'll send you the name of a trainer, I know. He's pretty well known in the industry. In fact, he trained the last Triple Crown winner. If anyone can help Katie to improve her odds at winning the Derby, it's him."

"Great, that would be helpful. Let me run that by her and Sammy, and I'll get back to you regarding a date."

"Good deal. Just don't let too much time lapse. Sometimes, it's the little things that trainers do initially that improve the success of a championship win. Let me know within a week or two."

When Claire returned to the table, Teddy invited her and Frank to the farm on Saturday afternoon for a casual dinner on the porch. "Frank, I want you to meet Mattie Grace and Sammy, and we'll show you around the farm." Then, thinking of Mr. Zee, he added, "I'd also like your opinion on another horse we have in our stable."

More importantly, Frank could talk with Katie and Sammy about the trainer. An offer of this magnitude would be better received coming from Frank.

Chapter Sixteen

T eddy pulled into the parking space behind Andrew's law office. Since returning from Savannah, he'd been busy with his medical practice, the real estate business, and the farm. He looked up at the gutters on the building. Someone had cleaned them since his last visit. A promising sign that Andrew was paying attention to the details.

He walked through the back door and stuck his head in the break room. Andrew was brewing a cup of coffee. He turned toward the door when it clicked shut. "Hi, Teddy. I was thinking of you just this morning. So glad you stopped by."

Teddy extended his hand. "It's been a few weeks. How've you been?"

Andrew nodded, a gesture that could have meant *fine* or *don't ask* or anything in between. "Would you like a cup of coffee? We've got this new Keurig machine. I'm not sure about brewing one cup of coffee at a time, but my staff's been wanting one of these machines for a while. So last week, I was at Target and bought one." He chuckled. "The ladies were so excited. You would've thought it was Christmas."

Teddy followed Andrew back to his office. As usual, Andrew closed the door and settled into a chair across from his desk. He motioned for Teddy to sit in the chair beside him.

"How's Daisy doing?" Teddy asked.

Thoughtfully, Andrew stirred his coffee. "We're still discussing how best to help Colleen move on with her life." He wrapped his napkin around the spoon and laid it on his desk. "It's a process, Teddy. A long process, but something dawned on me this weekend when Daisy and I were having lunch downtown. I'm seriously rethinking my retirement date."

"I never thought you'd retire," Teddy said. "You're legal counsel for most of the corporations in Abington. Who would take your place?"

Andrew walked over to the window and sipped his coffee. "I'd planned on Drew replacing me one day. But I realized the other day that we'll never see him again... not in this lifetime."

Teddy uncrossed his legs and placed his elbows on his knees—his knuckles supporting his chin. He'd accepted that truth years ago, but hearing Andrew say it aloud sent an ache through his chest. "Perhaps you should talk to Jacob over the Christmas holiday. Maybe he knows of a classmate who would like to move to a small town and start his career in an established firm."

Andrew laughed out loud. "That's a brilliant idea. Two bright, young minds are just what this firm needs to go to the next level." He walked across the room and sat down in the same chair he'd occupied earlier. "There's one more thing I need to discuss with you—if you have time."

"Of course," Teddy said. "What is it?"

"Colleen needs to move on with her life." Andrew drew in a steadying breath. "And Daisy and I need to do the same. We need to file the declaration of death claim so Colleen can have closure. But...."

Teddy nodded. "But?"

"But Daisy continues to resist. You know how much she loves her boy!"

It was Teddy's turn to walk around the room. The suggestion about Jacob taking over Andrew's corporate clients was just common sense. Jacob was currently studying law and was their only grandson. But this thing with Daisy would require more critical thought.

Teddy turned around and leaned back against the windowsill. He pulled a couple of coins from his pocket and studied them intently. "You're right, Andrew. Daisy may never agree to give up on finding Drew. But have you considered approaching this from another angle?"

Andrew cocked his head to the right and waited.

"Maybe you should present it in the reverse order."

"What do you mean, reverse order?"

"Well, if Colleen were missing, wouldn't Daisy want Drew to move on with his life?" Teddy looked back at a coin he held in his hands. After a moment, he looked up at Andrew. "The next time the subject comes up... casually pose that question. Hopefully, once she gives it some thought, she'll see it from a different perspective."

Slowly, Andrew nodded. "That's an excellent strategy."

"Daisy loves Colleen like a daughter." Teddy flipped one coin and then slid it into his pocket. "And I know she wants only the best for her grandchildren, but she isn't looking at the big picture."

Andrew jumped up from his seat and crossed the room to place his hands on Teddy's shoulders. "Thank you, son. I think that may very well be the answer."

Chapter Seventeen

Nic watched as Little Jimmy Levinson lit his second cigarette of the day. They got thirty minutes of daylight time each day, and during the break, LJ, as Nic began calling him because he was too old to be called Little Jimmy, usually smoked three to four cigarettes. LJ seemed sane enough. Intelligent, too. At one time, he'd owned a thriving insurance agency and was a competitive fisherman. He'd also had a family. Nic had seen them in a picture LJ carried around in his pocket. Beautiful wife. Three precious daughters.

But he'd got twisted somehow.

Little Jimmy had admitted to killing three other women and six girls in a six-month orgy of violence that came to a horrific conclusion with the murders of his wife and children.

Nic had done his share of killing, but he couldn't understand a man who would murder his own flesh and blood. Family was everything.

Nic glanced at LJ. He seemed perfectly normal, sitting on the bench watching the exhaled smoke release from his cigarette. He was still lean and fit, like the star student and athlete he'd been at his high school, but somewhere along the way, the demented part of his brain had taken control. Bad wiring, Nic figured. The crazy gene seemed to run in families, but maybe it was part environmental, too. That age old question—nature versus nurture?

Either way, Little Jimmy was a damaged soul.

Nic shook the thought from his mind. He didn't have to be best friends with the man. He needed information from LJ about a farm in

Abington he was interested in buying. If LJ didn't know the answers, his father, the longstanding mayor of the town, could find out for him.

Nic glanced at the security guard standing outside the door.

Little Jimmy asked, "What made you guys open up shop in Abington? We're a small town for an operation of your size."

"True enough. But we'd been looking for property in a small town for several years. Abington's access to the Atlanta airport was perfect for this type of business."

"Dad says you bought the farm," Little Jimmy said, lighting another cigarette. "How did you find out about Henry's place?"

Nic looked at his shoes, not sure how much information he should share about the deal, but he'd have to tell LJ enough to get him to open up about the Hawkins' farm.

Finally, Nic explained that his nephew, Fitz, had met Whelchel's daughter, Julia when his mother was in the hospital. She took care of his mom until they called in hospice.

"Yeah, Julia's a nice girl. A real beauty, too."

Nic asked, "What do you know about the adjoining farm?"

"The Hawkins' place?" Little Jimmy blew a circle of smoke into the air.

Nic looked back at the guard. "Yeah, the Hawkins' place."

"Katie and her husband own it. Katie's grandparents left the house and part of the acreage to her when they died, and she and her uncle turned it into a Thoroughbred race farm."

"Hmmm," Nic said. "How big is it? Do you know?"

LJ stumped out the cigarette, raised his arms above his head, and stretched. Then he plucked a speck of tobacco from his tongue. "Maybe sixty-seventy acres. Almost twice as large as Henry's place. Dad said they've got a horse that'll be old enough to race in the Derby next year. Some speculate she'll win the Triple Crown."

Nic stood and looked around the grounds, as the guard motioned their time was up. He needed that property. Seventy acres would allow him to build an airport large enough to transport drugs worldwide.

They owned one other airport in Colombia, South America. They needed another one in North America, and Abington, Georgia, was the perfect place.

"Interesting," he said. "Does the property back up to Henry's place?"

"Yes," Little Jimmy said. "Yes, it does."

Walking toward the back door, Nic said, "Those Thoroughbreds are expensive animals. I wonder how attached they are to their horses?"

Little Jimmy cocked his head to the side. "They're training for the Derby. Does that answer your question?"

Chapter Eighteen

S ilver Circle and their most experienced stable boy were already in the training arena when Sammy brought Mr. Zee out to train. Although their temperaments were different, the animals worked well together. Sammy noticed a renewed spirit in Mr. Zee, a competitive edge that he'd not recognized before. He was brave and inquisitive, but he was gentle in his approach to Silver Circle, and it seemed the filly pushed harder when Mr. Zee was around.

Suddenly, the stable boy let loose of Mr. Zee's rope, slapped him on his hindquarters, and let him run. Sammy stopped and watched. He moved just like Black Gold, the 1924 winner of The Kentucky Derby.

Sammy envisioned the tall, black horse posed in the Winner's Circle, saddled with a lush blanket of red roses across his back. A total of 554 roses, to be exact.

Maybe it was time to discuss the idea with Katie.

****

Later in the afternoon, when his mom and Frank arrived, his mom stayed in the house and visited with Mattie Grace while Teddy and Frank took the Gator down to the stables.

Teddy and Frank leaned against the fence and watched the training exercise. When Mr. Zee took off running across the pasture, the hairs on Teddy's neck stood up. It was a pivotal moment. Mr. Zee had finally turned the corner in his recovery. The stem cell therapy was working.

Sammy walked over and extended a hand. "Hello there. I'm Sammy Hawkins. You must be Frank?"

Frank returned the handshake. "That's a fine-looking animal you got there."

"Thanks. He's recovering from a leg injury."

"That's unfortunate. He looks like a championship horse."

Sammy looked at Teddy and laughed. "Well, he thinks he *is* a championship horse. His sire was a former Kentucky Derby winner, one of the country's top Thoroughbred stallions."

Frank took a closer look at the colt. "Is that Kentucky Star you've got there?"

Sammy nodded. "His barn name is Mr. Zee."

Frank said, "Well, I'll be damned. I was at the farm the day he was born." He turned to Teddy. "I didn't realize you bought him too."

"I didn't buy him. One of our previous trainers asked Sammy if he could stay in our barn. One thing led to another, and when the trainer left, the horse stayed. So, now we've got another horse to feed."

Teddy purposely downplayed the value of the horse. He wanted to find out what Frank knew about the colt's ability.

Frank continued to study the horse. "You got plans for this big fella?"

"We're thinking pace horse," Sammy said. They discussed the stem cell therapy Teddy and Dr. Scott had used on him.

Frank showed more interest in Mr. Zee than he did in Silver Circle, which both pleased and surprised Teddy. Sammy, on the other hand, grew more reticent as they talked, an occasional frown crossing his face.

Frank flicked his gaze from Mr. Zee to Silver Circle and back again. "Sammy, I don't think I'd train those two animals together every day. Maybe one session a week. Horses tend to develop a herd mentality… you don't want them to get too dependent on each other."

"Good point," Sammy said, his voice tight.

Frank cleared his throat and spat, then smiled. "And as you well know, Sammy, every horse is different. Some may be lazy in the morning and energetic in the afternoon. Others just need time to acclimate to their surroundings or new routines. Some are just ornery enough to try anyone's patience. Still, I think they might establish a pecking order whereby one might defer to the other on the track. Especially when they get in a big race."

Sammy was quiet as he listened to Frank's suggestions.

Teddy could tell Sammy didn't appreciate Frank coming onto his turf, much less telling him how to train.

Frank didn't seem to notice. "I tell you what, Sammy. We've got a world-class trainer at my brother's farm who has won a couple of derby races and a Triple Crown. What do you say I send him down here next week to work with your horses? He can design a training program for each animal based on their individual strengths and weaknesses. He may be able to give you some pointers on how to train for a big win."

Katie suddenly appeared from behind the barn. "Hi, Frank. So, who is this so-called world-class trainer?" She looked at Sammy and winked.

"Katie, it's great to see you. You've got an amazing place here. It's state of the art."

"Thanks. We're proud of it."

"I was just telling Teddy and Sammy that we've got a world-class trainer at my brother's farm. You may have heard of him. His name is Cicero Cappelletti. He might be able to lend a hand with training these two for the Derby."

Teddy looked down at the ground to avoid her eyes.

Katie looked at Teddy and back at Frank. "Are you kidding me? You know Cicero Cappelletti... *the Cicero Cappelletti?* The Italian who trained the last Triple Crown winner?"

Although Teddy had known Frank would mention the trainer sometime during the evening, he hadn't expected him to broach the subject so early in the afternoon.

She touched his arm and said, "Cicero Cappelletti is coming to the Hawkins Farm!"

Teddy shrugged and looked at Frank.

Katie flashed her prettiest smile. "If you guys will excuse me, I'm going up to the house to clean up. Frank, I'll look forward to talking more about it at dinner."

As she turned to leave, she lightly tapped Sammy's elbow and said, "Can you believe our good fortune? Frank just handed us an opportunity of a lifetime."

The color in Sammy's face reddened as he shuffled his feet. "Yes... our good fortune," Sammy said. Then he gave Katie a sideways glance.

Sammy reached for Mr. Zee's bridle. "I think he's had enough for one day. We don't want to over stress that leg." He led the colt toward the barn. A stiff smile planted on his face.

Katie went upstairs and showered while Claire stayed in the sunroom and read the paper. When she came back downstairs, she poured them a glass of lemonade and motioned for Claire to move into the kitchen while she made the salad and scrubbed the potatoes for baking.

"Tell me, Claire, what's up with you and Frank?"

Claire smiled. "Frank's a nice guy. He's asked for my input regarding the marketing for the condominiums he's building off the square downtown."

Katie hesitated. Her mother-in-law had been clinging to the past for way too long. It would be just like her to push Frank away, but maybe if she would admit her interest, she could finally move on. Katie softened her voice. "Seriously, Claire. Are you interested in seeing him in more than a professional setting?"

Claire looked down at the wedding rings on her left hand. For a moment, Katie thought she wasn't going to answer. Then Claire said quietly, "Seriously? I think I might be. It's just…" She hesitated, tilted her hand so her wedding band glinted in the light. "Every time I look at this, it feels like I'm burying Theo all over again."

Katie laid her hand on the older woman's forearm. She couldn't imagine what it would be like to lose a husband. If it were Teddy, she wasn't sure she could ever move on. Maybe she too would need a push from someone who loved her. "It's all right if you're not ready, Claire," she said. "But it's also okay if you are."

Claire nodded. Then, slowly, she slipped the rings from her finger and gave them one last glance. "I've held on to these too long. Katie, I want you to have my wedding band."

Katie's mouth dropped open, but she seemed to have lost the power of speech.

Claire smiled and dropped both rings into Katie's open hand. "Will you save my diamond for when Mattie Grace gets married? Perhaps her fiancé will use my stone for her engagement ring."

"Fiancé?" Katie laughed, cupping the rings gently in her palm. "Mattie Grace will be lucky if Teddy lets a boy get close enough to ask her out, let alone propose."

Through the shimmer of tears, Claire laughed too.

By the time the men stepped onto the back porch, Katie had tucked the rings in her purse for safekeeping. She'd already tenderized the steaks and had them ready for the grill.

She glanced at Claire—hands clutched tightly, a mix of hope and caution on her face—and reached to clasp her mother-in-law in an encouraging embrace.

While Frank and Sammy waited on the porch, Teddy came into the kitchen and smiled when he saw that Katie had everything well under way for dinner.

His mom cleared her throat, "Son, I've just given Katie my wedding band, and I've asked her to save my engagement ring for Mattie Grace."

He looked from his mother to his wife and back again. Clearly something big had happened here while he was at the barn. He leaned over and kissed his mother's cheek. "Good move, Mom. It's time you moved on. Frank's a great guy."

His mom patted his face. "Thanks, Son. I appreciate your support." She gave him a mischievous smile. "And your permission. Now I'm going outside to check on Frank." As Claire turned to leave, she looked over her shoulder and winked at Katie.

As soon as Claire was out of earshot, Katie pointed her finger at Teddy and said in that sassy tone that drove him wild, "I told you! Did I not tell you she liked Frank?"

"Yes, you told me." Teddy chuckled.

"I knew before you did, Teddy! You know, my dear, females are more intuitive than our male counterparts."

"Yeah, tell me about it," Teddy said. "You better run upstairs and put those rings in the safe before you forget about it."

While Teddy gathered a tray of supplies he'd need for grilling and went outside to put the steaks on the grill, Katie carried a tray of drinks to the porch. Everyone snacked on the goodies from the charcuterie board while Teddy grilled dinner.

Sammy seemed subdued, but Frank and Claire were chatting like old friends.

About halfway through dinner, Frank looked at Katie and said, "My brother, Philip, was quite taken with you, Katie."

She gave him an appreciative smile. "We enjoyed meeting him, Frank. He runs an impressive operation up there."

"He told me something today that you might find interesting." He took a sip of his water and said, "Seems he got a call from Talking Jack's attorney. The owner needs to sell some assets to cover the gambling debts of his youngest son. Debts that could cause his son some serious problems if not settled within a short period of time. He asked that we not mention the terms of the deal with anyone outside those present, but the owner needs to move quickly to meet the deadline. It's still not cheap, but he's cut the price by quite a bit."

He named a price. Like he'd said, not cheap. But not a million dollars.

Teddy and Katie exchanged glances.

Teddy asked, "Is the kid in trouble?"

At first, Frank was hesitant to say too much, but finally, he told them the owner had three children. The oldest two sons were married with families and had success in their respected professions.

"The youngest son is a total mess," he said. "He flunked out of college, been married twice, and has an addictive personality."

Teddy asked, "Drugs?"

"No drugs—just gambling." Frank finished the last bite of his steak and said, "Philip told me the price for Talking Jack might still be out of your reach, but when these types of deals come along, it's hard to ignore. Perhaps you guys could find a few more investors, pool your money together, and purchase the horse."

Frank leaned toward Katie, and he spoke in a low voice. "You know you won't be happy until you buy Talking Jack, Katie."

Katie glanced at Teddy. She'd known this day would come. When you wanted something as much as she'd wanted Talking Jack, somehow the universe delivered.

Teddy must have seen the determination on her face. He patted her hand and said to Frank, "Can you give us a day or two to see what we can work out?"

Frank walked out into the yard to place the call to his brother. A few minutes later, he returned to the table and said, "He'll need to know within forty-eight hours if you are moving forward with the purchase. He agreed not to mention the deal to anyone else until he hears from you."

Chapter Nineteen

The Syndicated Purchase

Katie sat at the kitchen counter, listening as Teddy made several calls about the syndicated purchase. Hearing only the one-sided conversation was nerve-racking.

Teddy had just apologized to one of his golf friends for taking his time to listen to a financial opportunity.

Their friends in Abington, Georgia, had different cultural endeavors from those living in Louisville, Kentucky. Their culture leaned toward the arts, not equestrian sports. Perhaps they should reach outside their local pool of friends to make this work.

The following afternoon, Angie sat with Mattie Grace while Teddy worked the phones to find investors.

When Colleen came in later in the afternoon to pick up Angie, Teddy was finishing a call with his banker, Don Johnson. Colleen peered into the sunroom, then turned to Katie, "What's Teddy doing home so early on a Tuesday afternoon?"

"We've got an opportunity to buy a championship racehorse, but the price is a little out of our reach. Teddy's trying to find some investors to go in with us on a syndicate purchase."

"Will this horse be ready to race in the next Derby?"

"Yeah, he should be." An image of the gorgeous chestnut colt rose in her mind. In her heart, he was already hers, but unless they could persuade enough investors to take a chance on him, she was going to lose him again.

Katie could tell the conversation intrigued Colleen. "I've got a pan of lasagna cooking in the oven. Why don't you stay for dinner? You guys can eat and be on your way in an hour or so, and you won't have to worry about making dinner."

Teddy walked into the kitchen just as Colleen plopped down at the bar. "Since you're staying for dinner, I'll open a bottle of wine."

He handed Colleen a glass and asked, in an exaggerated voice, "You don't want to buy a few shares of a racehorse, do you?" Teddy laughed at his negative sales approach.

Colleen laughed with him. Then she took a sip of wine and said, "Oooh, that's tasty... how much is a share of a racehorse these days?"

Katie's eyebrows shot up. "Are you serious, Colleen? Would you really be interested?"

Colleen nodded. "Maybe. Who else is on board?"

Teddy said, "Right now... Katie, Sammy, me, and possibly Mom." He gained some confidence as he explained how the partnership would work with five investors, although they had hoped for ten.

Over dinner, they discussed why the owner had decided to sell the horse. When Teddy finished telling the story, Colleen wiped her eyes. "Can you imagine having to sell a Thoroughbred to settle the gambling debts of your son?"

Katie nodded. "I know, right?"

"How old is the boy?" Colleen asked.

"Around twenty-five." Teddy said. "Flunked out of college, married twice. Fortunately, no children."

Colleen clucked her tongue in sympathy. "He's the same age as Jacob. I'm so glad Jacob didn't get derailed by Drew's disappearance."

"You have nothing to worry about with Jacob," Teddy said. "He's doing great in law school."

"Drew would be so proud of him," Colleen said. Then she continued, "Teddy, I've been talking with Andrew. The State of Georgia recently amended their statutes to reduce the time to four consecutive years for missing persons. This new ruling made me realize it's time to file a petition to declare Drew legally dead. What are your thoughts?"

Teddy stepped closer to the bar. "I think it's a good idea, Colleen. Drew would want you to move on with your life."

"Thank you." Colleen continued to sip her wine. "So tell me more about this kid who flunked out of college."

Teddy said, "The kid was lucky to have a father with the resources to redeem him from his gambling debts."

Colleen said, "Talk about redemption."

Katie said, "Colleen, what did you say?"

"I said, talk about redemption. The dad sells his prized horse to bail his son out of financial ruin. That's the definition of redemption."

Katie looked at Teddy and said, "Do you know if changing Talking Jack's name to Redemption would cause any psychological damage to a horse?"

"I doubt it would matter, as long as you file the appropriate paperwork."

Katie removed the lasagna from the oven. "A new owner—a new home—and a new name."

"Okay. That settles it," Colleen said, looking from one to the other. "I want in, too."

On Wednesday morning, after Teddy left to take Mattie Grace to school, Katie went into his office. She rummaged through the messages until she found Frank's phone number.

She slumped down in the chair and looked at the number. If Frank could explain the formula for the syndicated purchase, she thought she could sell enough shares to buy Talking Jack.

Katie studied her list of names. Frugal. Cautious. Professional. Successful. They each had the money to invest, but they might view this investment as a wild card.

Frank's rich, baritone voice answered on the second ring.

"Frank, this is Katie. I've called to ask you about organizing a syndicate purchase for Talking Jack. I understand it in theory, but I have a few questions. We've passed the forty-eight-hour window, but can you help me?"

"We've still got time, Katie, and I'll be happy to help you."

He explained how the purchase would work. First, Katie would decide the percentage she, Teddy, and Sammy would own based on the money they had available to invest. Then she would need to figure out the number of shares and how much each must bring to complete the purchase.

It was an easy formula. The horse cost $900,000. They needed $400,000 more to complete the sale.

"Okay," Frank said. "At ten thousand dollars for each share, you'll either need eight investors with $50,000 each or four investors with $100,000 each. In a syndicated purchase, it's best to keep the minimum investment at $50,000."

Once Katie understood how it worked, she said, "Thanks so much for your help. I just know I'll find enough investors to make the numbers work."

"Katie, you're almost there." She heard the smile in his tone. "Remember, just be yourself. Don't appear anxious. Your friends will hear the passion in your voice, and if *you* believe you'll get the horse, it'll happen."

After lunch, Katie finished the colorful one-page PowerPoint presentation. She completed a list of ten names to contact, including her former boss, Clayton Thomas.

When she finished her chores on Thursday morning, Katie went into the sunroom and composed a speech to go along with the presentation.

Mid-morning, she stopped to check on Sammy. When she got back to Teddy's office, she read through the speech once more and smiled. Her confidence soared.

She made a light meal and poured a glass of iced tea for lunch. As she ate her salad, she read the script several times. By the end of her break, she'd committed it to memory and was ready to make calls.

She started with Clayton. Her stomach fluttered at the thought of asking him to invest such a large sum of money. Of all the people on the list, he was the one who shared her love for horses.

First, they exchanged a few pleasantries. Then she went straight into the reason for the call. As soon as she started reciting the script, she felt a surge of energy. She was so excited. She wanted to blurt out the words, but she disciplined herself to enunciate each word. Still, after a minute or so, she abandoned the script and just talked from her heart.

Talking about her passion had never been easier.

Clayton asked her to repeat the script once more while he reviewed the PowerPoint.

There went that flutter again.

She took a deep breath and plunged into her hook. "What would it take to convince you to invest in a Triple Crown winner?" She slid into the rest of her presentation, and when she finished, she paused.

For a moment he was silent. Then he said, "Yes. This is a brilliant idea."

Wait. Had he just said…? She forced the words out of her mouth. "Excuse me."

"Yes," Clayton said. "I hear the passion in your voice. If you're willing to invest in a racehorse, then I'm comfortable buying ten shares."

If he'd been in the room, she would have hugged him. "Thank you, Clayton. I appreciate your faith in me."

"Oh, and my college roommate might be interested. If you don't mind, I'll give him a call while you send over a copy of the contract."

The contract.

Katie had almost forgotten about that. When they hung up, she called Frank and asked him to email the contract.

"Sure thing," he said. "And since you're so close to getting this done, Philip will give you until Friday evening at seven. The owner will need the money by Wednesday of next week."

They signed off, and Katie immediately downloaded a copy. Walking onto the back porch, she leaned against the post to read through the contract. There were a few areas that needed tweaking, but otherwise, she was comfortable with the document.

Katie scanned a copy to Andrew for review.

By the time Mattie Grace got home from school, Katie had agreements with six more individuals. Clayton and his friend Daniel were the first on board, with Rhett Louis, Marsha Whelchel, Letrell Winters, and Jim Brody. Before Teddy got home, Katie hoped to contact the last four people on the list. Fortunately, they were clients she represented at the firm, but they all loved horse racing.

She could almost feel Talking Jack's satin coat beneath her palm.

Friday morning, Katie turned on the desk lamp to get to work. She was down to the wire, waiting to hear from two people.

An email from Andrew Byrd popped up on her phone. He'd attached a revised contract. Quickly, she sent off an email to the investor list, requesting a signed copy be returned within twenty-four hours. The hard copies would arrive in the mail a few days later.

Katie spent the morning discussing the language in the document. Finally, late that afternoon, the last two people sent emails requesting a copy of the contract.

Then, Frank called. "I talked to Philip today," he said without preamble. "We've decided to buy ten shares each."

Ten shares each! That was enough to reduce hers and Sammy's investment by two hundred thousand dollars.

She stammered a thanks and sank back in her chair, trying to absorb what had just happened. A smile spread across her face. Talking Jack—Redemption—was finally hers.

Katie ran through the house singing, "We're buying Talking Jack! We're buying Talking Jack!"

When she ran back through the kitchen, Teddy stood inside the back door, smiling as he watched her with excitement.

Katie flung her arms around his neck, and said, "I've got enough investors to buy Talking Jack, and you won't have to invest any of your money!"

Teddy swept her into a hug that lifted her off the ground. "Congratulations, sweetheart. You're finally getting your horse."

"Oh, Teddy, I'm so excited. I've spent the last three days putting this deal together."

He chuckled. "Have you told Sammy?"

"Not yet. I was waiting to tell you first."

Teddy held her face in his hands. "Katie-girl, I'm so proud of you." She closed her eyes and smiled.

He finally released her hold. "While I'm upstairs changing, why don't you call Sammy and tell him the good news?"

Chapter Twenty

Sept 2021

As they waited in the library above the courtroom, Nicolas Suarez watched their defense attorney, Braydon Stone, shuffle a stack of papers on the table. The attorney's assistant had rushed them up the back staircase because Stone had not wanted to be in the courtroom when the cartel's brass arrived. After years of appeals, the cartel had hired him to defend Nic and his nephew, Fitzgerald Romano.

Stone had the jitters. He'd been to the men's room twice in the past twenty minutes. "Where did they find this guy?" Nic mumbled to himself. He couldn't believe Stone had secured a retrial, established on the earlier guilty verdict. It was bold, but he'd done it.

Stone wiped his face with a handkerchief as he glanced in their direction.

Nic smirked. Stone clearly thought his clients were guilty, yet he'd prepared a decent defense. Admittedly, he'd performed well, but now they were ready for closing arguments, and if he wasn't careful, he could lose the jurors.

First in his class at Georgetown, the brass had told them. Nic shuddered as he walked over to the window. God, he hoped Stone could pull this off.

He'd been away from the business for too long. The man he left behind had kept the operation moving smoothly. So smoothly, in fact, they needed to expand. The owner of the farmhouse had been unwilling to include that tract of land. However, there was a horse farm next door that would meet their needs, if the owners would agree to sell. He was sure they would because he could be very persuasive and was prepared to make them an offer they couldn't refuse.

At the window, he turned and looked over Stone's shoulder at the notes laid out on the table:

Model prisoners from the very first day.

Nic chuckled under his breath. Of course, they were model prisoners. If the *'endeble'* only knew every illegal infringement he'd ordered, he wouldn't have agreed to represent them. Nic and his nephew had known the consequences of being detained in an American penal system would be difficult. They'd wasted no time making friends with their fellow inmates. Because of their congenial manner, they soon gained comprehensive information about each inmate that lived on their cell block, along with the guards who supervised their activities.

The library door opened, and Stone's assistant, James, stuck his head inside to tell his boss they were gathering downstairs.

Stone nodded to his clients. "Gentlemen, it's time." He hurriedly assembled his papers and looked around the room for any items he might have missed.

While straightening his tie, Stone walked to the door. "Let's go win this one, James. I called in a bunch of favors to secure an impartial venue."

Following the attorney's lead, Nic headed toward the door. He raised his eyebrow and said to Fitz, "Yes. Let's do!"

Nic and Fitz, dressed in crisp khaki pants and new Polo shirts, walked behind the suits. The only noise as the four men descended the two flights of stairs to the main level was the sound of their footsteps.

Walking into the US District Courtroom in Washington, DC, Stone nodded to the prosecuting attorney before approaching the defense table. No sooner had the legal team settled in the chairs, the door to the judge's chamber opened, and The Honorable Robert Hardy appeared.

After the attorneys gave their closing arguments, the jurors deliberated for less than fifty minutes. When the jurors returned, there was a scurry of activity. The many spectators who lined the walls of the courtroom hadn't expected a decision to be reached so quickly.

Judge Hardy lifted his gavel and lowered it with one hard slam. "This court will come to order."

The courtroom quieted as everyone took a seat, eager to hear the verdict.

Nic opened his hands and rubbed his sweaty palms on his pants. He couldn't breathe. At the beginning of the trial, he'd been so confident, but now, as he watched the stoic expressions of the jurors, he wasn't so sure. Of course, it didn't help that Stone's face had drained of all color while sweat dripped from his forehead. He'd delivered the closing argument with calm and eloquence—no one could have done it better—but now he looked as uncomfortable as a bad girl at church.

"Will the foreman please stand at this time?" Judge Hardy said.

Nic watched as the foreman stood and shifted his weight back and forth. The fix was supposed to be in, but what if the jurors had voted against them?

The foreman removed a folded piece of paper from his shirt pocket. Then he looked at the judge and nodded. He was ready.

Get on with it.

Finally, after receiving instructions from the judge, the foreman announced a unanimous decision of not guilty.

There was a buzz of disbelief when the verdict was read.

It was as theatrical a scene as Nic had ever seen in a movie, complete with shaking hands and a quivering chin.

A brilliant performance—one Nic would not soon forget.

Nic slowly exhaled and glanced at his nephew. Fitz was smiling, obviously never doubting the outcome.

The *endeble* had done it—he'd won the case. True to form, Stone had pulled a miracle from his sleeve at the last moment, proving "beyond a reasonable doubt" the rogue Special Agent Bill Bowen had acted alone with regard to both the kidnapping and human trafficking charges and was not a member of the cartel. Part of that was actually true—no need to confuse the jurors with details of their drug operation.

The buzz surged to a clamor. Then, a thunderous shock from the gallery at the jurors' decision of innocence disrupted the courtroom. Judge Hardy banged his gavel until the spectators' excitement finally calmed. He ordered the immediate release of both Nicolas Suarez and Fitzgerald Romano from federal custody. Then he ordered all charges related to their sentence dropped and their convictions expunged from the record.

The trial had taken two weeks from start to finish.

Stone turned and extended his hand, first to Nic, then to Fitz, and congratulated them on their good luck. Then he opened his briefcase and reached inside. "Special courier delivered these to my office this morning... it's from Matteo Suarez."

Stone glanced at Nic searching for any sign of recognition. He never flinched. Stone continued, "Um, he attached a note explaining that you would need identification, credit cards, licenses, and cash. It seems the family was betting on your release today."

After serving seven years of a thirty-year sentence, Nic Suarez and Fitz Romano walked out of the US District Court as free men.

****

Nic and Fitz hailed a cab outside the US District Court building in Washington. Nic looked at his nephew, Fitz, and said, "Don't know about you, but freedom never felt so sweet."

Fitz stretched his arms and took a deep cleansing breath as he looked up to the clear, blue sky. "You got that right!"

"Where are we going?" Nic asked.

Fitz shrugged. "It doesn't really matter..." Then, he suddenly changed his mind. "Let's go over to Georgetown. There's a cool brewpub where I used to go with my buddies. Let's find out if it's still open."

"Sure, why not?"

The cab pulled in front of Galvin's on West Main Street. After paying the fare, they hopped out of the cab, and hesitated before going inside. Although it was October, the temperature was in the seventies. The air flirted with a touch of autumn, and the foliage was turning from green to varying shades of gold, orange, and red.

They sat in silence as they enjoyed the first round of drinks. The noise increased as people came in after work for a drink or a meal.

The flat-screen TV suspended from the ceiling above the bar announced 6:00 p.m., the local news was about to start. A brief picture of Nic and Fitz flashed across the screen as the news commentator announced their release from federal custody. Fortunately, the news clip lasted only fifteen seconds.

Fitz looked around the place and noticed that only one person was paying attention to the news. It was the guy at the end of the bar, three seats from where they sat down when they came in an hour earlier.

The guy wore khaki pants and a navy-blue sports jacket. The top button of his white oxford shirt was unbuttoned. When they made eye contact, the guy reached up and loosened his blue-and-yellow-striped tie. Fitz couldn't tell if the guy was an attorney or worked in the business community, but definitely a white-collar professional.

Fitz continued to watch the door. He was possibly paranoid, but the FBI would do everything they could to get them back inside the prison walls. He eyeballed the mirror behind the bar and studied the guy more closely. He had all the earmarks of an undercover cop. His hair was too long for someone practicing law in the DC area. He sipped a draft beer and repeatedly looked at his cellphone, but as Fitz watched, the guy's interest in the local news broadcast heightened.

Fitz told Nic that he was interested in getting back to Georgia, particularly Abington.

Nic's contacts within the cartel had kept tabs on the Whelchel farm and reported they had not yet sold the farmhouse.

"I agree," Nic said. "I want to make another offer on that farmhouse. But this time, I'd like to buy the adjoining farm along with it."

"Which farm is that? The Whelchel farm borders several properties."

Nic motioned for the bartender to bring them another round.

"You're right." He drew a diagram on a cocktail napkin. "There's the property that belongs to the Industrial Park. The other side belonged to the Hawkins family until the elder Hawkinses died. Now, the property belongs to their granddaughter. It's over twice the size of the Whelchel farm. Put'em together, and we'll have room to build a small airport—if we can get the plans passed through zoning."

"How did you learn about the other piece of property?"

"Do you remember Little Jimmy?" Nic asked. "The dark-haired guy at the end of the cellblock? They moved him from solitary confinement to our block because there was a shortage of cells in solitary."

"Of course, I remember Jimmy," Fitz said. "Wasn't he responsible for a string of murders that included his wife and children?"

"Yep, that's the guy."

"There was talk that someone pulled some strings with the governor to get him moved out of solitary," Fitz said.

"Yeah, I heard that, too," Nic said. "We spent an hour together twice a week during our daylight time. Jimmy was from the town of Abington. His father was the mayor for a lotta years, and he wrote to Little Jimmy every week—talked a lot about land transactions. It seemed Jimmy owned a property and casualty insurance agency, so his old man kept him abreast of the goings-on in the small town. One day, Jimmy told me about the transfer of ownership of the Hawkins farm. I understand it's a pretty big operation."

"Yeah?" Fitz said. "What kind of horses do they have?"

"I'm assuming Thoroughbreds. According to Little Jimmy, they've bought a horse to compete in the Derby. Some people think the horse has the makings of a Triple Crown winner."

"That could play well," Fitz said. "Especially if they resist selling the property to the cartel."

Joe, according to the tag on the bartender's shirt, sat their drinks down on the counter and said, "Should I add this to your tab, sir?"

Fitz nodded and glanced at the guy sitting a few seats down. Then Fitz realized the man was watching them through the mirror.

"Yes, please, and can we get a couple of your specials, too?"

"Coming up."

As Joe wiped the countertop, he nodded at the guy sitting at the end of the bar and said, "Hey Drew, do you need another beer?"

Chapter Twenty-One

Joe, the bartender, slid the mug in Drew's direction. The object of the game was to see how fast the glass could glide down the slick bar top without spilling. Drew had thought it was a silly game until he saw how much Joe enjoyed it. Over time, he'd come to appreciate the skill it took to move a full mug of liquid without spilling a drop. It was silly, but Joe enjoyed it. Bartenders, it seemed, were easily bored.

"Whatcha got going on this weekend, Drew?"

"I'm thinking about going back home."

Joe looked at him sideways as he poured a couple of drafts for the guys sitting at the table to his right. "Umm, you've never mentioned home before."

"Yeah, I know. There's a lot I haven't told you." Hard to believe, after all the years he'd been coming here, Joe still knew so little about him. "Maybe it's time."

The two guys at the other end of the bar had just finished their bar-b-que plates, pulled out a roll of money, and laid a few bills on the bar. They had the look of prison on them—the prison yard watchfulness, the institutional pallor.... As soon as they started toward the door, Drew let out a sigh of relief.

Joe cleared their plates and wiped the bar where they'd sat. Then, he walked down to Drew's end and said, "And... umm... so where is home?"

Drew took a long swallow of his beer and set the mug on the bar harder than he intended. "Abington, Georgia."

"Near Atlanta... right?"

"Right." Drew wiped his mouth with the napkin. "You probably hear a lot of crazy stories from your customers, don't you?"

Joe nodded. "I've heard some interesting stories, that's for sure, but I've never heard yours."

Drew looked around and noticed the businessmen sitting at the table to his right had moved to the main dining room for dinner. The bar area was empty except for him and Joe.

"It's a sordid story," Drew said. "You may not want to hear it."

Joe wiped the bar once more and then threw the towel over his shoulder. "Try me."

Drew lowered his voice and looked around. "I got involved with my best friend's wife."

Joe gave him a sideways glance and raised an eyebrow. "That's never good."

"No," Drew said. "Nothing like that. I got caught up in a scheme to steal his inheritance. It started as a game to see if I could manipulate this girl into marrying my friend. Anyway, it worked, she married him, and greed got the best of her." He shook his head, "I should've...umm... known better. She was a psychopath."

He still couldn't believe he'd let himself go as far as he had. At first, he'd told himself he had Teddy's best interest at heart, but even a child should have seen how things were bound to go wrong.

He loosened his tie a little more, and said, "She snapped... and then she went postal and killed a couple of people."

"Seriously? What did you do?"

Drew took a long swallow of his drink and wiped his mouth with the sleeve of his jacket. "I took the coward's way out. I got scared... and left the scene, knowing I'd already compromised my career... my family... and my standing in the community."

Joe stared at Drew, his expression more curious than judgmental, then reached for a handful of nuts and popped a few in his mouth.

Drew lowered his head and sighed. "Worst of all, I'd screwed my best friend. The very best friend a guy could ever have. All because of greed. I relive that nightmare every day. Can you believe it? I ran out the backdoor of that farmhouse and ended up in Washington. The next week, I answered an ad for a legal clerk position, and I've been hiding up here ever since."

The bartender licked the salt from his fingers. "What happened to the girl?"

Drew looked at the rich caramel liquid in his mug and said, "She killed herself."

Joe absently wiped his mouth, then poured Drew another drink and set it gently in front of him. "I can see why it took you so long to share all that. What a shame... for both of you."

"Yeah. A shame." Drew looked at his friend with wide eyes. "I gotta fix this."

Joe leaned his forearms on the bar and fixed Drew with a quizzical gaze. "How you gonna fix a thing like that, man?"

"I'll find a way," Drew said. "But first, I gotta get back home."

Instead of showing up for work the following day, Drew packed the few items he'd acquired while in D.C., and for the next two days, he enjoyed a road trip back to Georgia.

He was going home. Or at least going to his hometown.

He'd thought about going back a thousand times in recent years, but after what happened that night at the farm, he wasn't sure he'd be welcomed.

Drew had been hiding out in the D.C. area, providing research for a sick, elderly attorney in exchange for food, rent, a cell phone, and access to an eighteen-year-old Chevrolet Tahoe. When he got his envelope each week, which contained one hundred dollars in cash, he stashed away most of his money, but he kept out enough for a visit to the pub. Every Friday afternoon at 4:30p.m., he left for Georgetown. It was literally the highlight of his week.

For all of these years, the old man had been Drew's person. The only human on the face of the earth who knew Drew was alive, except, of course, the bartender, but Joe didn't even know his last name. It surprised him at how liberated he'd felt after telling the bartender his story. Joe had shown minimal emotion in learning his regular customer was basically a 43-year-old criminal who had fallen entirely off the grid.

After two days of traveling, he finally saw the sign. As he crossed the Georgia state line, he blew the car horn in celebration.

He was home.

Coming home was a long shot, he knew. Still, if he understood the men in the bar correctly, it sounded like Teddy and Katie had married and bought a racehorse. Luckily, the men had mentioned the Whelchel place while he was at the bar in Georgetown. Drew felt he owed it to Teddy to keep an eye on those guys. Perhaps his efforts could help even the score and redeem himself if his plan worked out.

When he arrived in Abington on Sunday at noon, he drove by the street where he'd lived. He turned left at the light and drove back around to his house. What if the kids were playing outside? Would they even recognize him? Then he laughed. Rebecca would be in high school and Angie in middle. It wasn't likely either of his girls would play in the front yard at their age. The house looked the same. The shrubs in front of the house needed pruning, and the magnolia tree had grown another four feet.

When he finished touring the neighborhood, he scoped out the situation at the Whelchel's barn and was pleased to find a half bath adjoining the small office. Walking to the steps leading up to the loft, he realized the space was perfect for a livable place. Henry Whelchel would turn over in his grave if he knew his law partner was hiding in his barn.

It didn't take long for the drug operation to become exposed. The second Monday morning he was at the farm, he heard a vehicle coming down the graveled road. He snuck out the backdoor before being caught by the visitors.

Drew spent his nights in the loft and usually hid deep in the woods, waiting in an old deer stand until the four thugs who snuck drugs in and out of the barn finished their daily business. Then they would load up and leave the property until the same time the following day. He hadn't seen the two men from the bar yet, but he was sure it would only be a matter of time.

The men were resourceful, using entrance points from other farms and particularly the area belonging to the Corps of Engineers.

Drew climbed up to the loft on rare occasions and listened as they discussed the drug drops on the property. Sometimes, he found large quantities of cocaine in the precise area they had discussed in their meetings. Each time he kept watch, making sure no one came close to the site. Still, one afternoon when he went out to investigate the evidence he'd overheard them discussing, he found the hiding place empty.

He frowned as he looked into the clearing beyond the pine trees. Had he misheard?

Drew sensed a movement. The scuff of the boot on the wooden steps coming down from the deer stand froze him. Before he could turn, rough hands grabbed him from behind, and someone else yanked a musty hood over his head.

"My lucky day," a harsh voice growled in his ear. "Somebody to play with."

Drew twisted and bucked, but the man's grip was steel. This was bad. Very bad. How could he have been so stupid?

"Try not to kill this one so fast," a second voice said. "The last time, I hardly even got a turn."

A burst of pain exploded in Drew's head, and he lurched forward, landing hard on his hands and knees. As the air whooshed out of him, a second man jerked Drew's arms behind his back. Steel cuffs bit into his wrists.

"Look," he said. "It's not—

"Shut up." The first man gave Drew a sharp cuff to the ear, then they dragged him across a gravel drive and a patch of grass.

A deeper darkness inside the hood told Drew they'd taken him back to the barn. He heard a chair scrape. Without a preamble, they shoved him into it.

"Listen, man." His voice felt strained, but—thankfully—held steady. "It's not what you think. I'm an attorney. Or I *was* an attorney. I got into some trouble several years ago, and I've been on the run ever since."

"Yeah, that's an interesting story, Batman!" said the second thug. "Why should we believe you?"

Drew licked his lips. His mouth had never felt so dry. "Okay, well. I can help you guys if you'll just listen. You give me a place to hide out, and I can provide legal advice to you and the boys here. I might even be able to help you avoid the feds. Considering the amount of cocaine you dropped out there, you'll need my help if the FBI gets on your trail."

They were listening. Or at least they weren't sawing off pieces of him. He gave them a second to think about what he'd said, then added, "However, there is one caveat."

A sharp bark of laughter. "What's that?"

Drew felt stronger now. They were asking questions, or at least one of them was, and the other hadn't hit him in a while. "I can't appear with anyone from the cartel in a public place or in court. I'm sure the authorities think I'm dead. If I'm discovered, I'll be officially disbarred and could face a prison sentence. Believe me, that wouldn't help me *or* your bosses. So, I can't take any unnecessary risks, but if you need legal advice, I'm your man."

The first thug's voice took on a dangerous tone. "Who said anything about the cartel?"

"Come on, man. Who else could run an operation like this?"

Drew held his breath until the thugs stepped away to talk between themselves. Their voices were muffled, but Drew thought one of them might have made a phone call. It seemed to drag on for hours, but he couldn't tell if that was so, or if the sensation was a trick of his mind. He spent the time calming his mind and easing the tension from his muscles. He'd made his play, and they'd take it or not. If this was his day to die, he wasn't going to spend his last moments in a state of panic.

Seemingly a thousand years later, the heavy footsteps drew closer. "Guess it's not my lucky day after all," Thug One said. "Boss decided we could use some legal counsel from a local." Thug Two searched Drew for firearms, then pulled the hood from his head. Drew sucked in a delicious breath.

"Keep the barn floor clean." Thug Two said. "We sometimes bring in pallets of products for storage. Not for a long period. A day or two at the most, and we don't like this area to get too dusty." Then, they threw him a couple of blankets and a sleeping bag from the back of their van, released the handcuffs, and told him they would bring a microwave and some food on their next trip to the farm.

The following morning, after he'd bathed and changed clothes, Drew waited in the lower part of the barn when the van pulled up. This was the most rustic place he'd ever stayed, other than the occasional weekend trip he'd made in the vehicle the old man allowed him to drive. The back of the truck was too cramped for his long legs, so he preferred the barn.

The two thugs, along with a wiry guy about Drew's age, came inside. Thug Two said, "Batman, this is Fitz. He's our leader. We discussed your terms. Fitz wanted to meet with you before making this official."

Drew immediately recognized the leader from the bar, but he could tell the guy didn't remember him.

They discussed the terms of the agreement with ease.

Fitz asked, "Is Drew short for Andrew?"

"Yeah. It is."

"I had some indirect dealings with Andrew Byrd, an attorney here in Abington. You remind me of him. Any relation?"

Drew blinked, not sure how much information he should divulge until he was confident of their deal. Would divulging the relationship endanger his father? Fitz's flat gaze said he'd already suspected the truth. Which meant the truth could earn his trust, but lying might destroy any chance of an alliance. Drew took a deep breath and said, "I'm his son."

Fitz gave a barely noticeable nod. "So, you're interested in offering legal advice in exchange for staying in our barn. Is that correct?"

Drew said, "Yes. That is correct."

"I like it. Access to a local attorney will be helpful." Fitz looked at the other two men and then nodded to Drew. "Here's the deal. You can stay in the barn, as discussed. We'll bring in some blackout stripping for the windows."

Fitz climbed the steps to the loft. "Is this where you sleep?"

Drew nodded.

"My men can put up a wall to give you some privacy up there and bring in an air mattress for you to sleep on."

Fitz came back down the steps and motioned to the small office. He opened the door leading to the half bath. The area immediately to the left was a small, empty closet. He pointed to the site and said, "We can tear down that wall and install a shower. Nothing fancy, there's no hot-water heater, but it would give you a place to shower."

"A cold shower is better than no shower," Drew said.

When he finished discussing the renovation plans, Fitz turned to Drew and said, "Are you familiar with international law?"

"I studied international law in school. Of course, in a limited capacity. I practiced criminal law, but mine were all domestic cases."

"Well, we're going to need you to brush up on your international law. I'll try to find some law books for you to study. I may need your help in locating these books."

"Of course." Drew said. "I might borrow a few books from my dad's firm."

"Are you crazy! You can't just go into your dad's firm and borrow some books."

"As a matter of fact..." He produced a key from his pocket. "I have a key to the office. Unless they've changed the code on the alarm system, I should have no problem getting in there."

Fitz grinned. "I like your chutzpah."

Chapter Twenty-Two

The Breeders' Cup Juvenile

M attie Grace," Katie said. "Please put away the Halloween candy and go upstairs and get your bath. You need to get packed tonight. We leave early in the morning for California."

"I don't want to go to the race," Mattie Grace cried. "Please let me stay with Angie and Becky! Colleen doesn't mind if I stay with them."

Katie frowned. "Don't tell me you asked Colleen before asking me."

Mattie Grace hung her head.

Katie bit the inside of her cheek to keep from saying something she'd regret. Once again, Mattie Grace had gone around her mother to get her own way. It put Katie in a difficult situation, but the more she thought about it, the more she realized it would be best for Mattie Grace to stay home.

Part of her wanted to call Colleen and ask if Mattie Grace could stay with her for the week. The other part was afraid giving in would reinforce her daughter's inappropriate behavior. So here she was, waffling at the last minute about something she should've handled weeks ago.

The silence stretched while she weighed the pros and cons. This was the Breeders' Cup Juvenile. The race that often determines if a horse qualifies for the Derby. As one of the trainers, Katie needed to be accessible to Redemption and Mr. Zee during the days leading up to the race.

Silver Circle hadn't made the cross-country trip to the Thoroughbred Club in Del Mar, California, since the Breeders' Cup was only for two-year-old colts and geldings.

Teddy walked into the kitchen with a copy of the local newspaper under his arm. He looked from Mattie Grace to Katie. "What's going on in here?"

"Mattie Grace asked Colleen if she could stay with Angie and Becky while we're in California."

Teddy patted his daughter's head. "Go on up and get your bath while we discuss this plan of yours."

Mattie Grace brightened. "Thanks, Daddy."

Katie turned away to hide her frustration.

Teddy said, "I've just finished reading the article about The Breeders' Cup Juvenile. Can you believe the editor printed an article about Mr. Zee and Redemption? He even mentioned Dr. Scott and Mr. Zee's stem cell therapy."

Katie glanced at the newspaper, but was unable to focus. Her daughter knew exactly how to push her buttons—and how to wrap Teddy around her little finger.

Teddy pointed to the paper. "Did you read the part where Doctor Scott said Mr. Zee's tendons are sturdier than before, and that his legs are as strong as Redemption's?"

Katie folded the paper and put it on the counter. "Yes. It's a great article."

When they heard the water cut off in the upstairs bathroom, Teddy took a bottle of water from the refrigerator and lowered his voice. "Honestly, Katie. I wondered why we hadn't already asked Colleen about her staying with them." He took a long swallow from the bottle. "A horse race is no place for a young girl."

"You're right about that."

"Remember the last time? You spent two days before the race in the room with Mattie Grace trying to entertain her. It wasn't fair to her, and it certainly wasn't fair to you."

"It would have been nice if you'd mentioned that earlier."

He shrugged. "I didn't want to step on your toes."

"Well, now we either have to take her with us or show her that doing an end-run around her parents works. Neither option sounds especially appealing."

"We'll make it clear she should have asked you first," Teddy said. "But she was miserable the last time. Making her go would be like cutting off your nose to spite your face."

Katie sighed. "You're right. I'll call Colleen right quick and make sure it's okay with her. A week is a long time to wrestle with three young girls, though."

"Yeah, well…" Teddy winked. "Better her than us."

****

It was after midnight when Katie and Teddy got into bed. It seemed they'd just dozed off when the clock sounded at five o'clock. They rushed through their morning routine, and left the house in time to take Mattie Grace to school and drop her clothes off at Colleen's house.

Fortunately, the early morning traffic had cleared and they arrived at the airport in record time.

Teddy had managed the travel details for Sammy, Cappelletti, and the farmhands. Their crew had left ten days earlier with the horses. Making a cross-country trip with two trainers, four farmhands, and two Thoroughbred horses required a good bit of planning.

He'd also managed the flights and hotel reservations for him and Katie and arranged for a car to transport them from the airport to Del Mar. In addition to taking care of his medical practice, scheduling the travel arrangements for the trip had been time-consuming. By the time they boarded the aircraft, Teddy felt a sudden wave of relief. It was the first time he'd been able to relax in over a week.

As soon as the pilot reached the cruising altitude of 30,000 feet, Katie asked, "Teddy, there's something..." She quickly turned her face toward the window.

Teddy reached for her hand. "What is it, honey? Did we forget something?"

She shook her head. "No. It's just that I'm chilly. Will you reach in the overhead compartment and get the beach towel out of my carry-on bag?"

"Of course."

Katie snuggled down in her seat and closed her eyes. Teddy watched her for a while, wondering what was on her mind. He finally found a comfortable position, and they slept through the entire flight.

Once they hit the ground in California, the pace was hectic. On Monday afternoon and Tuesday morning, they got acclimated to the new routine. By Tuesday afternoon, the temperatures on the west coast soared into the eighties.

On Wednesday morning, Katie slipped out of bed and dressed in the dark, careful to not wake Teddy. She stopped by the restaurant off the lobby of the hotel, purchased a large coffee, and headed to the stables. Cappelletti and Sammy were already there, feeding the horses and grooming them for the day. As soon as they led Mr. Zee out of his stall, Katie knew something wasn't right. He seemed lethargic.

Sammy walked up to Katie and said, "We need to talk."

"What's up?"

"Not here. Let's go outside."

Katie motioned to Cappelletti that they would be out back. When she turned to look for Sammy, he'd already taken off. He was halfway out of the stable when she caught up with him.

"Sammy, wait for me, please. Why are you walking so fast?"

He stopped. "Let's walk around back." When they got outside, Sammy looked around the corner of the stable and watched as Cappelletti and Mr. Zee walked down to the track.

"Cappelletti is working Mr. Zee too hard."

Katie wasn't sure what he meant. She thought Sammy and Cappelletti made a good team, but clearly something had changed between them.

"Sammy, we hired a professional trainer to get the horses conditioned to race. So I can't just go out there and question his tactics. This is our first big race." She looked around the area as if she thought Cappelletti might overhear their conversation. "But in many ways it's the most important race of the season because it often determines which of the horses gets invited to the Derby."

Sammy looked at the ground as he shuffled his feet. "It's not right to work a horse this hard. He had him on the track early the past two mornings and kept him out there two hours after I'd finished with Redemption." He let out a deep breath. "I'm telling you, Katie, this heat is too much for Mr. Zee, and he's pushing him too hard."

"Why isn't Cappelletti spending more time with Redemption? He should give them equal time."

Sammy shrugged. He was shutting down. He'd said what he'd meant to say, and he would not say anymore.

Katie touched his arm. "Okay. I'll talk to him. But keep in mind, this is a very delicate matter, and we can't afford to alienate Cappelletti. We've got too much invested in these horses."

When Katie walked onto the track, Cappelletti was already working with Mr. Zee.

Katie said. "Sammy's concerned that you're working Mr. Zee too hard. He may be right. It looks like he's having difficulty handling the heat."

"I know what I'm doing."

Katie smiled and rubbed Mr. Zee's withers. "I know you do, but it could take him a couple of days to recover from getting overheated."

"I appreciate your opinion," Cappelletti said. "I do."

Katie looked out over the track. "One other thing, I've noticed you've not been spending as much time with Redemption this week."

Cappelletti smiled. "Sammy's been handling Redemption, and he's doing a good job. Mr. Zee requires a different type of workout because of the stem cell therapy."

Katie looked confused.

"I can understand why Sammy thinks I'm overworking Mr. Zee, but I'm not pushing him that hard during our sessions. I'm just allowing him extra time to train."

"Well, that makes sense. We're both worried that he won't be able to stand up to the heat on the day of the race. The temperatures are supposed to be in the mid-eighties."

Cappelletti ran a hand down Mr. Zee's back. "Allowing him extra time each day is helping him to acclimate to the heat." He paused. "Why don't we walk him around the track for a few minutes? If he doesn't work through his fatigue, then we'll take him back to the stables. He'll have this afternoon, tomorrow, and Friday to rest before the race."

Katie nodded. "Okay. That sounds like an excellent plan." But, first, she'd get Teddy to text Dr. Scott and ask him what they should do. It could be the stem cell therapy had affected his ability to sweat.

The long days were hectic working with the horses, but their evenings were more leisurely spent, relaxing and dining at one of the many restaurants overlooking the Pacific Ocean.

While Katie was dressing for dinner on Wednesday evening, Teddy's phone rang. It was Cappelletti. Teddy laid the phone on the dresser.

"Excuse me, Teddy," Cappelletti said. "I've got you on speaker so both Sammy and I can hear you. We're down at the stables and thought you should know Mr. Zee has refused his oats for the second time today. Katie asked us to keep you in the loop."

"Thanks for letting me know, guys. I'm waiting to hear from Dr. Scott. We're not sure if any of the medications he took while going through therapy would affect his performance in warmer weather. So when you leave the stables tonight, text me an update, and I'll let you know what I found out from Scott."

Cappelletti said, "When we get back from eating, we'll come down and check on Mr. Zee and send you a text."

On Thursday morning, when the sun peeked through the drapes, Teddy lay in bed and decided it would be a good day for sightseeing and shopping. Katie had been at the stables early each morning and had worked late into the afternoon, and she deserved a break. He flipped over to the weather channel. It projected temperatures to reach the mid-70s. As he quietly got out of bed, he looked out the window and noticed the morning sky was perfectly blue and absent of any cloud coverage.

As he finished dressing, there was a knock on the door. Teddy quietly opened it and helped the steward roll the breakfast table into the suite.

Katie sat up in bed and glanced at the beautiful tabletop. "Are you trying to spoil me, Teddy Williams?"

"Not at all. I just thought we'd start the day off with breakfast in the room."

She lifted the lid from the platter of French toast. "Yummy. Let me get a quick shower, and I'll be right back." Katie inhaled a deep breath on the way to the bathroom. "The cinnamon and nutmeg smell wonderful."

She turned at the bathroom door. "You look nice. Why are you dressed in khakis and polo? Aren't you going down to the stables this morning?"

Teddy poured a glass of ice water. "We're going to spend the day touring the city."

"Remember, Mr. Zee hasn't been eating. I need to check on him before I head off to the city."

"But Scott confirmed he might be slower to adjust to the warmer temperatures. Besides, Cappelletti was able to get him to eat a handful of oats late last night." He smiled. "Sweetheart, I know you're concerned about Sammy and Cappelletti. But they need to learn to work together and draw from each other's strengths."

After they finished breakfast, Katie dried her hair and dressed. She chose a white t-shirt, a pair of faded jeans, and a navy jacket. She put on a pair of boots, blew Teddy a kiss, and went out the door, promising to be back within forty-five minutes.

When she got down there, Cappelletti and Sammy were leaning on the fence watching Mr. Zee and Redemption. Mr. Zee seemed to have improved. Not one hundred percent—but improved.

When she got back to the room, she changed shoes, grabbed her pocketbook, and was ready to go.

Teddy looked at her and said, "You look beautiful."

She smiled and cut her eyes at him. "Well, for the record, you're the one who wants to spend the day in the city. I'd just as soon stay here and sleep all day."

"We'll sleep tomorrow. Today, we're going to spend the day sightseeing and shopping."

They rode through the town area in an authentic trolley while listening to a guided narration of the sights. The tour included the homes from the original Mexican settlements in Old Town San Diego State Historic Park.

Then, they were off to the San Diego Zoo.

"Mattie Grace would love seeing the animals here."

"I just had that same thought," Teddy said. "She'd be screaming at the sight of those panda bears."

****

After lunch, they spent the afternoon shopping in the 16-block section of downtown in the national historic district. They purchased a panda bear for Mattie Grace from the owner of a small boutique. Teddy found a jacket to wear on the dinner cruise in a men's shop two doors down.

When they walked out of the men's store, Katie pointed to the brick building across the street. "Oh, Teddy, let's go to this art gallery. The brochure says they have the finest selection of art in the entire city."

Teddy watched as she leisurely strolled through the gallery, examining the detail of each painting. Finally, he picked up a brochure to read. When he put it back in the display stand, Katie had moved on to a picture of a woman in a bright blue dress holding a young boy. He went up behind her and put his arms around her waist, and said, "That's a nice picture."

Katie quickly wiped a tear from her eyes. "Yes. This artist is world-renowned. She's known for her ability to depict Expressionism in her work."

Teddy chuckled. "What does that mean?"

Katie reached and brushed the side of his face with her hand. "It means she captures the essence of her subjects with absolute brilliance. Look at the clarity of those eyes. You can almost feel the love passing from the mother to her son and from him back to her. That's an example of true Expressionism."

They spent another hour in the gallery, and then he said, "We should probably leave soon. We'll need to find a trolley over to the port."

****

The late afternoon air was crisp as the ship departed the port. The sunlight sparkled across the water as the guests lined the railing to watch the vessel slowly move out to sea.

Teddy leaned on the rails as his hands extended over the water. Watching the skyline disappear into the distance was the perfect ending to their day. He missed Mattie Grace terribly, but time alone as a couple was what they'd needed.

Katie moved in close enough for their bodies to touch. "Babe, thank you for today. It's been nice just strolling along unhurriedly with you. It reminds me of that afternoon at Hilton Head Island before we married."

Teddy smiled.

She looked out over the water, her back against his chest. "I know I've been distant lately," Katie said. "It's just... I've got so much going on inside my head right now."

He slid his hands around her waist. "Go on."

"All these decisions we've made about bringing in Cappelletti, changing veterinarians, and leaving Mattie Grace behind with Colleen. I'm glad we made them. But I'm used to making choices on my own, and now it takes a quorum to make a simple decision. I made my own decisions back when I was working, but now it feels like I'm just one small part of one big machine. I feel that I've lost my identity as a person."

Teddy wasn't sure he'd heard her correctly. "Are you saying this has been bothering you since you quit work?"

"No... no. It's just something I've been feeling lately. I'm grateful we were able to buy Silver Circle and Redemption, and you know how much I love Mattie Grace."

Teddy listened carefully.

Katie smiled. "You also know how headstrong she is, and it makes me nervous when she starts challenging me. I love her creativity and high spirits, but sometimes her intense nature makes her difficult to parent." She continued to look out over the water. "And bringing in Cappelletti has added an extra dimension to our little enterprise, but I know he's going to make a winner out of Redemption and Silver Circle. If he and Sammy can work through their differences, they could make a good team." She lifted her glass to her lips. "Sometimes, I yearn for the days of locking myself in an office and working on clients' files. It was a much simpler time."

"I don't understand. You said you wanted to quit your job and stay home with Mattie Grace."

"I did, but..."

They moved inside for their dinner and continued their conversation over the candlelit table. As the ship cruised along at a slow speed, dinner music played in the background. They saw famous landmarks, such as the Coronado Bridge, the Cabrillo National Monument, and the infamous California sea lions, while enjoying a 3-course plated meal.

Teddy could tell Katie was struggling to tell him something more. The candlelight flickered, and her watery eyes danced from the light as she searched for words. This was as intimate a conversation as they'd had in a long time.

He reached for her hand and touched her fingers ever so lightly, hoping the intimacy would encourage further conversation. "Talk to me, sweetie. Please tell me what's *really* bothering you."

"I just feel inadequate."

"In...inadequate? Honey, what do you mean?"

She ran a finger over the rim of her glass. "When I was working, people depended on me. My clients depended on me. When I quit work, my opinion and advice were no longer needed." She looked up at Teddy, her eyes filled with tears.

Teddy wasn't sure where she was going with this conversation. He'd made it as easy as possible for her to leave the CPA firm. His mom had come over and stayed with Mattie Grace for two weeks while Katie went to work to interview a replacement and clear her office of personal items.

Then one day, without any warning, she mentioned that she'd always dreamed of training racehorses. So Teddy hired a contractor and began making improvements to the farm so she could train in a state-of-the-art facility.

"I'm sorry, Teddy," Katie said. "You planned this beautiful day, and here I sit moaning about my wonderful life."

"It's fine, Katie. I just don't understand what it will take to make you happy. We have a great life together."

Katie nodded.

Teddy's frustration showed in his tone. "Mattie Grace, Sammy, and I depend on you every day. Even Cappelletti and the other farmhands defer to you. You're the glue that keeps our little world together. What more do you want?"

She removed the tissue from her pocketbook. "I'm fine, honey. Really. I'm fine."

Teddy finished the last of his key lime pie and folded his napkin. "Looks like the port is up ahead. Would you like to go out onto the deck and watch the lights?"

Katie smiled, "That sounds lovely." She was quiet as they left the restaurant, and although she let Teddy hold her hand while they watched the distant lights from the ship's deck, it seemed she was a thousand miles away.

They didn't talk much on the way back to the hotel, and she remained quiet even as they prepared for bed.

When Teddy awakened the following morning, he replayed his conversation with Katie at dinner. He'd never considered Katie might have missed her career. Instead, she'd worked up until the day before Mattie Grace was born, trying to get her files organized for the part-time staffer who would handle her cases during the maternity leave.

Once she got home from the hospital, the calls from the office became more frequent. Finally, toward the end of her leave, Teddy had come home one day for lunch and found his wife in tears. "I can't go back to work," she sobbed. "I can't leave our baby!"

He stared at the ceiling. Everything about the previous day had been perfect up until that moment at the end of their dessert. There had been several times in the past few weeks that she'd start a conversation and then change her mind. He thought the problem somehow involved Mattie Grace as they were butting heads lately. Their daughter was strong-willed—that was for sure.

Teddy slipped out of bed and looked out the window. There was a rhythm to the ocean waves as they rolled onto the nearby beach. He reached for his phone, opened the French doors, and stepped outside. The breeze from the ocean was cool, but the warmth from the sun as it loomed across the water provided enough heat to stay on the porch a while longer.

When he heard the gentle knock on the door, he quietly let the steward enter their suite and set up the simple breakfast.

"Is there anything more you require, Mr. Williams?"

"No, thank you. This is perfect. Please ask the maid service to postpone our cleaning until mid-afternoon."

A few minutes later, Katie stretched her arms and yawned as she opened the drapes. Then she stepped outside and saw the beautiful table of food. The breakfast quiche had just the right amount of browned cheese on top, and the melons looked vivid and fresh. Teddy poured her a cup of coffee and held her chair while she sat down. Katie looked out across the water as she hugged the cup in her hands. "The first cup of the morning… it's the absolute best part of the day."

As she bit into the quiche, she said, "This is delicious." She wiped her mouth with her napkin. "I dreamed about the little boy in the picture at the art exhibit we saw yesterday." She cut her eyes at Teddy. "I woke up feeling relaxed, as if I'd lifted a burden."

Teddy said, "That was a beautiful piece of art."

When they finished breakfast, Katie went into the bathroom and showered while Teddy placed the tray of dirty dishes outside the door of their suite.

As Katie combed through her hair, Teddy came into the bathroom carrying two flutes of mimosas. He handed a glass to Katie.

"Thank you. I didn't see this earlier."

"I saved it for now." He took a swallow of his drink and stepped into the shower.

When he turned off the water, Katie hummed a cheery tune while rubbing lotion onto her body.

Teddy wrapped the oversized towel around his waist, "You sure are chipper this morning."

"I know. Sometimes we just need to clear the air. Thanks for letting me vent last night."

"No problem. Do you feel better now?"

Katie nodded and smiled as she brushed his face with her hand.

Teddy pointed to the counter, "Grab your mimosa and follow me."

Katie giggled and reached for her glass. "Teddy, I need to get to the stables this morning."

"Why don't you let Sammy and Cappelletti handle it today. They need to get this worked out before the race, and they'll never work out their differences if you keep interfering." He placed his arm around her waist and pulled her close. "I promised you yesterday that we'd rest today," he whispered. "I've placed the *Do Not Disturb* sign on the door." He took her hand and led her into the bedroom.

****

The week rushed by, and before they had time to get acclimated to the Pacific Coast time zone, it was the afternoon before the race. They were standing with the other owners and trainers, awaiting the assignment of their jockey. Unfortunately, Katie had bitten her fingernails to the quick.

"This is the reason Cappelletti wants us to hire our own guys to train with Redemption and Silver Circle," Katie said. "Carrying a person with the appropriate weight during practice will make a big difference come race day. Our boys aren't used to carrying a 115-pound person in this heat."

"Well, I forwarded the list of names Cappelletti emailed to me this morning. You might want to look it over and start your own investigation while we're here. I recognized a few of the names on the list."

"Thanks," Katie said. "I'll do that." She knew she was more uptight about a jockey being assigned to Redemption than she cared to admit.

Teddy's hand slid through his blond hair, leaving only one tiny strand of hair on his forehead. She smiled. Of course, his concerns were justified about a jockey for Mr. Zee because of the black colt's leg injury.

Perhaps it was the exposure to the California sunshine and the added bronze sheen to his face. Or maybe it was the confidence he'd shown in Sammy and Cappelletti's ability to find a way to work together. Yet, for the first time in several months, Katie felt pure joy when she looked at her husband.

****

The morning of the race, Teddy and Katie were up early. They read the morning paper and enjoyed their coffee on the balcony before Katie went to the track.

After Teddy showered and made a few calls, he ate breakfast in the restaurant and then meandered down to the stable. He found Katie leaning against the fence next to the track.

"Here you are," Teddy said as he approached the fence. "I brought you some coffee."

"Thanks."

The area between her eyes bunched into a 'V' as she watched a grayish-white colt walking around the track with his manager.

"What's wrong?"

"Nothing. I'm just watching that big fellow over there." She moved further down the fence to get a better look. "He's Gray Ghost."

"They say he's fast," Teddy said as he followed her. "Listen, I have an idea."

"What's that?"

"We've enjoyed being at the beach this week."

Katie turned back to acknowledge his remark. "Yes, we have. I've felt more relaxed this week than I've been in months."

"I was thinking," Teddy said. "While Mattie Grace is out of school for Christmas break, we might take a quick trip to St. Simons the day after Christmas. What do you think?"

"She'll love it," Katie said as she continued to watch the horse. "But let's make it a surprise."

"Good idea." He leaned over and whispered in her ear. "Let's not worry about Gray Ghost. This is our last day in San Diego. I want us to enjoy the day to the fullest."

Beige stucco architectural buildings with red tile roofs surrounded the Del Mar Racetrack, a nod to the Spanish mission settlements which originally occupied the land. The placement and design of the buildings around the facility enhanced the racing experience. The elaborate spectators' stands stood on the opposite side of the track.

Teddy and Katie met with Cappelletti, Sammy, and their crew three hours before the two o'clock race.

Cappelletti said, "Mr. Zee ate well last night and finished his breakfast this morning. He's taken plenty of water and seems to have fully recovered. In fact, during our walk this morning he gave it all he had, so much so, I had to pull in the reins to keep him from exerting himself." He chuckled. "Redemption, now he's a different story. He walked around the track all week like he owned the place—he and Gray Ghost. One of those three will win the race today."

Katie smiled. "Well, I hope it's not Gray Ghost, but I'm delighted to hear the confidence in your voice."

The horses and their jockeys lined up and walked through the Del Mar Track ceremonial archway an hour before the race, heading to the starting gate. As the jockeys found their place in line, Katie went up to Redemption and spoke to him in a whisper.

She looked up at the jockey, the intelligence in the jockey's eyes confirmed she need not worry about his ability to handle Redemption. "Do you remember what we told you yesterday morning?"

"Yes, ma'am."

Katie smiled. "Just let him know it's his race. He'll start slower than the other horses, but when he gets comfortable with the track, he'll show you what he's got."

"He'll do fine."

"Good luck," Katie said as she walked a few feet to where Teddy was also giving the jockey instructions about how to handle Mr. Zee.

"Remember, Mr. Zee will fly out of the gate, but as soon as he sees Redemption moving to the front, he'll probably back off."

"Sir, this horse is a competitor. What if he doesn't back off?"

Teddy smiled as he patted Mr. Zee. "After all he's been through, let's just let him run the race."

"Let's go, boy. Let's show him what you're made of."

When the starting bell sounded, the gate doors swung open, and the horses rushed onto the track. Teddy's heart pounded in his chest as

Mr. Zee powered around the track. As usual, Mr. Zee jumped to the lead to set the pace, while Redemption was third from last as they rounded the first turn. The rain from the previous night left the track muddy, but Mr. Zee proved to be as sure-footed in the muck as he was on a dry dirt track.

As he rounded the last turn, Redemption appeared at his right. Mr. Zee looked Redemption in the eye and continued by his side.

Usually, he would back off and let Redemption and Silver Circle take the lead. But since Silver wasn't in the race, Mr. Zee seemed confused about his role.

That's it, boy. You stay right there. You and Redemption can race to the finish line together.

Teddy winced as Gray Ghost came around to the right side of Mr. Zee and finally passed him. Redemption moved to the inside. Mr. Zee followed close behind Gray Ghost and Redemption.

He looked over at Katie. She bit her fisted hand.

The horses ran neck and neck, then Gray Ghost dropped back, failing to keep the pace. Two other horses came from behind, and they, too, struggled to take the lead.

He's going to do it. He's passing Redemption!

At the last moment, Mr. Zee moved into the front-runner position.

He screamed. "Go, boy! Go! Go! Go!"

Teddy jumped in the air as Mr. Zee won the race by a nose.

Chapter Twenty-Three

K atie turned to Teddy and flung her arms around his neck. "We did it, Teddy! We won! Our boys won!" Tears streamed down her face, and she held Teddy's face next to her lips.

He gently pulled away from her embrace. "I'm not exactly sure of the quickest route to the Winner's Circle. But get your stuff, and I'll race you down there!"

After a late night of celebration, Katie wanted to sleep late. However, a light knock at their door awakened her. She heard the water from the shower and quickly slipped on a pair of sweatpants and a sweatshirt and ambled over to the door.

"Good morning, Mrs. Williams," the hotel manager was on the other side of the door, holding four copies of the morning papers as a steward stood next to him with their breakfast. "I hope you don't mind, but I wanted to deliver these papers to you and Mr. Williams personally. Also, we took the liberty to prepare room service for you guys to enjoy as you prepare to leave this morning."

After the hotel manager left, Katie unfolded the paper and immediately went into the bathroom just as Teddy stepped out of the shower. Holding the front page so he could see the large, bold print, she said, "Look, Teddy! We made the first of the local newspaper:

The Hawkins farm from Abington, Georgia, entered a new era in Thoroughbred racing receiving national attention for their first and second place wins at The Breeders' Cup Juvenile at Del Mar.

The phone rang, and she handed the paper to Teddy as she went back into the bedroom. The hours leading up to their departure from Del Mar were a litany of phone calls offering congratulatory remarks, poses for pictures with their horses, and interviews with reporters.

Their arrival at the airport was an unexpected experience. A crowd of photographers from the area's news outlets had gathered at the airport entrance. The cameras flashed as they snapped pictures of Katie and Teddy getting out of the limo.

"Mr. Zee! Mr. Zee!" The onlookers chanted as they made their way through the airport.

Another group of news reporters waited at the concourse as they approached their terminal.

On the flight home to Atlanta, the crew members stopped and congratulated them on their Del Mar wins. Then, as they departed the plane, the pilot came from the cockpit and chatted with them about the race.

"You guys, be careful as you depart. My co-pilot just heard that a hundred or more reporters are waiting to speak with you inside the terminal. They've come from all up the eastern seaboard to talk to the owners of Mr. Zee and Redemption, and I'm not surprised. I heard that your horses are favorites to dominate the Triple Crown this year."

"We've thought our other two horses might have a chance at winning the Triple Crown, but this win for Mr. Zee came out of nowhere. He injured his leg earlier in the year, and the medical community told us there was nothing more they could do. My husband found a veterinarian with stem cell research experience, and now he's the winner of the Breeders' Cup Juvenile."

"That's a great story," the pilot said. "My eight-year-old son watched all week as the news reporters talked about the horses leading up to the race on Saturday. There was something about Redemption that stole his heart. Every night at dinner, he'd tell us another interesting tidbit about the beautiful chestnut horse from Abington, Georgia. Finally, Terri, my wife, asked if we could place a small bet on the horse." The pilot chuckled. "She just wanted him to enjoy the full experience. So, early Saturday morning, I went online and placed a bet for our boy, and he won some money! He was thrilled, but now he wants to go to The Kentucky Derby."

"He sounds like an extraordinary young man," Katie said. "Please jot down your son's name and address. When we get home, we'll send him a picture of Redemption to put in his room."

The pilot reached for a pen and business card and scribbled down his son's name and their mailing address. He handed the paper to Katie and said, "Ma'am, this will make my son one happy little boy!"

When they entered the terminal, reporters surrounded them and yelled questions about the race. "Mr. Williams, what do you think about Mr. Zee? Is he a contender for the Triple Crown this year?"

The media attention was more than either of them would have expected. Katie paused and whispered in his ear. "We shouldn't waste this free press time. Perhaps you should respond to the reporter."

Teddy turned and walked back over to the reporter. "Sir, that's a good question. Mr. Zee is a fine horse, and he's got championship blood running through his veins. I won't try to predict his future—but I will say this: Mr. Zee never ceases to amaze me."

Teddy talked with ease to the reporters. As expected, he was an instant success. As they walked off, Katie hugged Teddy's arm. Her heart almost burst with pride as she whispered, "Well done, my love."

****

Teddy noticed Katie had slipped into her quiet mode as they left the Atlanta airport and pulled onto the interstate, heading north toward home.

When they came upon the exit to Abington, Teddy reached across the seat and squeezed her hand.. "Katie, dear, we're on the last leg of the trip. I can't wait to see Mattie Grace and sleep in our own bed tonight."

Katie opened her eyes. A slow smile formed on her lips. "I'm so tired. I just want to climb into bed with Mattie Grace between us and sleep for a week."

"Was Colleen bringing Mattie Grace home?" Teddy asked. "Or do we need to go by and pick her up?"

"I texted Colleen at the airport to let her know we had landed. They'll be at the house when we get home."

As they topped the hill, vehicles lined both sides of the road for a half a mile, going down to the farm's entrance.

Teddy looked at Katie, "What the hell?"

Katie's hand flew up and covered her mouth. "Oh, my gosh, I hope nothing's happened. I haven't seen this many cars out here since Papa died."

Teddy tapped on the brakes as he looked from one side of the road to the other.

When he turned into the farm, he stopped the car at the entrance before continuing up the blacktop drive. He counted another fifteen cars lining both sides of their driveway, going up to the house. Shaking his head as he stretched his neck to see over the embankment. "This looks like one of Mom's celebrations to me."

"You think Claire did this?"

Teddy nodded as his smile widened. "Yes, ma'am, this has Mom's name written all over it!"

Katie strained to see the setup in the backyard. "I wish she'd waited until next weekend to throw this party, or at least discussed it with us first."

"Oh, it'll be fine," he said.

When they pulled up to the house, people were hanging out on the back porch. Someone had set up a big white tent in the backyard.

Although it was only five o'clock, the white lights strung around the outside of the porch and throughout the tent sparkled as they drove into the garage.

Billowing smoke swelled from the other side of the garage. Teddy said, "Look at that smoke. I bet Frank and his buddies spent the day cooking a pig in the ground pit."

"I don't know about this, Teddy. She must've invited the entire town of Abington to this party!"

Teddy pulled the car into the garage and turned off the engine. "Listen, Katie. You've got to get it together before we get out of the car. I admit, it looks like a lot of people, but honey, this is a big deal for a small town like Abington. This farm, *your farm*, has made national news. Your picture was on the cover of every major newspaper in the world this morning."

"Oh, don't be ridiculous."

"You're playing on the big stage now. Just like at the Atlanta airport, when you told me we shouldn't waste press time. And you were right!"

"Well, I just wanted to come home and go to bed," she said, "but instead, it looks like everyone in three counties is in our backyard."

"That's true, but Mom and Frank have gone to a lot of trouble to include the people of Abington in this grand celebration."

Katie rolled her eyes

Teddy gave her a look he reserved for Mattie Grace when he meant business. "You know, Mom, Katie. She plans everything down to the letter."

"Well, this is over the top."

"Yes, but you have to love her heart. She's doing this for you!"

The men, who were filling aluminum pans with chopped meat, took turns taking the pans into the tent and placing them on the tables of the buffet line.

"Look out there!" The energy from the music was electrifying. "It looks like Frank called one of those Kentucky bluegrass bands to play for the evening."

They'd roped off a clearing in the pasture to the left of the stage. Firewood and kindling waited to be ignited. Hay bales topped with pieces of blue and white gingham fabric circled a fire pit.

Suddenly, the music stopped. Someone announced that the Breeders' Cup winners had just entered the property. Then a band member asked everyone to proceed to the white tent for announcements about dinner.

Everyone burst into applause as Teddy and Katie entered the vast tent. Teddy stepped forward, grabbed the microphone, and waited for the crowd to stop cheering. "As exciting as it is for the Hawkins farm to gain global recognition for winning the 2021 Breeders' Cup, nothing compares to coming back to Abington for this hometown welcome."

He spotted Cappelletti in the crowd. "Get up here, Cappelletti! We're celebrating you tonight, my man." He looked around the tent. "If we'd known you were planning this celebration, Katie and I would've been on the red-eye to Atlanta with Cappelletti."

The lanky Italian moved effortlessly through the crowd with a confidence few men could pull off without an air of arrogance. As soon as he got to the front, Teddy handed him the microphone as the crowd roared with applause.

After he thanked Teddy and Katie, he said, "It was a group effort getting Mr. Zee to this place. Because of his injury, no one expected him to perform at this level." He paused as his eyes rolled. "Well, no one except Mr. Zee." Raising his hands for emphasis, "He knew he was born for greatness."

The crowd exploded with applause.

Cappelletti shook Teddy's hand and gave him back the microphone.

Teddy winked at Katie and then mentioned her new elevated status as a major championship winner. "Like many women of our generation, my wife is now world-famous. Before we left California, she received a congratulatory call from the Queen of England. As you know, The Monarch is 94 years young, and she's an avid horse lover. She told Katie that she still rides every chance she gets. I'm sure my wife will soon receive an invitation from Buckingham Palace for 'Tea with the Queen'!"

Everyone broke into laughter. Then Teddy turned to Katie and said, "My dear, if there was ever any doubt about the impact you make on this world... our world, I hope now you understand."

Chapter Twenty-Four

A *ttendance by invitation only,* the engraved ivory paper stated. Katie smiled, mentally searching her wardrobe for the perfect outfit. This was the beauty supply company's annual event to introduce their new product line to the local salons. The women of Abington considered it one of the social events leading up to the holiday season. The invitation stated 3:30. Still, everyone would arrive well in advance to get a good seat or a place to stand to watch the representative styling of the models' hair while demonstrating the new products.

At exactly 3:00, Katie pulled into the parking lot at the salon. Laura Whelchel's champagne-colored Cadillac Escalade had stopped at the front door. Katie waved at Claire and Daisy as they got out of the car. Then she pulled around to the back of the salon to park. As she turned off the ignition, she noticed Colleen's vehicle a few spaces away.

That was a good sign.

Katie looked around the parking lot—but saw no sign of her friend. Colleen must already be inside. Katie was glad she'd shown up; she could never be sure Colleen would be up to a social event.

Katie walked into the salon. The first person she saw was Joan adding cookies to a large silver platter.

"Hi Katie," Joan said while refilling the punch container on the rectangular table in the reception area. "Glad you could make it."

Katie peeped inside the next room, but she didn't see Colleen anywhere.

The room had been the living room in its day, complete with a brick fireplace which the contractor had painted a cream color to match the walls in the salon. A tall table stood in front of the fireplace with a display of products to introduce during the presentation.

"Hi Vicki," Katie said.

"Hi, Katie. Love that outfit."

"Thanks! Have you seen Colleen?"

Vicki scrunched her nose. "She's in the back... and she's upset." She made one more change to the countertop and smiled at her display. Then she turned back to Katie. "On the way over, she went downtown for coffee, and she saw someone who looked just like Drew."

"Oh, goodness." Katie hurried to the back room, hoping she could get to Colleen before Daisy saw her crying. It was Daisy's 70th birthday, and Claire and Laura were planning a small celebration after the presentation. The last thing Daisy needed was to see Colleen upset.

Katie went straight to the kitchen area.

Laura stooped in front of the refrigerator. She rearranged a few items and placed the Prosecco on the top shelf and checked the plastic wrap, which covered the charcuterie board. She wore a classic turquoise and cream-colored outfit by Chanel. The short, blonde, messy bob was the perfect hairstyle for Laura's petite frame.

Colleen, in stark contrast, was a wreck—sitting at the bar with her face in her hands.

Katie's gaze swept past Laura and locked on Colleen. "Honey, are you okay?"

Colleen looked up with red-rimmed eyes. "Oh, Katie. You're finally here. I was just telling Laura I could've sworn I saw Drew walking out of the Coffee Shop downtown. His hair was much longer than he normally wore it, and he had a gray beard, but it looked just like him."

"Oh, honey. I'm so sorry."

Laura glanced at Katie. "I told Colleen that if Drew Byrd were anywhere around Abington, he would contact her."

Katie wiped a string of hair from her face. "I agree. He adored you!"

Colleen wiped her nose with a tissue and said, "I want to believe he would, but when he walked onto the sidewalk and looked up, our eyes met. He looked startled. Like I'd caught him doing something he shouldn't be doing. I've seen that same look on Drew's face so many times during our marriage."

Katie wished she could summon the words to help Colleen move past her grief, but all her mind would give her were platitudes. She gave her friend a sympathetic hug, then looked at her watch and said, "Colleen, aren't you supposed to model for the stylists today?"

Colleen clutched Laura's arm as she walked by and said, "Please don't tell Daisy about this. I don't want to upset her. Birthdays and holidays are especially hard for her."

"Okay, I won't mention it. But remember, half the ladies in Abington are already here." Laura handed Colleen a napkin. "Now, dry those tears before going out front."

Katie nodded to Colleen. "You know she's right. This event is a sort of '*who's who*' of Abington."

Colleen hesitated, nibbling at a thumbnail. "I don't know…"

"You'll be fine," Laura said, and gave Colleen a quick hug. "Now… I've got to run back to my car and get the birthday cake. Daisy doesn't know about the cake, so please don't say anything."

Colleen moved the stool back into place. She drew in a breath and let it out slowly. "Katie," she said, "there's one more thing I need to tell you."

"What's that?"

"Drew's pistol is missing."

As soon as Katie and Colleen came out of the break room, Jane grabbed Katie's hand and led her to the shampoo station.

"Girls, where have you been?" Jane handed them a black smock each. "You had me worried that you wouldn't get here in time."

"Okay. That's good." Jane said when both women had been shampooed, rinsed, and toweled. "You two go in there and introduce yourselves to Matt. He's the instructor for the class. Matt likes to meet each of the models before we get started."

Colleen rolled her eyes. "Do we have to meet him immediately? I'm a wreck, and besides, my hair's wet."

Jane smiled and hugged Colleen. "I know, but he needs to know a little more about the products you use at home every day. He's a nice man, Colleen. Who knows? You just might enjoy meeting him."

With a dismissive wave, Colleen looked at Katie and rolled her eyes.

As Colleen walked from the room, Jane whispered to Katie, "Matt's a sweetheart. I think they would make a great couple."

Katie opened her mouth and then hesitated. No. She wouldn't say a word. But maybe... just maybe, this was the opportunity Colleen needed to get on with her life.

Colleen was three steps into the next room before she realized Katie was still in conversation with Jane and Laura. Colleen faltered—she didn't want to meet the representative on her own—but she was already committed. Straightening her shoulders, she scanned the room. The man at the table in front of the mantle could only be Matt Kreuger. Medium build. Brown curly hair. He was the total opposite of Drew. His piercing blue eyes contrasted perfectly with the yellow Polo shirt and medium brown slacks. The only accessory was the black Apple watch on his left wrist.

He pointed to a bottle of the styling product as two older women asked questions. Then, thankfully, Katie turned the corner and walked in her direction.

"Looks like these ladies have Matt cornered," Colleen said. "Should we stand here and wait for them to finish?"

Matt looked over and smiled when he saw them waiting. He squeezed the older ladies' hands and thanked them for coming to the presentation, then sauntered over to Colleen and Katie.

"You finally made it! I was getting worried our models had stood us up today. My name is Matt Kreuger."

Katie extended her hand first as they introduced themselves.

Colleen had just wiped a single tear from her right eye when Matt looked at her. He shook her hand. He moved his left arm behind her, his arm barely brushing her back.

"Are you all right, Colleen?" Matt asked.

The whisper of her name caused an electric current to rush through her body.

Colleen took a step back. "Yes, I'm fine. Jane said you needed to know the hair products we use."

Matt laughed. "Jane said that... huh?" He turned toward the main room and smiled. "I can't believe she used that line on you ladies to get you over here. I just wanted to meet our models. The new products I'm introducing today are primarily for hair like yours. Natural, virgin hair that you can shampoo and go. I also have some new products for treated hair, but you obviously don't need that."

Matt's hand had settled on her back. How long had it been since someone other than her children and Andrew had hugged her?

He smelled manly. Was it Polo?

After a moment longer, she gently leaned forward to look at the products displayed on the table. Colleen read the label on the back of the bottle. "Abington is notorious for its high humidity levels. Does this *really* eliminate frizz?"

Matt reached for the bottle and sprayed her hair with the product, gently touching her scalp. "Yes, it does."

When the presentation was over, Claire circulated around the salon and asked everyone to hang around a few minutes for a toast to celebrate Daisy's birthday.

Claire and Laura then brought the food out from the back room, opened the bottles of Prosecco, and displayed everything on the table that Matt had used to demonstrate the new product line.

By the time Matt had finished with his orders and packed his vehicle, the party was in full swing. He joined in as the ladies sang happy birthday. Then he picked up a glass and waded through the salon until he found Colleen and Katie.

"This must be the occasion of the year," Matt said. "Whose birthday are we celebrating?"

"It's Daisy's 70th," Colleen said. "She didn't want a big party this year. So, her friends planned a birthday toast for today."

"Which one is Daisy?"

Colleen pointed to her mother-in-law.

"No way! She doesn't look a day over 60."

After a few minutes of small talk, he asked if they would like to join him at the local champagne bar for a drink.

Colleen shook her head, but before she could speak, Katie piped in, "We'd love to. But just one drink."

On the way downtown, Katie called Teddy and asked if he could pick up Mattie Grace while she went for a drink with Colleen and the hair rep.

Even though Teddy had considered Drew his best friend most of his life, Katie knew he wasn't likely to be the person to initiate a date for Colleen. He probably wouldn't want his wife to be that person, either.

Katie couldn't help herself. She was the hopeless matchmaker!

It was time, too. Colleen had waited long enough for a man who was never coming home.

Matt was reading the menu outside The Champagne Bar. Colleen craned her neck to look at him as Katie searched for a place to park. He didn't remind her of anyone she'd ever seen before. Handsome. Well-dressed. Nice build. He'd taken good care of himself.

Looking at her wedding rings, a tinge of guilt engulfed her. "I don't know if I can do this, Katie."

Katie pulled into the parking place and cut off the engine. "Well, we're here now. It won't hurt to have a drink with him."

Colleen nodded, remembering what Laura had said earlier—that if Drew had been anywhere near Abington, he would contact her. Laura was right, of course. After all this time, if he hadn't called or come home, he either couldn't or didn't want to.

"Okay," Katie said. "Just give me a signal when you're ready to leave."

Colleen nodded and stepped out of the car, aware of Matt's focused attention. He smiled as he watched them cross the street. "Shall we go in, ladies?" He held the door open and motioned for Katie to enter first.

Colleen's pulse quickened as he fell into step beside her and walked her to their table.

As the server seated them and handed each a menu, Colleen twisted her engagement ring around her finger. She shouldn't have come...

Scanning the menu, Matt joked, "What brilliant mind created so many bubbly concoctions?"

Colleen laughed and finally relaxed.

He shook his head in mock disbelief. "Just how many assorted drinks could one make with a splash of champagne?"

By the time the server delivered their water, they had already discussed the number of high-end hair salons in the Abington area and moved on to the previous presidential election.

It was already 8:15. Katie excused herself. On the way to the restroom, she called Teddy to check on Mattie Grace.

He'd already given Mattie Grace a bath and was tucking her into bed. "You're just in time to tell her good night." He said and passed their daughter the phone.

"Mommy," Mattie Grace said. "Me and daddy know what we're getting you for Christmas this year."

"That's exciting, sweetheart. I'm sure it will be wonderful, and I can hardly wait to see it. Anyway, it's time for you to go to sleep. Daddy will give you a big hug from both of us. I love you."

Katie yawned when she returned to the table.

Matt said, "Katie, if you need to get home, I'll be happy to give Colleen a ride."

He touched Colleen's hand and said, "Are you okay with that?"

Colleen smiled, cheeks reddening. "I... yes, that would be fine."

As Katie left the table, she looked back over her shoulder, and mouthed to Colleen, "Call me!"

Chapter Twenty-Five

Colleen was on her way down the steps with the empty clothes basket when Angie yelled. "Mom, the phone's for you. It's a man!"

She stopped mid-stairs, closed her eyes, and sighed. *What is wrong with that child? Is there no filter in that brain of hers?*

Colleen frowned at her daughter when she walked into the kitchen. "Thank you, Angie." She placed her hand over the receiver. "There's no reason to tell me the gender of a caller. Okay?"

Angie shrugged. "Just thought you'd want to know."

"Thank you. Now, go upstairs and finish your homework while I take this call." Colleen waited for Angie to leave the kitchen, then stuck her head around the door frame to watch her youngest daughter go up the stairs.

She stepped back into the kitchen and said, "Hello."

"Hi Colleen. It's Matt Kreuger."

A fluttering feeling settled in the pit of her stomach. Although he'd asked for her phone number, the night he brought her home from The Champagne Bar, she hadn't expected him to call. Especially when she told him she had three children: a son in law school and two younger daughters.

She finally answered, "Hi Matt. How are you?"

"I'm good. Listen, I know this is last minute, but I've got two tickets to the Georgia Tech-North Carolina game this Saturday. Would you like to go?"

A goofy smile spread across her face. "This Saturday?"

"That's right. I thought we might tailgate before the game. It's a three-thirty start time, we should be back at your house by nine o'clock."

Colleen glanced at the family calendar on the fridge. Angie had a soccer game at eight o'clock. But the afternoon was clear.

"Colleen. Are you there?"

"Sorry. Yes, I'm here. I was just thinking about the kids' schedule on Saturday. If I can get a sitter, then I should be able to go."

"Great! I'll pick you up around eleven o'clock."

She hung up the phone, thinking about who she could get to babysit. Rebecca would hang out with friends, but she needed to find someone to look after Angie. Perhaps Daisy would be available.

It felt strange, asking her mother-in-law to look after Angie so she could go out with another man. Especially in light of Daisy's reluctance to accept that Drew was really gone. But seven years was long enough to hope, wasn't it? For both of them?

Slowly, she dialed her in-laws' landline. They spent a few minutes talking about the children before Colleen sprang the question. "Daisy, could you look after Angie on Saturday. I've been asked to go to the Georgia Tech game in Atlanta, but I can't leave Angie at home all day by herself. Would you and Andrew keep her for me, please?"

Daisy didn't answer immediately.

Colleen knew what that meant.

She hadn't exactly said she had a date, but Daisy was an intelligent woman—she'd figured it out.

The silence stretched on. Colleen opened her mouth…

Then Daisy said, "Of course, sweetie. We'd love for Angie to stay with us while you go to the game."

****

Daisy hung up the phone and stared at the receiver. Her chin quivered as she wiped the tears from her eyes.

From the den, a television anchor blared the evening news. Andrew liked to watch it while he waited for dinner each night. He kept up with current events, which she supposed was a good thing for an attorney. Her own tastes ran to lighter fare, like cooking shows and vintage Hollywood movies. The world was ugly enough without seeking out more ugliness. Why couldn't things be simple again? All she wanted was her family safe and well, all gathered around the table for a home-cooked meal.

"Who was on the phone?" Andrew asked.

Daisy sat down on the sofa and choked back tears. She'd known it was just a matter of time. Colleen was a pretty girl, and Drew had been gone a long time. Long enough for everyone to presume he wouldn't be back.

"What's wrong?" Andrew asked. "Are you crying?"

She sniffled again. "I guess I should be happy for Colleen. But to tell you the truth—it really stings to think she might date again."

Andrew leaned forward in his chair. "Honey, what are you talking about?"

"That was Colleen on the phone. She asked if Angie could stay with us on Saturday while she goes to the Georgia Tech football game in Atlanta."

Andrew reached for the remote control and cut off the television. He got up from his chair and moved to the sofa. "She's still a young woman, honey." He reached for Daisy's hand. "It's time she moves on with her life"

"I know it's time." Daisy's voice broke. "But Drew's my boy, and he loved her so much."

He reached for his handkerchief and handed it to his wife. "I know. He's my boy, too. But it couldn't be easy running a household without him. Colleen deserves someone in her life right now. Someone to enjoy life with, and also someone to help her raise those girls."

"You're right, Andrew. I know you're right." And she did know, but that didn't make it any easier.

Chapter Twenty-Six

Before daybreak on Saturday morning, Drew slowly steered his truck around the barn to the access road next to the Corps of Engineers property and drove into town for the first time since returning to Abington.

Drew almost always rode in a cart for the eighteen holes of golf he'd played twice a week in his previous life, and he'd seldom walked down the street with his wife for exercise—but being back in Abington, living at the farm, he'd learned to appreciate a long walk. He usually walked five to six miles every day.

But not today. Today, he'd decided to drive into town.

He took his time on the drive to his father's office, immersing himself in the memories of the quaint little town he still thought of as home.

He'd enjoyed a charmed life.

He slowed as the sun peeked between the tree limbs, dappling the road and dotting the canopy with patches of gold. The beauty of it sent a pang of loss through his chest. He'd never intended to leave Abington.

Why would anyone want to leave this magical place?

Approaching downtown, Drew made a last-minute decision and drove by the stadium, where he'd played football in high school. He parked on the hill, which gave him a bird's-eye view of the field. The sun coming up behind the fieldhouse shone on what looked like a new scoreboard. Otherwise, the stadium looked the same as the first time he stepped foot on the field as a prospective player the summer before starting high school.

It was at this end of the field where he saw Colleen for the first time. She was a cheerleader. They were on the sidelines practicing their routine. Colleen had completed a triple somersault—he'd never seen anyone move with such grace. He remembered that moment as if it were yesterday.

The sunlight reflected off the turf, creating light and dark stripes on the field of freshly mowed grass bent in slightly different directions. Drew closed his eyes and took in a deep breath. A light scent of grass rose from the morning dew, reminding him of the odd composite of grass clippings, gasoline, and sweat from the players' uniforms and pads. In a town that had seen so much change, this was the one spot that remained the same, and it felt good. It felt good to be back.

He gave himself a few minutes to relive his glory days, then turned on the ignition and slowly drove toward his father's office.

When he got to the firm's parking lot, as expected, it was empty. Drew drove around the deserted town and went to the street adjacent to the firm's back entrance. Finally, he pulled behind the florist building, deciding their lot would be out of view. He locked the truck and walked through the woods to the back of the law office.

He stopped and looked around. Drew felt like he was home.

Carefully, he removed the key from his pocket and smiled when it actually worked. Then he gently opened the door and immediately punched the alarm code on the panel.

Again, he was surprised. The code still worked.

"Whew," he whispered. "I'm in."

The comforting smell of coffee still lingered in the air. Drew went straight to the break room in search of food. Unfortunately, someone had failed to empty the pot before leaving the previous day. On his way to the refrigerator, he stopped and poured the remaining coffee down the drain.

On Friday mornings, he'd always stopped by the local donut shop and picked up a couple of dozen donuts for the staff. The memory seemed like eons ago. Immediately, he turned and scanned the countertop. No donuts.

Nothing.

When he looked inside the refrigerator, he found the usual variety of soft drinks available for the staff and a case of bottled water filling one shelf. He guzzled an entire bottle of water and then stuffed another bottle in his backpack. Next, he grabbed a Diet Coke and scrounged around for something to eat. They'd stored a few sandwiches from a local deli inside the plastic serving tray provided by the restaurant. He squatted in front of the refrigerator, removed the plastic lid, and chose a sandwich.

He took a big bite and continued his walk through the building. He stopped in front of the partner pictures and traced Henry Whelchel's name plate with his finger. He still missed the old man. His dad loved to tell how he and his college roommate, Henry Whelchel, had formed a partnership when they finished law school in 1976. He'd died of pancreatic cancer, but he and Drew had gotten close working on the Industrial Park project together. He'd always been grateful for the way Henry had stood by him when he was struggling financially. If Henry were here now, Drew knew what he would say: *Son, you've got to make this right.*

When he got to his own office, he noticed the room was precisely as he had left it. His nameplate remained on the desk, but someone had removed the files he'd been working on. Otherwise, everything had stayed the same. Pictures of his family were still displayed on the bookshelf. His heart ached as he touched the portrait of his beautiful wife. But Drew grinned as he noticed Angie's goofy smile, contrasting Rebecca's and Jacob's serious expressions. Then he stared at his diplomas still hanging on the wall. Even his extra set of keys to his house and car, which he kept at the back of his middle drawer, remained unmoved.

His dad hadn't changed a thing. It was as if he'd never left Abington.

A feeling of nostalgia engulfed Drew as he walked down the hall. There was so much history in the building, particularly in his father's office. He hesitated before approaching his father's door. He took a deep breath and then slowly turned the knob. The smell of books, antique wood, and fine leather furnishings washed over him. There was another smell. Was it Old Spice? Surprised for a minute, he couldn't even remember the name of the aftershave his father had always used.

It *was* Old Spice. The buoy-shaped, cream-colored bottle with red lettering. His dad had always stored his aftershave next to the straight-edged razor in the medicine cabinet above their bathroom sink.

Drew pulled out his father's chair and plopped down. The smells of leather and Old Spice were stronger here, and the familiar fragrances evoked vivid memories. Sipping his cola and nibbling at the sandwich, he could almost hear his father's gentle, southern voice telling how he'd originally wanted to rent a smaller, more affordable office space on the outskirts of town. Henry's father-in-law had encouraged them to buy this house inside the city limits instead.

The advice had paid off. After six months in the growing business community, they had attracted a solid base of clients. Henry had landed a high-profile criminal case that attracted huge fees and brought notoriety to the firm. The property increased in value each year, so by the time Drew was in grade school, it had already paid for itself ten times over. Drew had heard the story numerous times throughout his lifetime. It was his father's favorite rags-to-riches tale.

He'd been sitting at his father's desk longer than he'd intended. Drew finished the last of the sandwich and crammed the wrapping in his pocket. Then he walked around the desk and picked up the soda can, before heading into the library.

A sudden noise from behind the building startled him. He peeped through the blinds and watched a man empty two bins of garbage into the back of the large pink truck.

The distraction unnerved Drew. Quickly, he retreated into the library and closed the door. The wood-paneled room was dark, but he refused to turn on the overhead fluorescent lights. It took a while to find what he was looking for in the dim room. He felt a pang of guilt for taking books from his father's library, but, when his father made him a partner he had told him that the firm would be his one day. So, in a way, wasn't it like stealing from himself? Of course, his dad might have changed his mind. But in the Byrd family, what belonged to one belonged to all. He scanned the shelves and finally found a few books on international law, placed them inside his backpack, and quietly left the room.

Something made him tiptoe through the hallway. When he got to his father's office, the door was open.

Drew stopped.

He could've sworn he'd closed the door behind him earlier. He held his breath as he peered around the door. His father sat at his desk with the chair facing the window. His elbow rested on the wooden chair arm, while his hand supported his head as he stared at the empty parking lot.

How had he gotten in here without Drew hearing him?

He looked so vulnerable. So different from the last time he'd seen him. It was the day before he left Abington, and they'd played golf at the club. At the time, his dad was a strong, virile man. Mr. Byrd had scored a round of 78 that day.

His father had never taken a golf lesson and had never paid for Drew to take lessons, either, but unlike himself, his dad was a natural at the game. Drew had never beaten his dad in golf, regardless of how much time he spent playing with The Tour Group.

For a minute, he wished he could go in and put his arms around his father and ask about his golf game, but he had to take these books and get the hell out—now.

If he didn't come through for these guys, they would kill him. They'd also kill everyone he loved.

There would be time later to reconcile with Dad. He hoped.

When the heating system kicked on, Drew quickly tiptoed out the back door, cautious to not make any noises as he left the building. Immediately, he turned left and walked toward the woods, careful to stay out of his father's line of vision.

He ambled around the woods until he found a fallen log hidden from his father's office. Then, sweating and out of breath, he sank onto the log and buried his head in his hands. He'd been within a few scant feet of his father, and yet he'd walked out without saying a word.

He couldn't get the image out of his mind. Sitting alone in his office, Drew's father looked like a broken man. He had aged considerably since Drew had last seen him. His dark hair, then heavily peppered with gray, was now snow white.

... and it's all my fault.

Drew downed the last of his drink before smashing the can and burying it in the rich, dark soil beneath his feet.

I'm such a jerk!

Chapter Twenty-Seven

Etched in his mind was the sight of his aged father. The slumped shoulders and particularly the white hair, but as soon as he pulled out into traffic, he dismissed the thought when he noticed a black extended cab pulling out from across the street. Immediately, he knew something was amiss. He turned right onto Green Street, and when he passed the post office, he took a hard right onto Green Street Place.

Drew watched his rearview mirror. Finally, he turned left on Boulevard and circled back to Green Street. Whew! He'd lost them.

He took the longer route and entered the farm from the graveled road adjoining the Corps of Engineers. The trip to town had taken longer than he'd expected. Relieved, Drew pulled up to the back of the barn and parked. Until… he saw the extended black cab parked on the other side of the barn.

Nic got out of the driver's side and leaned against the vehicle. "Did you get those law books?"

"Yep—got 'em," he said, "it was a piece of cake."

"Good deal."

Drew looked inside the truck, "Who's that?" He pointed to the guy on the passenger's side—he had the same small mouth, wide eyes with bushy eyebrows and a prominent widow's peak as Nic.

"That's Matteo…"

The guy pointed to his watch when Nic looked his way.

Drew made eye contact and nodded to the guy. "Is he working with you now?"

"You study those law books," Nic jerked the door handle, "and let me handle my cousin."

Chapter Twenty-Eight

C olleen looked at the clock on the bedside table. It was three o'clock. She covered her head with the comforter and tried to go back to sleep, but thoughts of Drew continued to fill her mind. He was spontaneous and fun. She would send him to the store for broccoli and he'd come home with three different flavors of ice cream instead. Then they'd stand at the kitchen sink and giggle over spoonsful of Rocky Road. He was also quick to fix a broken faucet and always eager to toss a ball with the kids, but he didn't always take her concerns seriously, and of course, there was that distance between them once he hooked up with that... witch, Nancy Leigh Williams.

What would he think of her dating again? They'd begun dating as teenagers, and she couldn't imagine being with anyone else.

Restless, she sat up in bed and grabbed her phone. Matt was nothing like Drew. Both men were tall, but Drew was built like a linebacker. He'd played football in high school. Matt's body was hard and lean, and he looked like a runner. Drew's hair was dark blond, while Matt's was almost black. Drew was loud, too loud, actually. Matt was soft-spoken, more reserved.

She had a missed call.

Her heart raced as she listened to Matt's voicemail. First, he'd called to make sure she'd been able to find a babysitter. Then, he'd ended the message saying that he couldn't wait to see her.

He couldn't wait to see her.

Colleen replayed the message to hear those exact words again. She was wide awake. It was like she'd taken a hit of espresso. There was no way she could go back to sleep now.

****

Matt skillfully pulled in between two vehicles and created a parking space that Colleen would have imagined no one could negotiate.

He raised the back door and spread out a small tablecloth and then he set out the food.

Matt pointed to the cooler. "Look inside and see if there's anything in there you'd like to drink with your lunch."

"Oh, you brought Prosecco!"

"You like that?"

"Yes, I do. But I'll drink water with my lunch. What do you want?"

"I'll drink water, too."

The conversation between Colleen and Matt flowed easily as they enjoyed their lunch.

When they reached their seats in the lower section on the 45-yard line, Colleen punched Matt and said, "How did you get these great seats?"

"A company incentive for exceeding my third quarter sales projections."

He was confident and self-assured, and she found his self-reliance extremely attractive.

After the game ended and they were leaving the stadium, it suddenly dawned on Colleen that perhaps she didn't want to find someone just like Drew, after all.

Chapter Twenty-Nine

Following an intense search for suitable jockeys, and with Cappelletti's leadership, Teddy and Katie decided on three men from the list of names Cappelletti had provided for them to interview.

Ricky Bailey and Peter Prado arrived at the farm in the same cab. Bailey was the taller of the two, a slim man with reddish hair and a colorful, artistic tattoo covering his right arm. Prado went around to the trunk to retrieve his luggage. His diminutive height was more pronounced as he stood next to Bailey. Prado was a swarthy, dark-haired man, whose muscular arms hinted at a natural athleticism enhanced by disciplined training.

Cappelletti showed them to their room and then suggested going back into town for lunch to get acquainted.

Over lunch, Cappelletti discovered that Bailey and Prado had worked together and shared some history as jockeys. When he mentioned that Leone would join the team later in the day, Bailey raised his eyebrows and glanced at Prado.

"Are you talking about Thomas Leone?" Bailey asked.

"That's correct," Cappelletti said. "Do you guys know Leone?"

Bailey looked at Prado and said, "No, sir, but we know of him. He—" the men exchanged another glance— "is very good with horses."

When they returned to the farm, the men settled in their room while expecting Leone to arrive. Bailey and Prado watched as the cab rounded the curb and pulled behind the big house. A handsome and dashing younger man jumped out of the car with unbound energy. Almost as short as Prado, with the same dark coloring, his dazzling smile clearly set him apart from the others. The bright yellow initials D.P.B. were inked prominently on his upper arm, which he proudly displayed because of his sleeveless white t-shirt.

Bailey turned to Prado and said, "Did someone forget to tell Leone that Georgia has four distinct seasons? It's November already."

Prado rolled his eyes. "He wears them for the ladies."

Cappelletti walked up to the cab, grabbed Leone's luggage, and directed him to the jockeys' room. He made the introductions and then took the men out to meet the horses. Sammy and Katie were waiting outside the stable when Cappelletti and the jockeys arrived.

Cappelletti lifted a hand in greeting. "Mrs. Williams, Sammy, our jockeys are here."

Bailey and Prado greeted Katie and Sammy with a handshake and a polite smile, but Leone held back a moment, watching Katie's exchange with the other two men. When she turned and extended her hand to Leone, he leaned forward to take it, then flashed that stunning smile. "I would've been here this morning," he said, his hand gently stroking the back of her hand, "had I known the owner would be so beautiful."

Katie blushed and smiled. After a moment, she drew her hand away, though not as promptly as Cappelletti would have liked.

Leone continued. "I look forward to working with you." He shot a quick glance at Sammy, then returned his gaze to Katie. "With both of you."

Cappelletti took a step forward. "Thank you for taking the time to meet our new jockeys, Mrs. Williams...Sammy. If you don't object, I'll show them around the barn."

He would have to keep an eye on Leone.

As the days went on, Cappelletti noticed Leone watching Katie with appreciation. Nevertheless, there were no signs of him overstepping. Apparently, Leone wasn't acting on his attraction to Katie. Aside from this minor detail, his horse skills were phenomenal, and they needed to get to work. It was true Leone thought himself to be a ladies' man, but it must not have caused a problem in the past. He came to them with impeccable references.

After an entire week of watching the interaction between the men and the individual horses, they paired Prado with Silver Circle, Bailey with Mr. Zee, and Leone with Redemption.

As Cappelletti watched him working alongside Katie while training Redemption, Leone was constantly touching her arm or back, or he'd brush up against her and look at her with those dreamy eyes. He noticed Leone had apparently developed a crush on her. Leone's reputation as the best in the business didn't add up with his behavior. Still, he'd worked with several world-class enterprises before coming to them. Cappelletti had to admit Leone had a way with the horses, though. In the short time he'd been there, Redemption's speed and focus had already improved. He was friendly and worked well with everyone at the farm, but seemed distracted when Katie appeared.

On Friday afternoon, as Katie led Redemption back to the stable, Leone ran up behind her and said, "Mrs. Williams, may I speak with you a moment?"

"Of course, Thomas. What's on your mind?"

Leone looked at the ground as he shuffled his feet. "Could you meet me down here in the morning? Redemption needs time to get used to my weight. He's not comfortable around me yet. He's almost there, but we need more time this week."

Katie hesitated. "Thomas, I appreciate your dedication, but I like to spend Saturday with Mattie Grace and Teddy."

His eyes flickered with disappointment. "One more workout should catch him up with Silver Circle and Mr. Zee."

She'd already seen how well Redemption was responding to his techniques, and she didn't want Leone to think they were not serious about winning. Perhaps Claire wouldn't mind watching Mattie Grace the following morning while she worked with Redemption and Thomas.

Katie sighed. "Okay, I'll be here around 10 o'clock, and we'll work with him for an hour or so before lunch."

Leone lifted his head toward the sky and folded his hands in a prayer-like form. "Yes!"

The following morning, Cappelletti was home with his wife while Sammy worked in the lower pasture with Mr. Zee and Silver Circle.

Alone in the stable, Leone and Katie worked side by side with Redemption. First, Leone meticulously cleaned his hooves. Then he brushed his coat in a circular motion as he led the animal to the corner of the stall. Next, he explained the need to massage the animal occasionally to develop a stronger bond, much like the need for lovers to explore each other's bodies.

The freedom with which he spoke caused Katie discomfort.

They remained in the stall, away from the door, taking longer than usual to prepare for the training session. Leone, a natural-born Italian, constantly talked in a heavy Italian accent about his native country and the village where he grew up. Katie had to pay close attention to follow his monologues. Today, the topic was his mother's cooking. "If you could only *zmell* de exquisite food baking in my mama's kitchen." He'd smile and look wantonly into the distance. "As soon as you enter the room, it hits you like a wave of joy. Watching her cook... like watching an artist at work. When she cooks for a big family celebration, a perfume of garlic and tomatoes permeates *de house* and beyond. As soon as you step foot into the yard, you can smell the delectable aromas flowing from Mama's kitchen." He kissed his fingers and continued, "She pairs each entree with wine from the region where I was born. Those family meals are spectacular."

Leone was apparently never at a loss for conversation. Still, after a while, Katie grew tired of his constant chatter. Conversation with Thomas required a level of concentration that often interfered with her work. She looked at her phone. They'd been in the barn for almost an hour already, and he had talked nonstop. Katie had errands to run and laundry to finish, and she wanted to get back to the house in time to have lunch with Teddy.

Still, Leone held the reins with his left hand in the stall as he held the brush with the other. Finally, Katie was ready to start the training session. Deciding to take charge of the situation, she reached for Redemption's reins. Leone pushed her away from the horse and grabbed her hands. Before her mind could grasp what was happening, he leaned in and pressed his lips to hers.

She froze. Her eyes opened wide. She was trapped in the corner of the stall with a man she barely knew and a thousand-pound colt.

Part of her mind registered Redemption's anxious energy.

Then the horse moved to the other side of the stall, even as she turned her head from side to side, avoiding Leone's insistent lips. She was a good three inches taller than he, but his body pinned her to the wall. She felt his breath on her chest as his fingers gripped her upper arms so tightly she could hardly move.

Finally, she threw her weight sideways as hard as she could, and his weight shifted slightly to the right. The pressure lifted from her right leg.

Now!

She drove her knee into his crotch with all her strength.

Leone grunted, and both hands flew to his groin as he doubled over in pain.

Katie slammed an elbow into his face, and he fell to the ground, groaning.

She turned and ran past Redemption, flew out of the stall, and raced for the house, sobbing with anger and humiliation. Was Leone behind her? She couldn't hear footsteps, but she could hardly hear anything over her own ragged breath. Then, heart racing, Katie stumbled inside the house and locked the door behind her. Next, she rushed to the foyer and locked the front door. Finally, Katie peeped out the kitchen window as she ripped layers of paper towels from underneath the cabinet.

Slow. Easy. Breathe.

She grabbed a bottled water from the refrigerator and sat down at the island. Her hands still shook as she rubbed the cold bottle over her tear-stained face. Why would Leone jeopardize an opportunity to work with a trainer like Cappelletti and ride a Triple Crown prospect?

It made no sense. Surely Leone knew they wouldn't keep him after this.

****

Teddy slowly pulled into the drive at the stables, and grabbed the two Yeti mugs of coffee from the cup holders. He'd puttered around the house most of the morning before finishing the breakfast dishes and making a fresh pot of coffee to share with Katie before lunch. Then he'd grabbed his AirPods and spent almost half an hour driving around the farm, looking for disasters in the making.

A beautiful Saturday morning, a cup of strong coffee, and the sounds of Journey. Sweet.

There were no disasters, but he'd noticed a few trees that had fallen since the previous month's windstorm and made a mental note to have those cleared away as soon as possible.

He stepped inside the stable. It was empty. Empty and unnaturally quiet.

"Katie, where are you?" He walked from stall to stall looking for her, but she didn't answer.

Oh, well. She must be out training.

Teddy walked to the other end of the stable and checked Mr. Zee's stall.

It was empty, too.

He opened the door and looked inside. Obviously, the cleaning crew hadn't shown up yet, but Teddy didn't mind cleaning the stalls.

The chore was a mindless exercise that required little to no thought. He went back for a stall rake and noticed Redemption's head stretching out from the open stall door. Teddy frowned. He'd heard of horses learning to open their stalls, but as far as he knew, that was a new trick for the big colt.

Teddy walked over and petted the animal, who seemed unusually nervous. "What's the matter, boy?"

He heard a low moan from inside. Leone lay curled on the floor in the corner, holding a hand over a bloody nose.

What the hell?

Had Redemption blown up and kicked the poor guy? Teddy cast a wary look at the horse.

Leone looked up and gingerly climbed to his feet.

"Are you all right?"

"I'll get my things and leave, Mr. Williams," Leone said, limping toward the door. "This is not... working for me."

"Man, are you okay?" Teddy asked.

Leone turned around and pointed to his bloody nose. "Do I look okay?"

Teddy followed him out of the stable. This was bad. Anyone who worked around horses had to sign a waiver saying they understood the dangers of equestrian sports and absolved the hosting facility of any liability, but a good lawyer could poke holes in it.

The last thing they needed was a lawsuit.

"Come on, Leone," Teddy said. "I'll give you a ride up to your room."

Leone hesitated, but then got on the Gator and grabbed the bar above his head, still holding his other hand over his nose.

Teddy reached under the seat and pulled out a box of tissues. "Here. You're going to need these." He knocked the vehicle out of gear, and they drove onto the blacktop drive.

When they stopped at the garage, Leone got off and rushed inside.

Ten minutes later, when he came out of the garage with his duffle bag, Teddy was still sitting on the Gator.

"Do you need a ride?" Teddy asked.

No, sir," Leone said. "My friend is coming."

Then he turned back toward the Gator. "Your wife…" He gestured to the area around him. "She has all of this, a beautiful home and family…but she's not happy. Sometimes when a woman is unhappy…." He hunched a shoulder and winced. "She was most upset when I rejected her advances."

Wait. What?

Had Katie done this to him?

Leone limped down the drive, presumably to wait for his friend. Watching the man's retreating back, Teddy tried to sort out his warring emotions. There had been truth in Leone's words. Katie was unhappy.

But the rest?

No. Maybe before the trip to California, but not now.

He felt guilty for even considering the possibility.

Teddy parked the Gator and headed toward the house. He found Katie in the kitchen, sitting on the stool at the island with her face in her hands.

"You okay?"

She lowered her hands and nodded.

She looked okay. A hell of a lot better than Leone did. If he'd been the aggressor, he had left no signs. But clearly, something had happened between them.

Teddy walked to the sink and washed his hands. Then he went to the refrigerator and surveyed the contents. "I'm getting hungry. How about a BLT?"

Katie wiped her nose with a tissue and said, "Teddy, I don't think Leone is going to work out."

"Yeah, well, I wouldn't worry about him hanging around here. Men rarely appreciate being assaulted by their bosses."

Katie's neck blotched with redness. "I... *assaulted* him?"

He removed the wrapper from the bacon and reached for the black iron skillet.

In a trembling voice, Katie said, "He tried to kiss me today."

Teddy flipped on the stove and then turned and looked at her. "He says you made advances."

Her mouth dropped open. Tears filled her eyes. "He pinned me in the corner and started kissing me. Trying to kiss me."

Teddy turned around toward the stove, not wanting her to see his face. He could only imagine the visual of the short Leone standing on his tiptoes as he tried to plant a kiss on Katie's lips.

"Kissing you, or trying to kiss you?"

He wiped his hands on a dish towel and turned to face her.

"I was trying to get away," Katie said. "But he was so strong. So, first I kneed him, and then I punched him in the nose." She gave a little laugh that sounded more like a sob and lifted one sleeve. Dark red bruises ringed her arm where Leone's fingers had dug in.

Teddy felt an enormous lump forming in his throat. It was followed by a long, slow burn. If he had Leone in front of him now...

He gently touched the skin beside the bruise with an index finger. "I think you broke his nose and hurt his manhood."

"What! You saw him, and you did nothing!"

Teddy cupped her chin in his hand and lifted her face. "Listen, you did the right thing. You hit him. I guess he was smart enough to know I'd never allow him to stay here after pulling such a stunt."

Katie's lips quivered. "You should have beat him up for what he did to me."

Softy, he said, "Let me see your hand," He kissed it, and then he kissed her nose. "I think you very ably took care of the situation."

Katie pulled away. "You should have defended my honor—hit him or something."

She was right. He should have. Maybe he should go after the guy right now and beat him to a pulp before his friend gets here. But those bruises on Katie's arms… Teddy was afraid if he started, he wouldn't stop.

He walked back to the sink and forced a smile as he reached for the tomato. "Seriously, I'm a surgeon. We insured my hands for two million dollars."

That brought a hint of a smile. A good sign. He went on. "The good thing is, neither of us had to fire him. He quit, and he's gone. So, let's put it behind us." He rinsed the tomato and dried it with a paper towel as he leaned on the island.

Katie was quiet for a moment. Then she said, "We'll have to find another jockey."

"We'll find a better jockey," he said, and pulled her into his arms.

There was a burning in Katie's throat just thinking about how Leone had pinned her against the wall. How could an assault happen on their own property? All three jockeys, including the trainer, Cappelletti, passed a vetting screen for criminal activity. What if Mattie Grace had been the subject of Leone's twisted behavior? Or perhaps Claire. She was a frequent visitor to the farm—always helping them transport Mattie Grace to her many activities.

What if Sammy had walked in? How would seeing her in a compromising position have affected him?

Her stomach churned. She needed time alone to process what had happened to her in the barn.

Abruptly, she withdrew from Teddy's embrace. "I'm going upstairs to take a bath."

She saw the hurt in Teddy's eyes as he turned back toward the sink, but she couldn't bring herself to comfort him. She was hurting, too.

As she started up the steps, she turned back toward the kitchen. "Do you think Claire would mind if Mattie Grace spent the night with her?"

"Of course not," he said. "I'll call her in a few minutes. Go on up and get your bath."

Katie barely had time to close the door to their master bath before waves of nausea bent her double. A sour taste filled her mouth, and she stumbled to the toilet, knees landing hard on the tiles as she heaved up her breakfast. She was scared. As scared as she'd ever been in her life. What if Leone hadn't shifted his grip? What if she'd recognized that opportunity a moment too late? A second at most, that was the difference between what was and what might have been.

Katie reached for a hand towel hanging above the sink.

The good towel.

Not the everyday towels they used to dry their hands. Wiping her mouth, Katie sat on the floor with her back to the deep bathtub. She lost all track of time as she waited for her stomach to settle down. Finally, she plugged the drain and turned on the water, turning it to the hottest possible setting. Then she removed her clothes and placed them in the small trash can next to the toilet.

She never wanted to see those clothes again. Leone's filthy hands were all over that shirt. If she'd had scissors handy, she would have cut it to shreds. She would never again, as long as she lived, wear a camisole under an opened shirt to the barn.

As the water filled the tub, Katie slipped inside and lay back. Thankfully, the claw-footed tub was deep enough for her to lie in. She grabbed another towel, this time a bath size towel. She held it over her face and screamed. The sound of the running water and the towel against her mouth drowned out her cries.

The water was rising, and the streaming water was now lukewarm, but she hardly noticed. Shivering, tears streaming, she only saw Leone's beady eyes and felt the warmth of his breath on her chest as he wrestled to secure her hands to the wall.

Suddenly, the door opened. She stifled a scream and lowered the bath towel enough to see Teddy enter the room holding a platter of sandwiches and two glasses of iced tea. He quickly placed the platter on the countertop and reached to turn off the water.

"Babe, are you okay?" he said. "You're shivering."

Was she okay? Katie choked on a laugh. She felt like she might never be okay again.

As soon as Katie removed the bath towel, Teddy saw the terror on her face. Her eyes red and swollen, and mucus streaming from her nose mixed with the flood of tears pouring from her eyes. He'd never seen her so distraught. How could he have misread the situation so badly?

Again, he fought the urge to hunt Leone down and beat the man to within an inch of his life. But while that might make him feel better, it wasn't what Katie needed right now.

He dropped beside the tub and reached for her. Wrapping his arms around her as her limp body melted into him. His gentle touch seemed to calm her. They rocked back and forth to the sound of his soothing voice. Finally, he took off his boots and slowly slid one leg over the side of the tub and then the other, careful not to disturb her. He immersed himself—clothes and all—and lay next to his wife, holding her as he might a hurting child.

"It's okay, sweetie. I'm here," he whispered in her ear. "We'll get through this."

Katie shook her head. "Just hold me."

They were in the tub for a while. Teddy stretched for the food tray and handed Katie half of a sandwich. Then he grabbed the other half for himself. Teddy finished his sandwich and took a long swallow of tea. The ice had melted, but the tea was still chilled.

It tasted good.

Katie nibbled at her sandwich and washed it down with the cold tea.

Teddy took her glass and placed it on the counter. "Let's get out of the bathtub and get you into some dry clothes. I talked to Mom. Mattie Grace is going to stay with her tonight."

Katie nodded.

"I'll give you something to help you sleep."

"Will you stay with me?" Katie asked.

Teddy brushed her hair from her face. "I won't leave your side. I promise."

It was dark when Katie finally woke. Teddy lay beside her, snoring softly. His right arm was around her waist, and his left arm was resting over his head. That stubborn strand of blond hair had fallen onto his forehead, and at that moment, Katie thought he was the most beautiful man she'd ever seen. She reached for the strand of hair and moved it in place.

When she came up to the house earlier, her emotionally charged thoughts about what could've happened in the barn had made her crazy. Even when she came upstairs to take her bath, she'd let herself get way out on a limb thinking about the what-ifs of the situation. Thankfully, Teddy was there to help reel her back in.

The sleeping meds had helped. She'd slept soundly for five hours, and now she felt better—felt stronger. She could see clearly now.

Watching him sleep, she wondered how he could've believed that she would have come on to Leone, or any man for that matter? Well, he really didn't say he believed it, but Leone had turned it around to make her out to be the aggressor. That was a textbook psychological move.

But how could Teddy have any sympathy for a man who almost assaulted his wife in their own stable? Perhaps he didn't realize the seriousness of the attack. Just because Leone hadn't succeeded in hurting her didn't mean he wouldn't have.

Teddy moved his arm tighter around her waist—his eyes slowly opened as he smiled.

"Are you okay?" he asked.

Katie nodded. "We need to talk."

Teddy leaned up on one elbow. "I know we do, but it can wait until morning. You need to rest now."

She closed her eyes and thought about the times they'd put off discussing problems in the past. It only caused more internal conflict for her, and probably him, too.

"I think we should talk now," Katie said. She snuggled closer, her hand resting on his chest. "I don't think you understand how serious the incident at the barn was. If Leone's weight hadn't shifted when it did, I'd never have gotten away. I thought he was going to rape me, Teddy. I've never been so scared."

Teddy moved closer to her and wrapped both of his arms around her. "I'm sorry, baby." His voice broke. "I'm so very sorry."

Katie felt a deep love for this man who stayed with her in a tub of cold water while she had a breakdown. Then, softly she asked, "Why did you believe I was the aggressor?"

Tears glistened in Teddy's eyes. "Leone said you were unhappy, and I know it's true. But I don't know how to fix it, and—" He stared up at the ceiling. His eyes shimmered in the moonlight. "I'm... afraid I'm going to lose you."

She laid a hand along his cheek. "You will not lose me, because I love you." She propped herself on one elbow and looked into his eyes. "I'm not going anywhere. But you need to understand that you can't always fix everything for me."

"So I'm just supposed to watch you struggle and not even try to help?"

"No, no. What you did tonight..." She brushed her thumb across his lower lip. "You were perfect. More than perfect. I needed that from you. But my... what you call unhappiness, it has nothing to do with you or our marriage. It's something in me, which means I have to be the one to figure it out. I think..."

He waited while she gathered her thoughts.

"I think it's about my feelings of inadequacy. About being a mother."

He kissed her forehead. "What do you mean?"

She didn't even know how to explain it to him. She loved Mattie Grace, but she was such a strong-headed little girl. Perhaps it's because her own mother had died when she was so young, and she was raised by a grandmother. Katie really didn't have anyone to model herself after. She fumbled her way through it, and the look on his face said he understood.

"Well, as long as we're being completely honest," he said, "my fear is that I can't make you happy, and you'll either leave me, or you'll remain in this marriage... miserable, just sticking it out. I don't want that for either of us."

Katie pushed to her knees, cupping his face in her hands. "Oh, no! No! No! Teddy, you're the best thing that's ever happened to me. I just need a little more time sorting through this internal conflict, and as soon as I make sense of it, I'll let you know."

Teddy said, "But you've been so quiet lately."

"Because I don't want to bother you with this until I can sit down and talk it through. But I swear to you, it has nothing to do with our marriage. You are my rock! I mean, how many husbands would have jumped into that bathtub with their clothes on?"

Teddy chuckled. "Let's be clear. I never jumped into the bathtub! Get that mental picture out of your mind." He gently pulled her on top of him. "I'm sorry I let my own insecurities override my ability to feel your pain today. I promise to never let that happen again."

She kissed him softly. "I'm sorry, too. Let's just try to put this behind us and move forward."

As his kisses grew more fervent, she wriggled out of her pajamas. "Close your eyes," Katie whispered. Then she reached for Teddy's t-shirt and lifted it over his head.

Chapter Thirty-One

The Monday morning before Thanksgiving, Teddy sat in his home office staring at the telephone. With the jockey debacle fresh on his mind, he sighed, took another swallow of coffee, and dialed Philip Nordstrom's cell number.

He needed to get the call behind him.

"Hello, Philip." He had hesitated to report Leone to the National Thoroughbred Racing Association, since calling out someone as successful and connected as Leone could come back to haunt him. Worse, it could cause problems for Katie—perhaps even derail her chances of making it in the racing business.

Still, he couldn't just let it go.

It was painful for Teddy to explain what had happened between Leone and Katie.

Katie was his wife, for God's sakes, and he still felt a tinge of guilt about not beating the crap out of the guy while he had the chance. He made himself go on, anyway.

Then, "Katie was a wreck," he finished. His hand ached, and he realized he was clenching the phone. "What are the odds this is the first time he's stepped over the line?"

After a long silence, Philip said, "He has a reputation as a ladies' man, but I've never caught a hint of anything like this."

Teddy blew out a frustrated breath. "I checked and double checked those jockeys' backgrounds. I wouldn't have hired him if his hadn't come back clean."

"Of course not," Phillip said. "He has a stellar reputation as a trainer. I doubt he'd jeopardize those credentials unless he was confident he could get away with it."

"Agreed," Teddy said. "He was careful. No other witnesses, just he said/she said. If he's assaulted other women, they must not have reported him to the authorities."

"Probably afraid of future repercussions. Who could blame them?"

Teddy hadn't reported Leone to the local authorities, either. Partly because Leone had already left Abington, and partly because of Leone's reputation. And partly because nothing had happened that couldn't be spun enough to create reasonable doubt. Leone must think he was untouchable.

Teddy had been slow to act, but after two sleepless nights thinking about Leone's actions, he suddenly had clarity about how to ensure it didn't happen again, and to make sure word spread throughout the industry.

"How is Katie?" Philip asked.

"Still a little shaken," Teddy said. Reluctantly, he admitted, "She hasn't been back to the stables since it happened."

That was natural, right?

"I wouldn't push her too much right now," Philip said. "But, if she hasn't gone down there by the weekend, maybe you could go with her and take the horses out for a ride. She needs to see that the only change on the farm is the absence of Leone."

Teddy dropped his head. Of course, she was afraid to go back to the barn. He'd been a fool to think it was just a kiss. It was only fast thinking that had kept it from becoming much more. "Excellent advice, Phil. I'll take it."

"And I'll get the word out about Leone to the members of the NTRA. I'll get back to you with any feedback."

Feeling like a weight had been lifted, Teddy ended the call and went into the kitchen to check on his wife.

****

On Wednesday morning, Sammy, and his dog, Ole Blue, slipped upstairs after breakfast and gazed out from the attic of the big house. Except for him, the house was empty. Teddy had already left for work. Katie and Mattie Grace had gone into town to shop for last-minute grocery items for their Thanksgiving dinner.

It had been about a month since Sammy noticed a pan missing from his apartment. Some utensils were gone, too. He rediscovered the missing items the very next day, and because of the pan's tarnished bottom, he'd wondered if someone had used the items for cooking over an open fire.

This pattern continued.

Being such a meticulous housekeeper, Sammy immediately knew when something was out of place or missing inside his apartment. It was unnerving to think a stranger would enter his apartment each morning.

The enormous clock in the foyer chimed, making Sammy jump. Then eight more chimes. He settled back into his watchful stance at the attic window while Ole Blue slept at his feet. Then, as the last chime faded, Sammy saw a scraggly-looking man coming from behind the garage. Sammy stepped away from the window to avoid being seen. He was a good hundred yards from the man, and his eyesight was not as good as it used to be. But the man seemed older and taller than any of the farm hands.

Sammy squinted at the stranger—trying to see his facial features. If he had to report the guy to the authorities, it would be difficult to identify him in a lineup.

The stranger carefully looked around the yard before going up the steps to Sammy's apartment. Sammy leaned forward to get a better look. The shirt the man wore looked like the one Katie had given him for Christmas the previous year, and the corduroy pants—his favorite pair—were the same ones he'd worn on Friday night.

As Sammy waited for the intruder to leave, he thought about how his laundry had increased over the past month. When his mother was alive, she'd handled his laundry. When she died, Katie managed it until she and Teddy married. Then, while they were away on their honeymoon, his brother, Roger, came to stay for a few days. That was when Sammy decided he should learn to do his own laundry.

The guy was inside less than fifteen minutes when he slipped out the back door, dressed in Sammy's clothes. The same red ball cap he'd worn earlier sat low on his forehead, just at the man's eyebrows. As he exited the apartment, he looked around before gently closing the door. When he started down the steps, he opened the top of a Coke can and guzzled the entire drink in one long gulp. Then he headed toward the old Whelchel farm.

Chapter Thirty-Two

T eddy closed his office at noon and sent his staff home to get ready for the Thanksgiving holiday. On his way home, he stopped by the local delicatessen and ordered a sack full of sandwiches.

Katie looked over her shoulder as Teddy walked through the back door. "What are you doing home? I wasn't expecting you until dinner."

"It was slow at the office, so I closed at noon."

Katie nodded toward his purchase. "What's in the bag?"

He leaned over and kissed her. "I brought lunch."

Katie smiled as she pulled the bottled water from the refrigerator, texted Sammy, and told him lunch was ready. Then she stuck her phone in her back pocket and said, "I know you've been busy, but have you had time to talk with Philip about...."

He nodded. "Called him first thing Monday morning. He's taking care of it."

Katie stretched to kiss his neck, and he squeezed her hand. "Is Mattie Grace joining us for lunch?"

"She ate earlier."

They both turned as Sammy came into the kitchen. "Redemption hasn't eaten anything all morning," he said. "I noticed last night he hadn't eaten his oats. At first, I thought he was just missing Katie, but when I got to the stable this morning, his eyes looked weak, and his ears weren't standing up straight."

Teddy, laying out the sandwiches on the breakfast table, frowned. "Should we call the vet?"

"That might be a good idea—with tomorrow being a holiday and all."

Teddy quickly sent a text to Dr. Scott, who quickly responded <Be there within the hour.> Sammy grabbed a sandwich and a Coke and returned to the stable to wait for the vet.

Teddy turned to Katie. "What can I do to help you get ready for Thanksgiving? I've got the afternoon off, and I'm here at your beck and call."

Katie giggled, though her eyes were still clouded with concern for Redemption. She wiggled her eyebrows and said, "Beck and call, huh? That sounds fun."

Teddy laughed. "Seriously, I'm here to help you get ready for Thanksgiving. Also, Mattie Grace and I will handle dinner this evening. We'll order pizza and wings from the pizzeria. Hopefully, you can put your feet up and watch a movie after dinner."

Katie brushed a hand against his cheek and gave him a grateful smile. "Claire and Frank are bringing the desserts around 5:30. She's making four pies and a carrot cake for Thanksgiving. I'm sure she'll not want to cook dinner, either. See if they want to eat pizza with us tonight."

"Good idea."

Katie looked toward the door, then hesitated. "I really want to check on Redemption, but I just don't think I can."

The helplessness on her face felt like a punch to Teddy's gut.

"When Dr. Scott gets here," Katie said. "Will you go down and find out what he thinks about the situation?"

Teddy nodded. Then he pulled her into his arms. It was all he knew to do, but it didn't feel like enough.

When Dr. Scott's truck pulled into the driveway, Teddy rushed out the kitchen door and followed the vet to the stable.

A heavy nasal discharge streamed from Redemption's nose, but the most notable symptom was his cough. He seemed lifeless, except for the heaving of his sides. When he coughed, his whole-body shook.

While Sammy stroked Redemption's back, Dr. Scott took the colt's temperature. He examined Redemption's eyes and gums, then drew three vials of blood to test for influenza. He looked at Teddy and said, "We need to move Redemption to the old barn to isolate him from the other horses. The results won't be ready until Friday morning because of the holiday, and if this is contagious, we don't want it to spread."

"We can't move him to the old barn," Teddy said. "We use it to store the hay."

Still rubbing Redemption's back, Sammy said, "How bout we use the trailer? It's clean. We can pull it down here and throw some hay in it."

"Good idea, Sammy," the doctor said. "But you'll need to wash the inside of the trailer with a mixture of white vinegar and warm soapy water... and be sure to dry it thoroughly before spreading the fresh hay on the floor."

When he'd gathered the blood samples, he turned to Teddy and said, "As an added precaution, get the farmhands to wash out the barn after they get Redemption settled. We won't know if this virus is contagious until the results come back."

Teddy nodded and watched the vet drive away. He looked toward the house. How was he going to break the news to Katie about Redemption? It was the day before Thanksgiving. After all she'd been through the past few days, this could set her back.

He trudged back to the house and slipped into the kitchen. Katie was staring down at a recipe card, verifying the exact measurements as she crumbled the cornbread and biscuits into a large aluminum bowl. Finally, she looked up at Teddy. "What did Dr. Scott say about Redemption?"

Teddy told her about the vials of blood Dr. Scott was taking over to the lab to analyze. Sammy was busy cleaning the trailer to isolate Redemption from the other horses.

"I should call Tommy Parker," Teddy said as he scrolled through his phone. "I need to ask if he can spare a couple of hands this afternoon to help Sammy and the men to scrub down the stables. We sure don't need the other horses to get sick."

Katie covered his phone with her hand and said, "Maybe we shouldn't alarm the neighbors at this point. If this is a contagious disease, Parker's men could carry the virus back to his farm."

"What do you suggest?"

Katie turned to the sink and washed her hands. "Give me just a second to slide on my work boots, and you and I can start cleaning the stalls."

Teddy stopped and gave her a searching look. Was she really ready to go back to the barn? He made a sweeping gesture with his arm. "Katie, you've got a Thanksgiving dinner to prepare. Are you sure you have time for this today?"

She slid the cornbread mixture into the refrigerator before reaching for her jacket and boots. "Let's go. We don't have time to waste." She turned to make sure he was following her. "Why don't you call the pizzeria and place the order for dinner? Tell them you'll pick it up around 5:15."

"Yes, ma'am." Teddy grinned. She sounded like her old self.

It took three hours to move the horses out to the field and wash down the stables. Sammy had cleaned the trailer for Redemption, laid fresh hay on the floor, and brought in fresh food. After he moved the trailer up the hill and parked it next to the garage, he went inside the big house to make a mixture of sugar water according to the directions from Dr. Scott. It would help keep the horse hydrated.

At 4:45, Teddy and Katie walked up the hill to the house. She sat down in one of the porch rockers and said, "You go on up and take your shower. I'm going to take off my boots and sit here just a minute."

Katie leaned her head against the rocker and closed her eyes. She hoped whatever Redemption had, he'd be over it soon, and if it turned out to be contagious, maybe they'd acted soon enough to keep the other horses from getting it.

She pushed herself out of the chair. She had a lot to catch up on before she'd be ready for Thanksgiving dinner.

When Teddy had finished his shower, and taken Mattie Grace to pick up dinner, Katie went into the kitchen and found some paper plates and napkins. She sat them on the breakfast table, then went upstairs to shower.

She was drying off when she saw Claire and Frank pull up the drive. Quickly, she slipped on a sweatshirt and an old pair of jeans, tied her wet hair up in a bun, and ran downstairs to open the back door.

"Perfect timing. Come on in."

While Frank brought in the desserts for their Thanksgiving dinner, Katie's cell phone rang.

It was Roger, her uncle from Athens. He hadn't responded to her earlier invitation to Thanksgiving dinner. Still, he was on his way to Abington and planned to spend the night.

A slow smile spread across her face. Roger was the fun uncle and a whiz in the kitchen. She suddenly felt the tension leave her body. Roger knew what needed doing and would just do it—without being asked. He always told exciting stories about his life at the university.

Roger said, "I wanted to surprise Mattie Grace and be there to watch the Macy's Thanksgiving Day Parade with her."

"Mattie Grace will love it," Katie said. "What time can you get here?"

"I'm turning onto your road as we speak."

Chapter Thirty-Three

Thanksgiving Day. The alarm clock on the bedside table buzzed at 6 a.m. Katie opened one eye and glared at the clock. It seemed she'd just fallen asleep. She forced herself out of the warmth of the down comforter, reached for her housecoat, and tip-toed down to the kitchen.

Katie poured a small glass of juice and reviewed the list she'd left on the counter. It listed the dishes waiting to be cooked and those needing to be prepared later in the morning.

She then got to work preparing the turkey.

After she'd slid the turkey into the oven, she ran back upstairs and slipped into bed for a few more minutes. Teddy turned over and smiled. "What've you been doing?"

"I put the turkey in to bake and started the coffee." She snuggled up to his warm body and played with a sprig of hair on his forehead. "I need you to do me a favor today."

"Sure. What do you need?"

"Do you remember that pretty brown sports jacket you bought in California?"

"Uh-huh."

"Would you wear it for Thanksgiving dinner? I thought we might dress up today."

Teddy stretched his arms, moved his head in a clockwise motion, and yawned. "Why do we need to dress up for *this* Thanksgiving dinner?"

Katie placed her hand on his chest. "Roger brought a jacket for dinner, and I'd hate for him to be the only guy wearing one."

Teddy laughed. "What is it with that guy? He grew up on this farm. So why can't he just throw on a pair of Levi's and a button-down shirt and forget it?"

Katie kissed his neck. "Because he's Roger, and he's always enjoyed dressing to the nines. Besides, his being here makes preparing a Thanksgiving meal much easier on me. It took us less than an hour after dinner to catch up for the time I lost yesterday cleaning out the barn." She smiled a wicked little grin and rubbed his chest. "Besides, I like to dress up for big holiday meals, too. It makes the occasion more festive."

Teddy pulled her close and smiled. "Okay, I'll think about it."

They were asleep when a knock at the door startled them awake.

"Who is it?" Teddy asked.

"It's *moi*," Roger said. "I've got a breakfast tray for you guys. Mattie Grace and I will be in the kitchen preparing the greens for the salad, if you need anything."

Teddy waited until he heard Roger's footsteps on the stairs. Then he opened the door. A large silver tray sat on the floor outside their bedroom. On it were two plates—identically arranged with French toast sprinkled with powdered sugar and banana slices. Beside them was a side of crisp bacon, a pot of hot coffee, and a small pitcher of juice.

Roger had left no detail to chance. A small bud vase filled with miniature yellow chrysanthemums sat on top of the linen napkins.

Teddy picked up the tray and returned to the bed. "Hell, let's just ask Uncle Roger to move in with us. This is like being at a five-star resort."

Katie grinned. She poured the coffee into the china cups and handed the pot to Teddy, motioning for him to place it on the nightstand. "Does this mean you'll wear the jacket for our Thanksgiving dinner?"

Teddy leaned over and kissed her nose. "Of course, I'll wear the jacket, but I'm not wearing dress slacks. You'll have to settle for jeans."

When Teddy finished his shower, Katie was gone. She'd made their bed and removed the breakfast dishes. The bedroom door was open and he overheard her and Roger laughing in the kitchen. Roger said that Sammy had eaten an enormous plate of French toast, wrapped a plate of leftovers, and had taken it to his apartment.

Before he could hear Katie's response, Teddy's phone pinged. He slowly reached into his pocket and then read the text message—a patient's name, followed by the results he'd dreaded. <Test results show enlarged appendix. Prepping for surgery now—the patient will be ready when you arrive.

"Crap, not today." He grabbed his wallet from the dresser and closed the door behind him.

At the bottom of the steps, Teddy said, "Got to go. I just got a text. A ten-year-old girl is waiting for an emergency appendectomy. If all goes well, I should be home by two o'clock—three at the latest." He kissed Katie and Mattie Grace, then nodded to Roger. "Man, that breakfast was fabulous. You're welcome to move into that suite in there." He gestured toward the addition at the end of the house. "Katie and I never use it."

"Don't tempt me. That's the best bed I've ever slept in." Roger took another sip of coffee and pushed his glasses up on his nose. Even at this hour, his silver hair was perfectly styled. "Don't worry about a thing, Teddy. I'll help Katie get ready for this holiday extravaganza."

"Don't take any sass from her, Roger." Teddy glanced at Katie and winked. Her face flushed as she turned back to the sink.

There was a glow about her this morning. I wonder... no, that's not possible. She'd had two glasses of wine last night, that's all.

Roger pointed his finger and said, "I'll just sass her right back!"

"That a boy," he said as he headed toward the door. "I'll be back as soon as I can."

After surgery, Teddy changed out of his scrubs and stopped by his patient's room to check on her.

As he pulled out of the hospital parking lot, his phone rang. "Teddy, this is Doc Scott. You'll never believe this, but the lab has the results of the blood test. Unfortunately, Redemption has a form of Coronavirus. It's a mild case. Still, it's a good thing we isolated him from the other horses yesterday. Keep following the same regimen until I get by there this afternoon with the meds, but he should be fine in a couple of weeks."

When Teddy pulled to the top of the driveway, five cars were parked next to the porch. He snuck in the back door and rushed up the backstairs to their bathroom, hoping no one had noticed him.

Through the fog on the shower glass, Teddy saw Katie slip into the bathroom and place a glass of iced tea on the counter next to the sink.

"How did the surgery go?"

Teddy stepped out of the shower, "It went well."

Katie was still standing in the bathroom, waiting for him to dry off. "I brought you a cool drink to enjoy while dressing. As soon as you come down and mingle a few minutes with our guests, we'll be ready to eat." She handed him the glass, placed her hand on his face, and kissed him softly.

Teddy closed his eyes as he drank the sweet nectar. "We could just stay up here the rest of the night. Just the two of us, up here alone. Roger can handle the dinner, and I don't think anyone would miss us."

"That's a thought." She smiled and squeezed his hand. "I'll meet you downstairs when you get dressed." When she got to the door, she turned and flashed that million-dollar smile. "Don't forget the jacket."

Teddy sat at one end of the dining room table, and Katie sat at the opposite end. The turkey she'd cooked earlier rested on a silver platter in the center of the dining room table. Small bunches of grapes, orange slices, and sprigs of rosemary completed the stunning presentation.

His mom and Frank sat to Teddy's right. While Andrew and Daisy were engaged in a conversation with Rhett, Teddy turned to his mother. "Mom, would you and Frank like to go with us to St. Simons Island the day after Christmas and stay through the New Year? Katie and I thought it would be a great time for a vacation since Mattie Grace will be out of school."

Frank touched Claire's hand and said, "Honey, that would be a perfect time for us to get married."

Wow! That was fast. Teddy knew they'd been seeing a lot of each other, but he wasn't prepared for such a brief engagement.

She flushed. Then she turned to Teddy and said, "That would be lovely."

Teddy looked at his future stepfather and grinned. "Well, Frank, welcome to the family."

"Son, I'm sorry I sprang that on you. I've been meaning to speak with you about your mother."

"Don't you worry about it, Frank. That's the best news I've heard in a while."

"I love her, Teddy."

"I know you do." Teddy coughed. "I'm glad both of you can go with us to the beach. Aside from getting you two married, I want to start looking for a beach house. Maybe you can help me find a good deal."

"Of course, and I'll call the K&P Resort in the morning about scheduling the ceremony. Then, Claire and I should call Philip and Celeste and let them know the good news."

"Hope they'll join us that week at the beach. Katie and I would love to meet Celeste."

Frank said. "It'll be nice for us all to be together over the holidays. From the looks of things, we'll need a large beach house. This family of ours is growing!"

Chapter Thirty-Four

K atie finished cleaning up the kitchen and made herself a hot cup of tea, waiting for Teddy to return home from the hospital.

She smiled at the memory of Mattie Grace giggling with Teddy before dinner.

As she sipped her tea, she walked through the house and considered the position of their Christmas tree. She and Roger had discussed it when he came at Thanksgiving, but she didn't want the tree in the kitchen because the heat from the fireplace would dry it out too fast. Katie walked through the rooms once more and stopped in the foyer. It was certainly big enough to accommodate a Christmas tree, and there was always a light draft from the front door. But, after second thought, she decided they would enjoy the tree more if it was in another room.

As she walked back through the kitchen toward the sunroom, she saw the perfect place. They would only need to move the two club chairs over a few feet and reposition the small table and lamp. The tree could stand in the middle of the windows at the end of the porch.

Satisfied, she sat down on the sofa, closed her eyes, and imagined their perfectly decorated tree. Then, as she clung to the warm mug, her mind drifted back to the first holiday season she spent with Teddy when her grandmother was still alive. It was a bittersweet Christmas Eve—but one she would remember with fond memories and gratitude to Teddy for making her grandmother's last Christmas a festive occasion.

She wished Nana were here to see Mattie Grace. She would be so thrilled to watch her great-granddaughter grow up. After Katie finished her tea, she washed out her cup and crept upstairs to her daughter's room. Quietly, she opened the door and peeped in. The little firebrand was lying on her stomach. The pink bunny was nestled under her chin as she clung to her favorite stuffed animal. At that moment, she looked like a little angel.

****

The traffic going into Atlanta was heavy for a Saturday afternoon, but Matt navigated the interstate like a pro.

Teddy was grateful to be a passenger for once, with a driver who clearly knew what he was doing. "Matt, how did you enjoy the North Carolina-Tech football game?"

Matt looked in the rearview mirror and grinned. "Man, it was awesome. Tech was behind 7-0 at the end of the first quarter. Then the referee blew his whistle on the very first play of the second quarter and called a personal foul on Georgia Tech."

"When I saw that call by the ref, I thought uh-oh, that's gonna be a problem. Then I got a text from the hospital, and I missed the rest of the game."

Matt chuckled. "Everyone in our section stood up and yelled at the referee. They were up and down the last half of the game. At the end of the third quarter Tech led 27-14. North Carolina scored again in the fourth quarter, but Tech came back and scored a field goal bringing the score to 38-22."

Colleen turned around in her seat and said, "Tech's final touchdown came with only 1:13 left in the quarter, they'd come from behind to win the game 45-22. It was so exciting."

Matt touched her hand and glanced at Teddy in the mirror, "Colleen's the first girl I've ever dated that loves college football as much as me."

As Matt pulled off the interstate, Colleen said, "Are we here already? It seems like we just left Abington."

"Teddy, are you comfortable parking in this lot? It's only a block from the theater."

"You're driving. Wherever you want to park is fine. I'm just grateful I didn't have to drive in this traffic."

The line going into the matinee extended down the street and around the corner. Matt suggested Teddy and the girls go into the café at the corner of Peachtree and Ponce and wait out of the cold. "I'll text you guys when the line starts to move."

Teddy found a small table next to the window. Light snow fell as they ordered three glasses of Prosecco.

Teddy lifted his glass and said, "Here's to the beginning of the Christmas season and lasting friendships."

Colleen grinned. "Oh, Teddy. Thank you."

By the time Teddy saw Matt outside the window, thirty minutes had passed. Teddy nudged Colleen. "There he is."

Colleen waved at Matt, and he winked at her.

Teddy said, "I like him, Colleen. But, at the risk of sounding like an old man, I must say, I appreciate how respectful he is of you."

Her face lit up. "He is, isn't he?"

She spent the next ten minutes talking about how different Matt was from Drew. "I feel a little guilty about enjoying Matt's company so much. It's like I'm being disloyal to Drew."

"Well..." Katie's eyes danced with mischief. "I knew he was a keeper when you told me he'd bought four tickets to The Nutcracker performance at The Fox Theatre."

"Yeah, we appreciate you guys inviting us," Teddy said. "And listen, Colleen. Drew wouldn't want you to spend the rest of your life in a shell. You have a life to live, and from the looks of it, Matt is interested in getting to know you. So just enjoy it. You don't have to marry the guy—just give him a chance."

Chapter Thirty-Five

Big Jim Levinson, the mayor of Abington, stared out the windows of his office at City Hall. The weather was dark and gloomy, even for a Christmas Eve. A light snow fell on the town square. It wasn't enough to stick, but enough to add to the season's excitement, if the Christmas season still caused one to be excited.

The mayor watched from his desk as the town folk hurried around the square shopping for last-minute gifts. The temperatures were in the mid-thirties, causing pain in his swollen arthritic joints.

He rubbed his forehead—another Christmas season without his family.

Delores, his wife, had recently transferred to a rehabilitation facility. The neatly stacked medical bills lay on the desk. Many of the envelopes remained unopened.

What was the use?

They had already met the lifetime limit on his health insurance. There was a letter in the stack from the insurance company explaining how the limit worked.

He'd been sitting at his desk since early morning, trying to think of a way to pay the bills. Their only son, Little Jimmy, was in prison for murdering thirteen people. The final blow was when Jimmy murdered his wife and three young daughters.

Big Jim missed those girls. They were the joy of his life.

Delores and Big Jim had burned through their savings trying to defend their son. As much as it hurt to lose the girls, they couldn't abandon their son.

What parent could?

As luck would have it, they'd just finished paying off a loan from the bank to cover Little Jimmy's legal fees when Delores ran a stop sign and plowed into the backend of a tractor-trailer that had just picked up a load of cocaine from a barn in Abington.

That was eighteen months ago, and Sheriff Riley, the only eyewitness to the wreck, had handled the investigation. Fortunately, the drug cartel was never implicated in the accident. They'd been silent ever since, and Big Jim was grateful they didn't seem to carry a grudge.

A fresh wave of dark clouds caused the streetlights around the square to flash on, breaking his trance. Big Jim finished the last sip of the cold coffee he bought earlier from the café. Then, as much as he hated to leave the warmth of his office, he reached for his keys, grabbed his overcoat, and walked toward the door.

A few moments later, he got into his silver Chevrolet 3500HD without being noticed by anyone at City Hall. Big Jim just wasn't in the Christmas mood, but he couldn't stay away from the prison, either. So when he turned the ignition, he couldn't think of a worse way to spend the holiday than to be incarcerated like his son.

It was hard to explain why he felt compelled to visit Jimmy. By doing so, he felt disloyal to the girls, but he couldn't just abandon his boy.

It was Patsy's fault, really. She'd quietly overlooked his indiscretions for years, but then she'd pushed Jimmy for a divorce he hadn't wanted. She'd even called him a psychopath in front of their children. His son had simply broken under the stress.

He checked the back seat at the red light to make sure he'd remembered to bring his presents: books and magazines mainly, a carton of cigarettes, a box of chocolate candy, and a bag of peppermints. Naturally, the security would check each package for any illegal substances.

Big Jim pulled inside the entrance to the prison. The security guard immediately opened the gate. He nodded and went on through, eager to talk to his son about their current situation.

After the usual security precautions, Big Jim slipped the guard a fifty-dollar bill. The guard reluctantly scanned the contents of the bag, unlocked the door to the large daylight area, and allowed him to go inside to visit. Little Jimmy was sitting in a metal chair, hands chained to the table in front of him. He looked thin sitting in his orange prison jumpsuit.

"You've got twenty minutes today," the guard said. "I'll be back when your time is up."

When the door locked, Big Jim walked over and sat across from his son. "Merry Christmas!"

Little Jimmy glanced at the bag. Then he looked up and smiled at his dad. "Thanks. Do you mind if I wait and open it tomorrow morning?"

Big Jim nodded. "Not at all."

After a few minutes of updates about the prison activities, Big Jim mentioned the cap on the insurance policy.

Little Jimmy owned a property and casualty insurance company in his previous life, so he understood lifetime caps on policies. "I hate that, Dad. It's hard to believe eighteen months of healthcare could cost that much. You'll just have to dip into your savings."

Big Jim got up and walked to the door and peeped through the glass. He felt his son's gaze following his steps.

Jimmy said, "How much are the total bills?"

"Somewhere around a hundred thousand, and then there's the monthly charge for your mother to stay in the rehab facility."

Little Jimmy got up and stretched his legs. "How will that affect your nest egg?"

Big Jim looked at his son and barked a laugh. "What nest egg?"

After a moment, Jimmy said, "Got a pen?"

Big Jim reached into his pocket.

Little Jimmy tore off the blank name tag from his gift bag. He wrote down a name and phone number and handed the pen and paper to his dad. "Call this guy, Dad. He'll help you."

Chapter Thirty-Six

Christmas Eve 2021

Teddy sat in the sanctuary where his family had been attending for the past four decades and tried to quieten his mind. Perhaps leaving for the beach the day after Christmas was too much. There was a lot to do to get ready for the trip.

He pulled himself back to the present, determined to enjoy the Christmas Eve service and the exquisite beauty of the 21st-century timber frame interior. The sweeping arches of the laminated wood stretched skyward, while vivid mosaic-stained glass windows lined each side. The Chrismon tree splashed thousands of tiny white lights on the wood-paneled walls.

He looked down the pew to his right and smiled. His mom and Frank chatted quietly among themselves. Next to his mom sat Katie. The late afternoon sunlight filtered through the stained glass and shimmered on her hair. He was next to her, followed by Mattie Grace and Sammy. Roger sat at the end of the pew.

It had been seven years since the first Christmas Eve service they'd all spent together, that was the year his dad and Katie's grandfather had passed. Katie's grandmother was still alive then—but wouldn't be for long. Her doctors had said only a few more weeks, at the most.

It was also the year of Drew's disappearance.

At the thought of Drew, Teddy instinctively swept the room for Andrew and Daisy. He spotted them two pews down, looking older and frailer than they should have. His heart hurt for them. Drew was their only child. If he were alive, he'd be sitting next to his mom telling her an outrageous story or digging through her pocketbook for a piece of candy. Forever the prankster, Drew would reach over and tickle the back of his dad's neck. Then Andrew would slap his neck and look at Drew with a suppressed grin.

Colleen sat next to Daisy, along with her girls, Jacob, and his girlfriend. Teddy stretched to see who sat on Colleen's other side. He tapped Katie's arm and whispered, "Is that Matt sitting beside Colleen?"

Katie shifted in her seat and nodded. "He's not going over to Andrew and Daisy's for dinner… Colleen's not happy about it, but at least he came to the service."

The first stanza of "Away in a Manger" rang from the organ, just as it had that Christmas Eve service in 2014, when he and Katie had attended with Sammy, Nora, and Claire. He laid his hand over Katie's and let his mind drift back in time.

He had walked in the back door of the farmhouse at six o'clock on Christmas Eve. His mom was at the house, adding the finishing touches to the meal, while he went to pick up Katie, Sammy, and Nora.

When they got into town, Teddy deliberately paced their trip for Nora to enjoy the Christmas lights along the route. He looked at her in the rear-view mirror. She looked weaker each day, but tonight her eyes danced with joy. It would be her last Christmas, so he turned left at the traffic light at the Butler Parkway and Washington Street intersection and drove through the downtown area.

An older gentleman had his Saint Bernard out for a nightly stroll. Otherwise, the square was vacant.

As large snowflakes peppered against the windshield, he decided it would be worth the extra few minutes to drive through the surrounding neighborhoods so Nora could see the professionally decorated homes. The snow-covered lawns of the large Victorian and Neoclassical dwellings in the center of town were sights worthy of a Hallmark Christmas card.

His mother came out the door as soon as she saw the car lights pull into her drive. Sammy helped Katie unload the trunk, while Teddy helped Nora out of the car. Nora placed her hand in the bend of his arm as he walked her toward the house.

Teddy said, "This is the first year Mom has decorated the house since Dad got sick."

"That's a good sign," Nora said.

While they enjoyed a few appetizers before dinner, Teddy opened the chilled bottle of champagne and placed the fluted glasses on a silver tray.

Teddy looked around the room, waiting for everyone to finish their conversations. Then he tapped the side of his glass. "It was my dad's tradition to give a toast each Christmas Eve before dinner." For a moment, his gaze rested tenderly on his mother.

As he recognized the room's somberness, something about the thoughts of Christmases past seemed to trigger a sense of reverence and reflection.

"We've been through many changes these last few months," Teddy said. "Admittedly, this is a sad Christmas in many ways. However, I hope we'll look back on this night as an evening to remember."

Everyone moved into the dining room to enjoy the meal. Following dessert, everyone prepared to leave for the ten-minute drive to the Methodist church.

The temperatures had already plummeted. Still, there was a special feeling in the air when they walked into the beautiful Gothic-style sanctuary. Tiny clear lights draped and cascaded the live twenty-foot Chrismon tree, and dozens of white poinsettias surrounded the bottom of the tree and scattered around the altar.

There was a sense of holiness in the sanctuary. Yet, a quiet stillness dominated the room as people arrived in anticipation of Christmas.

The congregation sang several carols before the minister delivered his message. When the sermon ended, a tall, dark-haired man dressed in a tuxedo came forward and sang, "Oh, Holy Night." At the end of the last verse, someone dimmed the sanctuary lights, and the minister lit his candle from the Christ candle in the advent circle. Then, he turned and lit the candle of the clergy standing next to him as the congregation sang *Silent Night, Holy Night, All is calm, All is bright.* An acute sense of unity permeated the sanctuary as the person at the end of each pew lit the next person's candle until everyone's candle glowed.

During the song's final stanza, the clergy members lifted their candles, and everyone in the church did the same as they raised their light to the Christ Child, the birth of whom they had each come to celebrate.

When the service ended, Teddy watched for signs that Nora was ready to leave. Instead, there was a look of awe on her face as she soaked in the beauty of the sanctuary. However, the real focus of her attention was on the massive wooden cross that hung behind the choir loft.

Smiling, she said, "I'm just trying to memorize the beauty of this lovely sanctuary and its twinkling lights. I'm certain I feel closer to God at this moment than at any other time in my life."

Teddy followed her moistened gaze to the wooden cross. On that holy night, celebrating the birth of our Lord, Nora was preparing to meet Him face to face.

As she sat quietly in the pew, she reached over and squeezed one of Claire's hands. Then her eyes shifted to the magnificent Chrismon tree and closed her eyes.

When the crowd had cleared, and only a few of the clergy remained, Teddy went to move the car to the front of the church.

When he came back in, he took Nora's arm and strolled with her to the front door. His mom and Katie walked ahead, and as Sammy reached the entrance of the church, he held open the heavy wooden door.

When they walked out into the wintery morning air, Teddy looked up at the sky. "It's Christmas Day," he said. Finally, he dropped to one knee in front of Katie and took her hand.

A smile spread across Nora's face. Then, she whispered to Claire, "Do you remember me telling you I prayed God would send our Katie a Prince to take care of her when I die?"

Claire nodded.

"God just answered my prayer."

Teddy pretended not to hear. Instead, he looked up at Katie, pulled out a little black box, and offered it to her. "Katie, I've been waiting for you all my life. Will you marry me?"

Katie stared at him, eyes wide, mouth half open.

Teddy's mouth went dry. Had he misread her cues? The ground felt hard and cold beneath his knees, and he suddenly felt foolish.

Nora squeezed Claire's hand and blinked back tears. "Give her a minute, Teddy. She's too emotionally charged or too cold to speak!"

Slowly, Katie sank to her knees in front of Teddy and cupped his face in her hands. When she kissed him, he thought his chest might explode with happiness.

Of all the kisses they'd shared, this was the one etched into memory. It seemed to last forever but was not nearly enough. When Katie finally drew away, her cheeks were wet.

Teddy cleared his throat, and said, "So, what do you think? There's a reason I asked you to marry me while we're all together as a family."

Katie laughed through her tears, and when she finally found her voice, she said, "Yes! Oh, yes, I will marry you!"

****

Katie's elbow jarred Teddy from his dream-like state. The service had begun, and it was time for the first reading.

He gave his wife a searching look. She looked beautiful, as always but her eyes lacked the sparkle he'd seen during the early years of their marriage. She was thinner, too.

Could it be she was just tired?

There had been a lot going on over the past few months, and now she was helping his mom plan her beachside wedding. Perhaps it was too much.

He'd lost his first wife to suicide. A fact that was never far from his train of thought. He could not lose Katie, too.

As if sensing his attention on her, Katie looked up at him and winked. It was that wicked little expression she reserved for when she had something up her sleeve.

He'd seen her slip a bottle of champagne into the freezer before they left the house. It would be icy cold when they returned home. He'd also found six chocolate-covered strawberries in the refrigerator earlier in the day. Of course, six strawberries weren't enough for the entire family to enjoy on Christmas day. But there they were, hidden in the crisper in a small white box tied with a red ribbon.

Katie slipped her hand through his arm. He wondered what she'd planned for them after they put Mattie Grace to bed. When he glanced at her face again, she was glowing. Not just smiling. There was definitely a glow about her.

She leaned over and whispered in his ear. "Merry Christmas, my love."

Chapter Thirty-Seven

They'd stopped by the restaurant and picked up the steak dinners. Nic had ordered the food after they left the mall. He specifically told the guy he wanted four separate meals with the largest rib-eyes in the house. So when he went to pick up the order, instead of finding four to-go boxes, he got a large tray weighted down with 3 lbs. of meat, a bag of Styrofoam containers filled with baked potatoes, four large garden salads, and garlic Texas bread.

Nic went around the back way, even though it took longer to get to the barn. When he made the last turn off the Corps of Engineers' property, they spotted Sheriff Riley's car parked behind the barn. Nic pulled in next to the Sheriff's car.

When he opened the back of the SUV and saw the cooler Fitz had filled with assorted beverages, he said, "How many people are you expecting tonight?"

Gripping his uncle's shoulder with his hand, Fitz said, "It's Christmas Eve, man. Let's live a little."

Nic laughed as they grabbed the bags of food and walked toward the barn.

When they opened the side door, Drew came down the steps with an envelope in his hand.

Nic nodded to Sheriff Riley, who was leaning back in a chair puffing on a fat cigar. He thought the sheriff's face was a little too red to have just finished working his shift.

They pulled the metal desk out to the middle of the room and set up a card table next to it. Nic set the food out on the table buffet style.

When they filled their plates and sat down to enjoy their meals, Nic offered each of them a thick envelope. "A little something to add to your Christmas cheer."

Once the meal was over, Nic opened up a beer and leaned back in his chair. "We've got a little housekeeping to take care of before it gets too late."

The men were quiet. The envelopes lay untouched. Perhaps they considered it bad manners to open the envelope in front of him. What the hell. It was a gift—a Christmas gift.

He let it go.

Looking at Drew, he said, "You sent the letter about purchasing the horse farm, right?"

"Here's a copy." He handed him an envelope. "I mailed it that same morning, just like you told me."

Nic nodded. "Now, we just have to wait for the reply. Which return address did you use?"

"The post office box in D.C.," Drew said. "Just like we discussed. I get a notification when an item is placed in the box."

A loud knock on the door startled Nic. He looked at the other men. "Are we expecting guests?"

Fitz reached for his pistol and motioned for Drew to do the same.

Nic went to the door and slowly opened it.

The man standing on the other side of the door was a big fellow. Nic glanced at Drew and then at Fitz. Both men drew their guns.

"Wait!" Sheriff Riley jumped to his feet, knocking over the beer next to his chair. "Don't shoot. He's a good guy."

Fitz and Drew lowered their guns but didn't put them away.

The big man tipped his hat, "I'm looking for Nic."

"I'm Nic. What can I do for you?"

"I'm Jim Levinson. Folks call me Big Jim." He explained his wife's mounting medical bills. He needed some part-time work.

Nic glanced at Riley.

Riley nodded.

"Do you know what we do?"

His eyes darted inside the barn before settling on Nic. It was nothing more than a slight twitch of one corner of his mouth, but it said all Nic needed to know.

The big man nodded and looked at the ground. "You're with the drug cartel. You've been dropping drugs on this property for several years. As the mayor, I've looked the other way, just like Sheriff Riley, but I need to make some extra money. My son says you can help me."

Nic looked at Fitz.

Fitz stepped to the door and said, "There's a family we need to watch. Are you interested?"

Chapter Thirty-Eight

A s he pulled onto the drive, Teddy glanced in the rearview mirror. Mattie Grace sat sandwiched between Sammy and Roger. Her eyelids were heavy, and her little head rested on Roger's upper arm. She'd had an exciting day from early morning, beginning with the daddy-daughter breakfast with Santa at the Art Center downtown. All social media networks had advertised the event, and the line had been nearly around the block, but Mattie Grace had borne it with uncharacteristic patience.

After pancakes and sausage with the big man himself, Teddy and Mattie Grace went by the pet store and bought a crate, a small collar, and leash for Katie's new puppy. Then they drove to Toccoa, to pick up the Yorkshire Terrier they'd picked out four weeks earlier.

Mattie Grace had spent the afternoon in the barn with Teddy and the puppy while Katie stayed at the house wrapping last-minute gifts, getting ready for Christmas. By the time they got to the Christmas Eve service, Mattie Grace was sleepy and ill-tempered. But what do you do? You just couldn't put a kid to bed at 5:30, because Christmas Eve was the most exciting evening of the entire year.

Teddy reached for Katie's hand. He motioned to the back seat. Katie turned and saw Mattie Grace dozing between her two favorite people.

Katie nodded. "She's had a big day!"

When they got out of the car, Roger immediately left for home, and Sammy went to his apartment. Teddy removed Mattie Grace from the backseat and carried her into the house while Katie walked ahead to unlock the back door.

****

Katie slipped into their bedroom and put on a pair of pajamas, while Teddy was upstairs putting Mattie Grace to bed. She grabbed the bag of gifts she'd hidden under the bed and went downstairs to the kitchen. She immediately added a couple of sticks of wood and ignited the flame. Then she slid the sofa a few feet over so they would face the warm fire. After that, she went into the kitchen and pulled the cheese, fruit, and a box of chocolate-covered strawberries from the crisper.

Humming to herself, she arranged the charcuterie board for her and Teddy to enjoy, she then placed the board on the ottoman near the sofa. She set Teddy's gifts around the charcuterie board in graduated stages. She fiddled with each gift—careful to find just the right balance.

A thump came from the back porch. Startled, Katie froze.

It wasn't like Sammy to come back to the big house after he'd said goodnight. If something had happened at the stable, he'd typically just text her.

Katie tip-toed to the picture window and looked through the blinds. Someone was moving in the shadows. A dark silhouette crept past the windows, heading toward the master suite.

Her muscles felt like lead.

Suddenly, she heard Teddy jogging down the steps. It would be hard not to hear his footsteps; he sounded like a herd of cattle. When he reached the kitchen, she turned and placed her fingers on her lips.

She whispered, "Someone's out there, and it's *not* Sammy."

Teddy reached to calm her. "How do you know it's not Sammy?"

"He's taller than Sammy. Much taller, at least 6'5", maybe taller."

Teddy cut off the lamp. Then he peeped out the window. "Wonder where he went?"

Katie pointed toward the master suite. "He walked past the window… while you were coming downstairs. Should I call 911?"

Teddy shook his head. "No. You stay here. I'm going out there."

"It's too dangerous, Teddy. We don't know who it is."

He gave her that cocky, crooked grin she usually loved so much. "Don't worry. I'll be fine."

****

Before cracking the back door, Teddy reached behind the clock on the mantel and grabbed his pistol. Then he slipped out onto the porch. The screen door screeched, and he saw a figure disappearing into the darkness. He stepped down onto the grass, then he stopped and looked around.

It was pitch dark.

What was he thinking? He should have turned on the floodlights before coming outside.

Teddy turned back and looked toward the garage where the puppy was staying. He stopped at the door and heard the puppy's soft whimper. She must have heard the intruder too. Of course, Ole Blue could sleep through a hurricane. When he looked up toward Sammy's apartment, it was dark.

He stepped away from the door, and a fist connected with the side of his face. For a moment, all he saw were stars, and the next thing he knew, he was on the ground. He scrambled to his feet fumbling for his weapon, but his attacker was gone.

Chapter Thirty-Nine

Early Christmas morning, before Mattie Grace woke up, Teddy walked around the grounds to ensure there was no signs of the intruder. Maybe he should have called the police, but he hated to ruin someone's Christmas Eve for what might have been a homeless person who'd lost their way.

Later, after Mattie Grace had opened her gifts, Teddy gathered the gift wrap paper and bows into a large trash bag and slipped out of the house. He placed the garbage bag in the trash receptacle and unlocked the lower apartment. Since the jockeys had gone home to be with their own families for the holidays, Teddy had hidden the puppy there overnight.

As soon as Teddy opened the door, the little puppy jumped up in the crate to get a better look. She whimpered softly while Teddy placed the small collar around her neck and attached a leash to the silver ring. Teddy grabbed the crate and sat it outside the door, then walked around the back of the garage for the puppy to do her business.

When Teddy got back to the house, Mattie Grace had displayed her gifts on the sofa in the sunroom. Just like her mother, she was an organizer. Although Teddy and Katie just knew she would love the horse stable and house, complete with furniture and animals, the gift she loved the most was the Glitter Dots Charm Set. A second-best gift was the Rainbow Sandland, which was a collection of multicolored sand. Finally, the gift Teddy was most excited about was the Ooze Lab. It was a soap and bath bomb set. Even at his age, he still loved a good science experiment.

Mattie Grace looked up when Teddy came in the back door. She had changed into the Disney princess dress and had placed the sparkling tiara on top of her tangled hair. Her eyes danced with excitement. Teddy put a finger to his mouth and placed the crate in the nearby mudroom before going into the sunroom.

"Where are we going to hide her?" Mattie Grace asked as she waited for Katie to finish cooking their breakfast.

"Let's remove the leash," Teddy replied, "and give her a moment to get used to the room until your mother finds her."

"What if she pees on the floor?"

"I walked her around the garage earlier. She'll be fine."

"I can't wait to see Mom's face!"

"Now, remember, Mattie Grace, this is your mom's gift. We'll all get to enjoy her because she's a part of our family, but it's your mom's puppy. Do you understand?"

She nodded. "Yes, Daddy."

A few moments later, Katie walked in and placed a platter of homemade cinnamon rolls on the table.

The puppy whimpered. Katie stopped and looked around. Then her gaze fell on the Christmas Tree.

The puppy whimpered again.

****

Katie looked at the floor below the tree. A tiny brown and tan Yorkshire Terrier sat among the gifts, the colored lights reflecting in her hair. She would have fit in a coffee mug. Her little head tilted to the right as she looked at Katie, her eyes bright and innocent. Then she shivered, her little tail wagging with excitement.

"Oh, my goodness," Katie said, already smitten with the puppy. A silly smile spread across her face. "I can't believe you got Mattie Grace a puppy for Christmas."

Mattie Grace looked at her father.

"Daddy! Tell her!"

"What?" He said with a mischievous smile, Teddy took a bite of a warm cinnamon roll. "Tell her what?"

"You know," Mattie Grace said, bouncing on the balls of her feet with excitement. "Tell her!"

Teddy looked up at Katie. "It's your puppy."

"My…" Katie rushed to the tree and picked up the puppy. It squirmed against her chest and licked her chin.

"She's beautiful. Just look at that adorable face."

Katie's grin grew wider. Bubbling with excitement, she carried the puppy to the table, cradling her in one arm while she ate a cinnamon roll. The puppy stretched up and licked her nose, and a rush of warmth filled Katie's stomach. Maybe this was what she'd been missing.

She reached over and laid a hand on Teddy's arm. "How did I get so lucky? You always know exactly what I need."

He looked at her and winked. "I just know… does Sammy know breakfast is ready?"

"Yes. He went to the stables to check on the horses first thing. He was going to take a shower and should be here in a minute. I can't wait for him to see my puppy!"

When Sammy walked in, Katie began to tell him the about the pup.

Sammy laughed. "We've met. The puppy woke me up at midnight. Finally, about two o'clock, I went downstairs and took her outside."

"Did she go back to sleep when you went back in?" Katie asked.

"Yep. She slept the rest of the night." Sammy crammed a bite of the warmed cinnamon roll into his mouth. "Hope you don't mind getting up for a two o'clock feeding again?"

Katie smiled. "Teddy will get up with her, won't you, sweetie?"

Teddy raised his eyebrow at Katie, "We'll see about that."

Chapter Forty

L ater, while Katie prepared Christmas dinner, Teddy set the dining room table, and Mattie Grace played in the sunroom with the puppy. Katie toyed with different names throughout the day, but nothing seemed to stick.

They discussed and discarded Molly, Maggie, Missy, and Pepper. Finally, Katie walked toward the kitchen to check on a dish in the oven. She turned to the puppy and said, "Come on, Lucy. Let's go into the kitchen and check on our Christmas dinner."

The puppy followed—and with that one command, she was Lucy.

When Claire and Frank arrived, their hands were loaded with bags of gifts and a large platter filled with assorted sweets. Lucy ran around in circles, licking and sniffing at their shoes. Then, suddenly, she squatted next to the island in the kitchen, and a little puddle of urine spread beneath her.

Mattie Grace screamed. "The dog peed in the house!"

Unfazed by the puppy's behavior, Katie reached for a paper towel and a bottle of rubbing alcohol and cleaned up the mess.

Frank lifted the puppy to eye level. "Could you be any sweeter? You're just a little bundle of soft fur." As he cuddled the puppy in his arms, he took an envelope from his jacket and handed it to Teddy. "This was on my desk yesterday morning. I forgot to give it to you last night but thought you'd want to know about it."

Katie looked at Teddy and raised her shoulders, but he was trying to process the contents of the letter.

"What is it?" Katie asked.

Teddy glanced at Frank and back to his wife and said, "An offer to buy the farm."

"That's not gonna happen."

Frank gave the puppy one more hug before placing her on the floor. "I understand, Katie— but it's nice to know someone will pay five million dollars for your property. The improvements you've made here have really accelerated the value of the place."

Before Katie could answer, the door opened, and Roger walked in carrying a tall box in one hand and a couple of shopping bags in the other. Mattie Grace yelled, "Roger, Roger, come and meet Mom's new dog. Her name is Lucy, and me and Dad picked her out."

Roger stooped over to hug Mattie Grace and petted Lucy. Glancing up at Katie, he smiled. "Someone has been a *very good girl*!"

Katie cut her eyes at Roger, but couldn't stop her grin. "Mattie Grace, wash your hands and get ready for dinner. The rolls are almost ready."

Mattie Grace placed her hands on her hips and jutted out her chin. "My hands aren't dirty!"

Katie's face felt hot. She didn't want to disturb the festive atmosphere. Yet, as much as she hated to ignore the outburst, she knew that was what Teddy would tell her to do.

"That's up to you. You can join us for dinner when your hands are washed."

Roger laughed. "I hate to say this, but she's a spitting image of your mother."

Katie turned and stared at Roger in disbelief. "Seriously?"

Roger nodded. "Oh, yeah. She sounds just like a sixteen-year-old Katherine." He looked at Sammy and raised his eyebrows.

Sammy grinned. "She's just like her. What was it Stephen used to say about her?"

Roger and Sammy yelled, "Beauty, brains, and spunk!" Everyone turned and looked toward the kitchen while the brothers laughed at the memory.

"In a few more years," Sammy said, "it'll be like having the silver circle all over again."

Silver circle. Katie remembered her grandmother talking about her mother, Roger, and Sammy being inseparable as teenagers. Their friends had coined the term silver circle because their bond was as strong as the precious metal.

"Yeah," Roger said, "but the silver will be more about our hair color than us leading Mattie Grace around to our way of thinking. She's way smarter than Katherine!"

Katie glanced at her daughter. Why hadn't she thought of that? It made perfect sense that Mattie Grace would share some similarities with her grandmother. Katie had quickly recognized a few of Claire's traits in her daughter, but she remembered very little about her own mother's personality. She'd never thought of her mother as a tough knot.

Mattie Grace was a beautiful child and smart, too, but that spunk... that's where it got tricky. Teddy knew precisely how to tame that rebellious spirit, but Katie struggled to reach the same balance. Somehow, that minor bit of information Roger and Sammy had imparted allowed her to look at Mattie Grace through a different lens... a paradigm shift.

Behind her, Roger cleared his throat. Katie glanced in his direction, and he motioned toward Mattie Grace. The outburst was over, and without another word from Katie, Mattie Grace was walking toward the powder room.

Children really should come with instructions. Katie let out a relieved sigh as she removed the rolls from the oven. She wasn't a bad mother, after all. She'd just been using the wrong techniques to manage her child.

Katie smiled and made a sweeping gesture toward the dining area. "It's time to eat!"

Teddy's eyes met hers, and she wondered what it would be like to have a little boy just like him. A blond-haired, blue-eyed boy with that adorable charm. She imagined that he, too, would rake his chubby little fingers through his windswept hair.

Suddenly, her arms ached for a baby.

Chapter Forty-One

T he movement of the ceiling fan caused a humming sound as Teddy stood on the back porch of the beach house and looked out at the ocean. The mid-afternoon cloud coverage was heavy, and the air was cool, still several families were on the beach.

Teddy pressed a number on his cellphone and waited. "Hi, Sammy. We just got here. On the way down, I thought we needed to make sure the farmhands understood the importance of watching out for any intruders. We're not sure if the Christmas Eve incident was just a random occurrence. But we can't be too careful."

"News travels fast in these parts. Tommy Parker dropped by this morning asking about it."

"I should've called him," Teddy said. "Anyway, call Sheriff Riley if you need him. Also, let us know if anyone out of the ordinary shows up while we're away."

After roaming around inside the house, Lucy discovered the porch. Her curious nature held Teddy spellbound as she sniffed out every object in sight. Finally, she found a comfortable spot on the rug. Her little body walked around in circles before curling up into a small, furry ball.

She was adorable.

Suddenly, a shaft of blinding sunlight cut through a gap in the clouds. Shielding his eyes with one hand, Teddy watched the clouds waft apart and drift away from the beach. The air warmed as the sun claimed its place in the sky.

The beach house had three levels. The ground level was where the owner stored the beach chairs, umbrellas, and pool supplies. The middle floor had a large, open kitchen and family area surrounded by two bedrooms and a full bath on either side. Due to the easy access to the steps going out into the yard, he, Katie, and Mattie Grace had taken the bedrooms on the left side of the middle floor.

Frank and Claire stayed in the bedrooms opposite Teddy and Katie, leaving one side of the identical third level available for Claire's oldest friends, Daisy Byrd, her husband Andrew, Laura Lewis, and her husband, Rhett. Frank's brother Phil, his sister Celeste, and her husband would occupy the other side of the third floor unless they'd prefer to stay at a nearby resort.

Teddy had reserved a large room off the King and Prince's main dining area for the rehearsal dinner on Thursday evening. The wedding rehearsal was scheduled for 4:00, and since the sun would set an hour later, Claire felt they would have plenty of time to show everyone where to stand and allow a few walk-throughs before dusk.

Katie stood inside the French doors, looking out over the beach. "Wow, what a view! How did you find this place?"

Teddy smiled and explained that one of the surgeons at the hospital had stayed there the previous summer.

"Well, I'm glad you found it. The layout is perfect for us!"

His friend had mentioned a beachside restaurant within walking distance of the house. In the other direction was a donut shop that served the best coffee on the island.

Katie said, "Will you and Frank watch Mattie Grace and Lucy while Claire and I go to the market? Mattie Grace fell asleep on our bed while I unpacked the suitcases, and I'm not sure about Lucy."

Teddy pointed to the corner of the rug. There she lay, curled up in a small ball.

Katie smiled.

"Of course," Teddy replied. "I may take a short nap, myself. Would you mind stopping by the seafood market and see if they have any fresh fish this afternoon?"

"Sure. Can you think of anything else?"

Teddy grinned and pulled her into his arms. "I could think of a few things!"

The following day, Teddy laced up his shoes for a run after breakfast and asked Frank if he wanted to join him. They each grabbed a bottle of water and took off down the steps. When they got to the beach, they turned right toward The Do-Nut Shoppe.

As they ran, the conversation was easy between the two men.

"By the way," Frank said, "On the way down here, I dictated a letter for my assistant to send in response to the offer we got about the farm."

"Thanks." Teddy shook his head. "I still can't believe we got a random offer of five million dollars. Who knew those upgrades and renovations would raise the value of the farm so quickly?"

Frank smiled. "Offers like that don't come around too often. I was telling Claire it was almost too good to be true."

A mile or so into their run, Teddy motioned ahead. "Looks like another new construction up there." They stopped to catch their breath.

Frank said, "It's very similar to the rental we're staying in. I wonder if it's the same contractor?"

The house had a medium-brown shaker exterior, which blended well with the stained wood of the wrap-around porches. They screened the portion of the porch facing the beach and added steps leading down to a small pool area. The most impressive part of the structure was the pitch of the roof.

Could it be a custom home? Giant sand dunes provided privacy for both sides of the house, and the seven palm trees they'd saved during the clearing process made it look like the structure had been there for years.

"You wanna go take a look inside?" Frank asked.

"Sure."

While Frank checked out the upper level, Teddy walked outside and found the contractor's name and phone number on the yellow builder's permit nailed to a tree beside the driveway. He pulled out his phone and took a picture of the yellow sign.

When he walked through the front door, Frank was looking up at the ceilings. "This is what you need, Teddy. Looks like it's over seventy-five percent done. You may have to pay a premium for a new structure like this, but this is a magnificent house."

Teddy showed Frank the picture of the permit. "Have you ever heard of this guy?"

"Nope. But I have a feeling that will change before the week is out.

Chapter Forty-Two

On Wednesday morning, Drew got a ping on his phone. The United States Postal Service had received an article of mail for his box number. Drew texted his contact in Washington and asked him to text a copy of the letter.

An hour later, Drew received another ping. He downloaded the attachment from the realtor.

We received your letter dated December 20th. My client appreciates your generous offer but has no interest in selling.

No joke.

Nic and Fitz pulled into the graveled drive just as Drew received the text. Nic looked at the message on Drew's phone. "Is he a freaking idiot? He just turned down five mil!"

He shook his head as he looked out over the farm. They'd only found the Whelchel farm after Henry Whelchel passed away from cancer... thanks to his nephew Fitz's relationship with Henry's daughter, Julia.

Julia was the nurse for Nic's sister. Fitz soon discovered a commonality with Julia when her father's cancer took a turn for the worse. A few days later, she became emotional talking about her father's recent assignment to hospice. Fitz invited her to coffee. Julie mentioned her mother would probably not keep the family farm once her dad died. Because of Fitz, the property had more or less been dropped in the cartel's lap.

Nic knew the Hawkins farm would cost more and be much harder to negotiate. An additional seventy-five acres would allow the cartel to build a small airport. The stateside facility would reduce the enormous transportation cost by half and allow greater expediency for their larger drug shipments back and forth from Colombia.

Nic thought about the recent dilemma as he and Drew walked around the barn.

Suddenly, Nic stopped. A huge grin spread across his face.

"What is it?" Drew asked.

"We've got the leverage here. We just need to get one of those prized Thoroughbreds from their stable and use it as a negotiating tool."

Drew looked down at the ground.

"What do you think, Drew?" Nic asked.

"Well, it depends on their security system… how sophisticated it is and how difficult it would be to bypass it. Some of those systems, I understand, are extremely hard to crack."

Nic pondered his next move. "We'll get Fitz involved. He grew up during the technological age and is very knowledgeable about electronic devices."

"You're serious about this, aren't you?"

Nic stopped, his face reddened, "You damn right, I'm serious. Who turns down a five million dollar offer? I'm going to get that farm, even if I have to blow it up to get them out of there."

Chapter Forty-Three

On Wednesday afternoon, Katie and Mattie Grace surprised Claire with a ladies' day in town. They went to lunch at the K&P Resort and afterward treated her to a mani-pedi at the local spa.

Late in the afternoon, Teddy and Frank went down to the beachside bar and grill to meet with the contractor. While Frank took a call, Teddy stepped back out into the sunshine and selected a table near the edge of the porch.

A tall gentleman dressed in jeans walked onto the porch. He wore a gray pullover sweater that zipped from his chest up. His ocean blue eyes were piercing and his neatly trimmed blond hair was much longer than either Teddy or Frank.

"Are you Teddy Williams?"

Teddy immediately stood. "Yes, you must be Luke Sullivan."

Then, he introduced Frank and asked Luke if he'd like a drink.

"An iced tea will be great," Sullivan said. "I don't have long… need to get back to my crew as soon as we finish. The men are waiting for their paychecks." Sullivan told them about the beach house. As Frank had guessed, the construction was seventy-five percent complete. Sullivan, however, was reluctant to commit to a completion date.

They were expecting a lot of rain in the forecast for January, but the landscaping could take as long as two months, especially if the rains continued into February.

"So, you expect a completion date of perhaps April 1st?" Teddy asked.

"If all goes well, that sounds about right."

Sullivan explained the extras in completing the patio area included a rock barbeque area that would double as a fire pit. In addition, a wrought-iron fence would protect the lot's perimeter.

"Is anyone interested in this house?" Teddy asked.

"Not yet, but we've had a lot of lookers. People get ready to talk price at about eighty percent completion. When they contact me, they've already walked through the place several times."

Teddy looked at Frank for a signal. Frank bunched his eyebrows, which meant he should let the man keep talking.

And Sullivan did just that.

They weren't surprised to learn that Sullivan had also built the house they were renting for the week. He mentioned several items that would not be included in the new structure, mainly because of the need to cut costs.

Frank was apprehensive about the cost-cutting strategy and probed a bit further. "Which amenities are you cutting? Anything we may want to negotiate?"

"The sub-zero refrigerator," Sullivan said, "but I'm adding a tankless water heater on both levels and a gas range in the main kitchen." When families rented for a large group, he'd learned everyone congregated on the main level to prepare meals. So on the top floor, Sullivan planned an efficiency-sized kitchen, a regular-sized refrigerator, microwave, and a bar area to double as a coffee station.

After he'd run through the list of changes, he said he needed to get back to the job. He slipped a card across the table to each of them and said if they had any questions to shoot him a text message.

When Sullivan drove away, Teddy picked up the card. He'd written $2.3M on the back. That was the information he needed.

He showed the number to Frank. "What do you think?"

Frank nodded. "Sounds reasonable."

Teddy and Frank picked up pizza on the way home. When they got back to the beach house, the ladies were already back from their afternoon at the spa.

While on the porch eating dinner, Teddy mentioned the beach house to Katie and Claire. They were so busy talking about the wedding plans they hardly acknowledged his remark.

Bouncing with excitement, Mattie Grace said, "Can we go for a walk on the beach after dinner and see the house?'

Teddy looked over at Frank. "What do you think? It'll allow us to see what the house looks like at night." One of the contractor's changes was to eliminate the windows on the family room side. It would give them a chance to see how it affected the view at night.

He smiled down at his daughter. "Sounds good. Let's take Lucy with us. Perhaps a long walk on the beach will help her sleep tonight."

****

When they returned to the rental house, he carried a sleepy Mattie Grace up the steps while Frank followed, cradling Lucy in his arms like a newborn.

When he returned to their bedroom, Katie was reading an article in a magazine.

He bent to kiss the top of her head. "I'm glad you're still awake. I want to tell you about a beach house we found."

Katie turned on her side to face him. Her eyelids looked heavy, and when he turned to get into bed, her eyes were closed and she was breathing softly.

Her focus for the next forty-eight hours would be on the rehearsal dinner and wedding. The beach house discussion would just have to wait until after the wedding.

Chapter Forty-Four

A t noon on Thursday, Andrew, Betsy, Rhett, and Laura arrived on the island. As they rolled their luggage into the elevator, Teddy said, "When you get settled, we'll grab a bite of lunch at the Beachside Bar and Grill. But first, we'll need to swing by the resort and pick up Frank's brother. He drove down from Kentucky yesterday afternoon, and he'll be joining us today for lunch."

"Where's Mattie Grace?" Laura asked. "I hope she's not out catching baby crabs in her pretty white flower girl dress."

Teddy laughed. "I wouldn't put it past her, but no, she went with Katie and Mom to take care of the last-minute decorations."

They chatted about family news on the way to the resort. But as soon as Philip Nordstrom got into the car, their attention turned to the man whose booming voice dominated the conversation on the drive over to the restaurant.

"This is a beautiful place. When I drove onto the island, the first thing I saw were those giant oak trees covered in Spanish moss. It was breathtaking."

Teddy nodded. "The entire island is that way. It's easy to fall in love with it."

"After I got settled in yesterday afternoon, I drove around the island to see the beautiful marshes. This island is a diamond."

Teddy parked the car, and they went inside. As they completed their lunch orders, Luke Sullivan came in with a couple and sat in a booth to their right. The couple placed a legal pad on the table, and as the developer launched into his spiel, Teddy spotted a long list of items.

He tried not to eavesdrop on their conversation, but it was hard not to listen. He wanted that beach house.

The man said, "We love this house and especially the location."

Luke said, "There's another couple interested in it."

The man pointed to his pad and looked back at Luke. "If we can agree on these items, we'll be ready to make an offer."

Teddy pulled his attention back to Andrew and Rhett, but they were chatting among themselves. Frank and Philip chatted about the family business.

Teddy looked toward the booth and overheard the man say, "A rock fireplace at the end of the screened porch is an absolute must!"

She flashed a smile. "Absolutely! And we'll pay for a larger swimming pool, Luke. We've got eight grandchildren who'd much rather play in a pool than in the ocean."

Teddy's back was to the booth, which muffled Sullivan's response. Teddy's stomach churned as they discussed the beach house.

HIS beach house.

As soon as they finished lunch, Teddy paid the check while the ladies stopped by the restroom. Folding the receipt neatly and placing it inside his wallet, he looked over his shoulder and made eye contact with the contractor.

Perhaps seeing Sullivan and the other couple was an omen.

There was nothing he could do about the beach house right now. He had a rehearsal dinner and his mother's wedding to attend. It would be New Year's Day before he could talk with Katie and get back to Sullivan.

Teddy glanced at the booth one last time before walking toward the door to leave. He locked eyes with Luke. Luke nodded. While the couple talked among themselves, Luke leaned back in the booth to stretch, then he discreetly put his hand to his ear and mouthed, "Call me."

****

The rehearsal dinner was a small but elegant affair with only twelve people in attendance. The men wore dress slacks, golf shirts, and jackets, but the women were more formally dressed. Even Mattie Grace wore a fancy dress with creamed color Elephantito shoes.

They were all seated when Philip arrived. His deep, baritone voice resounded throughout the dining room. He hurried over to thank Katie for inviting him to the rehearsal dinner.

"Where is my little princess?" he said. "That's the main reason I agreed to come to this wedding." He gave a robust laugh.

As soon as Philip asked about her role as the flower girl, Mattie Grace warmed up to him. "I'm wearing a white dress with a long sash that ties in a gigantic bow in the back." Her eyes twinkled as she stretched her little arms and explained the size of the sash. "I've got a white basket full of pink rose petals, and when Mr. Frank points his finger, I'll start spreading the petals before Ci-Ci walks in."

Philip hung on every word.

When Teddy announced they were ready for dinner, Philip asked Katie if Mattie Grace could sit with him and his sister and brother-in-law.

Mattie Grace clapped her hands with delight. "Can I, Mama? Please let me sit at their table."

"Of course, you can." Katie winked at Philip and said, "We're family now."

Teddy tapped the side of his glass. "I'd like to propose a toast."

He looked down at his mother. As much as he hated to admit it, she looked much younger since meeting Frank. "Mom may be small, but she's a tower of strength with a great capacity to love." He glanced at Frank and continued. "She's always said that your ability to love someone—says more about you than the other person. Her love is unconditional."

He looked toward Frank. "From the first time we met, I knew we would become great friends. So all I ask of you is to love and cherish her—and understand from the start that Mom's usually right!"

Teddy lifted his glass. "Please join me as we toast Claire and Frank… We love you both!"

When he'd finished his toast, Celeste stood and winked at her brother. She was four years younger than Frank and the CEO of a major pharmaceutical company. Teddy had never seen a woman so immaculately put together from her sleek, blonde bob to her polished turquoise pumps.

She tapped her glass with a spoon. Then she made a short toast to her older brother and his soon-to-be bride.

As the wait staff cleared the dinner plates, the guests enjoyed an assortment of desserts.

Just before eight o'clock, Katie announced, "We hate to break up this grand party, but tomorrow is a big day and our bride needs a good night's rest." Katie nodded at Mattie Grace and grinned. "I also need to get our six-year-old in bed before she falls asleep on the table."

****

Katie opened her eyes. Lucy was a warm presence on the pillow above her head; her tiny rib cage moved with each breath. Katie knew she should get up, but her body wouldn't budge.

Looking up at the ceiling, she thought about Claire.

It was her wedding day.

Whew, it had all happened so fast. They had planned a small, yet simple, destination wedding in thirty-five days. But, regardless of the size, it was a wedding just the same.

The bed was so comfortable. Why was it she always slept better on vacation? Five more minutes, and then she'd get in the shower and start her day. She inhaled the sweet smell of bacon frying and coffee brewing. Teddy was already in the kitchen preparing breakfast for their guests.

The guy was a saint.

Katie closed her eyes once more—she almost drifted back to sleep. Almost.

The ping from the nightstand startled her. She opened one eye as she reached for her phone. <Redemption's sick again. He's back in the trailer. I didn't bother you last night—it was late.>

That was her wake-up call.

She jumped out of bed. The next thirty minutes were a blur.

Her hair was still damp when she swept through the kitchen. She grabbed a cup of coffee and listened to Sammy retell the conversation with Dr. Scott. Katie rubbed her temples and wondered if Redemption had a previous propensity for ailments. That was all she needed—an ailing racehorse.

Teddy whispered, "Let me know what's going on with Redemption, okay?"

When she'd hung up the phone, she drained the last of her coffee and yelled, "Let's go, ladies! You gals have hair appointments starting in twenty minutes."

Teddy glanced over his shoulder while flipping a pancake. "Be careful on the road."

Katie leaned in and kissed his cheek, "Sammy's got it under control, but I'll text you the details when I get everyone settled at the salon." She headed toward the door, then quickly sprinted back to the kitchen.

How could she forget her own daughter?

"Teddy, Mattie Grace needs a bath after she finishes breakfast. Okay?"

Teddy smiled and reached for a slice of bacon. "Go," he said, pointing to the front door. "I've got this."

****

At 11:30 am, they were all dressed and pulling into the K&P Resort for the outdoor ceremony. As Teddy held the car door for his mother, he looked out over the ocean and said, "Mom, it's a perfect day for a beachside wedding!"

"It *is* a perfect day, Teddy." She reached up and brushed his face with her hand.

As he made his entrance through the elegant French doors, the local Methodist minister Tom Ward looked quite regal in his long white robe and broad white stole. A large silver cross hung from his neck. The minister was around the age of fifty. Medium build. Sandy blond hair. Warm brown eyes.

As they started over to the beachside arbor, Teddy overheard the minister say to Frank, "We've got to get this done before the end of the year, so you'll have an extra dependent on your tax return!"

Frank grinned, his ears turning pink, and grasped the minister's hand in a quick handshake. Teddy could already tell the two men had an instant bond.

Indeed, a good omen.

The violinist, seated to the right of the arbor, played her instrument as everyone found a seat facing the ocean. The vibrant, cloudless sky was the perfect backdrop for the white pavilion.

Almost time.

Teddy tucked his mother's hand in the crook of his arm. "Mom, you look stunning."

His mom beamed. "Thank you, Son."

"I don't think I've ever seen you so happy."

"Well, I admit, it's been a long time."

"I wouldn't hand you over to just anyone, but Frank Nordstrom is a good man."

His mom stopped and looked down at the ground.

Teddy reached for his handkerchief and wiped the sweat from his forehead. She'd been so careful in making this decision, and she and Frank were perfectly paired.

Please, Lord, don't let her back out of this marriage.

Frank was the best thing to happen to her since his dad died. To all of them, really.

"I was just thinking about your dad... and Bobby and Beth."

He forced a smile. "I'm sure you think of them every day, don't you?"

She patted the corner of her eyes with a tissue. "I'm not sure your daddy ever liked Frank, but I hope he'd be happy for us."

Thankfully, she wasn't having second thoughts. But why hadn't his dad liked Frank?

The minister and Frank approached the arbor. He glanced at Teddy and his mother, then nodded to Frank with a calming smile.

Teddy couldn't think of anything appropriate to say.

Of course, he had questions—but those questions would have to wait for another day.

Teddy breathed deeply, looked down at his mother, and saw fresh tears in her eyes.

"I'm sure he would. You were a good wife, and you deserve to be happy now."

"Thank you, Son." She squeezed his arm, a relieved smile brightening her face. "Frank's good for me. He makes me happy." Then she spotted Frank toward the arbor, and a sparkle lit her eyes.

"That's all that matters," he said.

Right on cue, Mattie Grace stepped in front of Teddy and his mother.

A princess. His beautiful little girl looked like a miniature princess wearing a white dress with a pretty bow tied in the back. In her left hand, she carried a white wicker basket. Her hair was perfectly curled, and the plastic tiara sat on her head.

Teddy whispered, "Honey, you look like a Disney princess." Mattie Grace looked up at him triumphantly.

He and Katie exchanged a smile as she walked to her seat. When Teddy looked back at his daughter, Mattie Grace stood tall, dropping rose petals on the white aisle covering. At the end of the aisle, she took her place next to the minister.

Teddy glanced at Frank standing at the arbor, smiling at his mother. It really didn't matter if his father had liked Frank or not. His father was gone.

Chapter Forty-Five

Turn off that flashlight!" the taller man said. "The lights are still on downstairs, and you can see the barn from any room on this side of the house."

"Okay, already," the other man barked. "But it's pitch dark out here."

The manicured ground outside the barn was identical to the yard around the big house. Although no flowers were blooming, the farmhands had long-since removed the dead plants from the previous season. The scent of fresh soil hung in the air.

As the taller man moved closer to the barn, he was careful to stay on the blacktop drive. "Stay out of that circular flower bed," the man said. "We can't leave any shoe tracks."

He pushed open the side door and smiled. "They left it unlocked. I told you it was just a matter of time." It had taken three visits to find the barn unlocked.

Removing a blue bandana from his pocket, he said, "Give me the flashlight." He placed the bandana over the lens and secured the rag with a rubber band before turning it on. The cloth dimmed the light enough to see the names on the doors of each stall.

"You got the peppermint?"

Looking down at his opened hand, he said, "Yeah, I got it." He removed a plastic bag from his pocket. "Here are the sugar cubes. I've already added the serum."

There was a loud click, followed by a humming sound. The first man stuck out his arm to impede the other man's movements.

Suddenly, bright lights came on and illuminated the middle area of the barn. The two men exchanged glances, then quietly retreated. When they got outside the door, they ran into the woods.

Chapter Forty-Six

As the sun peeked through the bedroom blinds, Teddy reached for the blanket folded across the foot of the bed.

Sensing his movement, Lucy jumped onto his chest. She licked his face as he crooned to her and rubbed the area behind her ears. When he found the sweet spot, she sat perfectly still, pressing her head into his hand. Lucy had bonded with everyone in the family, but her loyalty mainly depended upon whose lap she occupied.

"Do you need to go out?" he asked and scooped her into the crook of his arm.

When they returned, Teddy crawled under the covers, and Lucy climbed onto Katie's pillow and drifted off to sleep.

Katie turned over and snuggled up next to him. Wide awake, Teddy thought about the start of another year together. That was what New Year's Day was all about—new beginnings—an opportunity to start over with a clean slate.

Would this be the year Silver Circle or Redemption won a big race? Could they qualify for The Kentucky Derby, The Preakness, or The Belmont? Or perhaps all three—he hoped.

He was a big dreamer.

Was winning the Derby too much to ask?

Would he be able to convince Katie they should make an offer on the beach house? He really wanted that house. As much as they both loved the horse farm, it could be an overwhelming responsibility. They ate, slept, and breathed it. The beach house would give them a retreat from the humdrum, everyday stuff that seemed to drag so many couples down.

And he could afford to make an offer now. Earlier in December, he'd gotten an offer on Uncle Frederick's office building in Savannah. It was twenty percent higher than the asking price. When he showed it to his future stepfather, Frank said, "Sign the offer and return it before the buyer changes his mind."

Teddy had sent his e-signature less than an hour later, and the money was to be wired on the fifth day of January.

Katie's phone pinged. Yawning, she removed her arm from Teddy's chest and rolled toward the bedside table. "What are you doing awake so early this morning?"

"I'm just excited about the new year."

She gave him a sleepy smile. "Well, *I was* excited about getting another hour or two of sleep."

She fumbled her phone from the nightstand and blinked. "Oh, great. It's Sammy. I hope Redemption's viral infection hasn't spread to the other animals."

By the time she answered, Sammy had already hung up. No message.

Sighing, she got out of bed and fumbled for her house shoes. "Has Lucy been outside yet?"

"Yeah. About thirty minutes ago."

Reaching for a robe, she said, "I'll go make the coffee and call Sammy from the kitchen."

Out of respect for Frank, she'd invited his family to join their other guests for a New Year's Day brunch.

With the breakfast casseroles she'd made the previous night out of the way, she only had to make the shrimp and grits. Daisy and Laura would arrange the fruit platter, warm the yeast rolls, and make the mimosas.

She poured herself a cup of coffee, opened the door to the screened porch, and pressed Sammy's cell number.

He immediately picked up the phone and said, "Happy New Year, Katie!"

"Thank you. It looks like we're off to a good start."

Sammy told her that he and Roger had spotted a light in the woods after midnight, had gone down to the barn, and scared off two intruders.

She listened as she sipped her coffee. "Was anyone in the barn when you went inside?"

"Two men, but they ran out the side door when the lights came on. We didn't call the police because they would've been halfway to Atlanta before a car could get here."

Teddy placed a slice of leftover wedding cake on the table. She looked at him and smiled. Then Katie sat up straight in her chair. "Sammy, this makes me nervous. Please, take your phone with you when you go back to the barn."

Teddy tapped on the table and mouthed, "I'm going for a run."

Katie winked at him as she licked the frosting from her finger and mouthed, "Thank you!" She sat back in the wicker chair and shoved a bite of cake into her mouth.

As Teddy jogged down the steps to the beach, he pulled his cell from his pocket.

Sullivan answered on the second ring. He explained they'd spent the past two days with a rehearsal dinner and his mother's wedding.

Sullivan mentioned the couple he had met earlier at the Beachside Bar and Grill was about to make an offer. Still, they wanted a larger pool, a rock fireplace added to the end of the screened porch, and a Sub-Zero refrigerator on the main floor of the house.

"How close are they to making an offer?"

"I'm expecting one today."

Teddy nodded as he considered his response.

"With all the wedding activities going on here, I still haven't spoken to my wife yet."

"Man, I'd love to work with you, but if you want this house, you might want to get an offer together this morning."

"I understand, Luke. I'll see what I can do." Teddy stood with his phone to his ear as he wrote *my beach house* in the sand with his foot. "One more thing, you might want to show them the rental house we're staying in since it already has the Sub-Zero refrigerator and a fireplace on the porch… it's just a thought."

When Teddy finished his run, he brushed off his shoes, and left them in the back of his vehicle. The beach house would still be there in a few hours. He could make his case then and have an offer to Sullivan by early afternoon.

If that was too late, he'd deal with that, too.

Chapter Forty-Seven

Sammy stood at the dining room window watching for the SUV to come up the long drive. As soon as he saw the headlights, he was out the kitchen door, eager to discuss the events of the past week.

When Teddy cut off the ignition, Mattie Grace jumped out of the vehicle and ran toward the porch. "I missed you, Sammy! It wasn't the same without you."

Sammy broke into a wide smile. "I missed you, too, but you know I don't like weddings."

"But you'd *like* the beach house. Daddy said we're going back for spring break."

Katie and Teddy walked onto the porch, each pulling a piece of luggage. Katie and Sammy hugged. "Where's Roger?"

"He left about an hour ago… said he'll call you in a day or two."

Teddy handed Lucy's leash to Mattie Grace. "Here, sweetie, you need to walk Lucy around the yard for a few minutes before we go inside."

Sammy smiled as Lucy jumped around on the grass like a small bunny rabbit. He couldn't believe how much he'd missed the little puppy.

Teddy flopped down in the rocker and leaned his head back. "Talk to me, Sammy. Is it true someone was in the barn last night?"

"Sure is."

Katie set her suitcase down beside the door and turned to listen to what Sammy had to say.

Sammy leaned against the column on the porch. The night air had been unusually mild for New Year's Eve, and he and Roger had sat on the porch and made a fire after dinner. His arms waved as he talked about seeing a light in the woods.

Shortly after midnight, when they were getting ready to go inside, Roger had noticed the light again. "First, it was over here," Sammy noted as he pointed to the woods behind the pasture, "like they were coming up from the creek." He turned, pointing in the opposite direction. "Then it moved to the far side of the barn."

"Do you think it was some kids pranking around after the fireworks ended?"

"Don't know. The dogs from the other farms barked in the distance. Ole Blue got my attention when he started barking."

Teddy rubbed the dog's ears. "Ole Blue isn't easily excited."

Sammy looked down at his dog and grinned. "The light finally disappeared, but the leaves crunching in the woods didn't sound like an animal."

He'd never admit it to Teddy, but he'd been a little spooked out there in the woods. He hoped they'd catch these guys fast.

****

Teddy looked down at Ole Blue sitting at his feet. "Did you call 911?"

Sammy shook his head. "We snuck down to the barn in the dark... did I ever tell you about that time me and Roger and Katie's mama, Katherine, snuck out of the house late one night to spook the horses in the neighbor's barn?"

Teddy looked out across the pasture. Sammy was doing it again... getting off track. He didn't need to hear about Sammy's teenaged wild oats when there were important matters to discuss. But that was Sammy's way of dealing with stress. To lighten the mood, Teddy said, "The three of you were just a tribe of rebels, weren't you?"

"I guess so," Sammy said. He straightened his back and squared his shoulders, a serious expression on his face. "Roger thought it was some kids that got bored and were out pranking around—but I felt all along it was someone trying to get to our horses."

Katie wore a hint of a grin as she picked up the suitcase and opened the screened door. "I'm going to take my stuff upstairs while you guys catch up. Then I'll make us a pizza for dinner."

Teddy looked at her and winked. Then he looked back at Sammy. "Did you and Roger go inside the barn?"

Sammy nodded. "When we got down there, we unlocked the side door and went inside. I went over to turn on the lights, and then Roger told me to leave 'em off for a minute." Sammy drew in a long breath. "As soon as we went to check on the racehorses, we heard the side door open. You know it's got that squeak to it."

Teddy raised his eyebrows. "Yeah, we need to get that door fixed."

Sammy looked down at the ground, shuffling his feet.

"Well, what happened to the intruders, Sammy?"

"Roger flipped the light switch, the one on the back wall. When the lights came on, we saw two shadowy figures backing out of the barn."

"That must've been scary."

"You should've seen Roger." Sammy chuckled. "He took off toward the door, and then we heard a gunshot in the distance. It startled him, and he tripped over a bale of hay someone had left outside the stall, and by the time he got his footing, they were long gone!"

"Wait, did you say you heard a gunshot? Was it outside the barn or from one of the adjoining farms?"

Sammy hesitated, and then he shrugged.

He was good with horses, but it was probably too much to ask of Sammy to pinpoint the location of a gunshot.

"When did you discover Hershey was missing?"

"This morning. Me and Roger went to the barn as soon as the sun came up. Yesterday, after we got the stall disinfected, we moved

Hershey into Redemption's stall, and just to be safe, we moved Silver Circle and Mr. Zee to the other end of the barn."

"That was smart thinking. So, Hershey was in Redemption's stall, is that right?"

Sammy nodded.

"And none of the neighbors have reported seeing Hershey?"

Sammy shook his head.

"Are you sure you locked the barn door last night?"

Sammy looked at him with that blank look on his face.

"It's all right," Teddy said quickly. He had seen that look a thousand times, and he knew not to push the older man. If they'd locked the door before coming up to the house, the thieves would've broken a window or pried open the door to gain entry.

Teddy stuck his head inside the kitchen. "How much longer until dinner?"

"Another hour or so."

He looked at the pizza pan lying on the counter. "Sammy and I are going down to the barn to look around."

When they opened the barn's side door and turned the corner, Teddy barely missed stepping on a small bunch of candy canes on the floor. He laughed. "Have you been feeding the horses the candy canes from the house?"

Sammy shook his head, a slow, back-and-forth sweep of denial. Then, he stepped back—putting distance between himself and the peppermint candy.

"What's wrong?" Teddy asked. "Your face is white as a ghost."

He followed Sammy to the area where Silver Circle had stayed the past two nights.

Teddy poked his head inside. She had plenty of food and water, but the stall looked like it hadn't been mucked in a couple of days. He decided not to push the issue.

He stepped across to where Mr. Zee was staying, but his stall was dirty, too. Redemption's stall was almost spotless, but then they'd sterilized it after moving him to the trailer, and Hershey had only been there for a few hours.

As he looked around, Teddy realized whoever came into the barn had mistaken Hershey for Redemption. It would be a simple mistake to make in a dimly lit barn. Both horses were dark, but Redemption was at least a hand taller than Hershey, maybe more. Fortunately, the horses being moved around to different stalls had kept Redemption from being taken.

Only someone with knowledge of horses would know how much they liked peppermint.

"You were right, Sammy. These weren't kids out looking for a little mischief." As Teddy continued to ponder the situation, he rushed back to the pile of peppermint and found a small pail. When he knelt to scoop up the candy, he noticed several sticky sugar cubes on the floor underneath. That was odd.

He removed a tissue from his pocket and picked up one cube. It had a distinct odor of soured milk and dead fish. When he glanced toward the door, he saw a Ziplock bag on the floor. He picked it up and sniffed. It smelled the same as the sugar cubes.

Teddy reached for his phone and punched a button.

"Hi Doc, it's Teddy Williams. Hate to bother you, but we may have a problem." Teddy filled him in on the events of the last two nights. "Let's send these cubes to the lab for evaluation."

Chapter Forty-Eight

A t first light," Teddy said, "we'll organize a search for Hershey. I'll text the neighbors and find out if they've seen any signs of him on their properties. I can't believe he hasn't shown up by now."

The following morning, Teddy and Katie were sitting in the kitchen before 6 o'clock, waiting for the sun to come up.

Sammy ambled through the back door a few minutes later. "Morning."

"Good morning," Katie said. "Do you want some breakfast?"

"No, thanks. Just coffee."

As soon as the sun broke through the horizon, Teddy and Sammy took the Gator and went to the barn. The neighbors were already gathering and discussing the best way to search for the missing horse. Teddy held up copies of a grid he'd created of the surrounding properties within a five-mile radius.

"Thank you, guys, for your help this morning," he said. "We're not exactly sure how Hershey got out of the barn, but someone has been sneaking around our property while we've been away." He explained the barn would serve as Ground Zero, and he asked each group to report their findings every thirty minutes or so.

At their consent, he asked for the contact information of the fifteen volunteers helping in the search. Then they developed a coding system to use as they notified him of their progress.

They paired off and scattered in every direction. As Teddy heard the horses' hooves stomping throughout the woods surrounding his farm, he wondered who was behind the break-in that caused such a horrid nightmare.

He'd communicated with Tommy Parker several times throughout the morning, but Teddy was getting anxious. After three hours, there was still no sign of Hershey. He dialed his friend's number. "Tommy, have you seen anything out of the way since we last talked?"

"I rode around the perimeter of the property, and there are no fences down. Nothing that would suggest Hershey ventured outside your farm."

"It doesn't make sense. Where could Hershey be?"

"I can't answer, Teddy. But I saw one thing that raised my suspicions."

"What is it?"

"That old barn where you store your extra hay has a large red circle painted on the roof. The same marking I found on the side of my barn awhile back."

Teddy's mouth went dry. Those markings sounded like something a gang member might affix to a target. He had to find a way to secure his property and protect his family.

He'd just gotten off the phone with Katie when he received a ping. He looked at his phone. The bold X showed they'd found the horse.

He immediately called the number. "Talk to me."

"Teddy, you might want to call the police. We're down here at the road on the Corps of Engineers' property, near the edge of the old Whelchel farm."

He drew in a deep breath. "Is Hershey alive?"

"Yeah. Yeah, he's alive. Someone's tied his legs together, and he's heavily drugged. When we arrived, a scraggly-looking guy was trying to get the ropes unknotted. But as soon as he saw us, he darted into the woods toward the Whelchel's place."

Teddy paused, for a minute he couldn't breathe. The Whelchel place... it seemed like every bad thing in his life started there.

Chapter Forty-Nine

Teddy picked up the stack of mail, flipped through the envelopes, and spotted one from the lab. The report stated Trazodone as the active drug found in the sugar cubes, the same drug Doctor Scott had found in Hershey during the exam.

At dinner that night, Teddy said, "Doc thinks Hershey licked a cube laced with Trazodone and ingested enough serum to cause lethargic behavior. If he'd eaten all three sugar cubes, they would have made him deathly ill. He also said it could've caused extreme dehydration and maybe even death."

From the moment they'd bought Redemption and Silver Circle, there had been discussions about increasing the security at the farm. Now, after the incident on Christmas Eve and the break-in at the barn, he couldn't delay it any longer.

He squeezed a slice of lemon into his tea. "It's time we give serious thought to adding a security system."

Katie reached for the platter of pork chops and passed them to Sammy. "Maybe we should call Phil Nordstrom and ask him about the safety protocols they have in place. When we were there last, one of the trainers mentioned that, after dark, if anyone comes within ten feet of the property's perimeter, the auxiliary lights come on and a silent alarm notifies the guard in the security house."

A security house—he hadn't thought of that....

"That's a good idea," Teddy said. "Will you have time to call Phil tomorrow? Or should I?"

"I'll do it," Katie said. "First thing in the morning." She smiled at Teddy and looked around the table. "Anyone ready for dessert?"

Sammy and Mattie Grace cleared the plates while Katie brought the dessert dishes and pudding to the table. As she placed a bowl in front of Teddy, Sammy said, "I'll handle the chores in the morning while you contact Phil."

As Katie settled in her chair, she said, "You know, Sammy. Maybe you should be here when I talk to Phil. We need to discuss the pre-race protocol they use for the upcoming races. We have approximately eight weeks before the first race of the season."

"Sure," Sammy said. "When will Cappelletti get back from his holiday?"

Katie scrunched her nose and said, "I'm not sure." She looked over at Teddy. "Do you know, Teddy?"

He shrugged. "Don't know when they'll be back. He only said they'd be gone a month."

Sammy said, "How 'bout Mr. Zee? Are we going to include him in the training with Silver Circle and Redemption?"

Teddy wiped his mouth with his napkin. "Of course! He's got a big ole heart and a desire to win, and Cappelletti favors him since he won the Breeder's Juvenile."

"That's for sure. Cappelletti took a shine to Mr. Zee the very first day."

****

It took less than a week for the security company to install the sophisticated cameras and lighting system Phil Nordstrom suggested. The plan was pricey, but as Phil pointed out to Katie and Sammy when they called for his recommendation, "You've got to be prepared for the future. All it takes is one Derby win to elevate the profile of your facility. As soon as that happens, people will flock to Abington to see the winner. It will happen sooner than you think, believe me."

Katie asked. "So, you really think Silver Circle can win the Derby this year?"

Phil let out a hearty laugh and said, "Yes, I believe like many others that little filly will pull it off. At this time of year, all we talk about is who's going to win the Derby?" She heard him shift in his chair. Then he asked if they would need additional help from his trainer as they prepare for the spring races.

"Cappelletti told us he thought we were competent to handle the training process," Katie said. "But when he returns from Italy, we'll talk to him about staying on until we see what happens at the Derby." She raised an eyebrow and glanced at Sammy, who nodded in agreement.

"I'm glad you're asking him to stay on through the Derby. He's primed your horses to win," Phil said. "It's critical to follow the feeding schedules beginning fourteen days before each race. Cappelletti will walk you through the daily routine and be there to oversee the process. But before he returns from Italy, make sure every person dealing with your horses understands the importance of maintaining tight security and keeping to the oral schedule, be it food, liquids, or meds."

Chapter Fifty

Drew was in the bathroom rinsing out the coffee pot when he heard a vehicle pull onto the graveled drive. It wasn't even eight o'clock yet. Who would be coming to the farm at this hour?

He stepped outside and waited for Nic to get out of the truck. "What's going on?" Drew asked.

Nic propped his hips against the bumper. The tension in his shoulders belied the relaxed posture. "I've been awake most of the night. Unfortunately, we can't find the closing documents for this farm."

Drew's eyebrows went up as his head tilted. "Who handled the land transactions for the cartel?"

"Me... but Fitz and I were taken into custody on the day before the closing."

"Did you sign the papers beforehand?"

"I signed nothing... and I thought Matteo had signed them when he came up here to take over, but all he remembers about the first couple of weeks was being drilled by our attorney. Of course, it's been almost eight years, so I can't expect him to remember every detail from that time."

Drew leaned against the front of the truck. "Have you checked with your attorney?"

"He's dead."

Dead. The word was like a splash of cold water. This wasn't a game. "What—the attorney you used for the land closing is dead?"

"Yep."

"Well, that's unfortunate. What happened?"

"Our stateside attorney was working late one night when the heat pump in his office building blew up. The explosion killed him. Unfortunately, the legal files burned as well."

Drew stretched his arms onto the hood of the truck. "What are the chances of that happening?" He looked up to the sky and continued, "Who else would be privy to information about the closing?"

"I checked with headquarters and talked to our legal department the day before yesterday. They have nothing." Nic spread his empty hands. "We have a new accountant, and all he found was the wire transaction he traced through the bank records. He said they'd normally keep a copy of the closing documents on file in his department. Unfortunately, he can't find where we've paid any property taxes, either. The good news is the barn is covered by our insurance. It was added to the policy a month before the closing."

Drew picked up a twig from the ground. It sounded like the cartel ran a sloppy operation. They could carry out death assignments with precision, but preserving a legal document didn't seem to carry the same weight.

He pulled a knife from his pocket and whittled at the twig. If the cartel hadn't been paying the property taxes, that meant Mrs. Whelchel was still paying them.

"Your dad was Mrs. Whelchel's attorney," Nic said.

That much was true. Drew's dad had handled the closing for the sale of the farm. Drew wasn't involved, but he was in his dad's office when Mrs. Whelchel received a call from her banker that the money had arrived in her account. All he remembered about the closing was that the attorneys had agreed to a virtual close, but dates and times of real estate closings were often fluid.

Drew ran his hand through his hair as he considered the risk involved in getting those documents.

"My dad might've been old school, but he was meticulous about maintaining electronic files for every document produced by the firm. Of course, someone will need to contact the firm and request copies of the closing documents."

Nic straightened his stance and looked at Drew through beady eyes. "Well, that someone is *you!*"

The following week, Fitz showed up with a box in one hand and a pizza in the other. "Brought you lunch. And I got you the voice-altering machine you and Nic discussed." As he removed the device from the box, Fitz said, "Your calls can't be traced through phone records." He pointed to a button on the side of the machine. "You press this button to shut off the tracking function."

"Cool."

"This device will alter your voice to sound like you're from New England or the Midwest, or any dialect you choose. But just play with it until you're satisfied."

Drew spent the afternoon making calls to his cellphone. Finally, he found a voice with a dialect of someone from the northeastern part of the U. S. He liked it. It was a firm voice and very clear. His dad shouldn't have any trouble understanding him.

Next, he worked on the script. His father was so familiar with his speech pattern that he had to make sure he didn't give himself away. He read through the script several times, called his own cell phone, and recorded a message.

It sounded perfect! He pressed the number to the law firm and waited...

****

"Mr. Byrd, you have a call on line two."

"Thank you." Andrew drained the last of his coffee and wiped his mouth with a napkin. "Andrew Byrd," he said as he picked up the phone.

A man's voice came on the line. A smooth New England accent. There was a tinny quality to the sound, as if they had a weak connection.

Sam Smith and Nicolas Suarez, he scribbled. Then he jotted down a few more notes on his legal pad as he listened to the caller. Then, suddenly, he stopped writing. What did the caller just say? Did he ask for a certified copy of the original? His suspicions increased. How could Mr. Smith know he'd kept an original copy in his personal files?

Andrew placed his pen on the pad and rubbed his eyes. He wasn't about to take any chances. "Mr. Smith, I'll need a written request from Nicolas Suarez, along with a notarized copy of the request. Once I receive your request, I'll be happy to comply. My email is AndrewByrd@byrdandbyrdlawfirm.com."

"You'll have it," the caller said and promptly hung up.

Andrew stared at the phone, his hand still clamped on the receiver. That was a strange call.

He turned around and unlocked the safe. He went straight to the banker's box and found the file. The neatly organized folder had a federal express envelope protruding from the back. He removed the envelope.

Andrew pressed the refresh button on his computer, perhaps five times, waiting for an email to come through. Quickly, he flipped to his copy of the closing document and looked at the signatures. Matteo Suarez had signed the document. Andrew paused. Then he remembered questioning the name on the day of the signing. He read through the original document. It had Nicolas Suarez's name as the purchaser. They'd replaced the original documents at the last minute with copies bearing the name of Matteo Suarez.

He couldn't shake the thought that the tone and intonation of the attorney's speech was familiar. But he finally shook it off. His mind often played tricks on him.

The next fifteen minutes seemed like an eternity. Then, finally, an email popped up. Andrew clicked on the email, and read: *As discussed, this note serves as a request for certified copies of the original closing documents for Land Lot #405, belonging to Mrs. Henry Whelchel of Abington, Georgia.*

Mr. Smith represented a Washington, D. C firm. *DC—seems like nothing good ever comes from there.*

Chapter Fifty-One

Three weeks after Cappelletti returned from his visit to Italy, a snowstorm swept through the state. It was an early morning in January, exactly one month from Christmas Day.

Katie watched the last large, fluffy snowflakes falling from the sky. Then a peppering of smaller flakes, similar to sleet, began. The scene from the kitchen window was even more spectacular as the darkness faded away. A seven-inch blanket of white crystals had covered the pasture since midnight. Lit by the rising sun, it looked like the earth had been dusted with diamonds.

As Katie stood at the picture window and sipped her coffee, she marveled at the impeccable symmetry of the fallen snow. Only the hand of God could create such a brilliant scene. The perfectly covered ground looked as if He had opened the heavens, poured the snow with a measuring device, and eliminated the landscape's dips, crevices, and sharp angles with a smooth surface.

The screen door to Sammy's apartment opened, and Ole Blue ran down the steps. He paused, waiting for his master to follow. Sammy finally emerged wearing a toboggan cap, a heavy coat and scarf, and a pair of slick rain boots.

He walked toward the big house.

"Got any coffee?" Sammy asked as he stuck his head in the back door.

"Of course, come on in,"

****

Once the snow melted, Cappelletti, Katie, and Sammy settled into a daily routine with the horses. Unfortunately, the cold weather had affected Mr. Zee's agility. Since his injury, they worried that arthritis would settle in his bad leg and decrease his speed over time.

The extensive hours of training allowed Katie and Sammy to see first-hand how championship Thoroughbreds prepared to win the big races.

The stress of the long winter days wore on Katie, too. So she joined the gym to relieve some of the stress.

One day, while Colleen and Katie were leaving yoga, Colleen said, "I went online last night and bought two tickets to the Fox Theatre in Atlanta to see *Wicked*."

Katie stomped her feet with excitement as she held the door for her friend. "Oh, my gosh! We should've planned a couples' weekend."

Colleen scrunched her face. "But it could be a girls' weekend, instead."

****

On Wednesday before Valentine's weekend, Teddy ran into Matt at Andrew's office. They chatted just inside the foyer for a few minutes. "Are you free for lunch?" Teddy asked. "I have an idea I'd like to run by you."

They walked around the block to The Grill. It was only eleven o'clock, and the lunch crowd hadn't come in yet.

When the server took their orders, Teddy said, "I've been thinking about a surprise for the girls when they return from Atlanta. Perhaps a nice Valentine's dinner on Sunday night at the farm. We could hire a professional chef to prepare a gourmet meal. Is this something you'd like to do, or have you made other plans?"

Matt shook his head. "No. I haven't planned anything. We're kind of in-between that place in our relationship—we're not just friends, but we're not...."

Nodding, Teddy said, "I understand. I was wondering why you and Colleen didn't use those tickets at the Fox for a romantic Valentine's weekend."

Matt rolled his eyes and chuckled, "We've been through a rough patch lately."

When the server brought their lunch orders, Teddy reached for the ketchup and said, "Katie and I have been through rough patches, too. But we always get through it."

"It sounds like you guys make a good team."

Teddy crammed a french fry in his mouth. "You know women love romance much more than guys. Katie's worked hard getting our horses ready for this year's racing season, and Colleen's had a rough time of it since Drew disappeared. You're the first guy she's even looked at in almost eight years."

Matt unwrapped his burger. "I'm surprised to hear that. But then, I've never been good at reading members of the opposite sex."

Teddy chuckled. "Neither have I, but Colleen must see something in you she likes."

Matt shrugged and looked at his food in silence. He nibbled at his cheeseburger and took his time chewing it. "I don't know, Teddy. I'm not sure I'm getting anywhere with her, and I'd hate to keep wasting my time–and hers, too."

Teddy nodded. "I know the feeling. When Katie and I first met, it took a couple of years for us to get together. But it was totally worth the wait."

Matt glanced away and said, "I've never been very patient." Then he looked at the ceiling, his shoulders slumped. "At times, it feels so right... and other times, I feel like Drew is sitting in the room with us." He chuckled and raised his opened hands. "Damn guy's presence is everywhere—and I didn't even know him."

Teddy struggled to find the right words. "I won't lie to you, Matt. Colleen and Drew were close. They met in high school, built a great life together, and were the envy of all their friends. Then Drew went completely off the grid, and God only knows what happened to him. It was hard on her."

"When Colleen talks about it, she gets upset, and I hate to question her." Matt paused. "It must have been hard on you, too... never really knowing what happened between Drew and Nancy Leigh."

Teddy nodded. "It was. I'd just like to understand how they got together. Of course, we were all good friends." Teddy waved a dismissive hand. "But that part of my life is history."

Matt reached for his glass of tea. "How about you and Katie?"

Teddy smiled at the thought of his wife. "Katie and I were older. We met on the same day my marriage with Nancy Leigh ended."

Matt winced, and Teddy chuckled.

"Katie and I have a great marriage, but it's not perfect, and we're still growing into each other." He glanced at Matt. "But at the end of the day, we want to make each other happy. I've lived through one unhappy marriage, and I'll do whatever it takes to keep the peace in this one."

As they finished their lunch, they talked about Thoroughbred horses and the upcoming races required to qualify for the Derby.

Horse racing was a subject that interested Matt. "When is the next race?"

"The Florida Derby is March 6. Are you and Colleen interested in going?"

"Maybe." He checked the calendar on his phone and nodded. "Yes. I'm free that week. I'll ask Colleen if she'd like to go."

As the waitress cleared the table, Teddy punched something into his phone and said, "I just texted you the name of the hotel where we'll be staying. You may want to book a room as quickly as possible. They fill up pretty fast."

"Thanks, I'll do that," Matt said. "And let me know what I can contribute to this Valentine's dinner. I'm not much of a romantic, but I'm willing to try."

Chapter Fifty-Two

O n Sunday morning, Teddy took Mattie Grace over to his mom's to spend the night. He hurried home and got the barn chores out of the way, then went inside to inspect the house. The cleaning lady had been there on Friday, but he scrubbed the kitchen, anyway. When the fixtures and surfaces were gleaming, he roamed from room to room, straightening papers and wiping away invisible dust.

The dining room had to be perfect. That was the most critical room. He lifted the box of silver and placed it on the table. There was a lot more silverware than they usually used. Three forks, two spoons. He didn't know what went where.

He pulled his phone out of his pocket and pressed Roger's number.

"Hey, man. I need your help. Matt and I've hired a gourmet chef to prepare dinner for Katie and Colleen tonight. I thought I had it under control, but I need help with the table setting. Have you got time to help me?"

Following Roger's instructions, Teddy set the dining room table and placed the silver candelabras on each side of the flower arrangement.

He stepped away from the table and admired his work. The table looked just like something Katie would put together for a dinner party. Telling her he loved her wasn't enough. Tonight, he intended to show her!

Teddy took a moment to walk back through the house, then he rushed upstairs and removed his tuxedo from the closet. He had exactly twenty minutes to get a shower and dress before the chef and violinist arrived.

Teddy heard a car outside the kitchen. When he looked out the window, the Uber driver was turning around in the driveway. Matt was dressed in his tuxedo. Damn. Drew had never looked that comfortable in a tux. Even on his wedding day, he walked around with his tie loosened the entire day, an easy grin on his face like he was looking for a pickup basketball game.

Matt nodded to the driver and walked onto the back porch. When Teddy opened the door, Matt said, "Dang, I hope this works!"

Teddy laughed as he patted Matt on the back. "Me, too, my friend. Me, too."

****

When they turned onto the driveway, Katie got a fluttery feeling in her stomach. It was only when the car stopped in front of the garage that she saw the sign: "Katie and Colleen, please enter through the front door."

Katie rolled her eyes. "I hope Teddy didn't decide to paint the foyer this afternoon. He's been talking about it for weeks." She got out of the car and glanced around the yard. Everything looked normal—no signs of paint cans or dirty brushes at the back of the house. When Colleen opened the trunk, Katie grabbed the Nordstrom bag and grinned when she saw the silver negligee.

Colleen admired the back of her pink dress. "I'm so nervous. I want this to work out, but at the same time, I'm afraid because I want everything to be perfect." She turned around and said, "Does that make sense?"

"Of course. Just be yourself and let the relationship evolve."

Colleen twirled around, adding a flirty twist to her hips. "Well, if this doesn't do it. I don't know what will."

"Are you kidding? Matt's going to love that dress. It's gorgeous."

"I can only hope."

"Come on in, Colleen. Apparently, we're riding to the club together tonight." When they got to the front porch, Katie slowly turned the doorknob. The lights were low, and violin music played in the background. Katie looked at Colleen, and they both giggled. A simple arrangement of red roses sat in the center of the dining room table.

Colleen said, "Can you believe the guys have gone to this much trouble? I mean, you're married to Teddy, but Matt and I are... we've just started dating."

Katie stopped at the head of the table. Goodness. Teddy had positioned the crystal goblets perfectly. Water. Red wine. White wine. He'd even folded the napkins like a restaurant. The forks were in the correct order, too.

He did this for me...

"Look at the table, Colleen." Gingerly, Katie ran a hand across her nicest linen tablecloth. "This china belonged to Teddy's grandmother." Then rubbing a finger along the edge of the plate, she said, "It was a wedding gift from Claire."

The chef had quietly appeared, carrying a silver tray with four champagne flutes. He was tall and handsome and looked very regal in his white chef's jacket.

A knot formed in Katie's throat, and her eyes misted over. *We've never even used this china before.* She stepped back and looked at the table. He'd thought of every detail, including a scripted name card at each place setting.

She heard a movement in the foyer, looked up, and saw the hope in Teddy's eyes.

Katie fluttered her eyelids and did a flirty little twist of her mouth. A trademark sign that meant she loved it. Slowly, he walked over to her, his gaze skimming the beautiful cream-colored dress she'd worn for dinner. Oh, that look. There were no words needed… when he had that look on his face. It had been a little while since he'd looked at her with appreciation. But there it was….

Finally, he lifted her hands to his lips, "Happy Valentine's."

She smiled and nodded to the table. "Thank you," she managed to whisper.

Teddy gave her a princely half-bow. "You're welcome."

Katie stole a glance at Colleen. She was giggling at something Matt had just said. They made a good-looking couple.

The four chatted while the chef plated the food. When the chef finished, he looked from Teddy to Matt and said, "If you guys can take it from here, we need to get going."

Teddy handed the chef a white envelope. The men left through the kitchen door as everyone found their places at the table.

****

During dinner an alarm on Teddy's watch sounded. He excused himself from the table, went into the mudroom, and checked the video screens. The movement had come from the backyard, but the screen was now clear. The screen monitoring the barn was also clear, but screen number four showed someone walking through the pasture toward the Whelchel's farm. That seemed odd, but he watched the screen for several minutes, and the man never emerged from the woods.

He sent a quick text to Sammy asking him to keep an eye out.

When he returned to the table, Matt asked, "Is there a problem?"

"No, just someone cutting through to the Whelchel's farm."

Teddy picked up the napkin from the table, and said, "We almost forgot! Matt and I've been talking about the four of us going to the Florida Derby in March." Teddy swept his gaze from Katie to Colleen. "Would you ladies like that?"

Katie clapped. "Oh, Colleen, that would be such a fun trip. Please say yes!"

Colleen looked at Matt and tilted her head. A couple's trip—a long weekend with a room for each couple.

"It's just a race, Colleen." Matt chuckled as he picked up his water goblet. "We're not asking you to perform espionage."

She couldn't blow her response—but she didn't want to seem overly anxious either. "It sounds like a fun trip." Then she straightened her shoulders. "I'm a partial owner of a racehorse, you know."

Matt said, "What? You own a racehorse!"

When they'd eaten the last delicious morsel of the surf and turf, the guys cleared the dinner plates from the table. Matt removed two dessert plates from the sideboard, placed one on the table in front of Colleen. Then he grabbed a raspberry from his own plate and popped it into her mouth, his finger lingering on her lips a moment longer than necessary.

A surge of electricity coursed through Colleen's body.

Matt jerked his hand away. "Ouch, Colleen, you shouldn't bite!"

It was comical, and everyone laughed. He'd felt the spark, too. She felt her face redden.

He returned to his seat while Teddy served himself and Katie. A slow seductive smile spread across Matt's face as he reached for his dessert fork and placed it on his plate.

At ten o'clock, lights from a vehicle appeared through the side window. Teddy looked outside, "Matt, the limo is here."

As they prepared to leave, Matt wrapped his arm around Colleen's waist. "It's time to get this lady and her smoking pink dress home."

Colleen swatted at him, but she beamed all the way to the door.

Chapter Fifty-Three

On Sunday afternoon Drew arrived at the neighboring garage apartment later than normal. Unfortunately, he still didn't have a water heater in the newly constructed bathroom at the barn. Not that he'd ever get one.

It was later than expected when Sammy finally came out of his apartment and meandered down the road to the barn after finishing his midafternoon snack.

Drew couldn't linger.

He locked the door of the apartment and glanced toward the barn. He never knew when Sammy would return. The apartment was spotless… not even a few random breadcrumbs on the countertop.

Drew quickly showered, dried the shower stall, rolled up his towel, and stuffed it back inside the duffle bag. He looked around the bathroom one last time to make sure he'd left no traces of his visit. Then he noticed the stubble ring in the sink. Sammy must've forgotten to wipe it clean.

Just before Drew opened the door to leave, Teddy pulled into the garage and removed a long flower box tied with a red ribbon from the back of his SUV. Drew looked at the date on his watch.

Of course, it was Valentine's weekend.

As soon as Teddy went inside his house, Drew grabbed his duffle bag and closed the door behind him. Instead of going back to the barn, he hid out in the woods behind the garage. He wanted to see what Teddy had planned for Valentine's Day.

Shortly thereafter, an Uber car pulled up, a dark-haired guy dressed in a tuxedo got out. The guy was carrying a tote bag, a bottle of spirits extending from the top. It was the same guy he'd seen at Angie's soccer game. As he watched him walk onto the back porch of the farmhouse, Drew's stomach felt like he'd swallowed hot coals.

He might as well stay and see if Colleen showed up.

An hour passed when another car pulled up the drive. It was Colleen and Katie. Drew moved a few hundred feet to get a better view. Colleen bounced from the car, and then she checked herself out in the car window while Katie removed her luggage.

She looked entirely different with her hair pulled up in a fancy up-do, but Drew couldn't peel his eyes away from the tight-fitted dress.

Together, Colleen and Katie went around to the front of the house.

Colleen looked happy.

But how could that be?

He stifled a laugh. He would be foolish to think his wife had spent all this time grieving for him. They'd been soulmates... until he'd got tangled up with Nancy Leigh. He shook his head as he pulled a piece of bark from a fallen tree.

Who was he kidding? Of course, he wanted her to be happy.

As darkness fell upon the farm, Drew snuck around to the front porch. He tiptoed up the steps and watched from the window.

Hmm. A dining room.

It had been a parlor when Mr. and Mrs. Hawkins were alive. Then, just as he shook the memory, the dark-haired guy delicately moved a strand of Colleen's hair behind her ears and mumbled something. Colleen dropped her head, face as red as fire.

What had the guy said to cause her such embarrassment?

Teddy laughed, and Katie clapped her hands. This guy wasn't just a flash in the pan. He was a part of their lives. It seemed Teddy and Katie not only approved of this relationship, but they were a comfortable foursome—actively supporting it.

How could he have left such an amazing woman?

Colleen looked gorgeous in the hot pink dress. He wanted to reach out and touch her, but from the looks of things, that would never happen again.

It wasn't like she'd never seen a man in a tuxedo before. Drew had worn a tuxedo… on his wedding day and another time or two at the club. Anyway, it wasn't a big deal, but Colleen watched the guy as though she couldn't get enough of him.

Drew had a clear view of Colleen, and that dreamy look on her face made his stomach churn.

He knew that look.

Drew took one last glance at his beautiful wife.

He'd seen enough.

Drew left the porch and walked back around the house, not bothering to slip into the woods behind the garage. He was so despondent he'd failed to realize the full moon had provided a lighted path as he walked down the road to the barn and crossed over into the pasture toward the Whelchel's place.

Chapter Fifty-Four

(March 2022)

The Florida Bay Derby was the first of the calendar year. The March event was also the first Mr. Zee and Redemption were to take part in since November's Juvenile Breeders' Cup.

As determined as ever, Katie registered all three horses, to give them experience racing against championship Thoroughbreds on a professional track. With winnings from the November race in addition to the other races they had entered, Mr. Zee and Redemption were well on their way to qualifying for the Derby. Silver Circle needed this race for even a chance to qualify.

It would be a heck of an accomplishment if all three made it to the Derby. And as much as Teddy would love for Katie's horse to win, there was a part of him that was rooting for Mr. Zee. The colt had heart, and Teddy wouldn't be surprised if he turned out to be the most competitive of the three. What a thrill that would be!

The farm was humming with anticipation when Sammy, Cappelletti, and the crew left for the race on the last Saturday of February, two days earlier than scheduled to allow the horses to acclimate to the warmer weather. The early March temperatures in Tampa averaged between 73-79 degrees each day. Even a ten-degree difference in temperature could have a massive impact on a thousand-pound animal.

With the horses in good hands, Teddy and Katie, along with Colleen and Matt, left on the following Wednesday.

The plane touched down at the Tampa International Airport, and as soon as they walked into the terminal, reporters surrounded Teddy and Katie, yelling questions about Silver Circle. The media from all over the country, especially those from the East Coast, fed the frenzy within the equine community about Silver Circle winning the next Triple Crown.

Teddy marveled at the number of people in the terminal. If they attracted this much attention in March, just think how crazy it would be if one of their horses won the Derby. He hadn't fully grasped the extent of Phil Nordstrom's influence on the industry, but word of his endorsement for Silver Circle had clearly spread.

Katie shifted her carry-on bag and accepted a microphone. "Training three Thoroughbred horses to compete in the spring races is like having three children running in a high school track meet." She looked around at the press corps and grinned. "We want all three horses to win!"

Her final plug before the interview ended, "Keep your eyes on Silver Circle. She's a safe bet."

It was true, but Teddy was never one for a safe bet. He'd keep his money on Mr. Zee.

On the morning of the race, Katie woke early. She dressed quickly in her hooded sweatshirt and jeans and tip-toed out of their hotel suite. She stopped in the hotel lobby for coffee, poured the hot liquid into a Styrofoam cup, and took a cautious sip. Then she wandered over to where Sammy and Cappelletti sat eating their breakfast. Cappelletti seemed calm and confident as he scanned the sports section of the local newspaper. Across the table, Sammy stared down at his hands, tearing a paper napkin into tiny pieces.

"Are you guys ready to get started?"

Sammy immediately jumped up, but Cappelletti said, "Go ahead. I'm going to finish my breakfast and stop by the office before I go to the stables. I should be down there within the hour."

The air was clear, and the temperatures had already passed seventy degrees. The national weather forecast for the Tampa area predicted temperatures at race time in the low eighties.

As soon as she and Sammy got away from the main building, Katie asked, "What's going on? You look disturbed."

He took another sip of his coffee and finally said, "Something happened last night."

"Yes, you mentioned that much back at the restaurant. What happened?"

He stopped to remove the lid from his coffee. "Someone's mad about the jockey assignment."

Katie suppressed a laugh. "Sammy, seriously? Someone will always get upset about a jockey assignment. Come on—you know that. That's the reason jockeys have an agent."

He hunched a shoulder, not arguing, but not agreeing either. They walked in silence to the stables.

As they entered the northern end, six men huddled together at the opening on the opposite side of the barn.

Katie hesitated. She was too far away to hear what was said, but the looks on their faces showed concern. Were these the guys Sammy had said were upset? Or was there something else she should be worried about?

She put it from her mind and followed Sammy to Silver Circle's stall.

They were brushing the filly's coat when an official came around and asked Katie if she had a moment.

"Of course. Just give me a moment to sterilize my hands. Then, I'll be right out."

When she walked out of the stall, the official was standing outside the southern entrance, scrolling his phone.

She waited a polite couple of minutes for him to notice her, then gave a little cough and said, "Excuse me. I didn't catch your name earlier."

Without glancing up from the screen, he said, "I'm an official with The Florida Bay Derby."

"Right, you said that, but you didn't state your name."

He shuffled his feet and continued to stare at his phone. "Terrell Watson. There's been a development we need to discuss."

She suppressed a sigh. A 'development' was never a good thing. "Okay."

He glanced at the men moving away from the barn and then looked back at his phone. Finally, Katie said, "Sir. What about the development?"

He looked up this time, with a slight smirk on his face. "The jockey assigned to Silver Circle has been in the infirmary all night and can't race."

Katie looked around the stable and noticed the same group of men she'd seen earlier huddled under a tree a couple of hundred yards from where she and the official talked.

"Okay. Well, thank you for letting me know. How soon can you assign another jockey to her?"

The official's phone pinged. He said, "Excuse me, ma'am. I need to respond to this text. Just give me one minute."

Katie stepped a few feet away to allow him privacy to complete his text. When he finished, he stepped closer to Katie and said, "Okay. Here's the deal. We're one jockey short for the race, and unless you can pull some strings and have one flown in by two o'clock, in time to get tested and weighed, then your horse cannot race today."

"But bringing in a replacement is *your* responsibility!" Katie put her hand to her mouth and briefly turned her head away from the official. When she'd calmed herself, she continued, "Our registration documents state you provide a jockey for each animal." Then she pointed her index finger as if she were pecking on a keyboard, "It was in bold letters."

"There was an emergency." The official shrugged. "It happens sometimes. We normally bring in a couple of extras for an event of this size, but one had a death in the family and the other missed his flight. So, I'm sorry, ma'am, but if you don't find a jockey by two o'clock, your horse will get scratched from the race."

Katie went back inside the stable and found Sammy. "I've got to go back to the room and make some calls."

"Are you okay?" Sammy gave her a concerned look. "What's wrong, Katie? You're pulling at your lip, just like Mama used to do when she got upset."

Katie nodded. "Yes. I'm fine."

As she walked up the hill, Katie pulled out her phone and called Teddy about the jockey.

"What are we going to do?" she asked in a voice barely above a whisper.

"First, let's not panic. Something's not right about this situation. I've never heard of an official approaching an owner about getting their own jockey. It may be too late to contact the agent."

Katie said, "A jockey must meet certain credentials. You can't just pull someone in off the street."

"We'll make some calls," Teddy said. "We've paid the entrance fee, and we've got the registration papers. It seems someone is trying to get Silver Circle disqualified." She heard him scurrying around. "I'll be dressed by the time you get here."

"Okay. I'll stop by the restaurant and grab some fresh coffee."

"I wouldn't go back into the restaurant. Instead, I'll order room service when we hang up. By the way, if you run into anyone, smile and act like it's a normal day at the races."

Katie smiled as she walked into the lobby of the hotel, but she felt like she'd just had the air kicked out of her lungs.

****

Katie watched as Teddy poured coffee into their cups and served himself a healthy helping of eggs. "Do you want some eggs?"

"No. Thanks. I can't eat anything." She placed her hand over her mouth. "My stomach's in knots. I'm feeling nauseous."

Teddy reached for her plate and placed a piece of toast and a couple of strips of bacon on it. "You're not pregnant, are you?" he teased.

Katie smiled. "I wouldn't mind if I were. I've been thinking about it a lot lately."

"Me, too. And it just so happens, I know a doctor that can help with that..." He winked as he handed her the plate. Then he filled a small bowl with cheese grits and set it on the table. "Eat this," Teddy said. "You can't go through the day without food in your belly. I can't let my little mama get sick."

Katie slowly chewed a bite of toast as she looked at her plate, then she glanced across the table. "I think we should have another baby."

Teddy's eyes danced with excitement. "Great, let's get to it!"

She felt a rush of relief. "Really? I wasn't sure you would be on board with it, what with everything going on at the farm."

"I hadn't given it much thought, but when I saw you in that silver negligee on Valentine's night, I changed my mind."

"Is that the reason you said something about it being our lucky night?"

He gave her a mischievous grin. "In more ways than one."

His desire for another child wasn't completely unexpected. She was pleased that he, too, had been giving it some thought.

She sipped her ice water, trying to remember if she'd packed the silver negligee. Then she pulled herself back into the moment. "How could something like this happen?"

Teddy grinned. "Well, it's quite simple. You put on that little negligee you wore on Valentine's night, and *Voila*! It will happen quicker than you think."

Katie's eyes rolled. "Not that, silly. I'm talking about a jockey. You'd think they'd bring in extras for these big races. Anything could happen. Besides getting a virus, a jockey could get injured during training. It just seems so irresponsible!"

"Good point." Teddy took a bite of bacon. "Give me the name of the guy who approached you earlier."

"His name is Terrell Watson. But now that I think about it, he was holding a lanyard in his hand, but I couldn't tell if it was an official Florida Bay Derby lanyard or not."

Teddy shoved some eggs into his mouth and chewed. Then he washed it down with some juice. Finally, he looked at Katie and said, "Was Watson wearing an official green shirt, one with Florida Bay Derby on the front?"

Katie sipped her coffee and held the cup close to her chest. "Hmmm, it was a green shirt, but it didn't have any writing on the front. In fact, I'm pretty sure the shirt was a Lacoste."

Teddy reached for his phone and scrolled.

"What are you doing?"

"Hold on… I'm looking for Phil Nordstrom's number. He'll know what to do."

"Should we call the agent?"

Holding the phone with his right hand, Teddy asked, "And you're certain the logo on the shirt was an alligator?"

She nodded. "Yes. I'm certain."

He pressed the number to Nordstrom, then put the phone on speaker so Katie could hear the entire conversation.

"Hello, Teddy. How's it going down in Tampa?"

"It looks like the temperatures are going to be warm for the race later today."

Phil's robust laugh echoed throughout their suite.

"But that's not the reason I called. It seems we've run into a problem with the jockey assignment for Silver Circle. Do you have a few minutes to talk me through how to handle this situation?"

"Of course, Teddy. What's going on down there?"

Teddy explained the current state of affairs. When he finished, Phil was livid. "Give me a few minutes. I'll sort this out and call you back."

When the call disconnected, another immediately came through. Teddy glanced at the caller I.D. and said, "Hello, Sammy. How are you this morning?"

"Hi, Teddy. Listen, I think you might need to come down here."

"Talk to me, Sammy. What's going on?"

"The drug tests are all clear," Sammy said. "But someone just stopped by and asked me if I knew the owner of Silver Circle. I told him I did. Then, he told me to give you a message."

"What kind of message?"

"He said to tell you if you let Silver Circle race today, he would make sure your best friend didn't make it home tonight."

Silence.

Teddy wiped his mouth with the cloth napkin and placed his cup back on the saucer. "Is that all he said?"

Sammy hesitated, "... Something about your friend who disappeared from the farm. It didn't make any sense to me."

Teddy shook his head, not trusting himself to speak.

"What's he talking about, Teddy?"

Teddy got up and walked over to the French doors leading out to the small veranda. He continued to hold the phone to his ear with one hand while he rubbed his temples with the other. His head was pounding.

"Okay...," he said. "First things first. Make sure someone stays with Silver Circle at all times. Don't leave her alone... you got it?"

"Yeah. One of our team has been with Silver Circle since I got down here a couple of hours ago. The horses have just received the morning feeding and won't get anything more to eat until after the race this afternoon."

Teddy leaned against the railing and closed his eyes. "Okay, Sammy, since they've just received the final feeding before the race, hang up and call the vet and get him to give Silver Circle one more drug test. We need to make sure this guy didn't tamper with her feed."

Sammy said, "Should he repeat the test for all three?"

"Good point. Please do it. Call the vet, tell him I'll pay the extra cost. But go to the back of the stall so no one can hear you talking, okay? And don't leave Silver Circle alone for one minute. Call me back."

In five minutes, Teddy's phone rang. He went back inside the suite.

Teddy said, "Okay, Sammy. Great. Now, tell me what this guy looked like. I need to know everything—what he was wearing, his height, skin, and hair color—all of it. Tell me every minor detail you remember about this guy. And leave nothing out, okay?"

Teddy wrote *tall, shiny, black hair, dark complexion, green shirt, nice shoes, and a smooth talker.*

"You won't believe this, Teddy," Sammy added. "As the man walked off, he turned to me and said, 'tell your boss what I said. If the horse races, his friend dies.'"

Chapter Fifty-Five

When Phil Nordstrom called back with information about the jockey situation, he roared with laughter. "It seems there's been a misunderstanding, Teddy. Your jockey never went to the infirmary. He was out on the track first thing this morning and went through the pre-race workout."

"Something's not right, Phil," Teddy said. "Now, two of my people have been approached about Silver Circle not racing today. The first person tried to convince us the jockey was sick. The second guy used a little more threatening approach. He told Sammy if the horse raced this afternoon, my friend would die. The guy referenced a good friend of mine, who disappeared several years ago. The strange thing is, no one has seen or heard from the guy since he disappeared."

"That is unusual," Phil said. "But once you gain a certain level of recognition, people dig around until they find something they can use against you. So was the disappearance of your friend highly publicized in the news?"

Teddy said, "Yes, of course. Do you think someone's trying to sabotage the race?"

"Let me make another call," Phil said. "We have a special committee that handles threats, like the one you just mentioned. It's not an official committee. It's just a group of owners who look out for each other. We usually put a couple of thousand in a pot each year to cover any expenses the group incurs, but it's well worth the membership fee." He paused. "Do this—text me all you know about this guy. I'll take the information to the group and find out how we can protect your animal. We'll talk again before the race. Until then, proceed as if Silver Circle is racing today, but tell your team to limit their contact with outsiders."

When Teddy hung up from the call, it was after ten o'clock.

Katie came in from the porch. "What did he say?"

"He said for us to proceed like we're going to race Silver Circle this afternoon. Do you feel like going down to the stable to check on Sammy and the crew? I need to text the descriptions of that guy to Phil so he can contact the committee."

"Yeah, sure." Katie grinned as she brushed the side of his face with her hand. "I need the exercise."

When she approached the stable, Terrell Watson suddenly appeared from behind a large tree. He reached for her elbow. "Ma'am, I need you to follow me, please." Katie's eyes darted. No official derby lanyard—no name tag. Nothing showed his credentials. She was close enough to smell the sweat of his body. His phone was in the same hand he'd used to grab her elbow, and he didn't have a firm enough grip. Watson reeked of stale alcohol. She jerked her arm away from his grasp and ran toward the stable, straight for the security office.

The security guard looked up and said, "Ma'am, are you okay? Why are you running?"

Katie bent over and placed her hands on her knees as she tried to temper her breathing, "That guy... out there in the green shirt... just grabbed my arm and told me to follow him."

The security guard radioed backup, "You'll be safe here. Have a seat until I come back for you." He walked out and locked the door behind him.

Katie texted Teddy and told him what had happened. He was still on the phone with Phil and relayed the information to him. In a few moments, two officials for the Florida Bay Derby and another security guard unlocked the office door. They offered to escort her back to their suite.

"We're locking it down."

Katie said, "Locking what down?"

"The stables. To ensure the safety of the animals."

Before they left, the loudspeaker announced for everyone other than trainers to evacuate the stable until after the race.

When Katie walked out of the stable, the patrol door was open, and Terrell Watson sat handcuffed in the backseat. His gaze met her, his eyes blazing with such menace that she almost took a step back.

****

At one o'clock, Teddy and Katie left the hotel suite, and Katie texted Sammy on the way to the track: <"We're on our way down. Is everything okay down there?" >

Sammy shot back. <"Yep. The horses are ready to walk out.">

They waited for the horses to leave the stable and make their way to the starting gate. When Mr. Zee, Redemption, and Silver Circle came by, Katie whispered to each animal. Then she gave her final instruction to the jockeys. Mr. Zee would want to get out front fast, while Redemption would need to be held back, then give him a push toward the end.

Silver Circle's jockey was the last one to whom she spoke. "This girl is special," she said. "She needs a firm hand, but if you handle her correctly, she'll reward you. Let her get used to the pace of this one." Katie turned and patted Mr. Zee's back. "But when she gets close to this guy, let her go. Let's see how fast she can make it to the finish line."

"Yes, ma'am," he said. "I hope to deliver you a win today."

"I'll be one grateful lady if you do!"

He grinned. "Well, if she's as good as all the hype, it should be a cakewalk."

"All I ask—is for you to go out there and give it your best shot. Silver Circle will do the rest."

When Teddy and Katie found their seats, Matt and Colleen were waiting for them. Matt handed them each a bottle of water. "You're gonna need this," he said as he wiped the sweat from his forehead and looked at his phone. "The temperature is already 85 degrees, and the humidity from the cloud coverage that rolled in at lunchtime is wicked."

"Thanks, man."

Matt looked around the stands and said, "The energy in this place reminds me of being at a college football game. These people are serious, aren't they?"

Teddy watched with binoculars as they led the horses into the starting gate. "Yeah, that's true. There's a lot of time and money tied up in these animals. These races last only a few minutes, but they're high-intensity moments." He glanced at Matt. "Would you like to wager a bet this afternoon, my friend? Which horse do you think will win this race?"

"I know very little about horse racing, but since my lady here is part owner of Redemption, I placed a bet on him." Matt covered his mouth and pretended Colleen couldn't hear. "Don't tell Colleen, but I placed bets on Silver Circle and Mr. Zee, too!"

Everyone laughed.

"Can I use those binoculars for a moment?" Katie asked. "I want to make sure our horses are in the gates and get approved."

Matt asked, "What do you mean, approved?"

Teddy handed the binoculars to Katie and leaned forward. "On the day of the race, they assign an assistant starter to each horse, and he enters the starting gate with them to make sure the jockey is secure. They also make sure the horse's feet are firmly planted, and the head's pointed straight when the gates open."

"I'd never noticed," Matt said.

"You're not alone. Most spectators don't know this, but they issue each horse a gate card after approval. So they keep detailed records on each animal."

"Not sure I'd want that job...."

Teddy removed the top from his water bottle. "The gate crew has one of the most dangerous yet essential jobs at the racetrack. Having a solid gate crew ensures the safety of both equine and human participants." He took a long swallow of water and then turned his attention to the gates.

The bell sounded, and the gates opened. The horses were right out of the gate. Mr. Zee was number three in the lineup, Redemption at four, and Silver Circle came in at number eight.

The one to watch was Tiramisu, a big chestnut with a long stride and only one loss for the season. Katie gave the binoculars back to Teddy. She closed her eyes and clamped onto his arm. Teddy watched through the binoculars. Then, at the half-mile marker, he handed them back to her and said, "Katie, here, watch the ending of this race. Silver Circle is now within three horses of the lead."

Katie took the binoculars and watched as Silver Circle rushed by Mr. Zee. She then passed Sterling, who was narrowly leading Mr. Zee. Coming into the three-quarter-mile marker, she and Tiramisu raced neck and neck with the leader. Blackjack, the horse that had led throughout the race, showed signs of running out of gas. White lather poured from the animal's neck, and his breathing became labored from lack of oxygen. The second Blackjack fell behind, Silver Circle passed him, followed by Tiramisu, Sterling, and Redemption. Blackjack was no longer a contender.

"Look at that, Teddy," Katie said. "Two of our horses are in the lead. Even Mr. Zee is hanging in there today."

Katie had spent very little time in the stable because of the events earlier in the day, but for once, a jockey had taken her instructions seriously. He had followed her instructions to the letter and had actually listened.

Colleen hung onto her binoculars and yelled, "Go, Redemption! Go, boy! Make me proud!"

Silver Circle led narrowly. Katie yelled for her to get to the finish line. "Go, girl, go! You can do this!"

Redemption was three wide and trailing Tiramisu and Sterling, each by a nose. However, Mr. Zee was gaining speed with three furlongs to go.

Silver Circle got her second wind and shot ahead, going into the last turn. Redemption followed suit and snuck up from the outside as Mr. Zee appeared at his right.

Katie jumped up and down and grabbed Teddy's arm. "We might just win this race!"

She stared down at the track, as if she could '*will*' the little filly an extra burst of energy. Neck and neck, Silver Circle and Tiramisu pounded across the track. Tiramisu was ahead by a nose when he crossed the finish line and won the race!

Katie's breath froze in her throat as Silver Circle thundered across an instant later, and Redemption finished a solid third! The win had slipped from their grasp, but that couldn't diminish her pride in what they'd accomplished. As Mr. Zee crossed the line in fifth place, all three of their horses were on the path to eligibility for the Derby.

Chapter Fifty-Six

On Tuesday before the Louisiana Derby, Frankie Burel was carrying his breakfast tray to the table when Thomas Leone called to him from across the dining hall.

"Burel!" Leone gestured to an empty seat at the table he shared with Trent Smith, the jockey for Silver Circle, and three other jockeys. "Come join us."

Burel usually sat alone. He enjoyed reading the sports section of the paper during breakfast, but he knew Leone wouldn't stop until he went over to his table.

He hesitated and removed the toothpick from his lips, "Sure thing."

Burel sat down at the table and placed his newspaper under the breakfast tray. Unfortunately, the sports section would have to wait. Leone had already begun his discussion about a trial run Wednesday night before the race.

Leone, the lead jockey, was the unofficial leader of the group. The rumors had circulated among the jockeys that Leone would no longer receive preferential treatment because of the incident the previous fall involving Katie Williams. He was notably the best jockey in the pack, but the industry wouldn't tolerate unprofessional behavior, regardless of how good he was in the saddle. They had assigned him to Tiramisu, and he wasn't happy with the assignment.

On the other hand, Burel was highly pleased to be riding Redemption, because he had already established a great rapport with the owner and trainer.

Leone explained the details of the trial run while the jockeys seated around a large table in the common dining room reviewed their daily agenda.

For the first time in Trent Smith's career, he'd received one of the top horses in the race, and it didn't look like he was about to risk losing it. "Management will never go for it!" Smith said with an edge to his voice.

Leone shook his head. "Do you think you could've said that any louder, Smith?"

Smith looked around the dining room, then lowered his gaze. His voice softened. "The owners will never allow it. It's also a huge liability for management. An injury could cost the industry a lot of revenue."

"Who says we're going to ask management?" Leone said. "I've arranged to use the track after midnight tomorrow night. That will give us a better idea of how our horses will respond to the track."

Burel sipped his coffee as he listened to Leone's idea. Damn guy. The only time he could ever remember Leone being unhappy with his horse assignment, and he thought he deserved a trial run. Of course, he'd do anything to beat Silver Circle, but a trial run wasn't the answer. And neither was working the horse for eight hours each day. Leone was working that horse into the ground, and that was a recipe for failure. But Leone couldn't let Katie Williams beat him. Well, he should've kept his hands to himself when he'd worked at her farm. Then he wouldn't have to worry about needing a trial run, and Burel could be reading the sports section instead of listening to this ridiculous conversation.

"Are you crazy?" Smith said. "You know what will happen if we get caught."

Leone rolled his eyes. "We won't get caught." Then nodding at three of the jockeys across the table, he said, "We've got a plan."

Burel finished his breakfast and was headed toward the barn when a bearded man in a ball cap walked up to him.

"Listen, man. I overheard the conversation at the jockeys' table this morning. You don't know me, but I know for a fact that Leone doesn't care about you or your horse. He's just looking out for himself. He's a bitter man."

Burel removed the toothpick from his mouth. "Thanks for the warning."

The stranger waved a dismissive hand. "If you run your horse in the trial, your horse could get injured. Hell, anything could happen. Trust me, you don't want to get involved with Leone. Take the night off. Go into town. Whatever you do, stay away from the barn tomorrow evening."

He hurried away without waiting for a response.

Burel watched as the man walked toward the track. He'd never heard of a trial run until this morning, and he'd been a jockey for almost fifteen years. The majority of the jockeys might pretend to go along with the idea, but few would be willing to jeopardize their careers because of Thomas Leone's insecurities.

On Wednesday night, Leone stood at the edge of the pavement just outside the stables. Smith and the three other jockeys came over, leading their horses. There was an air of excitement within the little group. This just might give them the slight advantage they would need to place in the race. Many horses were racing at the Louisiana Derby for the first time, and the heavy humidity affected their speed. Most of them welcomed a chance to acclimate their horses to the climate and the track.

Where was Burel? Maybe it was just as well... he thought seeing Burel ride would give him some useful insight, but he really shouldn't be giving this advantage to his strongest competition.

At 12:45, the jockeys mounted their horses and walked in a straggly line toward the starting gate—Smith and his best buddy, Felix Mason, fell in line last. Of course, Leone led the way.

As Smith walked behind Mason, he commented he sensed an ominous intention from Leone. Mason brushed him off as he continued to the gate.

Everything was just like a race, except it was dark, there were no crowds, and the jockeys weren't wearing their silks, only the jodhpurs and riding boots. They'd listed Tiramisu among the top five contenders, and Leone needed to maintain that ranking to qualify for the Derby.

Leone felt the tension within Tiramisu as the horses entered the gate. He checked the stall—it appeared clear of any trash or debris.

He looked around to make sure everyone was inside the gate.

Something was wrong. Tiramisu kept rearing up. Finally, at precisely 1 a.m., the lights surrounding the track came on just as Leone had instructed. He'd paid the guy one hundred bucks to roll out the starting gate, and an additional hundred dollars to slip inside, flip the switch, and then run like hell! Hopefully, the trial run would be over before any members of the racing committee were the wiser.

As Leone continued to calm Tiramisu, he realized he hadn't considered the danger of the trial run without the assistant starters. He'd never given them the respect they deserved; he thought their role was a waste of time. But, on the other hand, there was so much media hype surrounding Silver Circle, Redemption, and Blackjack that Leone had to make sure he knew Tiramisu well enough to pull off a win. Leone's workouts with Tiramisu, the first two days of the week, were more rigorous than was typically done during race week, but he did it anyway.

Leone was the top jockey at the event; he'd won more races than several of the other jockeys combined, and his winnings surpassed any other jockey in the country. But this year, winning had become personal, and regardless of how it affected the horse, Leone wasn't about to let Katie Williams' horses win.

Tiramisu was struggling to look straight ahead. Then, looking over the top of the gate, Leone noticed someone was missing.

Who was missing? He did a mental count. How about Smith? A movement from the hill caught his attention, and there he saw Trent Smith leading Silver Circle back toward the barn. Maybe the lack of assistant starters had spooked him.

Leone couldn't understand that at all. Horse racing caused him to get out of bed every morning. At 5'1", he weighed in at 112 pounds on most days. His nutritional trainer kept him on a strict diet even during the off-season throughout the summer months. Winning a race was like a drug to Leone. Once he'd tasted a win, he needed a second, third, and a fourth. He especially needed *this* win!

He'd done well financially, but it wasn't just the extravagant lifestyle that Leone enjoyed. He loved the feeling of power as he mounted a thousand-pound animal and the pounding of the horses' hooves striking the ground as he sped across the track, causing a sudden surge of adrenalin to shoot through his body.

As he turned back around, something caught his eye on the ground. There was a dead rat at the side of his gate. He'd missed it before because it was hidden by the shadows. So this must be what was spooking Tiramisu.

Leone tried to calm the horse, to no avail. Then he heard the gate lock. It was too late to say anything. There was a fifteen-second delay between the time the gate closed and when the horn sounded.

Leone patted the horse and spoke to him in a slow, soothing voice, hoping he'd place his front legs on the ground before the bell sounded. But the horse refused to stand still.

When the bell rang, Tiramisu thrust out of the gate, but instead of running, he reared up and jerked around facing the gate. Leone struggled to hang on to the reins. When the horse finally settled its feet on the ground, Leone had slipped to the side of the horse. Slowly, he regained the position. The horses on either side barely missed a calamity.

The thousand-pound colt reared up one last time, but his front legs landed on the ground with such force that Leone somersaulted through the air.

He lay in a sea of darkness.

As soon as management found out about the accident, rumors circulated the committee would call off the race. Jockeys followed stringent rules—and the four of them had violated their contracts by agreeing to take part in an unauthorized run.

Teddy's phone pinged. "Look at this text, Katie." He explained the committee had voted unanimously to suspend the four jockeys for the rest of the season, and the industry imposed a ten thousand dollar fine. Teddy slid his phone back into his pocket.

"But it sounds like the race will take place as usual."

Katie rolled her eyes. "Thomas Leone has ruined his standing within the racing industry. There's a rumor going around that none of the other owners would agree to let Leone near their horses after Philip Nordstrom told them what happened to us. He's lucky his agent was friends with Tiramisu's owner."

"I know one thing," Teddy said. "The committee better get ready for a lawsuit. Tiramisu may never race again."

It didn't take long for several owners to circulate legal action. The trial run had caused unnecessary dissension among the owners, jockeys, and the officials.

There was excitement around the racetrack on the morning of the race. Together, Teddy and Katie went down to talk with their team. Teddy called their jockeys into Mr. Zee's stall and said, "We'd like to congratulate you guys for not taking part in the trial run the other night. Unfortunately, as you've probably heard, Thomas Leone is in critical condition at the hospital."

The jockeys glanced at each other while Teddy spoke, but no one remarked about Leone's condition. They were a tight-lipped group.

He gently stroked Mr. Zee's head as he explained that Tiramisu, the horse Leone was riding, was diagnosed with EIPH, exercise-induced pulmonary hemorrhage and scratched from the race. There were valid reasons for following exact measures of protocol in organized races, and safety was a top priority among the rules of the racing committee.

"Fortunately," he finished, "the committee agreed to let us race. So, let's focus on winning the Louisiana Derby so we can head back to Georgia!"

The following morning, the front page of the local newspaper featured a half-page color picture of Silver Circle and Mr. Zee approaching the finish line at the track. The caption stated the Thoroughbreds from the little town of Abington, Georgia, had placed first and second in the Louisiana Derby.

Silver Circle had once again lived up to the hype created by the media, which seemed more enamored with her than ever.

Chapter Fifty-Seven

The Santa Anita Derby was the last race before the Kentucky Derby.

Teddy's stomach lurched as the plane made a sudden dip. He glanced over at Katie. Her jaw was tight, her face pale.

Without warning, they'd flown into an unexpected pocket of wind as the plane began its descent into Arcadia. The air traffic control center had instructed the pilot to circle the airspace until the turbulence had died down. The plane circled the airport twice. Finally, the pilot made an extremely bumpy, unexpected landing on the third attempt. The Boeing 747 skidded across the runway, tires squealing as the pilot applied the brakes. It was an abrupt stop.

Teddy's hand was red from Katie's clutching it throughout the landing. The passengers on the plane were exceptionally quiet. Finally, when everyone on board had taken a collective breath, he asked, "Are you okay?"

Katie nodded and reached for her phone. Heavy static rattled the intercom as the pilot apologized for the rocky landing and thanked the passengers for their patience and relative calmness.

Katie nervously pulled at her bottom lip. As they remained seated and awaited instructions to eventually deplane, Teddy tried to create a diversion. He retrieved the small spiral-bound notepad from his pocket and studied the points accumulated by each of their three horses. Going into the Santa Anita Derby, Mr. Zee had 130 points, Redemption was at 100, and Silver Circle had amassed 155.

"Can you believe this is the last race before Churchill Downs?" Teddy continued in somewhat disbelief, "This racing season has flown by."

Katie leaned her head against the back of the seat, her eyes closing momentarily. "I'm exhausted. We need a few days at the beach to relax." Teddy had planned to take the family to St. Simons before the Santa Anita, but there was no time.

Soon, darkness descended upon the tarmac. He looked out the window of the plane, while Katie continued to rest her eyes. The land crew sped around in their carts, preparing to unload the luggage from the cargo area. Teddy's adrenalin increased as he noticed the sea of neon lights glowing in the distance. Perhaps Silver Circle's name would soon be in lights—if she won the Triple Crown. Although she had gotten a late start, she'd already accumulated enough points to qualify for The Kentucky Derby. Currently, she led the pack with total points. Blackjack, Tiramisu, Sterling, Mr. Zee, and Redemption were within thirty points of her, and more horses were gaining momentum with the completion of each race. The competition was fierce.

Another plane coming in for landing interrupted Teddy's thoughts. It was a chartered plane, much smaller judging from its length, with an estimated twenty to twenty-five passenger seats. The pilot was skilled. He landed the aircraft with precision—no bumps, no squealing of tires, no skidding across the runway. He just put the plane down on the tarmac with the accuracy of a fighter pilot.

Soon, the stairs released and locked. One passenger—medium build similar to Matt, but with a little longer hair length—appeared at the top of the landing and then descended the stairs. As he walked away from the plane, the lights of the aircraft allowed Teddy to see the aviator-type sunshades the man wore (even though it was already dark), and there were sprigs of hair sticking out from a NY baseball cap. He wore washed-out jeans and a dark jacket that might have been blue or black.

The man walked purposely to a shiny black car waiting a hundred yards away from the landing strip.

There was something familiar about his walk.

Teddy chuckled under his breath. Whoever the stranger was, he was a fast walker. Matt Krueger had never moved that fast.

As soon as the man entered the car, the driver cut the wheels a hard right and circled back to the main highway as if time were of the essence.

Teddy shuffled in his seat, unsettled by the scene. It was an ominous feeling—like a flashing warning sign, as if he were supposed to see the man who'd sped away in the back seat of the car.

The two days leading up to the race were uneventful. Fortunately, there were no incidents that required Teddy's assistance. He and Katie just enjoyed the time away from Abington, and when Katie wasn't at the track working with the horses, they'd spent their time relaxing. She slept more than usual. Perhaps all the travel involving the races had caused her fatigue.

On Thursday morning after Katie left for the stables, Teddy decided to surprise her with an afternoon picnic. A trip to St. Simons might not be possible until after the Derby, but they could enjoy Newport Beach for a few hours.

The concierge arranged transportation for them to the beach. Shortly after noon, they went downstairs and placed their items in the car. As the car pulled away from the portico, Teddy noticed a man coming toward the hotel who was wearing a blue NY baseball cap and washed-out jeans—same baseball cap and familiar walk as the man Teddy had seen at the airport. The man quickly turned away as if he'd sensed someone was watching him.

The ominous feeling… it had returned.

The morning of the race, Sammy texted Teddy. <We're in lockdown. They found marks on the back door like maybe

someone was trying to get in. I'll call you when we get the all-clear.>

Teddy read the text to Katie. "This is a little disturbing that someone would try to break into the stable."

"I know. Thank goodness they have good security here."

With the extra time caused by the lockdown, Katie started packing their suitcases. They had booked an 8 p.m. flight. As much as she enjoyed racing, she was ready to get back home to Mattie Grace.

"You know this lockdown will lift momentarily. Are you going down for the pre-race walk?" Teddy asked.

Katie paused and measured her answer. She felt washed out, and the pungent odors in the stable the previous day had made her sick to her stomach.

"No. Sammy and Cappelletti can handle it today."

They'd never been late to a race before, but Katie had fallen asleep after her shower, and Teddy had let her nap until one hour before race time. He'd allowed just enough time for her to get ready and walk to the track.

They found their seats just as the bell sounded.

Blackjack burst out of the gate and pulled out in front with a powerful, ground-covering stride. He led throughout the race. Just as Teddy had resigned himself for a loss, suddenly at the last furlong, Silver Circle rushed up from behind. Teddy's pulse quickened, and Katie's nails dug into his palm. Blackjack bumped the filly with his shoulder, and she stumbled. Teddy's breath caught in his throat. Then, the silver filly found her footing and thundered toward the finish line, her nose at Blackjack's haunches.

Blackjack crossed it first by half a body length. Silver Circle came in second, favoring her left foreleg, and Redemption finished third. Mr. Zee came in sixth.

As soon as the race ended, Teddy grabbed Katie's hand. "Let's go. Something's wrong with Silver's leg."

****

They rushed down to check on their horse. Smith had already slid out of the saddle and bent to examine Silver Circle's leg by the time they arrived. "This looks bad. You'd better call the vet."

The quarter mile to the stables felt like a thousand as Silver Circle hobbled on three legs. The vet was standing at the stable door. He hosed her leg with cold water, but it brought only minimal relief. Then, he alternated ice compresses with heat, which seemed to help. Next, he applied an anti-inflammatory ointment to help work out the soreness and minimize the swelling. "I don't think anything is broken," he said, "but I'll let you know as soon as we get the results from the X-rays and ultrasound tests."

They were too preoccupied to talk much as they loaded their luggage and headed for the airport.

As they settled into their seats on the plane, Teddy's phone buzzed. It was the veterinarian following up on Silver Circle's condition.

"It seems that bump during the race overstretched the tendon on her left front hoof, and it will need professional care. The good news is that it is a minor suspensory ligament injury and should heal quickly."

"Do you think she'll be ready to run in the Derby?"

"I can't make any guarantees, but I think she'll be sound by then." He'd promised to send copies of the x-rays and the medical report to Dr. Scott in Abington for further evaluation.

The pilot's voice came over the intercom, and after a quick goodbye, Teddy ended the call. He glanced at Katie. It was the same pilot who had flown them from Atlanta four days earlier. Katie seemed oblivious as she continued to read her phone texts.

Teddy checked his phone messages before the plane took off. Only one. He clicked on it and heard Luke Sullivan's voice talking so fast—as if the recorder would cut off before he could finish the message. First, he asked if they'd changed their minds about the beach house. He'd expected to see them the previous week during spring break. "Oh, by the way," Sullivan added, "the other couple interested in the beach house have backed out. They've found a house they liked better on Hilton Head."

Teddy smiled. Then he placed the phone in his jacket pocket and removed the small spiral notepad he'd carried with him since the beginning of September. He checked his entries for each horse. Their Thoroughbreds had participated in twenty races and accumulated one-hundred points in order to qualify for the Derby on the first Saturday of May.

Teddy glanced at Katie. She held her phone four inches from her face, glaring at the screen with tremendous concentration.

He strained to see her numbers.

"I've got Redemption at 115 points!"

Teddy continued to look at his notepad. "Me, too. Where's Mr. Zee and Silver Circle?"

"Silver's at 135." Then she hesitated. "This can't be right. Mr. Zee has 120 points, and he's ahead of Redemption. Is that possible?"

Teddy glanced at his wife and nodded.

She turned off her phone, and reached for a book from her pocketbook. "Are you going to read on the flight home?"

"Nope," Teddy smiled as he leaned back on the headrest and closed his eyes. "Right now, I'm just thinking about getting home to our little girl."

Chapter Fifty-Eight

S unday was the longest day of the week for Drew. Every other
day, he could fill with menial chores, read international law
books, and exercise by walking the perimeter of the farm.
People in town were working, shopping, and going about their
business Monday through Saturday, but on Sunday, well, Sunday was
in a category all its own. A day of rest. A day for families to worship
and enjoy a leisurely meal together.

It was the day Drew missed his family most.

This Sunday was like no other. Drew got into his Tahoe late in the
afternoon and drove into town. He pulled around the square and then
went to the street behind his father's law firm and parallel parked.

He pondered his next move. Oh, how he wanted to see his family.
He wanted to talk to them. Of course, it was a long shot, but they were
his family, after all. Finally, he locked the truck and walked toward
the house. It was a little over a mile by foot, and he was willing to do
anything to get them to accept him back.

When he got close enough, he darted into the woods behind their
house and watched from the old treehouse he'd built for Jacob when
he was just a young boy.

Colleen certainly hadn't lost her green thumb. He wondered who
was taking care of the lawn. He took a deep, cleansing breath and
inhaled the smell of freshly mowed grass. The flowers in the gardens
had already bloomed, and the Japanese maple had grown over six feet.

His family was involved in a game of volleyball. The children were quite athletic. Jacob, his girlfriend, and Rebecca faced Angie, Colleen, and a dark-haired man.

When the game ended, the kids went onto the porch while the adults went inside. Drew couldn't believe how tall Jacob had gotten. Rebecca was no longer a little girl, and Angie followed in her sister's footsteps. The girls laughed and joked just like old friends. They all appeared to be happy, well-adjusted kids.

Colleen came onto the porch carrying a tray of food, followed by the man who hung onto her every word.

Someone, possibly Jacob, had already lit the Green Egg on the patio. Colleen watched as the guy positioned the burgers on the grill. As the burgers sizzled, the smell filled the air. Suddenly, Drew was hungry for a homemade burger.

Colleen was wearing a pair of white shorts and a spaghetti strapped top. The man smiled at a comment she made, then he reached down and kissed her lips.

Drew cringed.

How could Colleen allow this guy to kiss her openly in front of their children? Drew glanced at his kids once again. Rebecca and Angie laughed as they set the dinner table. Jacob and his girlfriend were so enamored with each other they hardly even noticed anyone was around. It seemed the only person who cared that his wife was kissing another man was Drew.

When they removed the burgers from the grill, they sat around the table on the porch and enjoyed their meal. The children burst into laughter in response to a story the guy had told.

Drew leaned back against the treehouse wall, face in his hands. As much as he'd like to walk into the backyard and yell, "I'm back!" He knew it was too late.

He'd waited too long.

They had replaced him. His family had moved on.

The following Saturday, Drew stood in the coffee shop and stirred his drink. He looked at the front window of the shop as a petite woman walked by. The lady reminded him of Colleen. He had seen his wife outside the shop soon after returning to Abington. Yes, he could find cheaper coffee elsewhere in Abington, but he often returned hoping he'd run into her again.

He dropped his paper into the trash receptacle and walked out the door. Colleen turned around. It was an awkward moment. Drew froze when Colleen raised her sunglasses, and they made eye contact. All color drained from her face. She looked as if she'd seen a ghost.

And then she was gone.

Why hadn't he spoken to her? It was the perfect opportunity to approach her and explain that he was back in Abington, but after watching his family the previous Sunday, he felt any attempt would be futile.

As he drank his coffee, he contemplated the end of the weekend as an excellent time to sneak into the garage. First, he wanted to get his knife out of the glove compartment of his classic car, provided Colleen hadn't sold it.

As much as he wanted to be like Teddy Williams, he suddenly realized that he was just a darker reflection of his old friend.

Chapter Fifty-Nine

A round eight o'clock on Sunday evening, Drew drove behind his father's law firm and once again parked in the florist parking lot. He parked under an enormous oak tree, shielded from the road's view. He grabbed his flashlight and started on foot to the woods behind his house.

He watched as the lights on the main floor dimmed, signaling the end of dinner and preparation for bedtime. Drew could see Colleen and the man standing in the kitchen window. They appeared to be tidying up the kitchen. When the kitchen light went out, Drew rushed through the backyard and entered the garage. It was dark inside, and he couldn't see anything without a light.

He spotted the unlocked door.

What was Colleen thinking? The car was a classic.

Drew opened the car door and quickly surveyed the leather seats. Not a scratch anywhere, not even a speck of dust. Then he looked at the odometer. Once again, it appeared Colleen had driven the car very little.

Oh, how he missed that car. He leaned over to open the glove compartment when he heard a noise. Quickly, he jumped out of the car, careful not to slam the door. Instead, he shimmied under the car and hid.

The overhead light came on. It took a minute for the light to illuminate fully. He saw the gray Nike athletic shoes of the person inside the garage. It sounded like someone lifted the lid from the trash can, but then he watched as the Nike shoes went to the passenger's side of the car and stopped. Drew could have touched the toe of the left shoe as the person faced the car door. He thought to himself,

"What the hell?"

Quickly, the person walked away from the car, dumped the trash, and rolled the can toward the door. He cut off the overhead light and slammed the door shut.

Drew waited for a full five minutes before pulling himself out from under the car, then he gently opened the passenger door and removed the knife from the glove compartment.

Bang! From the sound of it, the lid had fallen off the trash can and landed on the concrete drive.

Drew slid the knife into his boot and gently closed the door to the car. Then he hunched behind the car and peeked out of the garage window. The upstairs lights were off except for Colleen's bathroom.

He waited a few more minutes, locked the doors on the driver's side, and raced back into the woods.

D aisy Byrd had discussed the trip to Churchill Downs at every dinner party and social affair since Mr. Zee won the Breeders' Cup Juvenile.

On Wednesday, May 4th, three days before the race, Andrew and Daisy boarded a limousine and swung by for Frank and Claire. They made a detour to pick up their good friends, Rhett and Laura, at their farmhouse at the edge of Abington, and the three couples settled in to enjoy the hour-long ride to the Atlanta Hartsfield-Jackson International Airport.

As they pulled away from the farmhouse, Daisy suggested picking up lunch from a drive-in on North Avenue on the way to the airport.

She said, "Just give me the word, and I'll place the order." Finally, she convinced the driver (who rolled his eyes at the unexpected stop) to exit the interstate and pull behind the restaurant to the curbside pickup area.

Andrew looked at Rhett and chuckled. "I probably should say something to her, but it's just so nice to watch her enjoying herself again. Finally, after all these years, she's finally got her joy back. Who knew a horse race would have this kind of effect on a woman!"

When the food arrived at the car, Daisy handed the driver a chili-cheese dog and coke. He grinned at her through the rear-view mirror.

They became instant friends.

Daisy passed out food to Rhett and Laura. She placed a hotdog in Andrew's hand, then gently pulled it back, laughing at his startled expression. "Just messing with you, big guy. You have a special order—there's extra cheese on yours."

Andrew opened his hotdog and smiled. "We're barely out of Abington, and you've already started your shenanigans. I have a feeling this is going to be an extraordinary trip."

Daisy laughed again. "Anytime a trip begins with a ride in a limo, you can rest assured it will be memorable."

****

Teddy stood in front of the window in their hotel suite. He could hardly believe they were already doing this again—the early morning flight, the swanky hotel suite, the flurry of texts from Sammy and Cappelletti. As much as he enjoyed these escapes with Katie, it had seemed harder this time to leave Mattie Grace behind. They still had the Preakness and the Belmont to go.

His phone vibrated. Andrew's name flashed on the screen. Teddy read his old friend's message and smiled. "The "six-pack" has landed, and they're at the Louisville airport."

Katie glanced at her watch. "They've made good time."

It took less than an hour from their landing in Louisville for the "six-pack" to arrive at Churchill Downs. Once they got settled in their rooms, they met in the lobby, ready to walk around and familiarize themselves with the facility. The discussion was lively among the friends, and although it was only mid-week leading up to "The Most Exciting Two Minutes in Sports," the momentum had already begun to build.

The remaining partners who'd invested in Redemption would arrive in time to attend the cocktail party at 7 p.m. in the small ballroom of the hotel.

Teddy and Katie stood at the door as their guests arrived, while Sammy stood off to the side and sipped a glass of ice water. Roger and his friend had arrived a day early to prepare for the reception. First, they'd decorated the center table with a tall crystal vase filled with five dozen long-stemmed red roses, along with statues of bronze and pewter horses. Then, as a surprise, Roger displayed large canvas pictures of Mr. Zee, Redemption, and Silver Circle on easels behind the serving table. He also supervised the placement of the heavy hors d'oeuvres by the waitstaff and kept the bar well-stocked. It was just one more thing Roger could do to help his niece.

Claire, Frank, and Rhett were all investors. Laura came as Rhett's plus-one. While Andrew and Daisy were ostensibly included because of Andrew's legal advice regarding contracts and negotiations, Teddy and Katie would have invited them even if he weren't their official business counselor.

Next to arrive was Philip Nordstrom. Teddy heard his loud voice when he stepped off the elevator and entered the hotel's lobby. "It's time to party!" As he entered the reception hall, he pulled a cap out of a tote bag and handed it to Teddy. It was a black cap with white lettering: *Redemption for President*. He handed out caps as he walked through the ballroom.

Teddy grinned and put his on. They had depended on Philip to keep the party lively for three or four hours, and it looked like their confidence was well placed. The party was officially underway.

Clayton Thomas and his college roommate, Daniel Bray, arrived next. They'd made the trip together. It was the first time Daniel had been to the Derby, and he couldn't thank Katie enough for considering him as an investor.

Laura's daughter, Marsha Whelchel, was also an investor. "I couldn't imagine attending The Kentucky Derby without my siblings!" Marsha said as she arrived at the cocktail party with Julia and Betsy at her side.

Laura and Rhett beamed when they saw Laura's girls.

Teddy had invited Frankie Burel, Redemption's jockey, at the last moment. It seemed only fitting to include him, since they hosted the party for the owners.

It was almost the perfect number for a successful cocktail party with twenty people in attendance. Only the absence of Colleen and Matt marred the evening. They were flying up on Thursday morning.

Teddy and Katie greeted Cappelletti and his wife, then went to the front of the room. As they passed a server circulating with a tray of champagne, Teddy grabbed two flutes and handed one to Katie. Then he reached for the live microphone that Roger had already tested and placed on the corner of the table. "Please grab a glass of bubbly, and we'll get this party started."

Teddy welcomed everyone to Churchill Downs and thanked their guests for making the trip to Louisville. It had been a wild and crazy year, he said, and when they'd started this journey, neither he nor Katie had any idea where the road would lead them.

"We'd like to thank each of you for your investment in Redemption." Teddy looked at Katie and winked. "I'm still not sure how my wife talked you into making an investment of this size on a horse you'd never seen—but I'm grateful you did."

He explained how Philip Nordstrom saw how badly Katie wanted that big chestnut colt and encouraged her to put a deal together to buy the horse of her dreams. Teddy told how he had tried to no avail, but in one afternoon, Katie had pitched the idea to enough investors to make the syndicate purchase. "I guess we know who the salesperson is in this family."

A chant started from the back of the room. Ka-tie! Ka-tie! Ka-tie!

Teddy waited for the chant to die down and continued. "Seriously, it must've been an awesome moment when you arrived at Churchill Downs today, knowing Redemption was among the twenty most celebrated three-year-old horses in the world." He paused. "That's right. In the world!" Another pause. "Very few horses make it to this level of competition."

Everyone cheered.

He motioned for Burel to step forward. "Burel, come up here, please. I want these fine people to meet you." As Burel approached, he shook his hand. "This man right here is Redemption's jockey. He's the most skilled jockey in the industry, and we're honored to have him riding our horse."

The room burst into chants. Bur-el! Bur-el! Bur-el!

Again, Teddy waited for the cheers to fade, then he announced the horses had received their last workout earlier in the afternoon and would enjoy two full days of rest before the race on Saturday.

Another loud cheer erupted.

Teddy discussed the point system used by the racing officials and gave the standings for Redemption. "The morning papers consider Redemption a long shot," he said, "but one thing is for sure. If Redemption wins on Saturday, you can pat yourself on the back for making such a wise investment."

He paused, and his face broke out in a huge grin. "But... even if he doesn't win, Cappelletti assures me—his stud fees will continue to roll in for the next twenty years."

The mention of stud fees increased the energy in the room. More cheering, a few whistles, and glasses clicking among the investors.

The timing was perfect. *The Atlanta Soundkeepers* band started their first set as the investors celebrated.

Teddy stepped closer to Katie and whispered in her ear, "You know they consider you a rockstar!"

She grinned. "Perhaps not tonight, but they certainly will if Redemption wins on Saturday."

Chapter Sixty-One

May 4, 2022

Colleen dialed the restaurant and ordered Chinese food for a 6:30 delivery. Matt had stopped by his loft apartment, picked up his luggage, and was on his way to her house.

Perfect timing. He pulled into the driveway as the delivery guy drove away.

Colleen struggled with the corkscrew when the doorbell rang. Although they'd been dating for six months, he still rang the doorbell when he came to her house. It was a thoughtful sign of respect for her and her children.

Rebecca answered the door, reached for the bag of food, and chatted with Matt as they walked into the kitchen.

The girls rummaged through the bag until they found the fortune cookies. Angie quickly opened the cellophane wrapper.

Matt patted the top of Angie's head and joked, "You know it's bad luck to eat the fortune cookie before dinner?"

"No, it's not!"

Matt looked over at Colleen and smiled. He reached for the bottle. "May I help you with that?" Then he leaned over and kissed her on the forehead.

Colleen glanced at the girls, but neither responded to their signs of affection. And why would they object? Matt was a nice guy. He blended into their lives seamlessly.

And yet …

Colleen looked down and realized her hands were shaking. Was she ready for this? She'd contacted Andrew the previous evening and asked if he could secure a suite for her and Matt. Andrew had been so gracious and non-judgmental. He had even congratulated his daughter-in-law for moving on with her life. It had taken so much courage for her to make that call. But in the end, she knew it was the most respectful way to handle the situation with her in-laws.

"Mom, can I eat up in the playroom tonight?" Rebecca asked.

"Me, too, Mom," Angie said. "Can I eat in the playroom with Rebecca?"

Realizing Colleen's mind was wandering, Matt looked at the girls and said, "I don't know, *can* you eat upstairs?" He smiled and continued, "Or, should that be, *may* I eat upstairs?"

Rebecca looked at Colleen and rolled her eyes.

"Of course," Colleen said, "but bring your plates downstairs and load them in the dishwasher when you finish. And before you go to bed tonight, go ahead and pack your suitcases. We've all got to be ready to leave the house by 7:45 in the morning."

Rebecca flashed a thumbs-up. Then the girls filled their plates, grabbed a bottle of water each from the refrigerator, and rushed up the steps to the playroom before Matt had time to pour two glasses of wine.

As Matt and Colleen ate their dinner at the bar, they discussed whether they should call an Uber to take them to the airport or drive one of their vehicles.

Colleen said, "The girls are so excited about this race. I hope they remember to watch it on Saturday night."

Matt assured her they wouldn't forget. Rebecca had a picture of Churchill Downs as her screen saver on her laptop. Angie had a picture of Redemption pasted to her ceiling next to images of Wyatt Oleff and Milo Manheim.

Investing in Katie's horse had turned out to be the best decision she'd ever made. The kids felt such a connection to the animal,

Rebecca's headaches had stopped, and Angie no longer had nightmares. Additionally, as a result of hanging out at the barn, they'd developed a close friendship with Mattie Grace.

Matt reached for her hand and lifted it to his lips. "I'm looking forward to this trip. It'll be fun watching the pomp and circumstance at Churchill Downs, but the main attraction is the chance to spend time with you."

Colleen quickly pulled away. She hoped Matt hadn't noticed her saddened mood.

When the girls brought their plates downstairs, Matt poured Colleen another glass of wine. "Go on up and finish packing," he said. "I'll clean up the kitchen while you get your bath."

He took his time loading the dishwasher. Then, before turning out the kitchen lights, he gathered the garbage and headed out to the garage, where Colleen kept the big can for the trash overload.

When he walked into the garage, something seemed amiss.

He looked around, trying to remember every detail of the garage as it had been on Sunday evening when he was last there—the night he sensed someone outside the garage. Her husband's car was parked in its usual place. He wished she'd trade the damn thing in. It might help her to move on—and she definitely needed to move on. The guy was never coming back.

Matt looked inside the vehicle, his gaze instinctively falling on the glove compartment he'd seen opened the previous Sunday night. Someone had locked the door on the driver's side, but when he walked around the vehicle, the silver push-button lever on the passenger's door of the old-fashioned model was unlocked.

Matt stared at the unlocked door, careful not to touch anything.

He hurried away from the vehicle, grabbed the garbage can, and rolled it out onto the street.

On his way up the driveway, Matt got his overnight bag out of his trunk and headed back into the house. He turned off the family room lamp and then went upstairs and checked on the girls. Rebecca chatted on her phone, but Angie was already asleep on the sofa. Matt blew a kiss to Rebecca and quietly closed the door.

The smell from the floral-scented bubble bath infused the landing above the family room. When he walked into Colleen's bedroom, she sat on the bed, holding a hand towel to her face.

At first, it was just a sniffle. Then she pressed the towel more tightly to her face and sobbed. Matt reached across the bed without saying a word and gently stroked her back.

Her sorrow struck him like a blow. He'd told her over the weekend exactly how he felt for her. The three little words every woman needed to hear. I. Love. You.

Matt still couldn't believe he'd said it out loud.

Lord knows, he'd been patient with her, but what she'd gone through would have lasting effects on anyone. Still, he wished she could find a way to move forward... with him.

Between sobs, she explained, there were two separate incidents where she thought she'd seen Drew downtown. Then when she got home on Saturday, she thought she saw someone behind the garage.

"And... you thought it was Drew?"

"Not at first. It was just a shadow, and then it was gone. It scared me half to death."

Matt's fist clenched at the thought of her fear. If he'd been here, he could've protected her.

"I got inside and got the garage door closed. My heart was pounding so hard! But, then..." her voice softened. "When I stepped out of the car, I knew Drew had been there. The scent of him... it lingered in the air."

The softness in her eyes hurt Matt's heart, but he pushed the hurt away and nodded for her to continue her story.

There wasn't much more to it. She knew it was bizarre, so she quickly removed the bags from the trunk, went into the house, and called Katie, who suggested that her mind was playing tricks on her.

Perhaps Katie was right. Matt hoped so. After eight years with no contact, surely Drew was dead. If not, why would he come back now?

No wonder Colleen felt crazy at times. Who wouldn't? Drew was the only man she'd ever known intimately.

Until Matt.

Matt had never been in love, but meeting Colleen had changed that. She was innocent, loyal, kind—everything he could hope for in a woman. Matt glared at the picture on the bedside table. He thought again of the open glove compartment and the unlocked passenger door.

What if Drew were still alive?

He loved Colleen, but could he afford to get involved in a love triangle with a weird psychopath?

He fumbled through his overnight bag and removed the envelope containing the two airline tickets. Since meeting Colleen, he'd manned up and assumed the role of head of the family. He acted like a father, although six months ago, he would have laughed at the thought.

In that role, he'd purchased the tickets for himself and Colleen.

It had taken his entire monthly expense check and a small part of his savings, but he hadn't cared. He loved Colleen, and he'd come to love her family, too.

Now he laid the envelope on the bed beside her. "If Drew were alive, he would've already come back home." He twisted a strand of hair around his finger. "Only a fool would leave a woman like you."

Tears streamed down her cheeks as she wrapped her housecoat tightly around her body.

Matt touched her cheek with the back of his hand. What more could he do to prove to her they could have a great life together?

"Why won't you let yourself move on with your life? Drew's gone, but... I'm here."

"I know, and I love you for it," Colleen said. "Every time I think I've gotten over Drew—he reappears—even if it's just in my mind. It's like he's messing with my head."

"The day you saw him—thought you saw him—behind the garage. What day was it?" While he waited for her answer, he zipped the overnight bag.

Colleen touched his arm. "I don't recall the day," she stifled a sob, "but please don't leave."

Matt turned and placed a hand on each of her shoulders. Gently, he wiped a single tear from her cheek. "I'm not leaving. Let's get some sleep. I promised you I'd go on this trip, and I'm a man of my word." Then he looked into those sad eyes. "I've got to be honest with you, Colleen—it's hard to compete with a ghost."

Chapter Sixty-Two

May 5, 2022

Teddy opened one eye and tried to get his bearings. The nightlight in the adjacent bathroom filtered into the bedroom, providing just enough light to make out the pieces of furniture. Finally, his eyes adjusted, but he couldn't remember where he was as he looked around the room. The clock showed 11:05 p.m.

Someone banged on the door of their suite, and Teddy sat straight up in bed. His first thought was how the loud noise would awaken Mattie Grace. Then he scratched his head, remembering his daughter had stayed in Abington with a friend.

Cautiously, he tip-toed over to look out the peephole. Then he opened the door. "Sammy, what the hell are you doing up at this hour?"

"Sorry to wake you," Sammy said, "but Silver's sick."

Teddy rubbed the sleep from his eyes. "What kind of sick?"

"Looks like some kind of virus," Sammy said, adding that he'd already called the veterinarian.

Teddy dressed quickly, then explained the situation to Katie.

"I'm going with you." Katie pushed back the covers and swung her legs over the side of the bed. She swayed, then slumped forward, hand to her forehead.

Teddy slid onto the bed beside her. "Are you okay?"

"Yes, I must have gotten up too quickly." She rubbed her temples. "I'm just so exhausted. It doesn't matter how much sleep I get. It's just not enough."

"Why don't you just stay here and get some rest?" He promised he'd be back as soon as he talked with the veterinarian and checked on the other horses.

"I don't know. I feel like I should..." She shook her head as if to clear away the fog.

Teddy brought her hand to his lips and kissed her palm. "Please, honey. You're exhausted. Let me take care of this for you."

For a long moment, she was silent. Then she nodded and let him tuck her in.

When he and Sammy got to the stable, Teddy was unprepared for what he saw. The silver filly stood with her head low and her ears drooping. He'd never seen her so lethargic. Had she contracted a virus? Or had someone managed to drug her?

Teddy covered his mouth with his fist. If anything happened to Silver, it would devastate Mattie Grace. Him, too, he realized. Perhaps because of her size, the beautiful silver horse had grown on him. Everyone in the family had a special relationship with her.

He moved closer to Silver Circle and rubbed her head. This couldn't be happening.

This week belonged to their little filly. The nugget Katie, Cappelletti, and Sammy had worked so hard to achieve.

Teddy looked up as the vet came into the stall. Dr. Boone was a tall man with peppered gray hair and dark-framed glasses that added an air of sophistication to his calloused hands and ruddy complexion. His tone was hushed as he performed the examination, moving his stethoscope over the filly's chest and belly. When he'd finished, he said, "There are no signs of a viral infection, but we should rule out the possibility just the same. As an added precaution, I'm ordering the food supply to be reviewed by one of the facility's officials, and I'll pull a vial of blood and a stool sample for the Equine Medical Center to analyze."

As he prepared the needle, he said, "You know, I've been a large animal vet for nearly thirty years, and I've never seen a horse run like this one did yesterday and experience such lethargy in less than twelve hours."

Teddy ran a hand over Silver's withers. "Could someone have drugged her?"

Dr. Boone shook his head. "I doubt it. The security at this venue is among the highest in the world."

"So I've heard."

The website advertised Churchill Downs as having the most intelligent security system on earth—in part because it was monitored at all times by the Jefferson County Sheriff Department, and in part because they brought in additional security personnel during the week leading up to the Derby. In addition, if anyone suspected skullduggery of any kind, all equipment, feed, hay bales, etc., were subject to search and seizure.

The list of precautions was impressive. A member of the security team was required to log the name of everyone who entered the stables and document the reason for their visit. Regardless of their role—grooms, veterinarians, trainers, assistant trainers, owners, or any other connections needed valid KHRC (Kentucky Horse Racing Commission) licenses for permission to enter a stall, engage in contact with the horse, or perform any service for the horse.

"Don't worry." The vet closed his medical bag. If someone deliberately tried to keep Silver Circle from competing in the race, I'll find out, and they'll be dealt with. Now... I need to go over to the medical center and drop off these samples."

Teddy rubbed the horse with a wet rag. Perhaps he wasn't a large animal veterinarian. Still, he was a medical doctor, and horses, just like humans, could become dehydrated when they were ill.

He tried to feed Silver a handful of fresh oats, but she turned her head away. "Come on, girl. You've got to eat something so you can get better. We've got a race to run."

When the veterinarian returned to the stall, he administered liquids through an intravenous line. Then he ordered two more bags of fluids to follow.

"I'll be back in a few hours to change out the bags. By that time, we should have the results from the blood work and know what we're dealing with." Dr. Boone stopped and placed his hand on Teddy's shoulder. "She'll be fine, Mr. Williams. We'll do everything we can to get her strong enough to race. There's a lot of money riding on this horse. Everyone's talking about Silver Circle winning the Derby."

Teddy shook his head. "Thanks, Doc. I hope you're right."

Chapter Sixty-Three

The night before the race, Churchill Downs held a festive black-tie affair for the owners and their families, managers, trainers, and jockeys.

During dinner, Teddy whispered to Katie. "I've decided to sleep in the stable with Silver tonight."

She looked up from buttering her roll and gave him a confused look. "Do you think that's necessary?"

He nodded. "I don't feel right about letting her race yet."

"But the blood work didn't show any signs of an infection or food poisoning."

"I know. But still…" He left the rest unsaid. The veterinarian's opinion was that Silver Circle simply needed a rest. Perhaps, they had overworked her the past few weeks, or maybe the trauma to her hoof required additional rest. He thought she would be sound by morning, but she'd still eaten very little. Teddy was concerned she wouldn't be able to race the next day without adequate food intake.

"I'll stay with you," Katie said, but he put his hand over hers and shook his head.

"You have a big day tomorrow. Please, let me do this for you."

He could tell she was torn, but exhaustion won out, and she agreed with a grateful smile.

When the meal ended, they walked back to their suite. Teddy changed clothes, grabbed a blanket, and headed to the stables.

The security guard posted at the stable entrance immediately recognized him. "Mr. Williams," the guard said, "what are you doing down here so late? You should be up at the party enjoying yourself with your family."

Teddy explained what had happened to one of his horses, and said he thought he should feed her small amounts every hour to make sure she would be ready for the race the following day. "I'm not violating any rules, am I?"

The security guy chuckled. "Well, I'll let you in on a little secret. You're not the first owner to sneak into the stable the night before the big race."

Teddy set his watch to wake him every hour. Each time, he encouraged the filly to eat a generous serving of oats. She still refused to drink, so he squeezed liquids into her mouth from a clean rag he had saturated in a bucket of water.

At about three o'clock in the morning, Teddy woke to a sound coming from Redemption's stall.

He held his breath as he squinted into the shadows. The stable was lit only by a dim light shining from the security office, but as his eyes adjusted, he could make out the curve of the filly's back and haunches. Finally, he spotted his flashlight next to the door. It was a long-handled, tactical flashlight like the ones used by law enforcement, and it doubled as a weapon. He quietly got up, grabbed the flashlight, and tiptoed out to the door of Redemption's stall.

Teddy paused. He listened carefully at the stirring from inside the stall. Finally, he peered inside.

Someone sat in the corner.

Teddy glanced around, then shone the flashlight toward the person's face. "What are you doing in here with my horse?"

The man stood and ambled toward Teddy. An easy, languid walk Teddy recognized with a start. Then the face came into focus.

He was a few pounds lighter than when Teddy had last seen him. He had a beard, and his hair was longer and grayer, but there was no mistaking the rugged features so much like his father's.

"Drew?"

"Yeah, man, it's me."

"Where in the hell have you been?"

"I heard someone was trying to poison your horses. So as soon as the cocktail hour started, I slipped in here, and sure enough, a big dude was hanging around outside your filly's stall door." Drew pointed toward Silver Circle's stall. "But, of course, he ran out the side door when he saw me. So I just stayed here in case he came back."

"Who told you someone was trying to poison my horses?"

"It's a long story."

Teddy's fist clenched.

A long story! Slowly, he turned off the flashlight. Well, the least he could do was to hear what his old friend had to say. "I've got plenty of time."

Drew and Teddy ended up in Silver Circle's stall. They took turns feeding the horse and watched for any movement inside the stable. Teddy watched Drew as closely as he was watching for intruders. He had never known Drew to hurt an animal, but then, Drew had done a lot of things Teddy had never imagined he would.

As they sat in the dark talking, Teddy asked Drew about what had happened the night he disappeared.

"I... it's hard to explain." Drew rubbed at a frayed spot on one knee of his jeans. "I always considered you one of my very best friends."

"I considered you my best friend, too," Teddy said.

"But there was another part of me that was always jealous of you. Everything in your life came easy. You were so smooth with the girls. And you graduated at the top of your class. I couldn't even get into med school; I swear sometimes it seemed like you were living my life." Drew dropped his head between his knees. "I'm sorry, man. I just... really didn't have my head on straight."

He ran through it all, how he'd persuaded Teddy's first wife (now deceased) to help him swindle Teddy out of his inheritance. Then convinced Katie's grandmother to give him an option on their farm in exchange for fifty-thousand dollars.

It was painful to listen to, but somehow Teddy kept from interrupting. When Drew had finished, Teddy got up and stood against the wall. "Where did you get the fifty-thousand dollars you gave to Katie's grandmother?"

Drew hesitated.

"Well?"

"I used the money from the girls' college funds."

"Did you put the money in an escrow account? That was standard for options on a property."

Drew's voice broke. "No. Mrs. Hawkins wouldn't sign the option unless I gave her a check for the fifty grand."

Teddy occupied his hands with two silver coins from his pocket. "Go on."

"That night everything went sideways... Katie's grandfather had just died, and I planned to intimidate Mrs. Hawkins into signing over the farm that night." Drew wiped his nose on his shirtsleeve. "It was idiotic and naïve."

"Yeah," Teddy agreed. "But I guess we all do stupid things when we're not thinking straight."

He didn't mean it. He wasn't even sure why he'd said it, except maybe to keep Drew talking. No way in hell would Teddy ever cheat a friend or threaten an old woman, no matter how messed up his head was. But while he didn't understand why Drew had done what he'd done, he wanted to.

Drew looked at the ground and said nothing for a few moments. "When I knocked on the door, I was expecting Mrs. Hawkins to answer, but instead, Nancy Leigh was standing there holding a .38 pistol. I almost pissed in my pants."

Drew's shoulders slumped. His entire posture had changed.

Teddy cleared his throat. "I imagine having a .38 pointed in your face would have that effect on you."

"Yeah. I was pretty shaken by that time. Then, when I walked inside and saw your mom and Mrs. Hawkins tied up in the parlor... I don't know. Something snapped in me."

Teddy blinked. Then his fists clenched. Something... snapped?

Fighting the urge to beat his old friend to a pulp, he gritted out, "Let me get this straight. You saw my mom—who was like a second mother to you—tied up with duct tape. And you just left them there. Do you have any idea how scared those two women were?"

Drew slowly shook his head.

"I'm sure this is hard for you to understand. But like I said earlier, I snapped. Later in the kitchen, I was lying on the sofa crying because I knew my family would disown me for plotting with Nancy Leigh. When I heard the gunshot and saw Nancy Leigh run out the back door, I knew that was my only chance to escape. If I'd hung around, I'd get arrested, bring shame and humiliation to my family, and lose everything I had worked so hard for."

"And running away? That didn't bring your family shame and humiliation?"

Teddy looked down, unable to keep the disgust from his face.

"Of course, it did." For the first time, there was an edge to Drew's voice. "But I couldn't see that then."

"Okay. Okay." Slowly, Teddy unclenched his fist. "After you ran, what then?"

Drew filled in the gaps, how he'd hitchhiked up to D.C. and found work with an attorney who'd paid his rent and a weekly cash allowance.

Teddy shook his head. There was no way Drew could've made this story up. "So, you've been living in D.C. all this time?"

"Yeah," Drew said. "Until September."

He told Teddy how he'd learned about the cartel's plot to buy the farm, and how, when Teddy refused to sell, they planned to sabotage Silver Circle in retaliation. They planned to put something in her food to impede her performance in the Derby, then dose Blackjack with something to enhance his. They'd bet on Blackjack and win millions.

Teddy couldn't believe what he was hearing.

A drug cartel had offered him five million dollars. It was an extravagant offer. They must really want the farm. Did they really think he'd give it up if Silver didn't win?

Drew continued, "Make no mistake, if this plan doesn't work, they have a Plan B."

"Plan B?"

Drew nodded.

They sat in silence for a long time.

Teddy knew what Drew meant. They wouldn't stop the intimidating tactics until he sold them the farm.

Teddy had to stop these guys. Plan B might involve actually hurting the horses—or worse, one of his girls, and he couldn't bear the thought of something happening to Katie or Mattie Grace.

Then Teddy said, "And you came here because…?"

"To stop them, of course."

They were silent for a few more moments. Then Teddy said, "Do you think these guys have tampered with the water supply?"

"I don't know, but the guy I saw earlier had a duffle bag over his shoulder… no telling what was inside."

Teddy was tired, but he had processed everything Drew had told him. "Did you ever try to contact Colleen or your parents?"

Drew shook his head. "I didn't. I knew it would be too much for them."

Too much for them, or too much for you?

Teddy bit back the question. Maybe he didn't want to hear the answer.

Teddy got up and walked over to the stall door, but he remained silent. He was waiting for Drew to finish his story. He hesitated to say anything for fear he would say too much.

The silence stretched on, even in the moonlit stall, Teddy knew Drew was hurting. He could hear the pain in his old friend's voice.

Teddy's mouth was dry. He needed a drink, but after all the hurt Drew had inflicted on him and his family, Teddy didn't know if he should leave him alone with Silver Circle.

He'd only be gone a minute, but he wasn't sure Drew could be trusted.

Still, Drew had shown remorse and acted in good faith when he came down to stand guard over Teddy's horses.

Finally, Teddy opened the stall door. "I'm going to get a drink from the machine at the end of the stable. Do you want anything?"

Drew shot him a grateful look. "A water would be great. Thanks."

As he went to get the drinks, Teddy thought back to the question Don Johnson had asked him. What would he do if Drew Byrd ever showed back up? That same sick feeling rolled over him as he pondered the question.

He'd always thought, if the moment presented itself, he would do the right thing. He would extend grace to the man who had betrayed him.

Instead, his stomach flipped, and he rushed to the nearest trash can.

Chapter Sixty-Four

Drew sat in silence, waiting for Teddy to return from the soft drink machine. He leaned his head against the wall, gazing toward the ceiling. Not that he could see anything important; the room was dark except for the exterior light that filtered through the window and danced off the opposite wall.

He pinched the bridge between his eyes. Teddy must've had a million questions, but his friend—if he still was a friend—was a classy guy. So far, he'd carefully measured each remark. A smaller man would not have been as tolerant.

Teddy returned and quietly handed Drew a bottle of water.

There was a notable change in his posture. He looked weak, holding his stomach as if it hurt.

What had happened to him?

Teddy plopped down against the wall next to a bale of hay. When he finished what he wanted of his soft drink, he laid his head on the hay and dozed off to sleep.

Whew, no more questions for now.

Drew welcomed the silence. He'd become used to a solitary existence, and he relished the quiet. But, as much as he owed Teddy an explanation, it mentally exhausted him to relive the events of those years and the uncertainty of Teddy's response.

He offered Silver another handful of oats. Her breathing had stabilized. Finally, it seemed Teddy's feeding plan had worked.

She seemed much better—fine, in fact.

Drew lay back on a soft pile of hay and closed his eyes. He'd almost drifted off to sleep when he heard a soft footstep.

Then there was a thump.

He lay still for a few seconds. When he opened his eyes, a shadow moved outside the stall.

Quietly, Drew got up, moved over to the wall, and listened for more movement.

He heard whispers. A brief chuckle. And finally, an expletive.

Drew reached for his gun at the side of his boot. Then he tiptoed out, peeked around the door frame, and looked inside Redemption's stall. He'd been waiting all night for these two, but in the dim light of the stable, they had entered the wrong stall.

One of them struggled to get a rope over Redemption's head. The older man was in the back trying to push Redemption out of the corner of the stall.

Drew glanced at Redemption. He was about the same height as Blackjack, but in the darkness, the chestnut-colored colt appeared black. Hearing a noise outside the building, Drew stepped away from the stall door.

He took in a deep breath, allowing himself a moment to reconsider his move. His pants and shirts were unremarkable, but the men would recognize his brown plaid wool jacket. It was the only jacket he owned, and they had seen it every time they'd been at the farm. Drew slipped back into Silver's stall and nudged Teddy's leg with his foot. When Teddy's eyes opened, Drew motioned for him to get up.

Teddy rubbed the sleep from his eyes and quietly stood.

There was another expletive from the other side of the wall. Drew pointed to it and mouthed. "I've got my gun."

"Don't!" Teddy whispered. "It'll traumatize these animals."

Drew took off his jacket and handed it to Teddy. "Here, give me your jacket."

Teddy hesitated and then switched jackets with Drew.

"Wait in the car," Drew whispered. He handed Teddy a set of keys. "I'm driving an older model black Tahoe, parked right outside the stable. Be ready to move. They probably have a getaway car waiting nearby."

Drew pulled a ski mask over his head and slipped the gun into his coat pocket. He waited for Teddy to get outside. Then he went back to Redemption's door and watched.

Were they trying to drug the horse?

The older man fumbled with a syringe and a vial of serum. He was either extremely nervous, or his gloves prevented him from keeping a grip on the vial.

The younger guy still struggled to get the rope over the animal's head.

Although he was a tall man, Redemption was a taller horse, at least sixteen hands, perhaps more.

He wouldn't budge. The horse was intelligent... and sensed trouble.

Drew entered the stall and deepened the pitch of his voice so the men wouldn't recognize him. "What are you doing in here?"

When Drew walked around the horse, the shorter man dropped the syringe, slipped out of the stall, and ran. The second man elbowed Drew in the face.

The impact of the blow caused Drew to stumble, but as he recovered, he removed the gun from his pocket. The taller man's eyes widened, and he bolted from the stable.

Two against one. The men hadn't even tried to tag-team him. He was sure they had weapons, so why hadn't they used them? After all this time, planning and plotting, had they finally lost their nerve? Perhaps they'd realized they were in the wrong stall. Or perhaps they simply didn't want the kind of attention a gunshot would bring.

He couldn't be sure.

But whatever the reason, their presence meant trouble. They had manipulated someone to gain access to the horses, and Drew wasn't about to let them harm one of Katie's.

The moment was his, and he was going after them.

When he got outside, Teddy flashed his lights, and Drew went over to the vehicle. "Get over. This could get ugly."

Teddy slid over the console for Drew to take the wheel. Drew jumped in and threw the rope over the back seat.

"Kill your lights, Drew. Here comes their truck."

"Are you sure?"

Teddy explained that someone was waiting in a nearby truck when the two men ran out of the stable. "When the first guy opened the truck door to get in, I got a good look at the driver."

When the long, black truck went by, Drew saw the outline of the men's heads through the rear window of the extended cab. The taller man was in the backseat behind the driver. Drew spotted security vehicles parked throughout the facility as the truck crept by.

The truck exited the lower parking area and turned right, moving at a creep.

With their headlights off, Drew followed along until they reached the main gate. The truck picked up speed as it turned onto the main road, and Drew let a few cars pass before he turned on the headlights and followed at a safe distance.

They'd gone a little over a mile when the truck in front slowed.

Did they suspect they had been followed? Or were they just being cautious?

Drew reduced his speed to match the truck.

Finally, the driver stepped on the gas. The truck hurtled down the mountain, and at every curve, the driver swerved a little wider of the median.

Drew increased his speed as well. The truck's rear window opened, and the tall man fired off several shots. A bullet pinged off Drew's side view mirror.

"Holy crap! He's firing at us!" Drew looked down at the dashboard. The needle hovered a fraction below eighty miles an hour.

"Man. Back off," Teddy said. "He's got the advantage here."

The truck suddenly shot forward, obscured by the mountain.

"I agree. It's dark out here." The steering wheel was damp from Drew's sweaty hands. "He's going at least ninety. That's way too fast on these roads." He wiped the sweat from his brow.

"Try backing off. Maybe he'll slow down when he finds out we're not playing his game. I don't want to be the reason he misses that next big curve."

As they approached the wicked curve, they heard tires squealing. The truck fishtailed around the bend and Drew yelled, "Watch out!" But the blinding lights from an eighteen-wheeler hit the vehicle. For a moment, Drew couldn't see. Then he heard a loud crash ahead as the eighteen-wheeler roared past their Tahoe.

"Pull over," Teddy said. "I think their truck hit something."

Drew slid the Tahoe onto the median just before the curve. A wide gap stretched between two ragged ends of the guardrail; the metal twisted into a grotesque parody of sculpture.

Drew jammed the Tahoe into park and ran to the guardrail without shutting off the engine. Teddy was close behind him. They watched in silence as the truck rolled down the embankment, then flipped over and burst into flames at the bottom of the ravine. The air was thick with dark smoke and smelled of burnt rubber. Drew suddenly couldn't breathe. His heart pounded so hard his chest hurt.

He ran his hand through his hair. Why hadn't the men tried to overpower him in the stable? Perhaps they'd heard the same noise he'd heard coming from outside the building. It could've spooked them. One thing about the cartel, they fought to win, but when they sensed defeat, they got the hell out of the sandbox. They'd been in the "big house" for one stint of time, with no intention of ever going back.

Drew shook his head. "The driver of the eighteen-wheeler must not have seen the truck leave the road. Otherwise, he would've stopped."

"It's the middle of the night," Teddy said. "I'm sure he wasn't expecting a truck to round that curve going 80 miles per hour." He calmly removed his cellphone from his jacket, and pressed 911.

When he'd made the report, he turned to Drew. "Did you recognize those guys as the two in the stall?"

"Yeah. That was them."

"How can you be certain?"

"Remember earlier when I told you about the two guys in the bar? The ones I overheard talking about kidnapping Katie's horse?"

"Yeah."

"Those were the guys I followed to Georgia. I've been providing them with legal counsel in exchange for a place to live."

Teddy paled. It must have finally hit him how close they'd come to a direct altercation with members of the drug cartel.

They waited in silence for the emergency vehicles to arrive.

Finally, Drew kicked a rock down the embankment. "Who was the big dude driving the truck?"

Teddy rubbed his forehead. "Do you remember Big Jim Levinson?"

Drew shook his head, confused. "The mayor of Abington?"

"Yep. That was the infamous Big Jim."

Chapter Sixty-Five

B y the time the authorities finished their questioning, Teddy felt wrung out. He and Drew drove back to the stable in silence, each lost in his individual thoughts. The stable was dark and quiet. It was an eerie quiet. And, for some reason, it looked different than it had just an hour earlier when two members of a drug cartel had attempted to drug Redemption.

Drew checked Redemption's stall while Teddy checked on Silver. Then they took their positions in Silver's stall and took turns feeding her oats. After the subsequent feedings, they settled in next to the wall.

Just before daylight, Teddy drifted off to sleep. The last thing he heard was Drew's even breathing.

When he awoke, Drew was climbing to his feet, and the vet stood at the stall door, waiting to come inside. It was half-past eight o'clock, and people were already gathering outside the window.

Dr. Boone methodically examined Silver Circle. "Did you guys spend the night down here?"

They both nodded.

The vet ran a hand over the filly's withers. "I don't understand it, but Silver Circle is one hundred percent improved. Her labs show no signs of a virus or food poisoning—and if she had either of those, she could never have recovered so quickly. But whatever she had; she seems to be over it."

He checked her mouth for any sign of infection in the gum area. Then he frowned and squinted into her right nostril. He reached for his flashlight and looked into both nostrils. Then, he removed an instrument from his medical bag. "Mr. Williams, I need you to hold her head still for me, please."

Teddy moved closer and took the lead rope, holding it close to the halter.

Carefully, the vet removed a piece of tan-colored sponge from Silver's right nostril. He looked again at the left one, but it was clear.

Still holding the piece with his instrument, he said. "Well, here is the problem. Someone inserted a piece of sponge into her nostril."

"I don't understand," Teddy said. "Why would someone do a thing like that?"

Dr. Boone explained that any foreign object inserted into her body could affect the animal's behavior, and the body responds similarly to having a viral infection. Then he leaned over and ran a hand over each of her legs.

Even with his limited experience, Teddy could tell there was no swelling. It appeared that the slight fetlock injury from the last race injury had completely healed.

It was a miracle.

The vet looked up, grinning. "This sponge incident might end up being a blessing for Silver Circle. There's nothing like a day of full rest to eliminate swelling from an animal's legs."

"Are you saying she can race today?"

"No guarantees, but it looks promising." Dr. Boone gave Silver's flank a pat. "Had the diagnosis been a viral infection, I would've had no choice but to scratch her from the roster. It would've been unconscionable to let an animal race immediately following an infection."

But this was a different scenario.

"Do you have any enemies, Mr. Williams? Perhaps someone who wouldn't want your horse to win today?"

Teddy looked at Drew. "Yeah, I think we know who might have done this."

The vet looked from Teddy to Drew. When they didn't offer more information, Dr. Boone sighed and promised to check on her throughout the day. If Teddy's team could make sure she ate small amounts for a few more hours, he thought she'd be ready to race by late afternoon.

As they walked toward the door, Teddy asked, "And if we can't get her to eat? What happens then?"

Dr. Boone turned toward Teddy and extended his hand, "Then she'll be ready to run in the Preakness."

When the vet had gone, Teddy placed his hand on Drew's shoulder. "You're coming to the race this afternoon, right?"

Drew laughed.

"No, man. I have nothing to wear. These clothes are all I've got."

"Come on," Teddy said. "Let's go up to our suite. You can get a shower and change. You look like you could wear a size 36."

When Teddy and Drew opened the door to the suite, the lights were off.

Katie had left a note on the nightstand.

Gone to breakfast with Frank and Claire.

Whew! Thank goodness. He had a lot to explain to her, but he didn't want to rush through it. He needed more time to do it justice.

Pointing to the bathroom, Teddy said, "There are plenty of fresh towels. You'll find a robe behind the door."

As soon as Drew closed the bathroom door, Teddy hung around long enough to hear the water from the shower. Then he went back into the living area and dialed Andrew's room.

"Hi Andrew, it's Teddy. I have a favor to ask. Could you and Daisy meet me in the restaurant downstairs at 9:30? There's something I need to talk to you about."

When the call ended, Teddy made a call to the registration desk. Then he went back to the bedroom and found Drew something to wear to breakfast. He opened the bathroom door, slipped inside the dressing area, and placed the clothes on the counter.

He hoped he was handling this the right way. It might be better to meet in Andrew's hotel room and have Drew wait outside while Teddy prepared Drew's parents for his appearance. But even though both sides had spent many years praying for this reunion, there was no way to predict how it would unfold. That there would be joy, he had no doubt, but there might also be resentment and recrimination. A more public meeting would encourage a more cautious approach and give everyone a chance to retreat if the situation became overwhelming.

Teddy quietly closed the door and started looking through the closet for a jacket for Drew to wear to the race. He'd never removed the brand-new jacket Katie had bought for him to wear from the black plastic bag.

Teddy didn't hesitate. He grabbed it, along with the new khaki slacks, and quickly removed the tags.

Next, he rummaged through his shirts until he found the pale blue polo and placed it next to the other articles of clothing.

Shoes. He'd need a decent pair of shoes. But Drew's feet were two sizes larger than his own, so he called down to the front desk. "Please connect me to the concierge's desk." He asked the concierge to deliver a pair of brown shoes and a belt to their suite ASAP. A few minutes later, a steward arrived with the items he'd ordered.

While Drew dressed, Teddy carefully placed the clothing in the hanging bag. Before he zipped it, he found an envelope in the desk drawer. He slipped a ticket to the race and a few bills inside the envelope and stuck it in the jacket's pocket.

He stepped back and smiled. Done.

When Drew walked out into the living area, he pointed to the black bag and said, "What's this?"

"Clothes for you to wear to the race. We'll drop them by your room before going to the restaurant."

Drew laughed. "Man, I don't have a room. I've been sleeping in the backseat of the Tahoe for the past two nights."

"Well, you have a room now. You're in room 2026. Here's the door code. You should keep this card with you at all times." Teddy looked at his watch. "Come on. We need to stop by your room before going down to eat breakfast."

Drew unzipped the bag and looked at the clothes with disbelief. "You put this together… while I was in the shower?"

Teddy nodded, then grabbed his keys and wallet from the table. "An envelope with your ticket is in the pocket inside the jacket."

Drew threw the black bag over his arm, then squeezed Teddy's shoulder. "Thanks, man. You didn't have to do this."

"Yes, I did," Teddy paused and walked toward the door. Then, he turned and said, "You'd do the same for me."

Chapter Sixty-Six

Drew double-checked the locked door when they left his hotel room. Then he looked at his watch. It was 9:35. His parents should already be at the restaurant.

They went straight to the hotel's main floor. The lobby was empty except for a couple of ladies going toward the gift shop.

As they approached the entrance to the restaurant, Drew's eye darted to the door and back to Teddy. "Why don't you go in first, talk to Mom and Dad for a few minutes, and let them know I'm here?"

Teddy agreed.

Drew walked over to a small sofa and picked up a copy of the morning paper. Then after ten minutes of trying to focus on an article about Silver Circle's run for the 2022 Triple Crown, he looked up as Teddy stood at the restaurant entrance.

Teddy motioned for him.

"How did it go?"

"Of course, they're in shock. But the tears in your mama's eyes are tears of joy." He chuckled. "Andrew is so emotional he can't even speak."

"But they're okay, right?" Drew hesitated, allowing his parents a moment to let it sink in before going inside the restaurant.

Teddy nodded. "Daisy wanted to call Colleen right away, but I asked them to wait and let you decide how to handle that." He looked around the lobby. "You and I should probably talk again before you talk to her."

"That sounds grim."

"Yeah, well. A lot has happened since you…" Teddy pointed to the sofa near the door. "Anyway. If you need anything, I'll be over there, reading the morning paper"

Drew looked around the restaurant and saw his parents sitting at a table near the window. His dad sat across the table from his mother. When he left Abington, his father stood tall, back straight as the handle of a gavel. Now his shoulders were rounded, his spine curved. The years had not been kind to him. With a trembling hand, he dabbed his eyes with a white handkerchief.

From his vantage point, he could only see the back of his mother's head. But he would have known her anywhere. A large silver clip secured her perfectly coiffed hair. It wasn't a ponytail like Colleen and the girls wore, but a stylish look that swept her hair away from her face. As he drew closer to the table, he could see her shoulders heaving from the sobs.

Drew choked and stopped in the middle of the restaurant, paralyzed by the hurt he had caused his parents.

A waiter approached him and asked, "Sir, can I show you to a table near the window?"

Drew lifted his fist to his mouth and coughed, misty eyed. He shook his head.

His parents got up from the table.

The waiter tipped his head in acknowledgement. "Of course. Please sit wherever you like, sir. Let us know if you need anything."

As the waiter walked away, Drew's dad approached with outstretched arms. His mom was close behind.

While he stood in the middle of the restaurant wrapped in his father's embrace, he glanced at the waiter, who quickly turned and walked into the kitchen.

Andrew held Drew close. The familiar smell of Old Spice permeated the space. His mother steadied herself by resting her hand on the back of the chair a few feet away, but he felt engulfed in her love just the same. It was the tenderness in her eyes that conveyed her feelings.

It was always her eyes.

Tears streamed down her cheeks as she watched them embrace. It had been a long time since they'd seen each other. Still, she hung back a bit, allowing Andrew a private moment with his son.

The last time Drew had seen his father was the day before he left Abington. They'd played golf that Friday afternoon. Normally, he would have spoken to his mother when he dropped his dad off at home, but that day, he was in a hurry to take Colleen out for dinner. It had been eight years since he'd seen them.

Eight years.

Eight years of memories he had missed.

There were eight years of birthdays, Thanksgiving feasts, Christmas Eve services, summer vacations, and various occasions in between.

He had missed them. All those memories he could never get back.

Lost. Gone.

His father released his embrace and led Drew back to their table.

Drew looked down at his mother and smiled.

"Hi, Mom. How are you?"

And that was all it took. Daisy took his face in both hands and kissed him. Then she told him to sit himself down and tell her everything he had been doing.

There were no interrogations. No reprimands—only sparkles of joy in her eyes that her son had returned.

"Have you eaten breakfast?" Daisy asked.

Drew shook his head.

"Well, let's get that waiter over here and order you something to eat. You look thin." Daisy reached for his hand. "The western omelet is fabulous, but so is the French toast. Oh, my goodness, the biscuits are even better than mine. They're so good you'll want to slap somebody."

Drew reached over and hugged her. "Mom, I've missed your sense of humor. And nobody's biscuits are better than yours."

Tears welled in her eyes. She quickly wiped them away.

"You won't believe this, Drew, but your father is talking about retiring at the end of the year."

"Dad, that's great news," Drew blinked away tears, then placed the napkin on his lap.

Andrew smiled, his gaze lingering on Drew as if he couldn't get enough of him. "Well, now that you're back, I may just put that retirement off. I want to work with my son for a few more years."

"But Andrew," Daisy said. "You promised me you'd hang it up at the end of the year so we can travel with Claire and Frank."

Drew's eyebrows lifted. "Frank? Who's Frank?"

Daisy and Andrew smiled at each other. Then she said, "Son, we've got a lot of catching up to do."

Chapter Sixty-Seven

While Drew enjoyed a hearty breakfast, his parents told him about all the changes in Abington. The next time the waiter walked by, Drew asked, "Can I get more coffee, please?" He couldn't seem to get enough. The restaurant blend tasted better than any he'd tried in a long time, and the juice tasted just like freshly squeezed oranges.

When the server had gone, his mom and dad resumed their narrative. Drew suppressed a smile, not wanting his parents to think he was being disrespectful, but it was cute how they talked over each other. Both sitting on the edge of their seats, eager to talk about the progress of their grandchildren. From all indications, the girls were doing well in school and sports. His mother passed across a wallet full of photos, and he savored each one, swallowing past the lump in his throat. He had missed so much.

"You won't believe this," his mom said, "but Jacob is the spitting image of you, Son." Drew grinned at the pride in his mother's voice. He'd also noticed the resemblance when he'd attended his son's college graduation, but he'd thought it might be wishful thinking,

They touched on Jacob's academic accomplishments and how much they looked forward to his joining the law firm upon graduation. Then Andrew changed gears.

"Your mom gave me a new grill for my birthday," he said, and added that he'd spent much of his spare time perfecting recipes.

His mom grabbed his father's hand and said, "Son, your father is quite the gourmet cook, as long as he's cooking on his Weber grill. I still won't let him use my gas stove!"

That stove was the same type used by a southern celebrity chef, and she wouldn't let anyone near her gas stove.

"You'll enjoy that grill even more, when you retire."

As Drew chewed the last of his bacon, the waiter came by and refilled his coffee. "How's Colleen doing? You guys haven't mentioned her at all."

Andrew looked toward the door. "See for yourself." He nodded to an area behind Drew.

Drew wiped his mouth with the napkins and pushed his chair away from the table. He stood and turned toward the entrance to the restaurant. Colleen stood just inside the door, next to a dark-haired guy waiting for someone to show them to a table. The guy had his arm around her waist, listening intently to whatever she was saying.

The guy looked taller than he'd remembered. Leaner, too. Then the guy pulled Colleen closer and kissed her hair.

It was intimate.

A gesture as intimate as he could make in public, short of kissing her on the lips.

It spoke volumes about their relationship as they were totally absorbed with each other and oblivious to anyone else in the room.

Drew sat back down and placed the napkin in his lap.

****

Colleen and Matt stepped off the elevator and walked straight to the restaurant. The lobby was empty, so they concentrated on the roster of horses Colleen held, which were scheduled to race later in the day. She'd allowed herself $1,000 to bet on Redemption. At the time she'd partnered with Katie and Teddy, there were high expectations for the young colt. Even though the bookies and clerks now considered Redemption a long shot to win the race, she had invested in him, and he was her horse.

When Matt asked her about a few of the other horses, she said, "It would be unconscionable of me not to put most of my money on Redemption. Besides, the owner of Nordstrom Farm said he could place high in the Derby."

Standing inside the restaurant, waiting to be shown to a table, Colleen looked around the room. "Where's the waiter? I'm starving already."

She saw Andrew, Daisy, and a bearded man she didn't recognize sitting at a table near the window. They seemed engrossed in conversation.

Looking back at her list of horses, she said, "How much should we bet on Silver Circle and Mr. Zee?"

Matt shrugged. He had reached for a menu and was scanning the breakfast items, clearly more interested in eating breakfast than betting. She explained that at least spreading the money among three horses would increase her odds of winning something back.

Matt smiled. "You're an efficient investor." He kissed her hair.

"Matt, would you mind if we sat with Andrew and Daisy this morning?"

Matt looked toward the big window. "I'd rather not."

She frowned. Colleen wanted Matt to get to know her in-laws—wanted them to see that he made her happy. "You've had me all to yourself for the past twenty-four hours. And we've spent very little time with them since we arrived yesterday."

Matt rolled his eyes. "Okay. If it makes you happy." Smiling, he brushed her cheek with the back of her hand.

Colleen leaned up and kissed him tenderly on the lips.

The waiter arrived and led them to the table.

Matt's hand rested at the small of her back as they approached the table. Breakfast with Andrew and Daisy couldn't be that bad. They were interesting people. Colleen was happy, and that was all that really mattered.

Colleen walked around the table and stood behind the chair next to Daisy, leaving the empty seat next to Andrew for Matt. "Good morning. Do you mind if Matt and I join you for breakfast?"

No one said a word. But Andrew and Daisy looked different—like they'd been crying.

Colleen smiled at Daisy, then at Andrew.

Matt removed his hand from his pocket, preparing to introduce himself to the man across the table from Andrew. Long hair. Scruffy beard. Then he immediately saw the resemblance to the pictures in Colleen's house. Who else could it be?

Andrew's eyes glistened as they darted to the other person at the table. He was about to burst with pride and relief that his son had shown up after so many years.

Great. Drew was back.

Colleen looked at the man, and her mouth dropped open. Her eyebrows shot up, and she looked back at Andrew in confusion.

Matt clenched his fist and shot Drew a stern look.

But Andrew's teary eyes danced with excitement as Colleen slowly stepped back and covered her mouth with her hand.

No words. Just a look of shock. An expression of disbelief replaced the joy on her face. Matt placed his arm around her waist to steady her.

Finally, Colleen said, "*Drew?*"

Drew nodded, looking from Colleen to Matt. Then he stood and extended his hand to Matt. "I'm Drew Byrd. I'm...,"

"Yeah, I know who you are." Matt glanced at Colleen. Her chin quivered, and the blood had drained from her face. He choked back the words that sprang to his lips—*You're the son of a bitch who walked out on his family.*

For a long, painful moment, the unspoken sentiment hung between them. Then Colleen stammered a greeting and, looking like she'd rather be anywhere else, pulled out the empty chair and joined Drew and his parents at the table.

****

Drew still couldn't believe the mother of his three children had a boyfriend. Not just a male friend, with whom she went out to dinner or to a movie, but an honest-to-goodness boyfriend.

As hard as it was for him to see them together as a couple, they'd gotten through it. At least they'd been civil to each other.

Drew quietly finished his breakfast while his mother conversed with Colleen and Matt about the upcoming race. He tried not to stare at the guy, but there was something about him that bothered Drew, aside from the obvious, of course.

He'd watched him from afar since returning to Abington. He had watched as he'd picked up Colleen for a date or taken the garbage out to the garage at night after dinner, and again when he arrived at Teddy and Katie's house on Valentine's night. Then there were the times he'd been at Rebecca's soccer games as Drew had watched from the nearby overpass. The guy was always around. Most recently, the night he came out the back door of the house while Drew was getting his knife out of the glove compartment of his classic car.

He chuckled, remembering hiding beneath the car while Matt dropped the garbage in the trash can. Matt had walked around the car to where the passenger door was ajar, but he hadn't bothered to slam it shut. As he sat across the table from Matt, Drew recognized something about him he'd not noticed earlier. It was the bushy eyebrows, the scar just above his right eye, and the prominent widow's peak. Was this guy... no, he couldn't be—no way.

As soon as Matt finished his breakfast, he kissed Colleen on the cheek and spoke to her in a soft voice. Then, he excused himself and left the restaurant. Her gaze followed as he left the restaurant. But what could the poor guy do? Continue to sit there? No, he'd made the right decision—it was best he'd left.

Technically, Colleen was still Drew's wife. They had not divorced, and she had never filed the paperwork to declare him legally dead. Nevertheless, he'd checked the website often.

Drew had every right to be sitting in the restaurant with his wife.

Not long after Matt left the table, Drew's dad suggested to his mom that they too should leave. "I've got a few calls to make, Daisy. Are you finished with your coffee?"

She looked at Drew and then Colleen and smiled. "Yes. I'm finished."

When they stood to leave, Drew stood and gave his mother a reluctant parting hug. Then, as his father walked by, he squeezed Drew's shoulder and gave him a meaningful smile.

Drew and Colleen were finally alone.

The silence was awkward. Colleen tugged at a lock of hair, still damp from the shower, a gesture he'd always found endearing. Drew slipped into the seat his mom had just occupied, and the scent of Colleen's shampoo filled the air.

After all the time he'd spent dreaming about this moment, Drew couldn't find the words to express his feelings. His love for her. Their home. The kids. Their grades. Their extracurricular activities. The questions were on the tip of his tongue, but he felt like a sixteen-year-old boy once again. He couldn't articulate his thoughts—the same as the first time he'd asked her to go to the Homecoming dance in high school.

He smiled at the memory. Colleen had finally asked him if he wanted her to go with him to the dance. They'd laughed about it for years!

Colleen was the first to speak. "Matt's a nice guy. We've been dating since last fall."

Drew only nodded and sipped his coffee—not trusting himself to speak yet.

"He's good to the kids... he owns a boat. Abington's temperatures have been in the low 80s, and we've been taking the girls out on the lake. Matt taught them to ski last weekend."

The waiter appeared and refilled their coffee. The sound of her voice drowned out the banging of pots and pans from the nearby kitchen. His father had never liked to sit near the kitchen. So why had he chosen this table today?

He glanced at the kitchen door and then back to Colleen.

When she next spoke, there was an edge to her voice as if she were trying to inflict pain. "Matt and Jacob play golf together."

The Saturday morning golf outings with Jacob were how Drew had finally bonded with his son. It was their special time. A couple of hours each week for father and son to enjoy each other's company.

Drew waited for the waiter to return to the kitchen. "I realize I owe you an explanation, Colleen."

Tears filled her eyes, and she bit her bottom lip. She seemed smaller than he remembered. There were no signs of aging, well, maybe a few fine lines around her eyes, but her hair looked beautiful in the longer style. The layered cut took years off her face.

She'd always looked like a little girl when she cried. The same was still true. "You can't just show up after vanishing for almost eight years and expect me to welcome you back with open arms!"

She covered her mouth with her hand and looked around the restaurant.

Drew could always read his wife like a book, but there was an obvious struggle going on inside her head. "We'll get to that, but for now, I wanted you to know that I'm moving back to Abington."

Her eyes widened, then she quickly glanced away.

Colleen loved Matt. Drew could tell by the way she'd looked at him. There was a tenderness in her glance. The same way she used to look at Drew.

He could accept that—he'd have to—but he was unprepared for what came next. Colleen wiped her nose and said, "I'm not sure I want you to come back to Abington to live. I don't want you around the children."

He dropped his head. He knew it would take time to regain her and the children's trust. Maybe he never could. But for now, his beautiful wife was sitting across the table, breathing the same air as he, looking as though she was trying hard not to climb over the table and hit him—or hug him. Either way would be fine with him; it would allow him to touch her. A brief touch of her hand would make him the happiest man in the world.

Her eyes glistened, but she wasn't moving. Instead, she sat upright, her back straight as an arrow and utterly poised, but she hadn't reached out to touch him. Not yet, but he was hopeful.

She was still sitting there. They were together.

Colleen had not followed Matt out of the restaurant.

She hadn't left with his mom and his dad, either.

She had stayed, and that was enough.

For now, that was enough.

Chapter Sixty-Eight

A fter their morning walks with the horses and talking with the jockeys, Teddy and Katie met Claire and Frank for lunch at an outdoor cafe. Then they stopped at the track to enjoy a couple of other races before heading up to their suite to change for the big race. It was the first time Teddy had an opportunity to speak privately with Katie about Drew.

As soon as they got into the elevator, Teddy felt the tension. He made a few casual remarks about their discussions with the jockeys, but Katie remained quiet.

His arm rested on the railing behind her back, but her spine remained stiff, her jaw tight.

Teddy unlocked the door to the suite and held it open while Katie walked ahead. He sat on the edge of the bed and put his face in his hands. It had been a long, tension-filled night and a lot of information to process, some of which he was still trying to wrap his head around.

Katie walked out of the bathroom, hands on hips, her head tilted to the right. "Are we going to talk about this or not?"

"Of course," he said. He removed his shoes and placed them in front of the nightstand. He'd hoped for a thirty-minute nap. Oh, well. "What exactly do you want to know?"

Katie walked around to the other side of the bed. "How about starting at the beginning?"

Teddy explained the previous night's events, beginning with his decision to spend the night in Silver's stall. When he described his meeting with Drew, her eyes grew wide, and when he got to the part where they chased the intruders onto the main highway, her mouth flew open. Clearly, she wasn't happy with her husband's involvement in a high-speed chase. When she learned Drew had risked his life and his cover to chase the vehicle, her eyes welled. A sob escaped her when Teddy described the truck's long tumble down the embankment.

"Why didn't you let me know what was happening last night? I always feel like I'm on the periphery of your decisions."

"What is that supposed to mean?" Teddy leaned against the coffee service station and poured himself a glass of water. "We were busy standing guard with your horses. Excuse me if I didn't stop and give you a play-by-play of what Drew told me. Geez! Should I have stopped and asked for your permission?" He knew that was a low blow. One he would likely pay for many years to come.

"Play-by-play! Are you kidding? Remember the LLC you created for the business? The one you conveniently forgot to tell me about. And the beach house you've been planning to buy? Did you ever once ask me about it?" She blew out a disgusted breath.

"It just seems like you go through life making decisions without even considering me."

Teddy turned and looked at his wife. What was going on with her? She was running the whole gamut of emotions, as if her hormones were in overdrive. Even the pitch and tone of voice sounded foreign to him.

Not that he'd ever say that. She'd bite his head off if he did. Still, he didn't like the inference that he made decisions without her input. "Seriously! Every decision I make is about you. You and Mattie Grace."

Teddy stomped into the bathroom and closed the door.

Chapter Sixty-Nine

A fter his shower, Teddy dressed in silence. When he went back to the nightstand to get his shoes, he noticed the partially opened drapes. Then his eyes darted to the dresser where a stream of light spotlighted Katie's hat, the one that coordinated with her new suit. He smiled to himself. She'd been so excited the day she'd brought it home from the store. Finally, she'd found the perfect hat.

It was also a perfect day for a horse race. The sky was clear. Another beautiful afternoon in Kentucky. But the temperature inside their suite was anything but perfect. Katie still hadn't looked at him since he'd gotten dressed.

Katie slipped the blue camisole over her head, shaking her long auburn curls as she looked at herself in the mirror.

Teddy leaned over to tie his shoes. Perhaps she needed a few moments alone. It had been a busy day, and he could use a few moments alone himself. "I'm heading out to the stables. Come on down when you finish dressing."

He grabbed his wallet and opened the door before she could object. He just couldn't stand another angry exchange. Not today. Not now.

He felt a sudden mood change as he entered the hotel's lobby. It was like walking into a mall at Christmastime, watching the excitement on the faces of the little children waiting in long lines to talk to Santa Claus.

At Churchill Downs, the adults experienced the excitement. The few small children in attendance rode around in strollers, and even

388 · RENEE PROPES

then, it wasn't a place a little one would want to spend the day. But, occasionally, he'd spot a young child in the crowd and was grateful Mattie Grace had stayed with a friend.

By the time Teddy got to the track, there was an electrifying wall of noise—excitement so thick you could almost cut it with a knife. He smiled as he, too, got caught up in the energy from the crowd.

He stopped and looked around at the masses of people in the concentrated area. An estimated 150,000 spectators attended the Derby each year. Security was tight. Each person admitted to the stables had gone through a vetting process, complete with criminal background checks. Only those who'd passed the stringent testing received official Churchill Downs lanyards.

The colorful outfits of the spectators added to the festivities. The ladies dressed in either strapless pantsuits or colorful sundresses with matching hats, and the men appeared dapper in their colorful ties and light-weight sports jackets and summer suits. Because of the high humidity, some opted to wear polo shirts instead of long-sleeved dress shirts. Men also wore funny-looking hats for the festivities. It was all just part of the horse racing culture. Whether the spectators liked it or not, they were required to wear the official lanyard without exception.

Teddy's thoughts of Katie softened, and he hoped she'd remembered to grab her new hat before leaving the hotel room. She'd looked stunning in her white pantsuit, but the blue straw hat with the white ribbon and the matching silk tank top underneath the jacket lifted the outfit to a different level of sophistication. It was an outfit reserved for a winner.

Perhaps that was an omen.

He arrived at the stable just in time to see Mr. Zee and his jockey preparing to walk toward the starting gate. The animal reared up, but the jockey immediately calmed him. Of the three horses, Mr. Zee had the most sensitive nature and was most affected by the noise of the crowd. Teddy pulled the jockey aside and said, "I've just got one more thing to tell you. Mr. Zee needs to set the pace. So, remember, keep him calm, because he'll need to go to the lead right out of the starting gate."

The jockey shot him a severe look. "Yes, sir. We've covered this already."

The noise was deafening. Teddy repeated. "You've got to keep him calm. Let him set the pace, so Silver Circle and Redemption can get comfortable in their surroundings. Then, when you feel him getting acclimated to the track, he'll instinctively know what to do. Normally, he backs off when the other two horses catch up with him, but if he wants to keep going today, just let him. Let's see what he can do."

The jockey smiled. "Mr. Williams, Silver Circle's odds are 5 to 1. Everyone is betting on your little filly today, her and, of course, Blackjack. But, trust me, Mr. Zee will do his part to get Silver across the finish line."

Frustrated, Teddy looked away and then back at the jockey. He needed the man to understand that Mr. Zee was a champion, too, and he deserved a chance to prove his ability. Of course, the jockey shouldn't deliberately push him too hard, but if he didn't back off, that'd be okay, too.

The jockey nodded. "I got it, sir. Anything else?"

"No. That's it."

The jockey saluted Teddy, and he and Mr. Zee walked off. Teddy returned the salute and then looked around for Katie. When he spotted her, he hurried to catch up. She seemed unaware of his presence as she started toward their box seats. He rushed ahead until he could reach out and touch her arm. Then he pulled her close and whispered in her ear, "Good luck today, pretty lady. Sorry about earlier—I'm just tired."

"I'm sorry, too. Good luck to Mr. Zee. I know how much you want him to win."

"Katie…" Teddy stopped and cocked his head. "Mr. Zee is your horse. He's just like Silver Circle and Redemption."

Katie scrunched her nose. "I just know how much you love Mr. Zee, that's all."

"I love all three horses. We—you've put your heart and soul into training these animals, but if the Hawkins Farm has a winner today, it'll be because of you. Not me. Assuming the financial responsibility for this business is far different from fulfilling a childhood dream."

Katie looked around; her face reddened when an older woman walked past them and had overheard their exchange. "Okay, Teddy," Her voice cracked. "I was wrong. I'm just trying to hold up my end of the business."

A staff member walked by, and Teddy called him over. "Sir, would you mind grabbing my wife and me a couple of those mint juleps?" He handed the steward a single bill and told him to keep the change. Then he turned back to Katie.

"Excuse me, sweetheart. You said you're just trying to hold up your end of the business. Tell me more about that."

As Teddy listened, he saw that vulnerable side of her, a side that was out of character for his strong, determined wife. Perhaps she felt they were competing to make the business work.

Teddy sighed as he rubbed his hand through his hair. "Listen, Katie. We are business partners. Understand? We're business partners who just happen to be married. These types of partnerships don't always work out." He touched her face. "But we love each other too much to let anything come between us, and all I've ever wanted was to help you fulfill *your* childhood dream. I am... I am not in competition with you."

When the steward returned, most people had cleared to find their seats or a place to watch the race.

"Thanks," Teddy said to the steward, and handed Katie her drink.

She looked at the ground. "Okay. I'm sorry. I admit I misunderstood your motives. When we win today, the first thing we'll do is buy that beach house you've been wanting."

"Sweetheart, I'm just waiting for you to give me the green light. The money from Uncle Frederick's property sale will cover the beach house. I thought a second home would be the best investment for our family and our future."

Katie set her drink down on the concrete wall and sighed. "I shouldn't have gotten so upset earlier, but, of course, you'd never finance that kind of purchase."

Teddy had that lopsided grin on his face as reached for her. "We're in this together, Katie. What's mine is yours, and what's yours..." Teddy smiled. "Is yours, too."

Katie giggled.

He pointed to the mint julep. "Why aren't you drinking that? It's a tradition here."

Kate laced her fingers through his. "Let's go. We need to find our seats. By the way, I like how you think." She rubbed her belly and smiled. "Our son will love having his very own beach house." Then she rushed off to find their seats. She was dragging Teddy by the hand.

Teddy's mind went numb. Trying to keep up, he thought, *son*?... What? What did she say?

Chapter Seventy

When Drew got to the track, he went straight to his seat to get out of the crowd. He looked around the stands as he stretched to see his family. His father had told him that his and Daisy's seats were in the same row as Colleen and Matt. That would be awkward—at least as awkward as breakfast—but he still got a little glow at the thought of seeing Colleen again.

He couldn't remember where he'd seen Matt before, but he was sure he had. Perhaps at the club during a member-guest tournament. There were always a bunch of guys from other areas playing in that tournament.

Finally, he spotted his parents sitting in the section across from him. Claire and presumably Frank sat in the same area. Laura, Rhett, and Roger were seated near the others. Drew wasn't sure where Teddy and Katie would sit. He hadn't seen them in several hours.

There were too many people here for his taste. After living a life of isolation for so many years, he'd much rather watch the crowd from a distance than be a part of it.

As he glanced at the section where his parents sat, he made eye contact with his dad. They raised a finger at each other in acknowledgment. Then he noticed two empty seats on the other side of Daisy. His gut instinct told him they had reserved those for Angie and Rebecca, but he wasn't even sure they were at the race. If not, he would've liked to have one of those seats himself. As far back as he could remember, his parents had enjoyed watching horse racing. He'd love to enjoy the banter with his mom and his dad while watching the horses pound the ground around the track.

As much as he wanted to talk to his children—hug them—tell them how much he loved and missed them—he restrained himself. Instead, he watched the empty seats. Hoping and praying he'd get a glimpse of them today. He'd have to be careful not to let them see him if they showed up.

He felt another pang of shame and sorrow. What kind of father was such a stranger to his children that they wouldn't even recognize him?

Andrew had asked him to wait until Colleen could figure out a way to tell the children that he was alive and well before contacting them. It had taken some persuasion, but finally, he'd agreed with his dad that they needed to hear the news from their mother that he planned to return to Abington.

He wondered how they would respond. Matt had been a constant in their lives for over six months. Yet, something wasn't right about him.

Again, he worried at that thought. It was the cadence of Matt's speech that sounded familiar. Drew had seen him before. He didn't seem like a D.C. type, though—not an attorney or a member of Congress.

Perhaps a lobbyist.

Drew stretched to see if he could see where Matt was sitting. The aisle seat next to Colleen was empty.

She was alone. Where were the children? Where was Matt?

Drew couldn't shake the thought that Matt looked familiar. He remembered the way Matt had turned to Colleen before leaving the breakfast table. What had he said to her?

Drew jumped up and left the stands.

He couldn't enjoy the race until he was sure about the man he'd seen earlier in the stable. Of course, he could be wrong—he hoped he was—but he had to make sure Silver Circle was well and ready to race.

Chapter Seventy-One

M att looked out over the track, arms resting on the rail. The encounter with Colleen's ex still chafed at him. He hadn't expected Drew to be such a rough-looking character.

The long hair. The beard. None of it looked like the man he'd imagined—the athletic, intellectual professional he'd seen in pictures scattered throughout Colleen's house.

Andrew, though—Andrew was the embodiment of an attorney. Conservative, well-spoken, calm, deliberate... the complete opposite of his son. Drew looked like anything but an attorney. A nomad, maybe, someone who'd lost his way and lived in the woods or under a bridge.

Matt stepped away from the rail and shook his head. Eight years. Why couldn't Drew have stayed missing?

And what was up with Colleen? From the way she'd talked about Drew for the past six months, Matt would've wagered she would've jumped into Drew's arms the moment she saw him.

The man's presence was everywhere. He was the ghost of Colleen's life—and now, Matt's too.

He could still see the pain on Colleen's face at breakfast, when he'd folded his napkin and excused himself. He couldn't have hurt more had someone reached inside his chest and stabbed his heart with an ice pick. But she had a decision to make, and him sitting there waiting for her to make it would only cause additional grief for everyone concerned.

396 · RENEE PROPES

Colleen had a family to consider. Matt only had himself, but he had a decision to make, too.

He glanced around to make sure no one was paying attention, then pulled his phone from his pocket and scrolled through his text messages. He'd only received one since Monday, and it was from his cousin—dated Tuesday afternoon.

It was a *what-if* type of message <Regardless of what happens, follow through with Plan B on Thursday afternoon.>

He'd already done that, but they'd expect him to follow up. Matt couldn't just relax now that Nic and the others had been killed. Quite the opposite. The cartel was a massive organization. There were always extra boots on the ground. Watching. Waiting.

Matt's shallow breaths continued as he examined his options. He was in love with Colleen. He had never felt about another person the way he felt toward her. Conflicted, he couldn't take his eyes off the screen. Should he return to Abington? Or play out his role and hope the cartel would let him walk away at the end?

The gun in his pocket suddenly felt heavy.

He'd stayed out of the family business up to this point. It wasn't the type of life he wanted. He lacked his cousin's nerves of steel. He'd agreed to this one time. But he'd told his cousin that, after this one, he was out. Never again. It was a simple assignment. No one could get hurt, but either way, now his life was about to change, and God only knew how bad it would get.

As he walked away from the railing, heading toward the stable, he touched his lanyard.

Wearing it had been a nuisance at first. But after a while, he'd just gotten used to it hanging around his neck. Since Colleen was part owner of Redemption, Matt's lanyard showed V.I.P. credentials. Same as before, entering the stables without Colleen felt like a betrayal. The security guard's back was to the window, and he didn't seem to notice when Matt came in and slipped into Silver Circle's stall. He'd been there only a few moments when he heard a movement outside.

He froze.

He turned and saw a man hurrying away from the stall door. Quickly, Matt removed the rubber gloves from his pocket and put them on. If he was lucky, the stranger hadn't noticed anything unusual, but he'd feel better once he'd finished.

He couldn't see the sponge he'd planted in the filly's nose on Thursday afternoon. Perhaps the trainers had removed it. When he tried to cram another piece into her nostril, she danced away, tossing her head, and snaking it from side to side. If he'd only thought to bring a flashlight, he could tell if the new sponge was securely lodged.

The animal seemed alert and well-rested. Yet, when Matt looked into her big, dark eyes, he felt the tension within the horse, as if she knew he wasn't her friend. He tamped down a pang of guilt. The sponge wouldn't hurt her, and once this was all over, he could devote himself to being the man Colleen needed him to be.

If she still wanted him.

He touched his breast pocket, where Colleen had slipped his ticket for today's race. That had to mean something. She could have given it to Drew, but she had given it to Matt instead. It meant he was still in the running.

A sound from the side of the building sent a jolt of adrenaline through him. He glanced back at Silver. Her head was bowed, sniffing at the piece of sponge on the ground in front of her. There was no time to reinsert it. Her jockey would be there any minute. Matt rushed out the side door and threw the rubber gloves and the remaining sponge into a nearby trash receptacle.

Then, like an apparition, someone appeared from behind the other building.

Drew.

Matt reached for his gun and engaged the silencer. The last thing he needed was to draw attention to himself, and the sound of a gun firing would upset every horse in the nearby stable and those lining up to take part in the big race.

Drew slowly walked toward him. He wore a creamed-colored sports jacket with a pale blue golf shirt underneath, and his beard was neatly trimmed. A complete transformation. His hair, jelled and combed straight back from his face, resembled the picture Colleen kept on the bedside table. A soft breeze announced his approach, carrying the scent of some woodsy aftershave.

Matt kept the gun concealed in his coat pocket, hoping he wouldn't need to use it.

Drew said, "Are you Matteo Suarez?"

Matt's pulse raced. How did Drew know his real name? His hand slid back into his pocket, finding the reassuring weight of his pistol.

"You're Nic Suarez's cousin, right? I assume you've heard he got killed last night in a car accident."

A heavy object in Drew's jacket pocket caught Matt's gaze. Drew quickly slipped his hand into his pocket, and the pointed object moved.

He's got a gun.

Matt slid the safety off, still hoping he wouldn't have to use the gun, but his heart was still pounding. All his senses channeled toward Drew.

Calmly, Drew withdrew his hand and pointed to the stable. "Why were you inside Silver Circle's stall on Thursday? Don't deny it because I saw you."

Just like a lawyer—never ask a question to which you don't already know the answer. His voice was steady when he spoke. No nervous tics or jerking hands—a question asked as calmly as someone might ask a child. Clearly, he already knew the answer.

Their eyes locked.

He should've known when he'd seen Drew at breakfast. The long hair. The coarse beard. Drew must have been the scraggly looking man he'd seen hanging around the stable since Thursday afternoon.

Now, Matt was sure Drew had seen him insert the sponge in Silver Circle's nostril on Thursday. His mind raced as it suddenly registered that Drew had also stopped the cartel's attempt to sabotage the race. Drew was a murderer. He was responsible for Nic's death. He'd been working against the cartel all along.

A deluge of emotions swept over him.

Drew reached into his pocket.

Gun!

Matt jerked the pistol from his pocket.

Drew's eyes widened. The gun accidentally went off in Matt's hand, and Drew fell backward. Matt doubted Drew had even had a moment to register the impact.

Slowly, it dawned on Matt that Drew was no longer a threat to him or Colleen. Matt felt a surge of relief as his breathing returned to normal. He quickly slid the safety off and returned the gun to his boot. A cell phone lay next to Drew's hand. Matt bent to pick it up.

A cell phone—it wasn't a gun. It was an older model...

He looked around the area. No one was in sight. His shirt was damp with perspiration, and his palpitations increased as guilt engulfed him. He'd just shot Angie's and Rebecca's father, and Jacob's, too. Colleen would never forgive him. He paced back and forth, then in a circle.

It wasn't self-defense. He'd shot an innocent man.

There was never a gun. It was his imagination.

He'd stopped pacing. He would lose everything if the authorities discovered he'd shot an unarmed man.

His life would be effectively over.

He had to hide what he'd done.

Fighting down panic, he scanned the area and noticed a gully a few feet away. Again, no one was in sight—no one hanging around the stable. They were at the track, getting ready for the race.

It was about to start. Matt looked back and saw Drew's bloody blue shirt. He went back over to the body, grabbed both feet, and dragged it to the edge of the gully.

He glanced at the hole in Drew's shirt—blood saturated the area. It was a perfect shot to the heart. But how could that be? He'd never intentionally fired the gun; it had just bucked in his hand. Finally, he dumped the body into the gully.

Matt took a moment to brush the dust from his clothing and ensure there were no grass stains or blood spots on his slacks. He heard a noise in the gully—a moan. Matt shook his head, knowing his mind was playing tricks on him. He shook it off. There was no way anyone could've survived that shot.

He looked around one last time. The coast was clear. Then he dashed toward the V.I.P. section and reached in his jacket for the ticket. Matt's hand shook as he surveyed the location of his seat. He walked to the end of the section and spun his head.

He felt someone watching him, but he did not see anyone from security. Just paranoia.

Get a hold of yourself, Matt.

He looked at the stands above where he stood.

Moving along the walkway, he moved far enough away to watch the Byrds' seats. Andrew and Daisy, and another couple—already seated.

He pinched the bridge of his nose. He should've wrapped the body, but there wasn't anything lying around that would serve the purpose. The landscape crew at Churchill Downs maintained meticulous grounds. Even with 150,000 people present, finding a tarp or a large enough piece of trash would be difficult.

Then he spotted Colleen looking around the grandstand. She looked exhausted.

Matt inched his way closer to the section.

As the crowd sang the first notes of "My Old Kentucky Home," Matt watched the two empty seats on the other side of Andrew. The end seat next to Colleen was still vacant.

He looked down at his jacket. There was a tiny spot of blood on the lapel. When he looked up, a security guard with a radio in his hand looked straight at him.

Matt turned and glanced toward the starting gate. The assistant starters were finishing their inspections. Finally, he spotted Redemption being loaded into the gate, waiting for the bell to sound. When he turned back around, Colleen had spotted him. A huge grin appeared on her face. Her eyes danced with joy.

Matt slipped into the seat next to Colleen. He took her hand.

Still smiling, she reached up and kissed him. "I'm so glad you're here. I was terrified you'd left."

"No, bebé. I'm not going anywhere, at least not by choice."

She squeezed his hand. "I love you, Matt."

A loud bell sounded, signaling the start of the race. Matt pulled her close and kissed her hair. He prayed she'd never find out what had just happened behind the stable. He promised himself, if they could get through this, he'd make it up to her and always be the man she thought he was.

Chapter Seventy-Two

Teddy and Katie arrived at the track just in time to join the contenders and their connections walk to the paddock, in preparation for race number twelve—the Kentucky Derby presented by Woodford Reserve.

Fortunately, they were in their seats in a section specifically reserved for the owners, for the call to post, a trumpeter's signal that all mounts should be at the paddock exit in order to proceed to the track to begin the post parade.

It had been an emotional few hours for Katie, beginning with the remarks she and Teddy exchanged in the hotel room. But, then, as she watched the garland and trophy procession and the official portrait of the jockeys, those words were already forgotten. Instead, the years of dreaming about racing in the Derby had arrived. Luckily, her senses were oblivious to the smells of cigar smoke, flowers, bourbon, mint, dirt, and horse manure—all distinctive smells on race day.

The pride she felt during the jockey walk and the excitement of hearing the words 'Riders' Up' exclaimed across the loudspeaker— the call where the jockeys are instructed to mount their horses—was beyond description. But nothing could have prepared her for the roller-coaster of emotions she felt as the horses stepped onto the track for the Kentucky Derby post parade, and when over 147,000 people joined their voices in perfect harmony to the words of 'My Old Kentucky Home.'

Katie looked around their section for Drew. Where could he be? Perhaps he'd traded his ticket for a better place to watch the race. She turned around and saw the droves of people standing against the back of the grandstands. Except for the luxury boxes, perhaps standing gave the best vantage point.

She leaned close to Teddy, then looked down and patted her belly. "What do you think about our little buddy here?"

Teddy put his arm around her waist and pulled her close. "I've had my suspicions, but I can't believe you kept it from me."

"Ha! I learned from the best."

He kissed her nose and said, "I'm ecstatic about our good news! Now let's win this race!"

When the bell sounded, the gates opened, and twenty horses bolted out onto the track.

Blackjack bumped Redemption straight out of the gate. Redemption faltered and fell behind, fifth from the last. Katie's hand tightened on Teddy's.

Fortunately, Cappelletti had trained their horses to withstand the inevitable bumps they'd received on the track. The big colt quickly regrouped.

The hooves of the twenty horses pounded the dirt track with such intensity that Katie could feel the vibration in the stands.

Mr. Zee had started at the far end of the gate, an advantage allowing him to exit without a horse running to his left. As usual, he was out front from the start. But wait…

What's he doing?

The jockey was seemingly pushing the horse too hard or else Mr. Zee's speed had improved since the last race.

Mr. Zee was still leading at the halfway marker, but the white foam was visible on his upper body. Gradually, Silver Circle closed the gap. All eyes had been on the feminine little filly from the start of the race. She'd moved with such grace. Watching Silver run around the track was like hearing a symphony—it was melodious. Perhaps because of her size, the spectators had enthusiastically cheered for her in every race leading up to the Derby. Newspapers from all over the country reported her track speed at thirty-four miles per hour compared to the average rate of thirty. A lot of money was riding on the little filly from Georgia.

Redemption had gained momentum and caught up with the leading horses. He fought to stay in the race to the three-fourths mile marker.

Mr. Zee must have sensed Silver's presence nearby. Slipping into his role, he slowed his pace and let her pass. Katie glanced at Teddy. If he was disappointed, his face didn't show it. Instead, he was leaning forward, watching the action with rapt attention. Katie pulled her focus back to the track.

Going into the last turn, Redemption let loose and pulled into the lead.

Blackjack stayed neck and neck with him, while a burst of speed put Tiramisu in third and Sterling in fourth.

Silver Circle fell into fifth place.

As her speed decreased and she fell behind, a collective groan echoed throughout Churchill Downs. Who would have thought the little filly would be in fifth place at this turn? Obviously, the events of the previous few days had compromised her performance.

Blackjack was suddenly out front, and it was clear he came from a championship line. He was a striking horse with great stamina.

As the horses rounded the track under the late afternoon sun, a shiny tinge of blue reflected off Blackjack's black coat. He was fast and solid. Ten years earlier, his father had won the Derby and the Preakness, but the upset at the Belmont was devastating for Blackjack's sire; he'd lost by a head. The sports media recounted that defeat at every race where Blackjack participated.

Blackjack now had a larger following than his father ten years previously.

Blackjack—Redemption! The crowd screamed as the horses rounded the curve.

At the final stretch, the crowd was so loud, Katie found it hard to hear her own thoughts. She dared not try to speak.

Her gaze found Sammy in the crowd near the finish line, watching the race intently, his hands clamped to his ears.

No one blinked as all eyes watched the track.

Blackjack, Redemption, and Tiramisu were three deep. Silver Circle had regained a bit of momentum and moved into fourth. She blasted ahead of Tiramisu and edged between Blackjack and Redemption. Blackjack sensed her presence and thrust his body to the right. Silver Circle outwitted the black colt and avoided his attempted bump.

Once again, the crowd chanted, *Silver, Silver!*

The crowd roared with excitement as Blackjack and Silver battled it out for the leading position. Redemption trailed by a hair. Then, the three horses stretched their graceful bodies, fighting to gain the lead.

Redemption sped up as he approached the finish line. The screaming spectators watched his body bunch, then make a miraculous leap ahead of Blackjack and Silver Circle.

The crowd exploded as Redemption crossed the finish line a second later and won the race!

Katie and Teddy stared at the track with their mouths open.

Finally, Teddy turned to Katie and said, "Congratulations. This is your moment!"

"It's *our* moment," Katie replied. "You're just as responsible for this win as me."

Teddy said, "It's not the same thing."

Katie put her hands on Teddy's face. Tears filled her eyes. "Sweetheart, you believed in my dream. You slept in the stable with our horses, fed Silver every hour, and kept Redemption and Mr. Zee hydrated throughout the night. You and Drew chased those awful men out of Redemption's stall. You kept him from being drugged, and because of your devotion, our horse won the race."

Where *was* Drew? She had to thank him for keeping her horse safe.

She hoped he'd watched the race. The security was tight, but with the ticket Teddy had given him, he should have been sitting in the same row with them. She looked all around, but no Drew.

Maybe he felt uncomfortable about sitting so close to Colleen and Matt. Or perhaps he'd simply found a better seat. Well, he'd probably catch up with Teddy after the race.

Katie smiled at Teddy. "We won!" Her heart felt so full she could hardly contain it. There was so much she wanted to say, but the words seemed inadequate. Corny. Sentimental. Like drugstore greeting cards. But sometimes, a drugstore greeting card was the best you could do. She slipped her arm through his and said, "Thank you, Teddy. For sticking with me through these last few years. I know it's been hard on you."

"It's been a fun ride... but I must admit, you sure know how to pick a winner!"

She tightened her grip on Teddy's hand. "I certainly do. Come on, lover boy, let's go to the Winner's Circle."

Teddy grinned. "Ooh, I like the sound of that!"

When they got to the circle, Cappelletti talked with members of the media. Sammy was petting Redemption and laughing with Frankie Burel. Their jockey couldn't wipe the grin from his face as the officials ceremoniously placed a garland of red roses onto Redemption's back.

As Teddy and Katie stepped forward, the television announcer quickly completed his interview with Cappelletti and turned toward Teddy to ask, "What are your thoughts about Redemption's performance at the Derby?"

Teddy gestured to Katie. "You should ask my wife that question. He's her horse. She's the one who found Redemption and trained him."

The reporter turned to Katie and repeated the question.

"Redemption ran a noble race," Katie said. "The greatest run of his life!"

The announcer asked if it surprised her that Redemption had won instead of Silver Circle.

Katie shook her head. "No, not at all."

She smiled, remembering the brief encounter between the horses at the paddock gate. She explained how Redemption had turned to Silver and nudged her. Innately, he knew she wasn't one hundred percent. Thoroughbred horses are intelligent creatures. Silver responded in her own sweet way... as if they were communicating. "She stepped back and bowed her head at him, just like a young bride might do for her groom."

"That's a beautiful story."

"It was at that moment, when Silver Circle bowed, that I knew Redemption could win the race."

"You instinctively knew that he would win?"

"Yes. As my grandmother used to say, I just felt it in my bones. But make no mistake—Mr. Zee cleared the way for Redemption to win this race."

The reporter recounted the efforts of Redemption, Blackjack, and Silver Circle. It had been a close race; one he would've never suspected to turn out as it did. "The ending of this story reads like a fairy tale."

"People all over the globe expected Silver Circle to win the Triple Crown," she said. "Redemption was a long shot. His performance in the races leading up to today was less than impressive, but Redemption got a second chance." She squeezed Teddy's hand and smiled.

A siren blasted in the background. Blue lights flashed from the patrol car as it stopped at the bottom of the hill.

The security guard stopped about twenty feet away. He was wearing dark glasses, but Matt could tell the man was watching him.

As everyone celebrated the race, Matt glanced around the crowd and saw the guards coming. He considered trying to maneuver his way out and escape, but that would put Colleen in danger, and he'd rather go to prison—he'd rather die—than do that.

As the spectators moved closer to hear the interview, four security guards deftly moved toward Matt. Quietly, one of the guards flashed his credentials. "Matteo Suarez, you have the right to remain silent...." They snapped the handcuffs on his wrists and quickly ushered him away.

It was a brilliant move. There were so many people in the area, no one in the crowd had time to process what had happened.

Matt looked back over his shoulder and mouthed, 'I love you. I'm sorry.'

Colleen stared back, trembling, fists clenched. Her eyes, usually soft and brown, were wild and red. Her pale, smooth face was splotchy and distorted. She was crying so hard she looked like she'd come face to face with the devil.

Remembering that low moan he'd heard—*imagined he'd heard*—from the gully, he was afraid maybe she had.

He turned away; head lowered. Whatever happened to him now, he knew he deserved it.

Another patrol car appeared—followed by an emergency vehicle.

The reporter moved closer to Katie and held the microphone closer to his lips. "Now that you're standing in the Winner's Circle, how does this feeling compare with your dreams?"

Katie smiled and shook her head. "I never got this far in my dreams."

As Katie thanked all those who had helped them reach this point, she scanned the crowd for Drew. There was still no sign of him, but— she spotted their friends and family from Abington. Colleen was standing away from the others. She looked so alone, as if someone had broken her heart into a million little pieces.

Katie motioned for Colleen to join them at the circle. Colleen's lower lip trembled as Katie reached for her hand and pulled her close.

When she'd finished her thank-you's, with special tributes to Sammy, Teddy, and Mattie Grace, she looked back at the reporter and said, "I also want to thank Drew Byrd, wherever he is, for watching over our horses this week."

Gathering the rest of her Abington friends and family, she added, "We have an unusual story. We are the best of friends, and we have been on a journey for the past eight years. However, today, standing in the Winner's Circle at this hallowed track, our efforts have brought us together to enjoy this win. Because of Redemption, we have all been granted a second chance."

Chapter Seventy-Three

Although the front door of the patrol car was open, the back seat area smelled of human sweat. Matt twisted and turned, straining to see Colleen. He couldn't completely turn around because his hands were cuffed behind his back. It was awkward. In all of his forty-three years, he'd never come close to being arrested—until today.

He'd never forget the look on Colleen's face as they ushered him away from the Winner's Circle in handcuffs. It was the most painful expression he'd ever seen on a human.

And he had caused that pain.

Matt leaned his head against the back of the seat. How could he have not seen this coming?

The ghost that had haunted them for the past six months had finally manifested himself in the flesh. It had taken almost six months for Colleen to tell Matt she loved him. Yet, in less than twelve hours, their relationship had crumbled into tiny pieces.

He'd loved her almost from the start. She was his first true love and would also be his last.

His heart hurt for her.

His heart hurt for both of them.

Teddy and Katie stayed close to Colleen in the emergency waiting room while doctors rushed Drew to surgery to remove the bullet from his chest. Teddy couldn't remain seated. He paced back and forth to the double door as if his presence could make the doctor appear sooner.

Andrew and Daisy stood against the wall, Andrew's arm draped around his wife's shoulder while she completed paperwork and assumed the financial responsibility for the services their son was receiving. Her lips quivered, but her hand was steady.

Colleen scrolled her phone as she tried to contact the local authorities about Matt's arrest.

Three hours later, two law enforcement officers walked into the waiting room. Their mere presence caused everyone in the area to stop and take notice. They were tall men, thick chested, immaculately dressed in starched uniforms and shiny black shoes.

One officer stepped forward, hat in one hand, while the other rested on his holster. "Is anyone from the Byrd family here?"

Colleen stood up. "I'm Colleen Byrd. And these are Drew's parents." She introduced Andrew and Daisy.

"Mrs. Byrd," the officer said as he approached her, "We need to talk with you privately."

Colleen followed the officers to an empty office, and just before they closed the door, Katie stuck her head inside. "Colleen, the doctor needs to speak with you."

The officers looked at each other and nodded. Then, they stood on the other side of the waiting room doors while Colleen discussed Drew's condition with the doctor.

"We removed the bullet from your husband's chest," the doctor explained, "but he's lost some blood. A good bit, in fact. We almost lost him... We've given him a transfusion." Teddy could tell the surgeon was careful in what he told Colleen. "If his vitals remain stable throughout the night, you can see him when he wakes up. But right now, he needs to rest."

They waited in a room outside the ICU wing throughout the night. Teddy paced the halls hoping for a sign from the nurses that there had been an improvement.

Finally, just after the sun came up, the surgeon walked into the waiting room. He went straight to Colleen and knelt in front of her chair. Then he smiled. "He's still asleep. He's breathing on his own and his vitals are looking better. I'm going to check back in a couple of hours, and if he's still improving, you can go in and see your husband for a few minutes."

The doctor got a page and was gone before anyone had a chance to ask questions.

Teddy and Katie went down to the cafeteria and got everyone a cup of coffee and a pastry. While they were gone, Colleen dozed in her chair. The first sleep she'd had all night.

Just before noon, the surgeon came back into the waiting room. A big smile spread across his face. "Mrs. Byrd, your husband is awake. And he wants to see you. NOW!" He laughed as he motioned for them to follow him into the unit.

Teddy extended his hand to the doctor. "Thanks for taking care of my friend."

The doctor placed his hand on Teddy's back. A slight smile crossed the doctor's lips. "He gave us a scare last night… it'll take a few weeks, but we're expecting a full recovery."

The next day, after they moved Drew to a private room, Teddy hovered over the rails of Drew's bed and said, "Man, what happened to you?"

Drew gave a rueful laugh. "I was talking to Matt outside the stable. My hand was in my pocket. I'd weighed it down with my wallet, a canned drink, and my old cell phone. You know it has an antenna that sticks up about three inches. He must've thought I had a gun. When he reached for his, it bucked on him. His finger must've slipped into the trigger guard."

Teddy's eyebrows went up. "Sloppy handling by a novice—I presume."

Drew nodded. "I could tell by the shock on his face he didn't mean for it to go off."

An officer opened the door.

Drew took a deep breath. "I must've passed out. When I woke up, a security guard was pulling me out of the gully."

Teddy asked, "Did you fall into the gully?"

Drew frowned as if trying to remember. "Guess so."

The officer went over to Drew, "Sir, we have a few questions for you. First, what can you tell us about the incident?"

Drew repeated what he'd told Teddy, then added, "After that, I must have passed out. When I woke up, they were pulling me out of the gully."

The officer asked, "Do you remember how you got into the gully?"

Drew frowned. "No, sorry."

The officer's pen hovered over his notepad. "Sir, are you sure Mr. Suarez didn't intend to shoot you?"

"I'm sure," Drew said. "He pulled his weapon in a panic. I'm certain he thought I had a gun." He looked at Colleen, and they shared a slight smile.

"Thank you, sir. We appreciate your statement."

The officer closed his notepad. "We'll take your statement to the district attorney, and together we'll decide if an arrest is warranted."

Teddy drove down to the police station when Drew drifted off to sleep.

An hour and a half later, he returned to the hospital. Matt walked in beside him.

At the nurses' station, Teddy asked about Drew's condition.

Room 342 was at the other end of the hall. When Teddy knocked, Andrew opened the door. His gaze went to Matt, then back to Teddy, a question in his eyes.

Teddy nodded, not only reassurance but an acknowledgment. He knew as well as Andrew did that, while Matt might not have intended to shoot Drew, there were still too many unanswered questions. Like, why had he gone to the barn when he was supposed to be watching the race, and why had he gone there armed? And why were the police calling him Matteo Suarez? But all that could be settled later. Right now, there were more important things… like those second chances.

Andrew sighed, then stepped aside to let them in.

Katie and Colleen sat on the window ledge, and Andrew returned to his place on the small sofa. Daisy was all over the room filling the plastic hospital cup with ice chips, opening cabinet doors, looking for extra blankets, asking Drew if he needed anything.

It was just what mothers did.

She froze when Matt walked in, then placed herself between Drew's bed and the man who had shot him.

Colleen stared at Matt in disbelief. Then a smile lit her face. She jumped off the window ledge, scooted around the bed, and ran into his arms.

Teddy looked away. Colleen's joy warmed his heart, but he no longer felt that easy trust he'd had in Matt. Maybe it would come in time. He hoped it would.

The lighting in the room was bright, and the air smelled of antiseptic. The nurses had hooked Drew up to a drip bag, delivering antibiotics and nourishment straight into his veins. They'd also inserted an oxygen tube into Drew's nostrils to aid his breathing. An angry scrape on his forehead required medical attention, but all in all, he looked pretty good for someone who'd been shot in the chest.

Teddy went and stood next to Katie. It seemed surreal to be here in the hospital mere hours after winning the Derby. He squeezed her hand, and she squeezed his back, a comforting pressure. Then, after a moment, he looked down at Drew and said, "I didn't think you'd mind if I posted Matt's bail since you seemed pretty intent on defending him."

"I'm glad you did." Drew motioned with his hand as he tried to sit up in bed. "Matt, y'all come on inside here. I just have one question to ask you."

Matt's face reddened. "Sure, okay."

"Were you ever involved in the family operation?"

"No. And I hate that I let myself get pulled into Nic's racing scheme."

"I didn't think so. I only saw you that one time."

"Now, do you mind if I ask you a question?" Matt paused, waiting for Drew to nod. "Were you responsible for my cousin's death?"

"No. They were going too fast when they entered a hairpin curve. They missed the curve and went off the embankment."

Matt looked at the floor and nodded. "I had to ask...."

Drew managed a weak smile. "Colleen tells me you've taught our girls to water ski. Man, thanks for being so good to my children."

"No problem. You've got some good kids."

Drew glanced at Colleen. "It looks like we're going to be seeing a lot of each other now that I'm back. Are you okay with that?"

She nodded.

Then Matt pulled her close and said, "That won't be a problem. Maybe we can all go out on the lake when you get out of here."

Teddy, Katie, Matt, and Colleen returned to Abington late the following day. Andrew and Daisy stayed a few days longer until Drew was well enough to travel.

The week before the Preakness, when Teddy got home from work, he took a stroll around the farm. When he got to the lower pasture, he leaned against the fence and watched Redemption, Silver, and Mr. Zee grazing. The red and orange light created a peaceful stillness over the farm as the sun made its descent, and the pungent smell from the freshly mowed lawn permeated the air.

It was springtime in Georgia—a sight to behold.

The azaleas were blooming all over the farm. Beautiful shades of pink, lavender, orange, and red bushes clustered together and individually, accentuated by thick layers of brown pine needles. The large snowball bushes were still in full bloom, but the threat of a storm coming in the next day would leave the ground covered with the delicate white flowers.

Katie had often said the beauty of their farm in the springtime was intoxicating.

Teddy couldn't have agreed more.

He felt at peace, too. Katie's exhaustion and morning sickness had improved. Mattie Grace, learning she would be a big sister, had jumped up from the table and turned a cartwheel in the kitchen, which caused much excitement the previous evening at dinner. Finally, the threat of losing their farm to the cartel was over. Drew was recuperating at Andrew and Daisy's house; he'd walked to the mailbox the past two days to retrieve the mail.

Teddy had already called Luke Sullivan to schedule a visit to St. Simons at the end of the month following The Preakness. He and Katie were finally ready to buy the beach house.

When Redemption meandered over to the fence, Teddy gave him a piece of peppermint. Then, as he rubbed the side of the horse's head, it dawned on him that purchasing Redemption was one of the best decisions he and Katie had ever made.

All because of this horse, Andrew and Daisy had their son back. Katie and Teddy had resolved their differences and even had a little one on the way. Teddy and Drew had renewed their friendship, and, as Matt worked to prove himself, Teddy's bond with him had grown even stronger. Drew and Colleen had signed their divorce papers, and Matt and Colleen could finally move forward as a couple. The investors were busy telling their friends about the brilliant investment they'd made in Redemption, and no one in Abington, Georgia, was happier than Drew. He was grateful to be a part of his children's lives again.

It was like Katie had said. They had all been given a second chance. Even Redemption. He'd overcome a less-than-stellar performance and come back strong to win the Derby.

Teddy dug in his pocket for another peppermint, musing about the turns their lives had taken. He'd thought of Redemption as an investment—both for his bank account and for his marriage. As it turned out, Redemption was a beautiful story of grace.

The End.

ABOUT THE AUTHOR

Renee Propes is a southern suspense author who lives in Gainesville, Georgia, with her husband, Hardy, and their Yorkshire Terrier, Lucy. Renee and Hardy have one son, Zachary, and a daughter-in-law, Katie.

Books by Renee Propes

Duplicity: A Story of Deadly Intent
Fractured: A Story of Broken Ties
Redemption: A Story of Grace.

authorreneepropes.com
rlpropes@bellsouth.net
rpropes17@icloud.com

Acknowledgements

Redemption: A Story of Grace is the third book in the Abington Series. The people in this fictitious southern town could be your next-door neighbor, a family member, or someone you do life with.

When I began the research for this book, the first person I contacted was Jenny Westmoreland of Westmoreland Paint Horses. Thank you, Jenny, for inviting me to tour your farm and answering the numerous questions about horses and their varied personalities.

Thanks to Danelle Griffin, owner of *JDG Quarter Horses* in Maysville, Georgia, for the many conversations about horses. Thank you, also for the information you contributed to the research for this book.

I would be remiss if I didn't mention Shelby Quackenbush for introducing me to a Thoroughbred filly for the first time. She also introduced me to Kay Alfrey, whose husband once trained horses that raced at The Kentucky Derby. Thanks for your contribution.

A special thanks to my editor, Beth Terrell. Thank you for sharing your exceptional editorial eye. As I've said many times: You are brilliant!

A very special thank you to Frank Norton for your eloquent description involving the sanctuary of the Gainesville First United Methodist Church.

Many thanks to Martha Megahee, William Venema, Mary Casper, Dr. Sidney Washington, and Laura Megahee for serving as beta readers before the polishing and proofing began. Thanks for the time and energy you gave to this project. I cannot thank you enough.

Thank you to Jean Ellis, my treasured friend, who provided edits and guidance for *Fractured* and *Redemption*. I am grateful for your honest assessments and your generosity of spirit.

Elizabeth Waidelich is another treasured friend and my grammar guru who always gets the final look. Liz provided guidance for all three books and has developed an innate ability to read my thoughts.

A special thank you to my publishers at The Kimmer Group for your encouragement and guidance. You guys are the best!

I am grateful to the people in my community and worldwide who have purchased copies of my books and supported me on this journey.

Last, but not least... to my husband, Hardy, you're always my first reader, muse, and sounding board. Thank you for believing in my ability and for your encouragement and constant support. And, to our extraordinary son, Zach, our greatest legacy, and our daughter-in-law, Katie, whose beauty and kindness complete our family—everything begins and ends with you!

Above all, to my sweet friend, Jesus, for His mercy and grace.

CPSIA information can be obtained
at www.ICGtesting.com
Printed in the USA
BVHW031526300622
640993BV00007B/73/J